To Anui

Happy memories of
Swanwick,
         Love, Eliza Jane Goés

ELIZA JANE GOÉS

`aka
         Liz
Aug 12ᵗʰ 09

Fusion

Enjoy!

Trafford
PUBLISHING

Order this book online at www.trafford.com/07-1058
or email orders@trafford.com

Most Trafford titles are also available at major online book retailers.

Note for Librarians: A cataloguing record for this book is available from Library
and Archives Canada at www.collectionscanada.ca/amicus/index-e.html

Printed in Victoria, BC, Canada.

ISBN: 978-1-4251-2968-2

*We at Trafford believe that it is the responsibility of us all, as both individuals
and corporations, to make choices that are environmentally and socially sound.
You, in turn, are supporting this responsible conduct each time you purchase a
Trafford book, or make use of our publishing services. To find out how you are
helping, please visit www.trafford.com/responsiblepublishing.html*

*Our mission is to efficiently provide the world's finest, most comprehensive
book publishing service, enabling every author to experience success.
To find out how to publish your book, your way, and have it available
worldwide, visit us online at www.trafford.com/10510*

 www.trafford.com

North America & international
toll-free: 1 888 232 4444 (USA & Canada)
phone: 250 383 6864 ♦ fax: 250 383 6804 ♦ email: info@trafford.com

The United Kingdom & Europe
phone: +44 (0)1865 722 113 ♦ local rate: 0845 230 9601
facsimile: +44 (0)1865 722 868 ♦ email: info.uk@trafford.com

10 9 8 7 6 5 4 3 2

Foreword

In these troubled days of terrorism, human trafficking, modern slavery and the anarchy of gang violence it is easy to forget that the benefits of human migration far outweigh the trouble it can cause. This has been true throughout history. It is also easy to forget that there are as many heart warming tales of migration as there are horror stories and that for the number of bigots that exist there are many more fair minds to challenge them.

The twenty first century is not the first time people have felt that their identity has been endangered by a shrinking planet and neither is it the first time there has been a search for a new definition of a British identity (or any other national identity). The snowball effect resulting from increasing air travel means this 'coming together' is more rapid than ever it was and at times it appears to be spiralling out of control.

Some communities have inevitably had to forego some traditions but hasn't this always been the case over the centuries?

This migratory explosion has caused a 'fusion' which, if well directed, could create an energy which could change the world significantly for the better. For this to happen, however, history would have to do something new. It would have to learn. Power would have to remain with the philanthropic and the greedy who lie behind arms trading and therefore war would have to be finally routed out. To quote Lord Buddha, 'Happy is he who has overcome all selfishness; happy is he who has found peace and happy is he who has found the truth.'

'Fusion', written in the bildungsroman form, tells the story of the growing upwards and outwards of Ella a member of that once warlike and adventurous tribe, the red heads. It describes her move from an isolated community into a 1960s cosmopolitan kaleidoscopic society and how from then on her life is bowled along from conflict to conflict until finally she is in the centre of multi-ethnic London society.

Ultimately Fusion is a celebration of the joy of cultural integration but with a fearful glance at the dangers lurking around the edges of this happy and optimistic world.

This novel is loosely autobiographical without letting the mundane truth spoil a good story. The characters and settings are mainly fictitious but may at times resemble real people and places. If by any chance you happen to read this book and think perhaps you recognise yourself, it isn't you. Any living well-known personalities who have been mentioned more than in the passing have been consulted and the situations that dead historical figures are placed in are fictitious except where there is well documented historical fact. Some place names are real but their settings have changed. Other real places have had their names changed.

Acknowledgements

My thanks go to Rebecca Smith, author and editor, for her wonderful support and advice: Gloria Hagberg and Harry Wanderi for being excited about being in the prologue: Effie and Celia Goes for delivering flowers to Gloria in Nairobi on her 94th birthday: Ros White for transcribing my 'singing' into sheet music: Surinder Thethy who persuaded me I could write a whole book: All the family, friends, colleagues and students who provided both encouragement and fodder for the composite characters and especially my husband Gerry, daughter Gemma and her boyfriend Gareth.

My good wishes go to all those unwilling migrants who have suffered over the years and to those brave people who have climbed the walls of convention to join in the cosmopolitan society of cultural integration. I hope that for them the following famous quotes will ring true in a special way.

'The weak can never forgive. Forgiveness is the attribute of the strong.'

—RABINDRANATH TAGORE

'Prejudice may be defined as the lazy man's substitute for thinking.'

—ANONYMOUS

'People who develop the habit of thinking of themselves as world citizens are fulfilling the first requirement of sanity in our time.'

—NORMAN COUSINS

'What is philosophy but a continual battle against custom?'

—THOMAS CARLYLE

But perhaps, 'Philosophy: unintelligible answers to insoluble problems.'

—HENRY ADAMS

I must not forget Robert Burns and Helen Keller who begin and end my story on different notes of hope.

ELIZA JANE GOÉS

Table of Contents

'For a' that and a' that
It's coming yet for a' that
That man to man the world o'er
Shall brothers be for a' that.'

—Robert Burns

Prologue

JANUARY 2007

An elderly lady is cloistered in a chair but in comfort in her Nairobi home at the United Kenya Club with nearly ninety four years of memories to keep her warm. She is Mwalimu Gloria 'Granny of the Airlifts' of the 1960s who prepared thousands of Kenyan scholarship students for their first ever experiences of flying and for the culture shock of becoming undergraduates in USA or Canada.

She has many memories, some proud, others disappointing, depending on the height of success or the level of corruption

1

reached by her young charges, the elite of Kenyan intelligentsia at that time. Right now, she is feeling very excited and her will to live has strengthened.

'Harry,' she asks her companion in a clear, unwavering voice, 'I'm sure that young man on the front of Time magazine was one of mine. His name was Barack Hussein Obama. I remember he came from a village called Nyangoma Kogal somewhere near Kisumu.'

Harry laughs and says kindly, 'Why is it that you can remember such a detail from fifty years ago and you can't remember if you took your pills this morning?'

'Because this is much more important than my silly pills,' Gloria says. 'He wants to be the President of America and some people are saying that he can do it. Can you read the article for me, my dear? My eyes are not what they used to be.'

Harry decides to pick out the main points. As usual her mind is as sharp as a razor and she is absolutely right except she has skipped a generation along the way.

'It's his son, Mrs Hagberg. You're right. He's Barack Obama Junior and he came back to visit his father's village near Kisumu not long ago. He's just written a book called 'The Audacity of Hope' and yes he's going to run for President.'

Harry Wanderi is getting excited too. He doesn't usually get time to keep up with international news but he is going to follow this particular story.

'Oh, I do hope he wins,' Gloria Hagberg cries excitedly with her eyes shining. 'I want to live to see that day.' With a touch of her old sense of humour she adds, 'You had better make sure that I take those pills now, Harry.'

By now, Harry is engrossed in the rest of the story.

'…His mother is white American and he was brought up in Hawaii but his parents split up…and his mother married an Indonesian so he has step sisters and brothers,' Harry continues.

'What happened to his father? Does it say? He must be very proud. He was such a charming boy. Very handsome as I remember,' Gloria reminisces.

'I'm afraid there's nothing about his father here–except that Barack Junior has written a book about him,' Harry says. 'I'll see what I can find out for you.'

After talking to one or two people, Harry confirms his suspicion that Obama Senior was the one who had died in car crash in 1982 after some years of drunken poverty.

'I'm afraid Barack Senior died in an accident twenty five years ago, Mrs Hagberg.'

'Such a pity,' Mrs Hagberg declares. 'He had such a wonderful future to look forward to.'

Who knows if Mwalimu Gloria knows exactly what went on and if she is in denial–rejecting the unwanted memories from her cosy dreams of a rosy future for all her protégés?

'Never mind, perhaps his son will do better,' she sighs smiling softly. 'I taught them all to be proud of their heritage but to always work towards helping the poor and underprivileged of the world,' she went on. 'I felt sure they were listening at the time. Now, my dear, am I ready for my next pills? I need to keep going. This is going to be fun.'

Harry sets off with uplifted spirits to make the arrangements for a very special cake to be baked–for Mwalimu Gloria's ninety fourth birthday on February 1st 2007.

JANUARY 2007

Winter hasn't yet arrived in London and already there are daffodils in Barnet. The Climate Change Gurus are issuing even stronger warnings about global warming leading to rising oceans, horrendous storms, dustbowls of desertification and massively destructive tectonic activity–so people plant a tree whenever they jump on an overseas flight. The connection seems tenuous and futile.

The race is on. Will there be peace amongst the peoples of this earth before mankind destroys itself? Will the heat of cultural fusion do its job in the melting pot brought on by human migration or will the greenhouse gases do the job of melting the polar ice caps first?

Will the human race, the only race, find a common identity amid its rich diversity and move forward in harmony to build a better world? Blond, brunette and auburn, once warring tribes, are now under one umbrella. Will white, brown and black homogenise while still retaining their unique identities which enrich the fascinating global human society of this third millennium?

Can we step forward saying, 'We're all different but we're all equal!'?

CHAPTER 1

That 'In Between' Place

AUGUST 1953

Six year old Isabella Mackay sat precariously on top of the wide stone dyke that separated the boys' playground from the girls' playground at Balnahuig Primary School and waited. The sun was just coming up over the still waters of the bay, bathing the entire horizon in varying shades of gold. A lingering chill in the air made her glad of her fairisle jumper underneath which lurked a sturdy liberty bodice with its suspenders which held up thick grey woollen stockings. Her wee tartan skirt was held up by shoulder straps which crossed over at the back and were securely buttoned in the front at the waist. Her sensible Start-Rite lace ups had been buffed up until they shone in the morning light.

She was usually up and around before everyone else–even the Headmaster (or the Dominie as the Head Teacher was always called in those days). In this case Ewan Cameron, the Dominie, was the only teacher at the school; he used to encourage all the parents to go home and have more bairns so that the school roll of thirty five could expand to that magic number of fifty. This would mean that the education authority could employ another teacher to share the burden.

Isabella's soft, shiny, ginger curls glistened in the bright August sun and she screwed up her green eyes in search of any boat that might be coming across the bay from Orkney or Shetland or maybe even some other faraway and more exotic land.

This was Isabella's thinking time. From the time she was a wee toddler, she had taken to hiding away in a quiet place with a bonny view to reflect on life's happenings.

Today she was wondering why the *loons* and *quines* had to go into school through different doors and spend playtimes with a big wall and a wee gate between them. She always played with her big brother Jamie at home on the farm so what was the difference? There had been a terrible hullabaloo the other day when Isabella had decided to join in the boys' football game in the boys' playground. It just wasn't done.

'ISABella Mackay, what DO you think you're doing? If you're not back in the girls' playground in three seconds, I'll be tellin' ye're Mam and Dad!'

Isabella hadn't thought that was much of a threat but she didn't 'say' anything and had scampered off back through the wee gate anyway.

So today she was in that 'in-between' place on top of the dyke. She wondered what the Dominie, Mr. Cameron, would have to say about that but didn't let it interrupt her thinking time for too long. She contemplated the fact that her own wee in-between place was safely hidden away in her mind and from there she could watch what was going on in the outside world without getting too involved unless it looked interesting enough. If only she could have seen into the future, she would have realized that her fate was going to find her in all kinds of 'in-between' situations throughout her long and turbulent life.

Sometimes the 'in between place' was just the right place to be because you could sometimes see what other people couldn't. Last week was an example. Wee Ally Fraser was only four and tiny for her age. Her long dark hair was messy and she could have done with a good bath. Nobody in the playground was speaking to her because Kathleen Spencer-Smith's mother had said the Frasers were tinkies. Isabella thought she was the bonniest wee girl she had ever seen. She was right. Ally was beautiful and when she smiled, which wasn't often, her black eyes sparkled. Isabella was watching her sitting on a rock with her knees up to her chin, hugging them for dear life. Her eyes were glimmering with tears and Isabella knew somebody had said something–again.

'What's the matter, Ally?' the new, brave Ella said coming out of that 'in between' place and putting her arm round the boney little shoulders. She was scared she would break her she felt so fragile.

'Ye're nae supposed to speak tae her!' sneered Davy Brown who lived in the big hoose on the corner between the only two streets in Balnahuig. Their garden was the only one in the god-forsaken wind swept place that had a big tree.

'Awa 'n bile yer heid!' Ella shot back at him.

Wee Ally stopped crying and stared at her new champion in astonishment. 'Ahm nae a tinky and ahm nae stinky,' she whispered.

'Stinky Tinky!' taunted Davy again.

This time Ella was mad and came right out of that in between place or, from the other point of view, went right into it.

'Right Davy Brown, I'm tellin' the Dominie on you, ye big bully!'

'Aye, ye're jist a big bully,' added wee Jeannie Macdonald.

'It's nae fair! Ye're stinky yersel,' was Jessie Thompson's

observation.

To cut a long story short, what happened next was an outside the playground spat that resulted in very prompt intervention by a distraught Ewan Cameron and the two dinner ladies who had to be dragged away from peeling the tatties. By the end of it the boys and girls were very relieved to be safely back in their own, separate playgrounds.

'Maybe the Dominie was right', Ella reflected when she was back on top of the wall contemplating recent events.

Some good did, however, come out of the little fracas; after the *'quines cliped on the loons'*, Mr. Cameron felt he had to have 'words' with Mrs. Spencer-Smith about her snobby remarks and persuade wee Ally's mam to do something about giving her ever-growing brood a good bath every now and again. To date Miz Fraser had six children from five dads and was later to end up with many more bairns and a similar number of dads for them. Even the adults were cruel. They called them the mixed drops.

But, for the moment, wee Ally was fine. She got a special bath and a new frock from Ella's mam and, with her new found confidence, she sang in the school concert revealing a beautiful singing voice which was to one day make her a local star.

One of Ella's proudest moments was when Patrick Smith-Jones from the Big House in the woods said, 'That was pretty impressive, Ella. I wish you could stand up for me like that.'

'Why would I need to?' asked the brave champion.

'Don't you think I get any stick for sounding posh?'

'Aye, I suppose so–but you're nice posh.'

Patrick felt his family were nice posh too and though they always joined in the community activities it wasn't always enough. They were different and sometimes the local folk were cruel.

Today Ella (who didn't want to be called Isabella any more) was looking out over the bay and wondering why she had red hair and green eyes while her sister Morag was blonde with blue eyes and her brother Jamie had brown hair and brown eyes. At six years old she found it confusing. She discounted the thought that they could be mixed drops (little ears had been listening to adult chat) because the three of them had definitely inherited the funny ears from their dad. She decided she'd ask the Dominie. She'd tried asking her Mam and Dad but they didn't seem to know much except that Grand Auntie Mag had had red hair before it turned white.

Ella's question for Mr. Cameron began a long series of fascinating lessons. In later years his pupils were to look back on their time at Balnahuig Primary School and realise just what a gifted teacher they had been privileged to have. The question had actually been a very earnest one which had drawn on poor Ewan Cameron's reserves of 'delicacy'. It was,

'Do you think I might be a mixed drop? How do we know we're not? And why am I the only one in the Mackays with red hair?'

'Well. Isabella,' he said, because he didn't know she was now Ella.

'Ahem. It's all about the history of people traveling across the land and sea and it'll take a very long time to answer your question properly.'

'But, can ye try?' she asked.

'I'll try,' he replied happy to have a few weeks of material to work on instead of the prescriptive and restrictive schemes of work imposed from above by people who knew very little about bairns.

The first job he asked his thirty five pupils to do, with the big ones, who were eleven, helping the wee ones, who were four, was to make a huge chart with all their names–with columns for their hair colour and eye colour and spaces for the hair and eye colours of their brothers, sisters, parents and grandparents This had maybe caused a few problems for the mixed drops but things got glossed over amicably.

The chart came up with blue, grey, green, hazel and brown eyes and blonde, sandy, mousey, reddish-blonde (salmon), ginger, strawberry blonde, auburn, brunette, dark brown and nearly black hair plus a few indeterminate shades like bluey-green or sort of or kin'a rusty. The task was something that everyone could get involved in as each one had a unique contribution. Willie and Haimish, who both had a twin and who were both Downs syndrome children, were lapping up the attention as the others peered into their eyes and stroked their hair. This was better than somebody always asking them to spell their name or say the alphabet or count to ten. Mr. Cameron, in his wisdom, had set up a rota for all the pupils for 'teaching' Willie and Haimish and of course, most of them assumed that they should start at the beginning–again. The Balnahuig pupils never thought there was anything very strange about the two Downs boys. They were accepted without question.

Many years later, however, in retrospect, Ella did think there might have been something strange about the coincidence of two sets of twin boys each with one normal child and one Downs child. From her secret, now adult, 'in between' place she reflected on the fact that the sets of twins had different mothers but only one of the mothers was married; the other mother lived alone with her boys in a wee cottage a stone's throw away from the other family. But Ella didn't 'say' anything. She wouldn't.

After the excitement of filling in the giant wall chart with all the hair and eye colours, Mr. Cameron decided he needed to bring in reinforcements in the shape of Mrs. Cameron, his dear wife who had probably been very relieved to give up her job teaching Maths to the big anes in the big school so that she could be a good wife to Ewan and mother to her three boys. Were it not for Hugh, Fergus and Bruce Cameron, the roll at

Balnahuig would be only thirty two.

Maggie Cameron was of a rather nervous disposition and her sentences were punctuated with, 'Shhst' which became, 'Wheesht now!' followed by a few seconds of frantic rapid blinking when conversations became more animated. It wasn't hard to guess why she had been pleased to give up teaching at the secondary school but the little ones loved her. She played the piano and sang on a Friday which was their only source of music except when they made it themselves. On special days she brought in mountains of home baking like millionaire's shortbread with toffee in the middle and chocolate on top and deep fried doughnuts with dates in the middle and rolled in caster sugar. Her brother was the dentist in the nearest wee town where the big school was.

Today Maggie was needed to make enormous basins full of 'paper mashy' as the Balnahuig bairns called papier mâché.

The pupils had been bringing in all the newspapers from home and the *shoppy manny* had been asked to bring his left-over papers and magazines (of which there were many) but nobody was saying why.

The next part of the project was to become indelibly imprinted on the impressionable minds of these youngsters from remotest Caithness. It had taken weeks to plan. First the van from Inverness had arrived with mountains of sugar paper, glue, thick sticky tape, big tins of powder paint in blue, green, brown, yellow, orange, red, black and white and a stock of (mostly large) artists' paintbrushes. The bairns were involved in the process of unloading the van but Ewan and Maggie wouldn't tell them what it was all for so, by the time everything was ready for them to start, curiosity was burning brightly.

The first job was to cover the floor of one end of the biggest room in the school with a gigantic sheet of stiff paper. To do this they needed to stick sheets of paper together with the parcel tape and turn the whole enormous sheet over. It needed at least half of the school's population to perform this feat amidst a great deal of laughter and shouting of instructions. Next, the sheet was divided into twenty numbered rectangles. Twenty of the older pupils were given a rectangle each inside which they had to copy a pattern but on a bigger scale–using chalk which could be rubbed off. Still they were on a voyage of discovery. What was going on? After all the patterns had been adjusted (inevitably) so that they joined up to Mrs. Cameron's satisfaction, out came the basins of (smelly) pâpier maché. Under strict instructions, lumps and ridges of the stuff were pummeled together and stuck in strategic positions. At last it began to dawn on the more observant in the group.

'Is it The World Mrs. Cameron?'

'Let's have a look,' was the still enigmatic reply.

Out came the tins of powder paint and brushes and by this time the children were suggesting putting blue on the oceans and green on the land and, of course, a red dot for Balnahuig. In a child's eye, there is no other place in the world more important than home, no matter how small or remote it is.

There was no stopping them. Atlases flew off the shelf and paints got mixed and slapped on in the right places. They were making all the decisions, the little ones listening to the more knowledgeable big ones. The result was a little less than perfect but still pretty accurate, three dimensional world map complete with the Rocky Mountains, the Andes, the Alps and the Himalayas sticking up a bit out of proportion but painted brown with white snowy caps. The continents were green and the oceans were blue and most major things had been named in black poster paint block capitals. Still, however, the only place named and marked by a red dot was Balnahuig.

Maggie's mathematical skills and creativity had laid the foundations for Ewan's next move. Now he was going to try to answer the question about hair and eye colour and mixed drops. He had raked through copies of The National

Geographic magazine and The Encyclopaedia Britannica and come up with pictures of people from all corners of the world. The pupils had to cut those out (sacrilege!) and stick them on little cardboard cards which were stuck into little wooden stands which the big boys (not girls) had been asked to shape at home using bits of 'kindlers' with a groove on top for the card and a base nailed on the bottom to make it stand up. All the boys had penknives (or Swiss army knives if they had rich uncles) which they used for sharpening pencils or carving out whistles or tweeks (catapults); this was before the time of 'arrest for possession of an offensive weapon'.

The bairns set about putting the Africans in Africa, the Chinese in China, the Indians in India, the Red Indians (that dreadful misnomer) in America, the Eskimos in Canada, the Viking red heads and blond Danes in Scandinavia, the brown eyed brunettes near the Mediterranean and the blue eyed, dark haired Celts near the Scottish Hebrides. So far this seemed simple and straightforward. But that still didn't answer the growing number of questions.

Why had there never been an African, Chinaman, Indian, Eskimo or Red Indian anywhere near Balnahuig in living memory? That one was easy to answer as the eager little beavers looked at their big map which was big enough to step all over and came to the conclusion that they were on the other side of the world—and not much happened in Balnahuig worth coming all that way for.

Where did all those different people in Balnahuig come from? Why wasn't everyone the same?

Ewan and Maggie had read 'The Origin of the Species' and anything else they could lay their hands on in remotest Caithness. Strangely, at that time in 1953 James Watson and Francis Crick had announced to the Eagle pub in Cambridge that they had 'discovered the secret of life'—which was true as they had just discovered DNA. The Balnahuig youngest generation and their teachers were quite unaware of that fact–but they were busy coming to terms with their own answers to their own big questions.

The kids were open to suggestion and inquisitive, like all children, and the Dominie and his wife were their only source of information.

Even better, Ewan sported a spectacular war wound and half an ear which was his legacy from Eritrea during the Second World War.

'Why have you only got half an ear, Mr. Cameron?' led to a very full answer after which the pupils knew about all the places Mr. Cameron had visited, what the people looked like and how kind they were and why he had to go there, which of course led to how bad Hitler was and how wrong it was to think that only people with blue eyes and blonde hair were good enough to live.

'Why do we all look different?' had conjured up this massive world map project which had been entirely pupil led and had lasted for months by the time it branched off in all manner of directions–not always logically. For example red-haired Vikings crossing the sea to trade and become farmers prompted an animated reading of 'The Ancient Mariner' every afternoon for fifteen minutes until it was finished. The underlying lesson here was Coleridge's–love for all God's creatures.

There seemed to be a smooth transition from mathematical scale and map-making into the study of the child-friendly rudiments of human migration, the theory of evolution, the recessive gene in blue eyes, the evil Nazis, the highland clearances engineered by the wicked Countess of Sutherland, the reading of 'Uncle Tom's Cabin' by Harriet Beecher Stowe (who was nearly conned into believing that Elizabeth the Duchess of Sutherland was a lovely lady who educated her people). Harriet Stowe was embarrassed to find out that the Countess had, in fact, burned their houses and hounded them towards the coastal plains so that her henchmen could put sheep on her land. She had declined the next invitation to Dunrobin Castle.

This led to a bus trip (the whole school fitting on one bus) to the Strathnaver museum to find out what had happened to the unfortunate farming families forced to live in and around Bettyhill where they had to supplement their meagre incomes from the poor farmland with fishing–which was a trade they knew nothing about. Here they learned a little bit of Gaelic 'Mo thruaighe ort a thir, tha'n caoraich mhor a' teachd' which meant, 'Woe to thee oh land, the Great Sheep is coming!' The lesson taught here was that it was wrong for the rich to persecute the poor and we should be brave enough not to let it happen.

Most of the time, however, lessons were less charged and concentrated on the three Rs and day to day topics. The homework for today had been to write a story with the title 'One day in my Life'. Ella had finished it and this is what she handed in.

One Day in My Life by Isabella Mackay

The day I'm writing was yesterday.

Mam woke me and Jamie at six o'clock to do our home jobies, Jamie's bigger than me because he's eleven and I'm only seven. Our big sister Morag is away somewhere I can't spell, studing something. She's the brany one.

My jobies are to fill the coal pails and stick baskets for liting the fires for the cold and put them in the back passage near the wellies and dungreez because theyr dirty too like the coal. Then I have to brush the shoes using the stuff in the box in the cubby hole near the back door. They have to be shiney when I finish. I can do my jobies at night but I'm nearly always too bisy. Mam says I'm nearly always too lazy.

The phone rang early and my Dad says Mackay Hillside or some-times just Hillside because ther are so many Mackays. Hillside is the name of the farm. Some people say I'm Isabella Hillside because it's

15

easier for them to no who I am.

I had my breakfast before my work because if you wait til after, the porrij is too thick as its bean on the ray burn for ages.

I walked to school down the brae because Morag's bike is old and rusty and it's a terrible job to push it back up again. I like walking anyway. Ye get piece to think. Jamie took his bike after his jobs on the farm because it's a good bike.

We're making a great big map of the world in the school with blue seas and green land and brown mountains and we're getin to no where all the places are and what the peple are like. You can walk across the Atlantic sea to America. One day I want to see all the places in the world before I come back and do Mr Cameron's job when he's ready for a rest. I'll have to be quite old tho. Today we put white paint on top of the Himalayas and a big red dot for Balnahuig.

After school me and Jeannie Macdonald picked brumles from near the waterfall and took them home in a jar each we got from Mrs. Scott at the shoppy. Mam gave me a kiss and said I was good not to eat them all before I got home. We ate them after our tea which was mince and tattys and peas.

Mam and Dad listened to the Archers at 7 oclock on the big wireless and Jamie and I played knock out whist before our supper and then we went to bed. I hope you like my story. I finished the last bit in my bed before I went to sleep. Good night.

Mr. Cameron did like the story and thought for a seven year old Ella showed a lot of potential. He wrote, 'What a lovely story,' in red pen and left it at that. The mistakes could get sorted later.

As for the original question from Ella, 'Why am I the only Mackay with red hair?' Ewan and Maggie could only do their best to unravel the mystery of mysteries of human biodiversity in simple terms for their young scholars. Somehow, although the Scottish culture was incredibly diverse and had its own in-equalities and prejudices, the Camerons got across the idea that it's good to be different and the underlying theme of all their history, geography, science and literature lessons (as they indeed were) was positive acceptance and not negative tolerance.

Ewan could not resist the temptation to try to make sure that this positive acceptance extended to all the peoples of the world. As the pupils stepped on Africa, China, Japan, India or any other part of their big world map (in stockinged feet) they were encouraged to accept the fact that the people there had the skin and hair colour which were most suited to their environment. Black and brown people were said to have dark skin, hair and eyes as a protection against the hot sun and blonds and redheads didn't need this protection. This was accepted by the youngsters as a fact which rang true somewhere deep within us. The Camerons were careful to add that there was no question of superiority or inferiority. We are just different. That's all.

This was the backdrop provided for Isabella Mackay's extraordinary future life. She and her schoolmates at Balnahuig Primary School each had a sense of their place in the universe according to their hair and eye colour.

Mary Macdonald's light blue eyes, light skin and black hair meant she was a Celt; they were probably the original inhabitants of Scotland pushed westwards to the Hebrides by the invasions of red-headed Picts and Vikings, Angles, Saxons, Normans but never the Romans. (The Scots were proud to boast that they'd kept the Romans out.) Mary thought it must be true because her granny and granda came from Eriskay in the Outer Hebrides.

Sandy Grant's dark hair and brown eyes were explained away by the Auld Alliance bringing a big tall Frenchman called 'Grand' who became his great, great, great granda. He was convinced it was true because he was easily the tallest boy in the school and Grant looked like Grand and he'd learned that meant big in French.

Jean Anderson's blonde hair and blue eyes were put down to her ancestors being Angles or Danes from Europe across the North Sea. Her dad liked boats so that had been enough to persuade her that this could be true.

Ella was pleased to hear that somewhere long ago she might have had an ancestor like Rob Roy McGregor and that red hair in her family had been hiding for a few generations before it came out in her. She was proud that Queen Elizabeth I was a red head too.

Any anomalies, in between colours and odd combinations were put down to never being sure what the genes were going to do.

Jamie's question was, 'How does it work for dogs, Mr. Cameron? Ye see my dog has one brown eye and one blue eye.'

That one stumped Ewan Cameron.

The Dominie and his teacher wife (voluntary because she was married) couldn't avoid instilling some good old-fashioned patriotism. The Scots were the best in the world and had invented all sorts of things from the telephone to tarmac roads to the latest new-fangled invention called television. The pupils would remember the first television set in the village on which they watched the coronation of the young Queen Elizabeth whose mother, they were proud to say, was a Scot. They were never to find out that Ewan Cameron had had his tongue firmly stuck in his cheek as he obediently handed out the gift of a coronation mug to each of his pupils–as publicly decreed by Sir Winston Churchill.

Balnahuig had only one religious establishment, the Church of Scotland–known as the Kirk. Most of the locals were barely aware of the fact that any other kind of Kirk existed. This was probably a good thing as a Wee Free or a Roman Catholic Church nearby might have caused havoc. The Kirk was the centre of the community. Anyone left outside was a source of concern, a lost lamb that had to be brought back into the flock. There was Sunday School for the bairns, Bible Class for the teenagers, the Women's Guild and a Presbytery of elders (all men) who helped to run the affairs of the Kirk. Everybody was expected to be involved.

Ewan Cameron the Dominie was very community minded. He kept himself up to date with world affairs by reading newspapers and 'Life and Work' the thought-provoking magazine of the Church of Scotland.

The pupils were not, always, sheltered from potentially upsetting events in the outside world of 1953. The execution of Julius and Ethel Rosenberg for selling the formula for the atomic bomb to the Soviets, Ariel Sharon's Unit 101 taking revenge for the deaths of an Israeli woman and her two children, the death of Stalin, the election of Nelson Mandela as national Chief of the Defiance Campaign in South Africa and the imprisonment of Jomo Kenyatta for seven years for his part in the Mau Mau uprising in Kenya were not on the curriculum at Balnahuig Primary School. However, they somehow managed to slip into the conversation and the youngsters were encouraged to question and criticise.

One thing that Ewan would not discuss, however, was a headline in a Caithness newspaper on Armistice Day, 1953. It announced the arrival of an 'Atom Plant for Dounereay'. He knew enough to be alarmed about the consequences and, although it was the best unkept secret in the area, he was angry enough to get himself into hot water. Politicians with gigantic egos were pushing it and if the Air Ministry were in charge, there would be no fighting the decision. Ewan wasn't about to bother little heads with anxious thoughts of nuclear threats. He did, however, suspect that Dounereay would become a piece in the Ministry of Defence's strategic jigsaw.

Crucially, for Ewan and Maggie, their hope was that their charges would be launched into life with the belief that there is a universal humanity and kinship which overcomes the diversity and prejudice which threatens to destroy that spirit. Most of all they hoped that the young ones had managed to develop a free mind to face the big, wide, wicked world and be able to fight for justice for themselves and others who were in need of it.

Many years later their pupils would remember Mr. and Mrs. Campbell as that wonderful, sensitive and far-seeing couple for doing just that.

Isabella Mackay's strong values and stubborn streak which, for now, were in that 'in between' place had been firmly set in stone.

CHAPTER 2

Mackay v. Macdonald

JUNE 1954

Jamie Mackay, at eleven, was in the top class at Balnahuig who were nearly ready to go on the bus to the big school fifteen miles away.

He wasn't looking forward to that. The journey to the primary school had been fine–a mile long race on his bike downhill along the narrow windy road by the side of the valley and across the wee bridge over the burn and into the village.

He was always late so he always had to race. His little sister Ella had always left ages before he was ready to go. He wondered what she found to do. She didn't take her bike, which was a rusty old hand me down from her sister Morag anyway. She wanted to look around at the views and the purple heather and yellow gorse. She liked listening out for birds too. Jamie thought she was daft but that was quines for ye.

It wasn't that he was lazy. It was just that he had better things to do than go to school. There was his sheepdog Ben, with his one brown eye and one blue eye, who needed a run, the orphan lambs that needed feeding, the eggs that needed collecting, the cows that needed milking or any number of real things to do that were more important than school.

And he needed 'just a wee minute' to stand on the bridge and listen to the babble of the tiny waterfall and look into the whisky coloured swirl to see if there were any fish. He always liked to do this and he never wanted to miss it. It set him up for the day. Jamie had always been a creature of habit.

Ella was only seven and she'd been thinking it would take forever to get to the big school. Her big sister Morag had been to the big school and now she was miles away in St Andrews at *varsity*; Ella felt she didn't know her. She never got to speak when she came home because everybody was listening to her big sister's stories–so she just listened too.

Ella might seem to have been only listening but, unlike her big brother Jamie, she was dreaming and dreaming of all those places in the big wide world that she wanted to see–starting with the big school that Jamie wasn't looking forward to. He was scared of change–any change–but Ella wanted to embrace new experiences and as many of them as possible.

AUGUST 1958

At long last the day came for Ella's first bus trip along the coast to the big school. Jamie could go on the bus with her because he still had a year to go; he felt proud because he was doing a real job looking after his wee sister.

They both had new bikes which they could leave in Mrs Scott's garden behind the Post Office near the bus stop. They had whizzed down the brae from the farm, freewheeling and yelling, which didn't disturb anybody but the birds and the sheep because there was nobody else around for miles.

Davy Brown was already at the bus stop looking spruce in his new uniform and brushed hair. He was embarrassed because his mother was there too to make sure he got on the bus. She and Kathleen Spencer-Smith's mother were good friends and they both wore Harris tweed suits and silk scarves with pheasants or horses on them—even to do the shopping at the Post Office. They usually looked as if they had a bit of a smell going on under their noses. Jamie and Ella called them the *twa snobby wifies* when nobody was listening.

You could hardly see Jeannie Macdonald beneath her bottle green blazer and yellow blouse. They were at least three sizes too big but maybe they would last until class five and the end of school.

Jessie Thompson had an enormous brown leather schoolbag with two straps and two big buckles to close it and two thick shoulder straps to carry it on her back. She only had a pencil case and her *piece* and a drink in case there wasn't enough lunch at the big school but she still looked as if her plump little body was going to fall backwards with the weight if she wasn't careful.

Ella brushed some dust off her new blazer and wondered how Wee Ally would get on without her. She had three new wee sisters now and she was still too thin but her hair was always shiny and she was getting bonnier every day. At least Davy Brown wouldn't be there to bully her anymore. Davy was looking uncomfortable. Maybe it was the thought of being a wee fish in a big pond where he couldn't be the boss anymore.

After the bus driver had waited for stragglers until he could wait no more, they set off along the road with the sea on their left and the changing landscape of heather moor, scrubby trees, gorse or tumbling waterfalls on the right. When the Castle overlooking the Pentland Firth came into view, there was only a mile to go. Ella could hardly contain her excitement.

This was the start of five years at Sinclair's Institution (for backward boys and forward girls) in the large village or small town, if you prefer, of Altnabervie. The school building was like a castle. It was said that an Andrew Sinclair, who had refused to cut off his red pigtail to please the Duke at Castle Malcolm, had gone to America and made his fortune. He had then sent $100,000, a princely sum at the time, to build a free school in Altnabervie for all the children of the poor. Ella thought he must have been a very nice man. She wasn't so sure when she found out that his name was connected with slave auctions. She was sure her Granny Sinclair didn't know that or she wouldn't be telling everybody that he was her ancestor. Then Ella had a moment of panic when she wondered if this man with the red pigtail was the ancestor who'd given her the red hair and the very worst thing she could imagine was that anyone, far less one of your own ancestors, could possibly be a slave trader. It was even harder to swallow the possibility that Sinclair's Institution was built using the profits from that unspeakable exploit. The young girl chose to believe that this simply couldn't have been true.

Sinclair's High School felt huge and very scary. In fact, there were nearly three hundred pupils in classes one to five and about five students in class six who had passed their Highers but were too young to go to varsity. Class One, the twelve year olds, was divided into ABC, T, P and R. You got put in one of those according to how you did in the dreaded eleven plus exams. It was well known that nearly all of Ewan Cameron's bairns from Balnahuig got into the ABC class unless there was something far wrong. By now, for example, the two Downs boys, Willie and Haimish had started going to St Andrew's Special School where they would be happier.

Ella was in 1A of the ABC class which meant she had Latin, French and all the other subjects. If you were in 1B you had French and no Latin and extra English. If you were in 1C you had no Latin or French and had extra English and extra needlework if you were a girl and woodwork if you were a boy. One drawback was that the ones in 1A had no lessons in needlework or woodwork for the whole year. T meant Technical which meant you got more needlework, cooking, woodwork or metalwork according to your sex, P meant Poor and R meant Remedial. Everybody knew this and if you were in R, you hated the school. Sometimes you weren't too happy in A either because you kept getting called, 'Teacher's pet,' or, 'Swotty swot'. At least everyone knew where they stood so they just got on with it and put up with it.

Ella Mackay coped. She shone in English composition and got by in Maths except for Algebra. She blamed the Maths teacher because he kept calling her Bella which was the name of one of her dad's Ayrshire *coos*. Finally she admitted she was just bad at Maths, full stop.

A few things annoyed Ella. She was finding it harder to hide away in that 'in between place' in her head because everything was so busy and the teachers kept saying it was time to go on to the next bit before she'd had time to think about the last bit. She wondered if anybody else thought like this but, as usual, she didn't 'say' anything. She just put on her wellies and took off on her own for a walk on the hill behind the farm, rain, shine or snow, whenever she got home from school.

'This is what she does—every day—or she won't speak to us,' her anxious Mam used to say.

'Och Mary, leave her be,' Ella's Dad would say. 'She just needs a wee while to sort things out in her head. She'll be fine.'

Charlie Mackay understood his daughter and let her get on with it as long as she took in the coal pails and the baskets of kindlers and did all the other jobs she was supposed to do. He too was a man of many thoughts but not so many words.

'I'd rather have something to say than have to say something,' he used to say which gave him the perfect excuse to sit and listen, sit and think or just sit.

Mary would say, 'Your father doesn't say a lot but when he does, it's been well worth waiting for.' What Mary didn't realise was that her daughter was very much the same.

Back at Altnabervie school, as Sinclair's Institution was sometimes called, the Scripture lesson was about to begin and Ella Mackay was about to come out of her 'in between place' and get into a spot of bother.

Mr Macdonald, who taught both Scripture and all the R classes, was a parody of himself which probably explained why the pupils in R hated school and half the school became budding atheists. Today Toffee Macdonald, as he was called, was leaning heavily, or at least his overhanging stomach was, on his huge carved oak desk with its sloping lid. As usual he was chewing. He looked a bit like the highland cow in the picture on the box of highland toffee he was always chewing and never offering anybody.

'I need to chew to concentrate,' he would declare. 'Though why I should bother, I don't know. Your tiny brains are quite incapable of absorbing my abstract thoughts.' It wasn't unusual to walk past his room and hear, 'Uneducable boy, that's what you are! Uneducable.'

Today he was ignoring a new carving on his desk which spelt out TOFFY MAKS YE FAT and was trying to organise the class.

'All you Catholic boys and girls from St Sylvester's can sit at the back of the room. We're reading the Bible and it's not for you. You can say your own Hail Marys in peace up there.'

'Please sir, is the Bible not for everybody? I thought it was.' This was Ella sticking her brave little nose out of her 'in between place'–with dire consequences.

'Well, Isabella, you know what thought did, don't you? It planted a feather and thought a chicken would grow. I'll thank you to keep your thoughts to yourself young lady–especially about things that don't concern you.'

The poor Catholics shuffled up to the back of the room one or two girls looking as if they were about to cry and some of the boys with ugly, angry expressions on their faces. Ella thought that her new best friend Nan being sent to the back of the room for being a Catholic was very much her concern. She went up to the back of the room too.

'Come out to the floor, Isabella Mackay.' Everybody had heard this before and knew exactly what was going to happen.

'Are you a Catholic?'

'No Mr Macdonald but I want to sit with Nan.'

'Hold out your hand. Either one, it doesn't matter.' With that he drew a long leather strap out of its usual resting place in the very ample inside pocket of his hairy green tweed jacket.

'Thwack'. The first belt caught Ella all the way up her arm to the inside of her elbow. 'Thwack. Thwack'. The other two tipped her fingers. Ella didn't cry. She tossed her red hair and flashed her green eyes but she didn't cry. She just glowered at the teacher until he had to avert his eyes.

'If you were a boy, you'd get double,' he added.

Then Ella did something that had never been done before as far as anybody could remember. She walked straight out of Toffee Macdonald's classroom and marched her little self all the way to the Headmaster's office. She was trembling with rage but there wasn't a tear anywhere.

Luckily John Gunn the Headmaster wasn't too busy and he took one look at Ella's face, raised one bushy black eyebrow over a bright blue eye and said, 'Would there be a problem that needs sorting now, Isabella?' His soft island lilt soothed Ella a bit. She knew that Mr Gunn and Mr Cameron from Balnahuig were the best of friends so she thought she'd cash in on this fact. What Ella didn't realise at the time was that John Gunn knew all about her as he knew all about all of his pupils, as much as there was to know. That was dedication–and he was a fair man and a brave one.

'Mr Cameron would have been proud of me today but Mr Macdonald gave me the strap for saying the same thing. Do you think that's fair, Mr Gunn?'

She wasn't making herself very clear and poor John Gunn was confused. He eyed, with dismay, the red welt on Ella's little white arm which was growing redder by the minute. Bill Macdonald had a reputation for being a bit too free with the belt and he'd been waiting for a chance to point out that at times this was unjustified. Maybe this was his chance if wee Ella could calm down enough to tell him what had happened. He couldn't imagine that she deserved to be belted–from what Ewan Cameron had told him. She'd been his star pupil.

Eventually, the truth was unearthed.

'I shouldna have got the strap for wanting to sit beside Nan,' Ella finally managed to get out, 'and the Catholics shouldna have to sit at the back of the room. I said I thought the Bible was for everybody and he said I was like a chicken that planted a feather and thought a hen would grow. That's not fair is it?'

'No, Ella, it certainly doesn't sound fair,' John Gunn replied feeling very sorry for this earnest wee lass, 'But wasn't it thought that planted the feather?' he added and was pleased to see she could still laugh despite feeling so upset. Ella was calmed down and John Gunn was in a quandary. He believed Ella and was horrified at what had happened and was thinking Ewan Cameron would indeed be proud of her. But how was he going to handle this and not be seen to be undermining a staff member in front of the pupils?

Ella was given a copy of 'Tales from Scottish Folklore' and

given permission to sit outside the office and not go back to the Scripture lesson and Mr Gunn returned to his office, shut the door and began to concoct a plan.

When it was time for Kirsty, the School Secretary to ring the big hand bell, he sent Ella off to her next lesson but still hadn't decided what to do–except that he would drive out to Balnahuig that very evening in his new Morris Oxford and visit his old friend Ewan Cameron.

The sunset was spreading over the cliffs and the sea in all shades of pink and purple as John Gunn meandered sedately along the coast road towards Balnahuig. He was running in his new car and wasn't expecting to see another car on the way there or back. His thinking cap was on. Toffee Mac, as his colleagues had taken to calling him, was becoming even more of a problem–and the complaints were coming in from irate parents.

'How can a man that disna like bairns be wantin' tae teach them?' was a common complaint. John had to agree but was duty bound to keep his professional mouth shut.

'I'll see what I can do Mrs Anderson. I'll have a word as soon as I can,' was the only pathetic response he could come up with and he was annoyed with himself.

The problem was, Toffee Mac was what you might call well-connected in the far north of Scotland and he thought he was somebody even though he wasn't–but his gentry friends thought he was 'somebody'.

John rounded the corner and saw the 'Dome of Discovery' dominating the horizon where once there had been nothing but sheep grazing and the ruined Dounreay castle. His heart sank and this awful feeling of unease swept over him whenever he saw it. Speaking of people who thought they were somebody–anybody who was anybody had wanted to see what was going on at this lonely seaside site and all kinds of Big Wigs had been giving lectures on atomic energy and putting up exhibitions in many of the local towns. Dounreay was now at the front line of research and a good employer which had transformed the economy of the area but John was haunted by the memory of a young woman, a Scottish Nationalist, who was brave enough to warn of the consequences of the project. Why was it that they wanted an area which was away from too many people? What was the reason for all the secrecy and the guard dogs?

Meantime there were a lot of people who had jobs who wouldn't have had, and Ewan Cameron had now employed a new teacher at Balnahuig Primary School as the roll was now fifty two when you counted the families of the Dounreay workers.

Ewan and Maggie were delighted to entertain their friend.

'My, what a lovely surprise on a week night, John,' was how Ewan greeted his great friend. 'Haven't you got enough work to do running that big school of yours?'

They'd had their tea of course–at half past five–so it was time for a 'tootie' of whisky by the time John arrived.

'Have you had your tea, John?' Maggie said. 'I can imagine what you bachelors are like.'

'Thank you kindly, Maggie' John answered, 'but I have been fed and watered.'

Maggie pottered off to put the boys to bed while Ewan did the honours.

'Will you have some water in your whisky, John? I've got a nice bottle of Glenfiddich here.'

'No, Ewan, I'll have it straight. They tell me the stuff's made from water so that'll do me.' Ewan could tell there was something more behind the gentle jokes. He'd known him a long time.

'Come on then. What is it?' he asked firmly, fixing him with a steady gaze.

'It's that dreadful man Bill Macdonald. He's belted wee

Isabella Mackay until she's black and blue–and her only in Class One. She'd been wanting to sit beside Nan Kilpatrick in the Scripture class and he wasn't about to let her.'

'For Heaven's sake why not?' asked Ewan and was promptly filled in with the details of the goings on.

'It would appear that Bill has told them that the Bible's not for Catholics and when Ella pointed out that it was for everyone, he lost his temper by the sounds of it. Anyway, she stuck to her guns and walked out of the classroom.'

'Well, she's a brave wee lass,' Ewan Cameron said sitting up straight and raising his eyebrows. 'She might be daft but I'm proud of her.'

'She said you would say that,' John replied relieved that his friend was on the same wave length. 'But the point is. What can I do about it, Ewan? The last time I complained about his bullying, a letter came back from the Authority to say that Mr Macdonald was a respected citizen who had every right to discipline his pupils as he saw fit. It was taken out of my hands. You know what it's like around here if you hob nob with the gentry. You can get away with murder–even bigotry.'

(The two men shared a laugh at how ridiculous that sounded.)

'Och, you know what I mean!' went on John, in sheer frustration.

By this time, Maggie had finished her chores and was coming through with the supper on a tray. A pot of tea, sugar, milk, her best teacups and saucers and a tray full of softies and jam, rock cakes, doughnuts and shortbread, all home baked. John would have been happier with another glass of whisky but he knew better than to mention that.

Of course, Maggie had to hear the story and she was the one to come up with a solution. It was Friday. She was due to be going up to the Mackay farm in the morning to see Mary about the Kirk Sale.

31

'I'll just take my camera up to Hillside Farm,' Maggie said in a conspiratorial whisper, 'to get a picture of the bonnie view down the valley and maybe, just maybe, I can take a photo of wee Ella's arm when I'm there. I think the film's nearly finished.'

Ewan cottoned on first. 'I'll just go round and see Jimmy Thurso in the morning. He was telling me about his new dark room last week.'

'Maggie, has anyone ever told you you're a genius?' John cried.

'Now, John, can you go into the Altnabervie Courier offices tomorrow and tell them there might be a story for them. But don't say it's definite until I–wheesht now–have words with Mary and Charlie–and wee Ella herself of course.' The excitement was getting to Maggie and she was blinking very fast and wheeshting all over the place.

The outcome was quite satisfactory. A suitably blurred photograph disguised Ella's identity (not intentional–only amateur) and an article with the headline BIGOT BULLIES BAIRNS AT SCHOOL was duly printed in the weekly Altnabervie Courier the following Thursday. This had the desired effect of getting the other parents with grievances against Toffee Macdonald out of their houses like woodworm out of a skirting board because they weren't scared any more.

The rumour was that Mr Macdonald had a new job somewhere way down near Edinburgh. Others said he'd taken early retirement. Jamie said, 'Maybe Toffee Mac's at hame mackin toffee.' He thought that was very funny–for some reason.

John Gunn, covering for the moment, was struggling with Scripture lessons. He began by asking all the children from the three different kirks to tell each other what happened in their respective services. The bairns decided there wasn't a lot of difference to talk about.

Ella Mackay thrived at Sinclair's Institution after the demise of Toffee Mac the bully. Jamie was proud of his wee sister and instead of having to look after her was pleased to bask in the reflected glory of her fame as a junior 'fighter for justice'.

Soon after the story was on the front page of The Courier a slightly bigger Wee Ally came rushing up to Ella in Balnahuig's only street calling, 'You've done it again haven't you? D'ye mind when ye sorted out Davy Brown for me? Oh ye were awfa brave then and ye're awfa brave now. I wish I was brave like you.'

Ella felt embarrassed. 'I think you're braver than I am, Ally. You're the one he bullied. Anyway I think I'm more daft than brave.'

The two girls laughed together and put their thumbs to their noses and wiggled all their fingers at Davy Brown's big house on the corner.

'I hate bullies,' Wee Ally cried.

'Me too,' cried Ella, 'and I hate snobs even more.'

As the girls grew through their teens together they were to share a love of singing and taught themselves and each other to play the guitar. They made up songs about bullies and what should be done to them. But mainly they sang the pop songs of the time, harmonising where they could–songs like 'Poetry in Motion' and 'Please Don't Tease'. The only arguments they had were over Elvis and Cliff. Ally liked Elvis and Ella liked Cliff.

Ella took to writing down her 'in between time' thoughts in secret diaries. Much as she loved Ally, she couldn't share all of her ideas.

Slowly Ella outgrew her younger friend. Whilst Ella went on to Kings College Aberdeen, Ally got a job in the kitchen at The Castle of May where she often met the Queen Mother and all her cronies. Ella was delighted that her friend was so happy.

At varsity, predictably, Ella found herself drawn towards the more militant and rebellious students (often the over-seas students) and found herself vociferously expressing a few opinions on Enoch Powell, Vietnam, Ian Smith and UDI, American Civil Rights, Women's Lib or whatever the current debate was on. As you might expect, she was always on the side of the underdog. She wasn't so much an activist–more an 'expresser of important views'.

On the lighter side, Ella and her friend Sue always watched Top of the Pops in the Student Union TV lounge–the only place in town, except for shop windows, where students could watch TV. Everyone was packed in like sardines and they loved it. Sue had a guitar too and she and Ella and three scruffy lads used to play and sing at the beer, cider and crisps parties when nobody could afford any other music. There was nothing very expert about their recitals; this mattered little as more often than not the singers drowned out the three chords needed for 'Blowin in the Wind', 'If I had a Hammer', 'Puff the Magic Dragon', 'Where have all the flowers gone?' or 'Lucy in the sky with Diamonds' or whatever the songs of the week were. Everybody knew the words and there were always arguments over what they meant. Up in Aberdeen the rebels sang. They didn't get around to Californian style protests but, including Ella, they did think about the issues.

Ella was, however, a bit of a prude when it came to her own sexual freedom so she didn't exactly embrace flower power. She was 'saving herself' for Rory at home in Caithness–and a fat lot of good it did her. (She'd promised, you see.) It must have been the influence of the Kirk and the fear of having a 'mixed drop' she reckoned later in life. The other reason she hadn't jumped on the make love not war band wagon was tragic. Her newly married cousin, Aileen, had taken the birth control pill endovin which was blamed for her having a stroke which killed her at the age of twenty seven. That was something that did scare Ella.

She did come close to falling for a very tall, red-headed Agri student from Shetland who made her laugh and a not very tall but very good looking almost white boy who could sing and had invited her to visit his exotic sounding home in Barbados–with its own private beach.

But she always went home to reliable Rory. She didn't notice until it was too late that they had drifted apart.

'You've changed, Ella,' Rory had said on their last date. 'I can't keep up with you.'

'I'm sorry Rory, but maybe you've changed too,' Ella had said sad but relieved that they could both move on. Ella was ready to fly. It was soon after that that she found the job in Kenya. Rory wasted no time in finding a suitable girl who could be the right wife to help him on Westerside, the farm next door to Hillside. Charlie Mackay had been dearly hoping that his youngest would be the one to marry into the neighbouring farm. He tried to hide his disappointment.

Big sister Morag had married an Englishman called Howard with a beard who knew nothing about farming and an awful lot about things her father Charlie wasn't much interested in. They lived way down in London and he wasn't going all the way down there to visit. Ella had been bridesmaid at the wedding when she was eighteen and liked Howard fine. Jamie accepted him and got on with feeding the cattle.

Of course when the first wee grandson came along Mary and Ella were down in London like a shot. Everything looked as if it was going to be fine. Charlie even said it was going to be 'fine'.

Ella emerged with an MA degree with respectable grades in English, Geography, Geology and Psychology and the class prize for Moral Philosophy. The following year she attended Aberdeen College of Education where she qualified to teach, English, Geography, Modern Studies and Speech and Drama. (She got a prize for being the best practical teacher in Geography but she didn't count that because the Headmaster of the school she did her 'crit' lesson at was her Uncle Jim's best pal. Ella hated nepotism so she never talked about it.)

During the Easter holidays before Ella's PGCE finished, Mary Mackay contacted John Gunn to see if there was a job for her youngest. Of course there was a job but if there hadn't been a job, John Gunn would have created one for his favourite ex pupil. Ella was having nothing to do with it.

'Mum, I don't need any strings pulled for me. I can manage by myself, thank you,' Ella looked at her mother's crestfallen face and felt guilty. 'Sorry, Mum. I know you're only trying to help.'

She told her mother she had already been offered a job and rushed off to the College library to start hunting. She wrote off to the MOD which at the time was the Ministry of Overseas Development and got herself an interview. Off she went on the train from Aberdeen to Kings Cross (without telling her parents) to be asked only three questions.

'Would you like a rural school or a city school?'

'Would you prefer a boys' school or a girls' school?'

'When can you be ready to go?'

The rest of the interview was spent discussing the Royal Dornoch Golf Club which she'd never seen and after twenty minutes she was sent off with (to save postage) the details of a girls' boarding school in the middle of the tea estates in a place called Kericho in Kenya. She would have to be ready for September and her train ticket from Altnabervie to London would be sent through the post. Then she would have to spend a week in London immersed in Swahili and East African culture before boarding a plane for Nairobi, via Entebbe in Uganda where it would need fuel to complete the journey.

The impact of Ella's news on the Mackay family was huge—especially as it had come completely out of the blue.

On the same day Jamie announced he was marrying Katy his latest girl friend who had qualified as a teacher at the same time as Ella. Ella wasn't at all sure whether that would be 'fine' but she agreed to be a bridesmaid and wished them well at the wedding. Time would tell. Katy was a townie and very brainy. Ella wondered how she would cope on the farm.

Mary had sailed through her son's wedding and now she appeared to be coping with Ella's news wonderfully. She usually fussed over little things like dust on the sideboard but not when it came to the big things. She had complete faith in Ella. She had no doubt that her daughter would come home in one piece and full of stories and told everybody how proud she was that Ella was doing her bit for humanity. Ella squirmed if she was within hearing distance–but her Mam seemed happy.

Jamie made a little Bon Voyage card with a message inside:

'I'll be thinking of the smile on the lion's face.'

'Thanks big brother,' she said giving him a shove–but she was used to his twisted sense of humour.

'Dinna worry,' was his comment, 'oor Ella could jump in a cess pool and come oot smelling o' roses. You wait an' see.'

No one was more overwhelmed than Ella herself. At first she had only been making sure that she was never going to go back and teach at Altnabervie where the top class could remember her as a pupil. Things had just got a little out of hand. Then she realised that this was her chance to see some of the places on the giant world map at Balnahuig Primary School. But she was sorry her Dad was so upset.

Family members they hadn't seen for a while were coming to visit to commiserate with the devastated Charlie and to wish Ella well on her journey.

'Now, Ella, don't you come back with coffee-coloured great grandchildren for me,' was Granny Mackay's useful contribution.

'Oh Jeannie, don't be silly,' was Aunty Lizzie's comment. 'Give it a century and we'll all be coffee-coloured.' Lizzie Hardy's rebuke for her sister carried some weight, she felt, as she had been a nurse to a Maharajah's baby in British India.

'Och, Lizzie. Just because every time the baby farted, you got another jewel, doesn't make you an expert,' was the cutting reply.

'Dinna worry. I'm only going for two years and I've no intention of having babies for a long while yet,' Ella assured the old dears.

Perhaps the best bit of advice (or the only one based on informed experience) was from Patrick Smith-Jones's father, wealthy and well-travelled international diplomat of Forestfield, a mansion hidden away behind some trees.

'The most important piece of advice anyone can give you, Isabella, is to always be discreet. Never let anyone know what your political beliefs are and never offer any comment on other people's convictions. You are going to come across all kinds of ideas that you won't agree with and some you'll be fired up about. If you value your safety and your sanity, keep your thoughts firmly under your hat, my dear–and you'll survive.' These words were delivered with such solemnity and passion that the young Ella was convinced that this man had discovered, from bitter experience, what it was like to stick your neck out in the wrong situation.

'Thank you for that. I'll certainly keep it in mind. I just hope I can recognise the situations where discretion is needed.'

'I hope so too,' added the wise but apprehensive diplomat.

Ewan Cameron was thrilled to bits that his protégée had such a spirit of adventure and had seen Ella in action so his words were simple:

'Enjoy yourself Ella. Be true to yourself and come back and educate us. But send us a few letters in between.'

An unexpected spin-off from Ella's hasty decision was a rash of articles in various local newspapers and magazines with headlines like

ELLA OFF TO EAST AFRICA and

LOCAL GRADUATE BECOMES MISSIONARY and

STUDENT FROM SINCLAIRS SETS OFF FOR KENYA,
After this Ella was hounded by schools, the Scouts and Guides, the Women's Guild (from the Kirk) and the WRI (the supposedly non-denominational Women's Rural Institute)–all wanting her to give 'talks'. According to the normally taciturn Charlie Mackay the WRI were 'Women Running Idle'. Ella hated being a mini-celebrity but kept everybody happy by saying she would take lots of pictures and tell them what it was like when she came back home again.

'I'm like you, Dad,' she told Charlie after escaping from the village hall one evening. 'I'd rather have something to say than just have to say something.' Father and daughter shared a rare moment of comradeship. Charlie went off to the town and bought his youngest a 35mm camera for taking slides and a powerful pair of binoculars to view wild game in situ–both of which were state of the art items for 1968. He was filled with apprehension for his daughter but by now he was proud. He'd always known she was a brave wee lass. He was hoping his heart wasn't going to be broken.

His daughter had never intended to do that.

CHAPTER 3

Total Immersion

AUGUST 1968

Mary's emotional state (not so calm after all) wouldn't allow her to come to the station, so Charlie and his daughter drove for twenty silent miles when the day came for Ella to take the train to London for her week of immersion in East African Culture. She would then fly on to remotest Africa for two whole years.

A much too large trunk with far too many household items (at Mary's insistence) had been despatched in advance to Kipsigis Girls School, P.O. Box 55, Kericho, Kenya, East Africa which sounded very exotic and exciting, so Ella was travelling light. A smallish suitcase, a haversack and her guitar in its case were all she carried and Charlie thought she looked far too small and fragile to be taking off on her first ever plane–and he secretly worried that she was never going to make it back. Hence his voice was stuck in his throat and he couldn't think what to say. Ella felt she knew what her father was going through and was ashamed to admit to herself that she wasn't so very sad to be leaving and couldn't wait to get on with the adventure.

'Dinna worry, Dad. I'll be back afore ye ken. Just think. You and Mam can come for a holiday that you'd never even have dreamt of.'

'Aye and pigs can fly,' Charlie said sadly. Ella, swallowing hard, gave her Dad a hug and managed a fairly breezy, 'I'll write when I get there.'

Then, with a perception that surprised and unsettled her father she added, 'I'm sorry things have to change and I'm sorry I didna marry Rory like you wanted me to.'

Charlie didn't think she knew.

The suitcase and the guitar were put in the charge of the guard in his van and Ella found a window seat and settled down for what seemed like endless hours of delicious thinking time and changing bonny views.

The six hundred and seventy odd miles to Kings Cross were expected to take around twenty four hours with a break in Inverness where Auntie Meg and Uncle Jim would give Ella bed and breakfast and put her on the train next morning at five to eight.

Her Auntie Meg and Uncle Jim were just the tonic Ella needed as they seemed to be just as excited at the prospect of their niece setting off for Africa as she was herself.

'Will ye be sleepin' in a mud hut an' eatin' giraffe twigs?' was her Auntie's daft question to which Ella replied she'd leave the twigs to the giraffes and she wasn't sure about the accommodation yet.

'Might you try and get to Rhodesia to visit Doctor Andrew, seeing as you'll be on the same continent at least?' Uncle Jim added in an effort to raise the tone of the conversation.

Doctor Andrew was Charlie and Meg Mackay's cousin. He was a doctor in a hospital in Rhodesia but found time to visit the family in Scotland every so often.

'It would be grand to go and visit him, but I'm not sure if the political situation would allow it,' Ella surmised.

As a partner in an Inverness firm of solicitors, Uncle Jim felt that it was befitting his status to take an interest in recent world politics which suited Ella fine as she'd recently been up to her neck in Aberdeen University Student debates.

The twenty two year old Ella gave her wily old Uncle a run for his money on American civil rights, Vietnam, UDI and a few other topics most significantly Enoch Powell's sacking for his 'Rivers of Blood' speech. They might not have agreed on everything but, after all the arguments, Ella's views had crystallised. No matter what, she'd always be on the side of equality and justice.

After porridge and honey for breakfast, Ella caught the train for Kings Cross and found a window seat again–but this time she kept her suitcase and guitar nearby as maybe there would be more people around than in the far north. She smiled at herself. If she was apprehensive about England, how was she going to cope with Africa? She told herself it would all be fine and settled down to take in the passing sights and daydream–her favourite occupation.

The high Cairngorm Mountains with their green and purple gave way to desolate moors around Dalwhinnie then the dramatic, steep-sided Glen Garry and the beautiful, dark green tree clad Tay Valley with its upside down trees in the glassy surface of the lochs–until the train crossed the brightly painted red Forth Bridge and chugged into Edinburgh. The workmen could be seen dangling dangerously as they painted. It was true that it was a never-ending job. When they finished at one end, the other end needed to be painted and so it went on. Ella had loved that story as a child. They'd still be painting it when she got back from Africa. Some things don't change.

Fifteen years ago Charlie and Mary had put a label on their six year old daughter which read: 'TO BE PICKED UP AT WAVERLEY STATION BY ANDREW MACKAY' and sent her off for her holidays to her Uncle Andrew's hill farm. Charlie and Mary were going to drive down a week later for a few days and bring Ella home. She remembered not being scared at all. Perhaps it had been the thought of the highland pony and the burn full of fish to be guddled for–as well as Auntie Betty's famous date and walnut ginger bread.

Ella still wasn't scared. Flying half way across the world to where she didn't know a soul didn't unnerve her–in the slightest. Perhaps it was the thought of all these exciting and exotic new people and places she expected to find.

Waverley Station to Kings Cross went by in a blur as exhaustion took over and Ella dozed her way past Newcastle and the Midlands which didn't seem exciting enough for her to fight to keep her eyes open.

At one minute to four, twenty four hours and seven minutes after leaving Wick, a sleepy, dishevelled Ella struggled out of Kings Cross Station and into a taxi–headed for total immersion in the Swahili language and the culture of the four year young new independent state of Kenya.

Twenty eight young teachers from all corners of UK had converged on the Study Centre at Eland House, Stag Place exhausted but fired up with anticipation. This was the evening reception for which they had been invited to dress up. Fresh-faced eager expressions beamed around the room. The main impression was of a swirling mass of bright colours clashing in a 1960s fashion parade; tie and dye, paisley patterns, velvet jackets, spots, stripes, bell bottoms, cat suits, chain belts, maxis, minis, dramatic socks, bright shoes, leather fringes, boleros, culottes and balloon sleeves, macramé, beads, more beads, body paint, crew cuts, flat cuts, long hippy hair, big curls, frizzy curls and Pocahontas hair bands.

For Ella think Altnabervie Draperies masquerading as trendy California—bright green jeans with white stitching, hip hugging with a wide white belt at the top and tight around the ankles, green and white striped T-shirt, tucked in, white and green stripy socks and white 'tackies' which is what plimsolls or sandshoes were called in Caithness. Green matched her eyes and her fashionably long auburn hair was her crowning glory and she stood out as the stunner of the group. Ella didn't think so. She took one look at the spectacle and rushed off back to the deserted dorm feeling very—well—Altnabervie. After she'd controlled the collywobbles in her stomach, she dived into her suitcase and dug out a green scarf, tied it Pocahontas style round her forehead, took a deep breath and went back to join her new world. She came back two seconds later to take off the tennis shoes and put on her only decent fashionable shoes which were navy blue with square toes.

The two gentlemen from the MOD (which was later to become the ODM, the Overseas Development Ministry to avoid confusion with the Ministry of Defence) were observing the results of their recruitment programme with a mixture of awe and consternation.

'What have we done Theodore?' Randolph hissed behind his hand. 'I hope this bunch of hippies will actually get down to a bit of work sometime. They all seemed to be so—um—clean cut when we interviewed them? How do you suppose they'll go down in Nairobi?'

Theodore had actually been thinking along the same lines and like Randolph, had been used to khakis and safari suits around Nairobi and suits and ties in the places they frequented in London. Such attire as was on display this evening they had simply associated with riff raff who wandered the streets and did nothing useful for a living.

'Nothing for it, Randolph, old man,' replied Theodore at his most pompous. 'We'll just have to mould them.'

'I wouldn't be too sure that they're mouldable, Teddy–or should that be malleable?' added Randolph, straightening his tie, which was quite unnecessary–in the circumstances.

What they hadn't realised was that Dorothy Watson, later to become Potty Dotty Watty, who had a PhD in Chemistry, by the way, had overheard this little conversation and relayed it to some of the others causing some hilarity. She was clad in tie and dye maxi skirt, leather waistcoat with a fringe and very large, wild curls in her long hair so looked just like the 'riff raff' the two post independence old colonials were referring to. She decided to get a few of the others to wind the two up–in the nicest possible way of course.

Meanwhile, armed with some Dutch courage, Randolph was saying,

'Come on Teddy; let's mingle before the welcome address.'

'Ah, Isabella isn't it? And how is the Royal Dornoch Golf Club, my dear? Still standing in the stormy north?'

'I still don't know because I still haven't been there. Sorry.' retorted Ella, verging on the impudent. But she gave him a wide smile before swiftly moving along to find some younger, more interesting company.

'Perhaps even that one isn't as biddable as I expected,' Randolph thought to himself before trying once more to find some conversation to help bridge the generation gap.

After some wine, beer or cider and a buffet meal, music was going to be provided to break the ice should the young people want to dance. Luckily the Study Centre wasn't staffed entirely by Randolphs and Theodores so there was a record player, an amplifier, some decent LPs and even a microphone. However, the welcome speech was to be first on the after dinner agenda and it was to be delivered by Randolph, the slightly more paranoid of the double act from the Ministry.

'May I say how, um, delighted we are to welcome you all

here as a precursor to the extremely important service you will be providing in Keenya,–uh Kenya–very soon. Before I go any further, there is one little, but vital thing that Theodore and I feel we ought to warn you about before you venture into the new culture of modern Africa. It has to be remembered that modest attire is most important and, as we look around us we can see a few outfits which, though very fine indeed for the London scene, perhaps, may cut rather too much of a dash in rural Kee–uh, Kenya. I do hope you will take my advice in the best possible spirit as we *do* think you are a wonderful bunch of young men and women and we *do* really believe you can be moulded into the kind of young people who will be suitable ambassadors for Great Britain or should I call it by its fashionable title–the United Kingdom.'

The unsuitably clad 'ambassadors' could hardly contain their amusement but somehow managed to soldier through to the end of this lengthy, pedantic speech and deliver a polite ripple of applause before the music was turned up and Potty Dotty Watty went into action. She'd collared another girl, discussed a plan, taken note of Randolph and Theodore's tipple and the two girls presented themselves in front of the two disconcerted men and offered them each a large glass of the red wine they had been downing fairly rapidly earlier on.

After some time, plan B was initiated. Randolph and Theodore were relieved of their wine glasses, jackets and ties, in that order and persuaded to take to the dance floor to leap around to The Marmalade singing 'Ob-la-Di Ob-la-Da' which they seemed to enjoy–quite a lot. They enjoyed 'Born to be Wild' even more and even knew it was sung by Steppenwolf.

Toby Pickles, green velvet trousers and paisley shirt was next on the scene. He could sing he thought so he grabbed the microphone and sang along to Amen Corner's 'Bend Me, Shape Me' the significance of which escaped the older men but otherwise brought the house down.

The penny was just beginning to drop but not quite when Toby took a scruffy bit of paper out of his pocket and started singing along to 'Congratulations' (Cliff Richards had got second place in the Eurovision Song Contest that year.) It went like this:

'Congratulations, Commiserations
You've found the biggest bunch of hippies
You could find.
Don't worry Randy, Don't worry Teddy
Let's hope our new employers will be blind.'

Their faces were a picture. Teddy stood there open-mouthed but Randy managed to blurt out,

'I say. You wouldn't be trying to tell us something, would you?'

They were left in no doubt of this by the time Toby Pickles had launched into the Frankie and Johnny theme but to the words, "Randy and Teddy were lovers–'.

To give them their due, Randolph and Theodore ended up appreciating the joke but assured everyone that they certainly were *not* lovers and produced pictures of their wives and children from their sturdy wallets–which made them seem more human; perhaps the generation gap had been bridged for the moment in one little corner of the world in 1968.

Bunk bed dormitories, shared lukewarm showers and the most basic of diets were doing nothing to dampen the spirits of the new ambassadors despite the hangovers after the eventful welcome reception of the previous evening. For six days and seven nights it was going to be Africa, Africa, Africa starting with a creaky 16mm film of the physical and human Geography of East Africa, followed by a slide show–or half a slide show before the projector had to be stopped because it was burning a hole in a picture of flamingos on Lake Nakuru.

The young teachers were also reminded that their job was

simply to provide the African students with the knowledge they needed to pass their school exams and they were advised to steer well clear of politics. Ella had heard that before somewhere.

After two days of discussions about African customs and culture school systems and making the most of very limited resources, the big experiment began. Everything was conducted in Kiswahili, absolutely everything. It was hard–especially not to cheat. The group tried their best. They had to resort to every kind of mime, gesture and facial expression to communicate–like babies learning to speak. It was amazing how many bits of language they picked up–and never forgot. Jambo, hello, kwaheri goodbye, asante, thank you and Gina yake nane? What's your name? presented no problems even though the learners couldn't see the words written down. One or two people gave up in sheer frustration and disappeared into a corner with a copy of the Teach Yourself Swahili.

Ella's mind kept going back to when she was six years old at Balnahuig School where they'd been building their giant world map that they could walk all over. Had she been subconsciously drawn to Africa because of those early lessons? Had she been wrong to feel that some inexplicable instinct beyond her control had brought her this far?

At the end of the induction week, the new recruits went their separate ways armed with a hefty pack of information and a list of the names and East African addresses of all the others.

CHAPTER 4

Journey to Kericho

All that could be seen out of the oval window was a thick mass of inky, midnight blue coming from underneath, then a slowly changing blood orange layer which was brightening and thickening as it was spreading into the silvery grey endless expanse above it.

It was dawn over the Sahara and Ella was waking up mid-flight to Nairobi, via Entebbe. She was thinking in world maps as usual, trying to work out where they were. The inky blue layer below was clearing to reveal the page in the atlas with the Nile flowing through Sudan. Ella could hardly believe her eyes. There was the blue river with its banks of green bending round in that distinctive, so familiar shape. And there was that huge expanse of golden desert. It was all true. It was real.

This was not just the first time for Ella to see the Nile, it was her first ever flight–and it was magic.

The heat was like a hammer on the faces of the passengers as they stepped off the plane at Entebbe. The creaky, wooden ceiling fans and the dusty aspidistras did little to cool down the little shack which served as a transit lounge while refuelling was done. Weary travellers flopped around on enormous very shabby brown leather sofas, kicking up some more dust as they moved. There didn't seem to be anywhere to have a drink and the queue for the single toilet was long. The place must have seen better days. Despite all of this, Ella could hardly contain her excitement. The adventure had begun.

Three hours later she was sitting on her suitcase with her knapsack on her back and her guitar upended between her knees. This was Embakasi Airport, Nairobi, and it was extremely crowded. She was feeling a little insecure as she realised that she had no idea what to do about getting to her school three hundred miles away. The new recruits had been told that their schools knew which flights they were on and that things would be sorted out in Nairobi but Ella had no idea who was supposed to meet her if anyone and she'd hunted around absolutely everywhere for an information desk which of course was non-existent.

So, here she was, sitting on her suitcase waiting for something to happen. She was in her favourite place again, watching the world go by and this time it was people watching. After Caithness where everyone was white and Aberdeen and London where only a few people weren't white, the spectacle of cosmopolitan Nairobi was fascinating. She had been expecting more faces to be African and was surprised at the variety of race, dress and language that surrounded her. She was passing time guessing what people did with their lives. She was thinking:

'That white man in khakis and red dust all over him must be a game warden. The woman in the turquoise sari and all that gold must have a rich businessman for a husband. The

Sikh with the beard and turban works in a bank. That's an American draft dodger with a rich father. Look at the lenses on that camera–and listen to him talking. I wonder if that one's a new teacher. She's nearly as white as I am–and she's got a big suitcase. Maybe that African guy's an MP. His suit and tie look brand new–'.

'*Memsaab?*'

'*Ndio.*' Ella surprised herself at her instinctive response after the total immersion in Swahili. A small African man in a dark suit and white shirt, with his earlobes tucked above his ears was looking at her and pointing at the label on her suitcase.

'Kipsigis Girls' School?'

'*Ndio.*' Again Ella was excited at being able to communicate and relieved that somebody was aware of her existence.

'*Kaa hapa,* sit here. *Ngoja Ngoja.* Wait here!' The only words she understood were 'Wait here!' but they did the trick. She wasn't going anywhere until someone came to the rescue.

That someone came in the shape of one white-haired bundle of energy, Mrs Haidee King of Solihull and now dynamic headmistress of Kipsigis Girls' School, a boarding school for the cream of African girls set within the tea estates of the Kericho Highlands.

'Oh, what a relief,' she flustered. 'I thought you weren't coming either. I don't know what that lot in London are up to. They sent our teacher to Nanyuki last time and we're all doubling up on lessons. Anyway, sweetie, you don't want to hear that, do you? Oh, I could hug you.' And she did, which was just what Ella needed. 'I like her,' she thought.

'Oh, I'm Haidee, by the way–Mrs King to the girls.'

'And I'm Ella. Miss Mackay to the girls I suppose'.

'And this is Arapngeno. I couldn't survive without him'.

'*Jambo Memsaab Kidogo*'. Ella was little madam. Mrs King was *Memsaab Mkubwa*, big Madam–not because she was bigger but because she was older and more important.

'*Jambo* Arapngeno,' said Ella and, now excelling herself, '*Asante sana*,' as she thanked him very much for carrying her suitcase.

'Ah, *mzuri mzuri* memsaab,' cried Arapngeno pleased that this rookie off the plane had made an effort to learn the language.

'Remind me to tell you a story or two about that lot in London sometime but not now. Let's get out of here.' Ella added.

Haidee finally drove her battered old white Peugeot 404 on to what passed for the main road after an endless battle to get out of the airport past ragged, disorganised, noisily honking piles of cars whose drivers didn't seem to have any idea of the concept of queuing or giving way or sticking to the correct side of the road. Ella had to ask which side of the road people drove on because it wasn't altogether apparent.

'The best side,' cried Haidee with her infectious giggle as she enjoyed her usual joke. 'But in theory it's the left side, like England. It depends on where the holes are and how big they are.'

Every sight, sound and smell was a new experience for Ella who, by now was covered in a thin layer of red dust like everyone else because it is impossible to sit in a car without open windows. The dust matched her freckles and hair and was acting as a protection against the tropical sun. The two women sat in the front seat finding out all about each other while Arapngeno slept soundly across the back seat.

Nairobi a few miles from the airport was every bit a modern city; this was in sudden and stark contrast with rural Kenya with its dry grassland peppered with acacias, which stretched beyond the smell of burning charcoal which filled the air near the shanty fringe of town with its rough, tumble down shacks, open sewers and overcrowding .

Wide avenues, neatly manicured lawns and tall clean

buildings gave the impression of affluence. It was only the vast curtains of deep red bougainvillea, the lilac of the jacaranda and the bright red of the flame trees that differentiated this city from London, Paris or New York.

Haidee swung the little car into what looked like a nonexistent parking spot, handed Arapngeno some shillingis and, when they all got out, locked the car. Haidee and Ella set off for lunch leaving the African man to fend for himself. Anticipating Ella's thoughts, Haidee remarked, 'He'd be uncomfortable. He'd hate it.'

Ella didn't believe that for a minute but she was remembering how important discretion was. She thought, 'Some things haven't changed since 1964 then.' Anyway, she was too tired to tackle her new boss on the subject.

'Is this the legendary Thorn Tree?' asked Ella noticing the tree growing up through the middle of the restaurant. The Thorn Tree had been described in the London press as an important world meeting place for expatriates and visitors to Kenya.

'You've heard of it? Yes it is–nothing but the best for your first meal in Kenya. It's part of The New Stanley hotel–five stars. Why don't you check the board?' Haidee suggested.

Ella wasn't expecting to find any messages but, to her surprise, there was a message from one of the recruits on the London induction course which read:

ANY TEACHER AT ELAND HOUSE IN AUGUST, PLEASE MEET ME HERE SAT. OCT. 14TH MIDDAY. HOPE LIFE GOOD FOR YOU.

It was signed Jim Sawyer, Kakamega School. She didn't remember him but made a note of the date and time and decided to try and come.

'I suppose that's what you call the bush telegraph,' she said to Haidee who just nodded as she'd been hearing it all before since 1959.

'That's amazing,' Ella had to add. She looked around to see

if there was anyone else around but that would have been too much of a coincidence.

However, the place was awash with young people from UK, Canada and USA mostly. This reflected the massive recruitment programmes for all kinds of very young professionals for work in East Africa in the late 1960s–and Ella was very conscious of this.

'How many of us are there?'

'Probably not enough' said Haidee, 'as long as they keep their noses out of the politics and keep their opinions to themselves. I think the theory is the younger they are the more apolitical they're likely to be.' Ella bit her tongue but did say, 'I don't know what makes people think that!' Her voice had risen and her eyes flashed which made the older women look at her curiously.

'With all the heartache that has been going on in Kenya, my dear, I think it's a case of least said soonest mended. I hope you'll come to understand that.'

'I do understand,' Ella said firmly, 'but any politics I have are about being fair and treating people equally–so that shouldn't be too much of a problem, should it?'

'Very admirable, I'm sure–but take care and watch and listen before you speak.' Haidee said gently, understanding this girl a little.

'Okay, I'll do that', Ella promised.

The spectacular journey from Nairobi to Kericho took them past the lush, flat, green carpet of the Limuru tea estates and on to the dramatic escarpment at the edge of the Great East African Rift Valley. No description could prepare any first time visitor for the sheer breathtaking scale of the topography: the sudden drop into the valley and the view of never ending flat plains of dry savannah with Mount Longonot protruding like a black carbuncle on the horizon.

Haidee seemed to have a story for every corner on the road;

her friend was headmistress at Limuru Girls School which was the best school in Kenya; it used to be for white girls only but now admitted African and Asian girls.

Here was the chapel built by the Italian road builders who constructed the windy road down the escarpment so that they could pray every morning. They stopped for a moment and indeed this tiny chapel was exquisite.

That was Lake Naivasha which is surrounded by the Delamere Estates. The present Lord Delamere's father was a crazy man who used to ride his horse through the bar at The Norfolk Hotel but the Delameres got away with murder because they were in cahoots with the new Kenya government especially since Jomo Kenyatta's forgive and forget speech in 1962 after the horrors of the Mau Mau rebellion.

She had heard there was a new baby grandson in the Delamere family. 'I think they've called him Thomas. And did Ella know that this Lord Delamere was six foot six tall—a real aristocrat? Over here's Lake Elementeita. That's where the family home is.

'I went there once,' Haidee said, 'It's so beautiful.'

Ella thought she detected a wistful note and as she looked sideways at the older lady; she decided she must have been very good looking in her day.

'This must be the famous happy valley of slow horses and fast ladies,' Ella couldn't resist the comment.

'Oh, you've heard about that, have you? These days are over now. No more champagne and pink gin, thank goodness. What a mess. I didn't get involved but I had a husband who did. I haven't seen him for years.'

'Ouch,' thought Ella.

And this was Lake Nakuru in the distance and could Ella see the pink fringes? Those were flamingos but there wasn't time to see them now because the schoolgirls would start arriving from tomorrow. They never knew how long it would take them to travel and could arrive a whole week before term started. Sometimes it was a two week walk. Ella was appalled. This intermittent stream of chatter was designed to drip feed the new expatriates with enough information to provide a background of the recent history of the newly independent Kenya and some reasons why their services were desperately wanted. After thirty years in Kenya, Mrs King knew exactly which facts to filter out of her wide knowledge to pass on. She knew that the first day in a new country was the day for brainwashing her excited and curious but naïve new recruits. She insisted on meeting them at the airport herself and by the time they had reached Kipsigis Girls' School, she hoped she had moulded them into a suitable frame of mind.

Ella wasn't bored but she wasn't always impressed.

'Over there,' went on Haidee, 'is St Andrews School at Turi. My daughter Felicity went there and she had every facility you could ever want. Horse riding lessons, swimming pool, outdoor theatre in the round. You name it they have it.'

'Very nice too,' mumbled Ella hoping she'd kept the sarcasm out of her voice. Her observations had registered more than Mrs King's spruced up, censored version of Kenyan society of 1968. With the windows open the smells and sounds as well as the sights of rural Africa were telling a truth which was much more fascinating than the prattle of a very British Colonial woman, however well intended it might be.

The car was slowed down by people, goats and cows most of the way along the road. Around Limuru, dust-caked, barefoot Kikuyu women were carrying enormous bundles of wood on their backs using straps across their foreheads that had worn deep furrows.

Little skinny boys in ragged khaki shorts were herding their goats with whistles and shouts waving excitedly as the car passed by.

The scene changed after Naivasha. Ella could not take her

eyes off the fine figure of a man by the roadside. He was well over six feet tall, dressed in a brick red toga over one shoulder, revealing a long limbed, almost naked athletic body on the other side. His handsome features with high cheekbones and a fine nose were set in an inscrutable expression close to arrogance. His hair was neatly plaited and, like the rest of his body, caked with greasy red clay and decorated with multicoloured beads. His face was dusted with a crimson powder and heavy earrings dangled from several piercings in his ears and he proudly carried a spear... 'Wow,' thought Ella. The only word she could think of was 'magnificent'.

'He's a Masai warrior,' Haidee told Ella.

'Lucky Masai ladies,' said Ella before she could stop herself.

'You can take the Masai out of Africa but you can't take Africa out of the Masai.' Haidee added using the old cliché.

In this case, Ella was inspired.

'You can't help but admire them for that,' she said. 'Who are we to decide which culture is most meaningful?'

Haidee told her that the Masai were the proudest tribe in Kenya, and closely related to the Kipsigis. Many had studied overseas in America and UK and come back with high degrees and chances of good jobs in the city but they couldn't wait to get home and drink their favourite cocktail of blood, milk, cow pee and charcoal ash and cover themselves in cow dung.

By the time the car had turned left off the Eldoret road on its way to Kericho, the day was coming to a close. A dramatic sunset was spreading a golden sheet across the entire horizon–but only for a very short time before focusing in on a huge vermilion ball which hovered for a few minutes and sank visibly inch by inch until it disappeared. There is nothing more startling than the first experience of a tropical sunset.

Arapngeno had been sleeping peacefully all the way but joined the others for a stretch while they all watched the theatrical show of the sun taking its bow for the day.

The young woman was aware of a strangely powerful bond drawing these three very different people together in their mutual admiration of nature's beauty–the tough ex-colonial, her wise old servant and the fresh off the plane, naïve expatriate. All different but all equal.

Ella's thoughts returned to Balnahuig Primary School and the values instilled by Ewan Cameron during the giant world map project. Despite all the hate, the violence and the horror, somewhere within us there are universal values–somewhere.

After the show was over the trio drove off into the solid, inky darkness. Tall fir trees with Spanish moss or old man's beard could be seen in the headlights indicating that they were climbing up into the highlands which were good for growing tea.

The car came to a stop. Through the smoke was a row of *dukahs* outside which fires burning in *ngikos* heated up maize cobs, meat pieces on skewers, skinny, tiny chicken legs, *mandazis* and pots of thick, sweet, milky tea. Arapngeno pointed out what he thought were the best pieces of meat for Memsaab Kidogo and she thanked him.

It was freezing cold after dark which surprised Ella and this African meal tasted wonderful. The very English sandwiches in the fancy Treetops restaurant in Nairobi were fine but this was much more memorable.

They were soon speeding off into the darkness again winding around the potholes but otherwise not slowed down by people and animals who by now had gone home to bed. Haidee must have known that road like the back of her hand because they only landed up in one hole which Ella and Arapngeno had to push the car out of.

'*Sukuma, Sukuma,*'–a new word to add to Ella's expanding Swahili vocabulary.

'We're in the middle of the tea table now. Pity it's dark,' Haidee said as they were nearing home. 'You'll see it in the morning.'

After much hooting, two *askaris* came running followed by three barking dogs to unlock the big wrought iron gates to the school grounds.

'You can't be too careful when you're looking after the cream of the country's teenage girls. They seem to have so many 'uncles' who want to give them a lift home to visit the 'family'.'

Her infectious giggle revealed that she wasn't a bit fooled. Nothing much got past Mrs Haidee King.

A steaming cup of cocoa in front of a roaring wood fire and a declined brandy nightcap later, Ella had a vague awareness of crisp white starched sheets and brown woolly blankets before her head hit the crisp white, starched pillow for the next solid twelve hours of blissful oblivion.

CHAPTER 5

Kipsigis Girls' School

The smell of charcoal burning and the sounds of rhythmic tapping and gentle singing in a strange language emanated through the metal mosquito netting which covered the open window. Someone must have been in the room earlier to open the curtains and windows and leave a cup of tea, now stone cold, by the bedside. Ella tried a mouthful, grimaced and gingerly put her toes out on to the polished red floor.

'I didn't hear a thing. I must have been exhausted,' she thought.

Her heart leapt with excitement as she remembered where she was. She went over to the wide but barred window at the other side of the room. As far as the eye could see, in all directions, there was the brightest, greenest, flattest carpet of green bushes imaginable. Above the carpet were a few taller tree-like bushes; dotted around were the tiny figures of women with their baskets on their backs, delicately picking the three little leaves from the top of the bushes.

'This must be the tea table,' gasped Ella in awe. 'All this so that people half way across the world can enjoy a cuppa.'

The sun was high in the sky; this meant that half the day had gone so, rather than explore the house in search of a bath, Ella threw on her green jeans and a clean T shirt and ventured out.

'You're still alive then.' This was Haidee being annoyingly bright and breezy. 'Come on. We've got lots to do.' Ella had a few minutes to down some tea and toast before being marched off on a round of the school classrooms, dormitories, assembly hall and staff housing–ending up at a newly built house at the end furthest away from Haidee's older house, the only substantial building on the 'campus'.

The newly built house was to be home for the time being for Ella and a Canadian girl called Janet Thompson who was a University student who could teach Drama and Music or, at a push, Religious Education. She was due back from a short break in Uganda that evening. It had three bedrooms, one of which was set up as a dining room, a bathroom, a kitchen with a big black wood stove, a living room with a huge open fireplace and French windows opening on to a veranda which overlooked a bit of wild looking bush land.

'So much for living in a mud hut and eating giraffe twigs,' Ella put in and related to Haidee what her Auntie Mary had said. 'I wasn't expecting running water and twenty four hour electricity but I'm not complaining.'

'You'd be surprised how many Americans complain about that,' Haidee said, 'and then you get the Englishman who wants his paper and milk delivered to the door.'

'Don't worry; your garden will look wonderful in no time. We've got a team of *shamba* boys all ready to attack it. We've got some money from the World Bank to sort the campus out.'

Haidee was very businesslike.

Soft furnishings were also included which meant cushions for the wooden armchairs and sofas and mattresses but no curtains, bedding or towels. Janet had already fixed up bedding and curtains for one of the bedrooms, presumably her own, and on the dining table was an old-fashioned singer sewing machine with a handle and a big pile of bright blue cotton (Jinja cotton from Uganda Ella was to discover) which matched the cushions in the living room. This seemed like a big job in progress.

'Janet's wonderful with a sewing machine,' Haidee pointed out. 'She helps me with the uniforms.'

'You mean you make all the uniforms.'

'Sure. How else would we get them at the price? Come on. The boys will bring all your stuff here and leave it in your bedroom so you won't have to lift a finger. Oh and I have some sheets and towels you can borrow until your trunk arrives. You're needed elsewhere. A few of our customers have arrived.'

Shadowing Haidee was an education. A visit to a fifty bed dormitory, uncovered two little girls dressed in identical long, white, kaftan- style nightdresses perching uncomfortably on one of the single metal beds all of which were made up with white sheets and pillows, blankets of a variety of colours, and tucked in with the tightest hospital corners you have ever seen. The whole place was spotless. The floors and windows shone and would stay that way as long as Mrs King was around.

'This is Mercy and this is Happy. They've walked two hundred miles in eight days from Kakamega to get here; we've had to throw their clothes away. They've been measured for their uniform.'

'Can I wear my uniform today, please?' begged an impatient Mercy.

'Soon,' laughed Haidee affectionately. 'We're not magicians.'

Ella didn't volunteer to wield a sewing machine but she

did ask where else she could be useful.

This is how Ella found herself thinking about preparing lessons for ten different subjects in Form One in her first year of teaching. She drew the line at Maths and Domestic Science on the grounds that she would probably do more harm than good.

'The other staff will be relieved to see you,' Elizabeth Kiprogot said to Ella with a firm African handshake. 'We're so short of teachers.'

Elizabeth, a plump and comfortable woman in her forties was Haidee's right hand woman, Ella discovered later, and apart from teaching Domestic Science, was a vital liaison person with the kitchen and ground staff and interpreter for the relatives of the school girls. The school would probably have collapsed without her.

On Ella's first day Elizabeth also took it upon herself to tell her something about the school and the pupils.

There were two hundred girls on role mainly Kipsigis, others Masai, Luo or Nandi but only three Kikuyus who were out of place in that part of the country. All should have passed the Kenya Primary exams and none should have been older than sixteen or younger than twelve when they joined form one. A tough little test on day one weeded out those who had probably got a cousin to sit the exam. With Mrs King around the elderly looking or pregnant girls were easily spotted at assembly.

Elizabeth laughed as she described a conversation with Mrs King.

'Do you see Rose Chebet's ankles, Elizabeth?' Mrs King had said, 'I'd better get her down to the hospital. And look at that new Margaret–she can't possibly be twelve.'

A quick trip to the hospital had confirmed Rose's pregnancy and the fact that Margaret had given birth to at least four children and was probably around forty. Rose had to be a non-starter but Haidee had to be very careful with Margaret; she was probably some politician's wife, sister or even aunt.

'Sometimes it's hard to deal with these situations, Ella.' Elizabeth explained. 'People are so desperate for an education.'

'I'll try to do my best,' Ella told Elizabeth feeling a little apprehensive about whether she was up to the task.

On that first day, after the shock of viewing her timetable with all its subjects and having a quick look at the resources available to her, Ella walked across the sports field to her new home with a heavy heart.

There was a yellow VW beetle parked outside her new home and beside it a haversack and a guitar case. Her housemate had just arrived. Ella's spirits lifted at the thought of some young company.

Janet turned out to be just the tonic Ella needed. She too was a redhead but almost blonde and she towered six inches above Ella.

'Hi there, I'm Janet Thompson,' she said in her Canadian accent, 'but call me Jan.'

'I'm Ella. I'm so glad I've got someone like you to share with–who's young I mean–and I see you've got a guitar too.'

'Oh, you're from Scotland,' observed Jan. 'Great. How was your journey? And before Ella could answer she added, 'My guess is you've been well and truly Haidee Kinged. Right?'

'Do you mean the crash course on how to be a good colonial and keep out trouble?' Ella answered thinking she was going to like this girl.

'Spot on Ella,' Jan answered. 'I reckon we two are gonna get along just fine. Has Haidee got you stitching, yet?'

'Not likely. I'd be hopeless. But I've just seen my timetable. They wanted me to take Form one for every subject until I put my foot down.'

'You'll manage,' Jan said detecting a note of panic, 'These kids are phenomenal. They'll teach themselves. You just need to keep two pages ahead of them. Have you seen your room?

I hope you don't mind blue.'

Ella was astonished to find that Haidee's servant, Arapngeno, had unpacked, hung up all her clothes, except her smalls which were left in the suitcase, made up her bed and hung a towel on a chair.

'When did this happen?' was all she could find to say.

'Isn't Arapngeno a treasure?' Janet commented. 'I've had to sleep at Haidee's house for three months because this house wasn't even built. I can't tell you how glad I am to escape and get in here. She's great but I sure need a break!'

'I can well imagine that,' Ella remarked. 'Thanks for all this Jan. I assume you did the curtains.'

'I'd nearly finished them before I left for Uganda so I just had to finish one seam, put the hooks on and Arapngeno hung them up. Are they OK? There was only blue cotton and some horrible bright orange colour at Kericho Stores so I hope you like them. They're a bit crushed but that'll drop out soon.'

It would have been churlish of Ella to say anything other than she was delighted.

'How about we down some scrambled eggs on toast and I tell you all about my trip to the Mountains of the Moon? Gee, but Uganda is beautiful. I can't wait for my pictures to come back.'

'I'm really relieved everything's all sorted out,' Ella told Jan, 'but there's no way I could get used to having a servant. I want to do my own chores. I thought *uhuru* was here.'

The two girls agreed that, in this modern, independent Kenya, they should make a stand and refuse to be like the old colonials and 'do' for themselves.

The doorbell rang and a small, elderly man announced that he was to be their *pishi* and he'd be reporting for duty at 5 am the next day. The girls said sorry, they wouldn't need a servant but thanked him anyway. The old man nodded, smiled and left with a twinkle in his eye. Twenty minutes later a bomb-shell hit the new housemates.

'What do you mean; you can't give Arapbet a job? If you don't give him a job, he won't be able to feed his wife and children and what's more, you won't be able to your jobs properly. I'm not having half fed, disorganised teachers messing up my school. Arapbet will be here in the morning. He already has a back door key. Good Night. Sleep well.' With that, the whirlwind left and nothing was ever said about it again. Haidee was her cheerful self and didn't seem to have held their thoughtlessness against them.

That was how Arapbet, a loyal and paternal Kipsigi came to be *Bwana Mkubwa* in the house of the two *Memsaabs Kidogo* even though even Ella at five foot three and half was bigger than he was and Janet towered over him. There was absolutely no doubt about who the boss was. The fire was lit at five am to heat the water and at around six am tea was delivered to each bedside. Breakfast, consisting of pawpaw, pineapple, some form of eggs, tea and toast was served on the dining table in the spare bedroom and at seven am the memsaabs were reminded that it was time to leave for *skooli* or they would be late. At ten am it was back home for coffee and home baking ready on a tray for morning break then straight back to the classroom. At twelve thirty pm lunch was laid out on the table, served, devoured and cleaned up after without the Memsaab Kidogos moving a muscle. Then they were sent to bed for a rest while the daily heavy rainstorm did its job and until the sun had come out again to shine on the rain washed land for the rest of the day. Usually, the whole world slept while it rained unless the noise was too loud on a tin roof or there was an urgent pile of marking or preparation to do. Arapbet's last job of the day was to send his two teachers off with a cup of tea inside them for afternoon sports or hobbies. Then he went home to his family until next day leaving the girls to fend for themselves with leftovers. This also gave them a chance to cook for friends if they wanted to in the evening.

All conversations were in Swahili–not the posh Kiswahili complete with grammar–but kitchen Swahili. Ella was surprised she'd remembered so much from her total immersion course in London. Jan was interested to hear that the tutor had been Canadian and wondered why CUSO (for volunteer students from Canadian Universities) hadn't organised such a Swahili course. Every time supplies were low Arapbet would point at empty packets and repeat the Swahili word so that a shopping list could be made.

All laundry was done before lunchtime every day. Floors were swept and polished a burnished red using half coconut shells and sheepskin footpads, firewood was piled up near the wood stove and the living room hearth, windows were polished with newspaper and of course all cooking and washing up was done and dusted before anyone else could even think of doing it.

After all that, when it came to pay day, Jan and Ella were embarrassed at the pittance they were expected to pay him. Ella hit on an idea. Why didn't they buy him a stock of flour, yeast and a few bread tins and get him to bake for all the other teachers who were always complaining about the lack of bread? Soon Arapbet was making a bit of extra money by selling his bread, the teachers were happy and the girls always had a hot oven and plenty of hot water. By ploughing back some of his profits to buy more ingredients he expanded his business to rock cakes and shortbread. The two little madams felt a little less guilty.

The work at school was daunting but, despite a few mini disasters, Ella coped. The students were a delight: They were desperate to hang on to every word uttered and soak everything up like sponges.

After class the girls flopped on the grass, noses in a book.

They knew what sacrifices their families had made to send them to school and weren't going to let them down. Four cows had to be sold to pay school fees for a year–but a father knew that he could sell his daughter for more cows if she had a School Certificate.

'Educate a man and you educate a person but educate a woman and you educate a family' was the common cry.

Also, which wasn't quite so apparent, there was the need for these girls to escape the oppression of their male-dominated society where the women did all the work and bowed down to rules made by men to suit men.

Meantime, the regime was tough and resources were limited. This was why Mrs King needed to wring every ounce of energy out of her young teachers and this was why she tried to free them from any kind of domestic hassle.

In one of her English lessons for the little ones Ella decided to set the task of writing a story with the title A Day in The Life of–. She wrote her own answer as an example. The students enjoyed it and produced wonderful essays of their own. This is what Ella wrote:

A Day in the Life of Miss Mackay

My name is Miss Mackay and I was born in Scotland. I came to Kipsigis Girls' School four weeks ago to teach. I think Kenya is a very beautiful country with much more sunshine than my country

My day begins at Kipsigis Girls' School with dormitory inspection at 5:30am to make sure that every girl is out of bed and the prefects have organised the cleaning rotas. It's still dark and I'm feeling very sleepy so I don't notice that Elizabeth Chebet is hiding under her blankets–but somebody else does and she's pulled out of bed.

When everything seems organised, I walk home for breakfast around sunrise at 6am across the wet grass, looking around at the white blanket of mist that clings to the tea table in the distance. It's there every morning and I know it's going to rise into the sky as the day gets hotter and eventually form clouds and fall as rain around midday. I can't believe it happens every day.

In my country in summer the sun comes up at 3:00am and doesn't go to bed until 10pm and in winter the sun stays asleep until 9am and goes down at 4pm and the weather is cold.

After breakfast, our Bwana Mkubwa sends Miss Thompson and me to school on time so that we will not be late for assembly at 7am.

Unless some teacher talks too much again after the hymns and prayers, I get to the first lesson at 7:15am. Today it is Geography which is lucky because it's one of the subjects I was specially trained to teach, However, Form One now know that I can teach anything anyone asks me to but that sometimes experiments can go a little wrong in Science and substances can turn out to be the wrong colour.

In Geography I am now pretty good at drawing an outline of the world map in a short time which is useful when there are only three atlases in school. I feel so lucky to have such hard-working pupils to teach–even if they do sometimes 'borrow' my chalk and don't return it.

Hey! Whoever you are, make sure you are using it well.

The next lesson is French and we are using a book called Pierre et Sedou which, thankfully, has lots of pictures and is quite easy. I always practise my lessons with Monsieur Duval and I think he thinks my accent is funny before he makes it better.

It's morning break and I'm going home for coffee and a short rest. Well I probably won't have time because I have to prepare the next lesson which is English.

In English we are preparing two poems for choral verse at Nairobi Music Festival next May. I hope the girls are enjoying them. One is 'Tarantella' by Hilaire Belloc and the other is 'Boots' by Rudyard Kipling. I don't know who chose the poems. I didn't.

The clouds are gathering so I know it's time to go home for lunch which is always tasty. Miss Thompson and I are both very tired so it's time for a rest while everyone else is resting–and who wants to be out in the rain?

My afternoon lesson is Music which is my favourite because I teach the pupils a song I know while I play the guitar and then I get to listen to all the African traditional songs which are new and exciting to me. I like when we go out on to the field and everyone can sing dance and drum as loudly as they like.

Today I'm not so lucky because it's my weekly duty day when I must supervise private studies in the evening between 8pm and 10pm. It was fun today because a swarm of **kumbi kumbi** *flew in through the open windows towards the classroom lights and I had my first experience of watching the girls make an extra meal out of them. I have decided I'm not ready to try them just yet.*

At 10pm Mrs King came along to send me home to bed which I was very happy about, Miss Thompson and I had a bit of a chat over a cup of cocoa and went to bed exhausted–but happy.

Tomorrow will be another day. Good Night.

Ella (and Jan) learned a huge amount from these stories. For some reason, most of the girls wanted to say *why* they wanted 'schooling'.

Happy Chepkirui wrote, 'I want to go to university so I can be the first wife of a chief's son. If I fail I might be the fourth wife of an old man.'

Tuesday Chebet began with, 'My name is Tuesday Chebet because I was born on Tuesday. Chebet means born when the sun goes down.'

Evelina Mboga's answer was revealing, 'A day in my life is full of study because when I become a politician there will be no circumcision for girls and my children will not cry for food.'

'I like Science best because I will be the doctor in a new clinic for my village,' Josephine Kiprogot wrote.

Other reasons for 'schooling' included, 'When I am rich I will live in a big house in a street with Jacaranda trees–' , 'My children will never have to walk for a week to go to school–' or ' I can teach English to my babies so it can be more easy–' and there were half a dozen who wrote 'Education is the key to life' and a few others who churned out, 'Educate a man and educate a person. Educate a woman and educate a family.'

When Ella was praising their work she said, 'I don't remember asking for all the reasons why you wanted to come to school but it was very interesting to read about them.'

'But Madam (not Miss),' Josephine Kiprogot informed her. 'We need all our teachers to know how important it is for us.'

'Madam' Mackay then felt duty bound to say, 'Then I must make sure that I do the best job I can.' When the whole class cheered, Ella thought back to the Caithness bairns who couldn't wait to get out of the classroom–especially the ones who 'hated the school'. If the Form Ones at Kipsigis Girls' were so mature and focused, what were her Literature classes in Form Four going to be like? The young Ella felt a huge sense of responsibility. They were, after all, the cream of Kenyan girls who were expected to be leaders in their society.

Routine established it was time for the young teachers to explore what exciting distractions life in Kenya had to offer.

CHAPTER 6

The Tea Hotel

SEPTEMBER 1968

First stop the Tea Hotel, one time haunt of white-only colo-
nialists, but now since *uhuru*, the visitors were a microcosm of
desegregated Kenyan Society, minus the hard-boiled *mzungus*
who had either left the country or been bumped off during
the Mau Mau rebellion.

The young and single of the teaching staff at Kipsigis
Girls' School were out for a drink. Haidee, Elizabeth, Darshan
Singh and Mary Lou and Brad, had declined the invitation
to join the others—probably on the grounds of age or a feel-
ing of 'been there, done that'. Brad's comment in his strong
American twang was,

'Geez, Guys, we wouldn't wanna cramp your style, now.
Go and enjoy.'

The youngsters, volunteers from VSO or CUSO, or early in

their teaching careers were discovering that this was a microcosm of *rich* desegregated Kenyan Society. Their sights had been forcibly lowered from the daiquiris or Gins and Tonic or even the wine of the first round as they realised they'd already made a substantial dent in the limited pay packet. So now it was local beer–or coke if you didn't like beer.

'Which beer would you recommend?' ventured Jean Pierre cautiously. 'And how much eez zat? ... Ah, I see. Then, perhaps we could try the local African beer?'

The group were now drinking the cheapest booze on the menu, hoping they hadn't lost face.

'Not sure I can handle this stuff,' David Lewis, English teacher, was saying. 'I think it's the real local *pombe*; I've heard it guarantees a massive hangover.'

The handsome (and amused) young Masai barman in the green uniform, that Jenny (wren) Mulrenan, History teacher, couldn't keep her eyes off, knew what the situation was.

'Try the Tusker,' he said in a deep velvet voice with a hint of an American accent. 'It's excellent and not that much more expensive than that poison you're drinking.'

Jean Pierre bravely ordered a half pint and everyone interested sipped it timidly.

'Not bad,' was David's verdict.

'A votre santé,' cried Jeanne Pierre, adding 'a palatable drink'–with emphasis on the 'table' of palatable *en français*.

'I'm glad my tipple's coke,' chipped in the teetotal Mitul.

'Cheers. *Slainte Vor*. Bottoms up,' from David, Ella and Janet.

'*Apki Lambi Umar Ke Liye*. That's Hindi,' piped up Mitul. 'Well, in Mauritius it is.'

Clever Jenny wren's contribution was, '*Maisha marefu*. That's Swahili, I think'

'Well done Memsaab *Mwalimu*,' said the barman whose name was Ole. 'You're right. It means good life. Or you could try the one on the Tusker bottle, *"Bia Yangu Nchi Yangu"*. That's "My beer, my country".'

'Here's tae ye,' added Ella, thinking it was all getting a bit too complicated. She wasn't sure if anyone understood.

From then on a cold Tusker was a firm favourite on evenings out–especially at a quarter of the price anywhere outside the Tea Hotel.

Meantime in the Tea Hotel bar, the newcomers were making themselves conspicuous. The lively chat and laughter were an attractive novelty for the regulars who were curious to find out more about this cheerful bunch. They would certainly relieve the boredom of the same old conversations about uhuru politics, Brooke Bond tea or the state of the roads to Nairobi or Kisumu.

A group of well dressed Kenyans were drinking whisky and eating chicken drumsticks from a basket. They'd been watching the young Mzungus suspiciously since they came in, perhaps expecting trouble but had decided they were harmless. One young man, Matthew Kiprui, wanted to talk to Jenny when he realised she was a teacher. He came over to make contact. After the introductions he said,

'I have a sister in the Girls' School, Evelina Chebet. She's in Form 4 Do you know her?'

Jenny said she did and then remembered that there were three Evelina Chebets at school. 'Do you know which number she is?'

Matthew laughed and replied, 'No I don't. So it's true is it? That crazy Mzungu head gives the girls numbers.'

'It's a bit hard to tell who's who when there are three Evelina Chebets and five Elizabeth Chebets,' Jenny pointed out in defence of Haidee. 'And, by the way, that crazy Mzungu really cares about the girls. She spends her whole life doing things for them.'

'Sorry. I suppose they do seem to like her,' was all that

Matthew could come up with.

'*Twende* Kip. Let's go. Time to move on. *Kwaheri.*' Matthew's companions had come to drag him away.

'See you. *Kwaheri,*' Matthew said with a smile–but a veil had dropped over his eyes. 'We're all working for Brooke Bond, in management. I hope to see you around.' His eyes rested on Jenny a little longer than on the others

'Kwaheri Matthew, *tutaonana,*' Jenny said revealing that her Swahili was improving. And as they left she couldn't help adding,

'I don't think his mates were too happy about him talking to us.'

A group of Sikh men with turbans, beards and healthy paunches were talking loudly over their drinks. They left soon after a flurry of pink and orange saris floated in and floated out again without sitting down.

The other crowd consisted of a tall, craggy older white man in a smart safari suit and cravat, a middle aged woman in a silk dress, a younger woman in cream trousers and tie and dye shirt, two good-looking young men in smart casual who looked like brothers, a tall African in neat khakis, a shorter African in a suit but no tie and a middle aged Asian couple in western dress, he in black trousers and white shirt, she in a silk dress and Kashmir cardigan casually but carefully perched on her shoulders.

Ella was people watching during a lull in the conversation and was fascinated by this fusion of people and cultures. All of them screamed elegance and money and they had obviously retired to the bar after dinner with the remnants of wine or brandy in their glasses.

'*Kahawa sasa, tafadhali,*' the taller of the two young men said to Ole with an air of quiet authority that commanded obedience but was still very polite. 'Who are our visitors?'

'They're all teachers from the Girls' school, Bwana Mike.

They seem to be worrying about our prices so I don't expect they'll be here for long.'

'Hang on a minute, Ole.' The two men, Mike and Ole, one black, one white had been friends since childhood and Ole was the one who had gone to university in USA and was doing bar work until the inevitable plum job in Brooke Bond landed on his lap.

The other man, Mike, had stayed at home after boarding school to keep things going on the family farm.

'Hi there. Welcome to the Tea Hotel. We don't often have the pleasure of the company of the local *walimu*. I'm Mike and this is my brother Drew. He's the big game hunter in the family and I'm the farmer. Would you like to join us all for coffee or can I get anyone a drink?'

Ella was charmed by his old fashioned courtesy and the tiny formal bow. Before anyone could say no she quickly jumped in and said, with the most charming smile she could muster,

'That's very kind of you. We'd be delighted. We'd been hoping to make contact with the local society.' Mike raised his eyebrows slightly but covered up his surprise at her bold confidence by organising some seating.

'Ole, we need–um–seven more chairs please–and can you come and take an order. *Asante.*'

Mike, with exaggerated aplomb, seated everyone boy girl boy girl and finally pulled up his chair next to Ella which made her feel slightly uncomfortable but more than a little excited. She found herself saying,'In Caithness we call this doing a Castle of May.' This seemed to intrigue everyone so she went on,

'The Queen Mum has a dining table for only twelve people at her holiday castle near my family home. She always sits everyone boy girl and then everyone waits for her to start talking. If she turns to speak to the person on her right, everyone else does the same. Then if she speaks to the person on her left, that's the cue for everyone to do the same. Seemingly she spends hours making sure that her guests aren't sitting beside anyone they won't get on with.'

'I've heard about this,' said the older lady. 'That's absolutely true my dear. Do you have any connections with the castle?'

'Oh no, but my brother used to help out in the castle gardens in his school holidays and my friend works there.'

'Oh really,' replied the older lady, perhaps with a slightly patronising or disappointed tone Ella felt.

'You can be Queen Mum tonight, Priscilla,' said Mike humouring her, 'and we'll follow your cue.'

Ella wished she hadn't brought it up–and was glad everyone laughed it off–except Priscilla who seemed to be enjoying her little delusion of royal grandeur. She wondered who exactly this woman was or had been at one time

Coffee arrived in a silver pot on a silver tray with a starched white tray cloth and was served in fine white china. The milk was fresh and the locally produced sugar looked like golden beach sand. Only Jean Pierre had ordered a fine Cognac; the others had been too polite to take advantage of a stranger's hospitality.

Ole served the brandy and another waiter in a long white kaftan and red fez served the coffee with a great deal of ceremony.

The older man and woman, Hugh and Priscilla Cavendish, turned out to be of Kenyan born farming stock and the younger woman was their daughter Emily who was taking a break from her vet studies in Bristol, The Asian couple turned out to be Dr and Mrs Agnelo and Carmen Menezes of Portuguese Indian origin whose families had left Goa in the 1940s. The two African men, Wilson Kirior and Ben Chepkwony were managing a system of smallholdings made up of subdivisions of the land once owned by the Kilpatrick family of Kisimot Dairy Farm. Mike and Drew Kilpatrick had a sister who lived at home on the farm with their parents. The ageing couple and their daughter hardly ever left the farm any more and relied on their two sons to bring home anything they needed which couldn't be produced from the land.

After these generalities had been dealt with within the whole group, Priscilla's cue came and Ella found herself sandwiched between David, the English teacher and Mike the farmer, but talking to David. Jan had Drew Kilpatrick to talk to.

'We seem to be hobnobbing with the higher echelons tonight.' David couldn't keep the mockery out of his voice.

'And some imagining they're higher than they are,' responded Ella. 'But interesting, don't you think?'

'Fascinating,' was David's flat reply ever the cynic. 'I wonder what they really think of us. I bet they say we're nothing but a bunch of do-gooders. Have you read Robert Ruark's "Uhuru"?' Ella said she'd started but couldn't get past the violence of the first chapter.

'These white farmers were horrible,' David ploughed on in a whisper.

'David! Can we choose a better time and place for this conversation, please? They *have* stretched out a hand of friendship.'

'Sorry. You're right. Change the subject. How are you getting on with "The River Between"?' David was obsessed with his reading and at the moment his reading was about Africa, for Africa and by Africans and, in his eyes, the African could do nothing wrong.

'I love the way he writes.' Ella was reading her first novel classed as African literature in English by a Kenyan writer called James Ngugi. 'I've never read anything quite like it–and I think I'm going to learn so much about how the Kenyans, or at least the Kikuyus, feel about what's been going on recently.'

'It's amazing isn't it', David put in. 'There's so much poetry in the prose and the conflict between the traditional and Christian Africans is far more interesting than the white black conflict, don't you think?'

'I met the fellow about six years ago, you know; in fact I knew him quite well,' interjected Ben Chepkwony loudly–completely destroying Priscilla's Castle of May etiquette.

'You mean Ngugi,' said David in a star struck fashion.

'He was studying English at Makerere when I was doing my Agri degree. I think he was the one who wrote a play called "The Black Hermit" which was put on in Kampala.'

'No way!' jumped in Canadian Janet, equally star struck. 'What's he like?'

Before Ben could answer, a curt comment from Hugh Cavendish put a different complexion on the matter,

'From what I've heard, he writes a load of Commy poppy cock. He's a reporter on the Daily Nation in Nairobi, you know. Bit of a trouble maker. Clever chap though, I hear.'

Ben and Wilson exchanged glances and thought better of bothering to contradict the older man.

Not so David. 'Have you actually read any of his stuff, Hugh? Or are you just passing on what someone else has said?'

'Oh, Dad only reads the papers and listens to the wireless these days,' piped up Emily addressing the whole group before turning to her father. 'Dad, you can borrow my copy of "Weep Not Child"–it's by Ngugi as well. You'll be surprised what you'll learn.'

Hugh muttered something that sounded like, 'I suppose I can try. Let it not be said I'm not open minded.'

Priscilla brought everyone back on an even keel.

'Excuse me everyone. I think we'll all converse with the person on our left now.' It was all the more amusing that she was being deadly serious. Ella was thinking the Queen Mum had a few good ideas and this was one.

'I heard what your colleague said earlier on,' Mike admitted but with a twinkle in his eye.

'Which bit?' Ella said feeling embarrassed.

'We're not all horrible.'

'Oh, that bit'. Ella pulled a face and Mike laughed.

'But some were worse than horrible.' Mike added ruefully. 'They were the characters who were the rejects in UK society-not nice people.'

'But you're one of the good guys?' Ella questioned.

'I try to be but it doesn't always work.' Michael Kilpatrick paused as if preparing to make an important speech. He looked into Ella's eyes and she thought she saw tears. 'Sometimes there seems to be too much to forgive and forget–on both sides.'

Ella stayed silent. She didn't understand enough to make any comment. Instinct told her there was a tragedy lingering there.

'Persevere with Ruark's book by the way.' Mike went on pulling himself together. 'Behind the horror of Mau Mau there's a glimmer of optimism somewhere–I hope.'

'Have you read any of the African writers?' Ella went on keen to relieve the tension.

'I can't get enough of them,' was the reply. 'I've got a shelf of them at home on the farm. You can come and borrow some if you like. They're not always easy to find.'

'I'd really like that. Thanks,' said Ella really meaning it. 'How come you're so keen?'

'Oh, I suppose I'm desperately trying to understand what went on.' Mike looked sad again but Ella didn't press the matter. 'Besides they're damn good stories. I started with Achebe's "Things Fall Apart" and then I had to read the others, One of my favourites is a Ugandan poem called "Song of Lawino". You'd like it.'

'I can't wait to start reading some African literature with the girls. I'm sure they're going to love "The River Between"–it's all about their own lives.' Ella went on. 'Do you know they're studying "A Man for all Seasons" at Kipsigis Girls' School?

Why would they want to know about Henry VIII rejecting the Catholic Church so he could get a divorce?'

'Why not?' Mike said. 'After all, polygamy annoying the missions is something that's part of their lives. It's not so different.'

'I suppose so', agreed Ella, 'And they could watch the film. Given half a chance though, I wouldn't choose to teach it here.'

Mike couldn't keep his eyes off this girl with the green eyes and masses of auburn hair and found himself saying, 'I hope you're not going to rush off as soon as you've arrived like most of these volunteers.'

'Well, I'm not exactly a volunteer. The Ministry of Overseas Development employed me. David's leaving at Christmas and I'm taking over the English teaching. He's ordered forty copies of "The River Between" so that should keep me here for a while.'

'Good,' Mike muttered. 'Where did you get that hair?'

Ella laughed as she remembered how she'd asked her primary school teacher that same question and if she'd been a mixed drop but she wasn't going to go into that now. 'That's a long story. Maybe I'll tell you sometime.'

'Can I call you Elsa–like the lioness?'

'Oh, I saw that film in London, just before we left–"Born Free" wasn't it–with Virginia McKenna and Bill Travers? He used to be my pin up when I was about ten when he was in "Wee Geordie". They even showed the film in the Kirk hall at Altnabervie.' Ella was getting carried away but something about the way this handsome young man was looking at her made her stop. 'Why Elsa?'

'Because you're a free spirit, Elsa–and your hair's the colour of a lioness in the sun.'

'Is that a good thing, then?' Ella asked to cover that mixture of embarrassment and excitement that was threatening to envelope her.

'Oh yes.' Mike still couldn't keep his eyes off her but then snapped out of his reverie suddenly. 'By the way, I didn't tell you two of my uncles are farming in Perthshire. We've been over to visit them a couple of times–though I don't suppose my parents will be up to the trip again. But I might.'

'Come on you two. Have you noticed what time it is or are you off in some cuckoo land?' interrupted Jan. 'Everyone's moved out to the lobby and they're waiting to say good night.'

'Can I come and visit you at the school?' Mike was asking, 'But I'll have to make a social call at Haidee's first. She's a family friend.'

'I think I'd like that,' said Ella demurely trying to ignore Jan's inane grins and nods behind Mike's back. 'Thanks for the coffee and the chat. I really enjoyed myself.' Ella continued.

The two brushed fingertips lightly before everyone dived into cheery goodbyes and poured themselves into cars–the teachers into two old VW Beetles, the brothers and their two African companions into a scruffy land rover, the Doctor into a flashy white Peugeot and the Cavendishes into a big, sleek, dark green saloon.

'Well, Ella,' Jan teased, 'you only seemed to have eyes for one person tonight. What did you find to talk about for all that time?'

'Would you believe it African literature? He's offered to lend me his Achebe books.' Ella was proud to name drop though it was the first time she'd come across Chinua Achebe. 'Oh and by the way David, he overheard your remark about white farmers.'

'Oh, did he?' was the flat reply. 'So what did he say?'

'Well he said they weren't all horrible but that some guys were horrendous.' Ella reported. 'He said something about there being too much to forgive and forget–on both sides. I liked him.'

'We noticed,' Jenny chimed in. 'But he's not as gorgeous as that Matthew guy from Brooke Bond. Did you see him?'

'We noticed you liked him too,' Ella chaffed. 'You'd better start improving your Swahili. He seemed impressed.'

'Oh, I don't think there can be any future there. He's got a sister at school–one of the Evelina Chebets; I wish I could remember his second name.'

'Kiprui,' David said. 'I'd watch out there, Jenny wren. His friends didn't seem to like him fraternising with the Mzungus.'

'I wondered about that too,' Jenny added sadly. 'Hope I'm wrong.'

Later on, over a cocoa nightcap, Jan and 'Elsa' swapped stories and discovered they both rather liked the Kilpatrick brothers.

'It's a pity I'm spoken for,' Jan admitted. 'Perhaps I could put that on hold.'

'I kept myself for someone for ages. I'm not making the same mistake again,' Ella said and told her new friend all about Rory and the farm and her father's disappointment.

'Sounds like you've had a lucky escape there Ella,' Jan said. 'You should never get married to please Daddy, right?'

'Right,' said Ella feeling a burden lifting from her heart and mind.

Jan's only reservation was, 'Drew says he much prefers animals to people. And, boy, does he know a lot about them. Fascinating.'

Ella wondered why. 'I think there must be some reason for that. Did you get a feeling there's something sad about the family?'

'Drew never mentioned them–even once. Strange.'

CHAPTER 7

A New Bridge Partner

Kericho Stores was waiting for deliveries to restock the shelves. Ella had been examining what was available and it wasn't a lot. There were huge quantities of carbolic soap, candles, clothes pegs and even, to Ella's amusement, tins of haggis and Walkers shortbread. Of bread, salt, coffee or sugar there seemed to be none.

Then Ella spotted a packet of sugar in the middle of an empty shelf. Arapbet had asked for sugar so she headed towards it. As she stretched out her hand to pick it up, she was aware of a quickening footstep and a brown hand just getting there before her, not exactly grabbing the bag of sugar, just making sure that it got possession of it. She couldn't be sure if the young man behind the hand had noticed that she was trying to pick it up but, despite a wide mischievous grin which might have been triumphant or might have been friendly, Ella

84

decided that she didn't like him and certainly wouldn't bother to be polite if she ever came across him again.

Jan had asked Ella if she'd help to cook for two male friends she'd invited over from a local mission school. The girls decided they could just about manage Spag Bol and salad followed by ice cream–without Arapbet's help. The old Kip was turning out to be a hard taskmaster. He refused to communicate in any other language apart from Swahili and was definitely the boss of the house. Thanks to him, the young teachers were never late and were always well fed, neat and clean. They weren't allowed to do any housework but he always reminded them to 'Funza kitabu. Saidia wana.' Roughly translated this was, 'Do your books and help the students.'

Today was Friday, however, and Arapbet had left his two Memsaabs Kidogo in peace but with a fully loaded stove enough to cook Spag Bol for an army and probably provide enough water to bath them.

Jan was describing their guests.

'I think you'll like them. They're from the boys' school along the Kisumu road. Bob's your all American Peace Corps conscientious objector. You know what I mean–the draft dodger with a big heart. Just don't bring up the subject of Vietnam if you want to get to bed early.

Now, John, I'm not sure about. I can't figure him out yet. He's big on athletics and teaches the PE at Cheptonge School and some Science–but I know he studied Political Science at York.'

'York?' Ella asked, 'In England? '

'No, it's the one in Toronto, Ontario. Quite a lively place I hear. Some of my friends went there from Montreal and they said there were all kinds of protests–like against LBJ Americanising the Vietnam War and Ian Smith's UDI and stuff. That must have been about 1965.'

'We had the same at Aberdeen University. There was a lot of talk but there weren't any demos. I think a lot of us felt this was all going on too far away for us.'

'We were the same in Montreal. Mind you, I think it only takes one charismatic character to change all that–or something to happen close to home.' Jan added.

'Too right,' said Ella, picking up Jan's Canadian lingo. 'Anyway, I'm not going to discuss politics if I can help it.'

The Bolognese sauce was safely unburnt at the side of the wood stove, the water was waiting for the spaghetti, the salad and the ice cream ready and waiting in the fridge freezer and the cheap plonk nicely chilling.

The girls dressed up in two similar little numbers that Jan had run up in an hour or so from two *kitenges* which are cotton cloths about the size of a blanket with exotic African designs in amazing colours. They can be worn round the waist, above the breasts, over one shoulder, round the neck or wherever you like. Most important, you can tie a knot in one corner to carry your money and tuck this away–anywhere you like.

Jan looked tall and stunning in dusky pink with a multi coloured pattern and she had cleverly folded the cloth in half, run up seams on either side leaving holes for butterfly sleeves. Then she'd cut a hole for the neckline making sure that it was 'plunging enough to tease' as she put it. On Jan the 'dress' was a just respectable knee length which Haidee had warned them was a requirement for 'her' teachers.

Ella had been so thrilled with Jan's dress that Jan, despite Ella's protests, had insisted on making one the same.

'But I gotta choose the colour for you. These amazing eyes and that gorgeous hair need to be enhanced.' Janet was doing wonders for Ella's confidence.

So Ella was now dressed in a similar pattern in bright emerald green but, at five foot three, her hemline was nearer the floor.

'Wow,' Jan gasped. She was right. Ella, with her exotic eyes and hair and, by now (with the help of lashings of Soltan on her fair skin) light golden tan and not too many freckles, looked lovelier than she had ever done before. She was unaware of this but feeling confident.

With a touch of 'Sergeant Pepper's Lonely Hearts Club' on the turntable and some Bob Dylan, Aretha Franklin and Janis Joplin as back up, the hostesses were waiting for their guests on two wooden armchairs with soft cushions on either side of a friendly, crackling wood fire.

'What shall we talk about with them?' Ella broke the silence.

'I know Bob likes to play bridge but I'm not sure about John.' Jan had been learning to play bridge in an effort to 'improve herself' as she put it so Ella admitted she could play a little better since her new brother-in-law had taught her and might be persuaded to have a go if they could find some partners.

'Well, I hope they don't have sugar in their coffee. Some berk watched me go for the last bag in the shop and he grabbed it. I think he enjoyed doing it by the look on his face.'

'No worries, I'm sure Mrs Singh can give us a cup of sugar if we need it later on. She's only twenty steps away.'

The rev of a car's engine announced the arrival of the 'guys', not exactly suited and booted, but at least clean and presentable. John hadn't been too sure about the evening but had reluctantly allowed himself to be dragged along. He wasn't too sure about Canadian connections but he was keeping this fact under his hat–as he was keeping a lot of things under his hat. Bob, as usual was enthusiastic.

'Jan's great fun–and what else are we gonna do? There's not exactly a lot going on in Kericho unless you're loaded. And I'm sure this new teacher will be fine too. They say she's Scottish'

'Hi guys, what kept you?' gushed hostess Jan.

'It's this new Ford Anglia John's got a hold of,' laughed Bob. 'The tailfins aren't long enough.'

'We don't need American style tailfins in this part of the

world,' John shot back good-naturedly, 'too extravagant. Anyway, the car's not new; a mate of mine fixed it up after the safari and I got it for a good price.'

'Do you mean the East African car rally?' Jan asked. 'It'll probably fall to bits soon then.'

'No way,' jibed John. 'My mate's the famous Joginder Singh of Kericho Motors–and he can fix anything–as well as win a few rallies.'

'Name dropper,' teased Bob.

'Come and meet Ella. She's opening up the plonk. Ella, this is Bob.'

'Good to meet you Bob.'

'And –.' Jan was interrupted by Ella's jaw dropping and a half guilty but mostly amused expression on John's face.

'I think we've almost met,' he said in a deep velvet resonant voice that churned up Ella's stomach and he looked at her with huge melting brown eyes to add to the assault. 'If I'd known *you* were going to be my hostess, I'd have brought my own sugar.'

Ella didn't say a word so he added, 'Sorry about that; it's dog eat dog in Africa, I'm afraid.' Ella thought she detected an American accent.

'Forget it,' Ella said calmly but, because she still hadn't forgiven him, she had to add, 'You probably needed sweetening.'

'Ah, so you're the berk that nicked the last bag of sugar. Oops, sorry Ella, it just slipped out.'

'Don't worry about it. Those *were* my exact words.'

'Right folks, how about a drink?' Jan said cheerfully feeling the evening's good will draining away. 'We've got Tusker– nothing but the best–and some–ahem–nice white wine,' flustered Janet papering over the cracks.

'Tusker'll do me, Jan,' Bob said.

'Ditto,' added John. This left the girls with a whole bottle of plonk to drink.

The evening progressed well after that with John trying his best to be forgiven by turning on his not inconsiderable charm and Ella trying her best to look as if she'd never succumb. She asked Bob lots of questions about Peace Corps and his school but it was left to Jan to bring John into the conversation.

'Bob tells me you did Political Science at York, John. That's not too far from my neck of the woods,' she began. 'How come you're teaching PE and Biology?'

Ella noticed John looking daggers at Bob. She had been unable to take her eyes off this exotic looking young man who was having such a strange effect on her despite her instincts screaming at her to steer clear. He was so unlike anyone she'd ever met before–and a far cry from the lads in Caithness. The brown which she had taken for sun tan on a white skin was a touch more than that but didn't seem quite Indian and his features were more Mediterranean than Asian. His tall body and long lean limbs were that of a trained athlete but the sheepish look on his face made him seem like a little boy. She thought she detected him blanch at Jan's question–only for a second.

'Oh, you know, um. They needed PE and that's my strength but when they heard I had Science in my degree they stuck me in Biology. It didn't seem to matter that it was Political Science. Anyway, that's boring. What's this about a game of bridge? Can someone run through the rules again to see if they're different in Scotland or Canada or USA?'

Ella decided that this guy had neatly side-stepped any more personal questions and wondered why.

There was just enough time to recap the very basics of bidding before supper and the rest of the conversation stayed light hearted until the game of bridge was underway. They drew for partners and it was Bob and Jan versus John and Ella.

Ella kept thinking of what her dad used to say, 'Never play bridge if you're angry–especially with your partner.'

'No bid'.

'No bid'.

'No bid.' There was a long pause.

'No bid' John said finally.

'Okay. Let's show,' cried Bob in frustration.

Three people had rubbish and John was sitting there with thirty points including all the Aces and Kings. Ella couldn't contain herself, having picked up the competitive spirit from her big sister's bridge-playing husband.

'What's your problem, John? That was our game. You didn't even have to think about it.'

'Sorry partner. Maybe I just need another explanation.'

'Okay, but listen this time,' Ella said rather too sharply. 'Are you sure you've played this game before?'

'Mmm,' John hummed. 'It was a long time ago. I'll tell you what. Pretend I'm a complete idiot and start from scratch.'

'That's not going to be hard,' Ella flashed back not noticing that Bob and Jan were almost exploding from suppressed giggles.

'I do know the names of the suits though,' John informed Ella trying to pretend he really knew it all and was only teasing.

'Right. Aces are worth four points, Kings three –'

Five minutes later the bidding started again and this time John landed Ella with five clubs to play but when he laid down the dummy hand there were six spades to the Ace, King, Queen and only the two and eight of clubs.

'What have you done, John?' Now Ella was really annoyed.

'What do you mean?' John protested. 'You can't get better than Ace King Queen and three others if you're bidding them?'

'These are spades, idiot, not clubs!'

'Oh, sorry. We call what you call clubs, flowers. I thought what you call spades must be clubs.

'So what do you call spades then?' Ella spat out.

'Leaves,' John spat back. 'It makes sense. Look at the shapes. Why should your description be any better than mine?'

'Anyway, there goes another rubber,' said Ella as she went three down on her contract.

Jan and Bob had thoroughly enjoyed the evening. Not only had they thrashed their opponents but they'd been entertained by the ding dong between the stormy Ella and the ducking and diving of the usually authoritarian and slightly pompous John.

'That was great fun.' Bob enthused. 'Let's make it a regular date–one week your place one week my place.'

'And one week my place,' said John. 'Great idea.'

Ella said nothing. She just smiled politely–but she didn't realise that John had been completely bowled over by this feisty red head and there was no way he was going to pass up this chance of seeing her again.

The evening came to a close over hot cocoa before the boys hit the road, the conversation turning to cars. Bob was envious of John's new car and wondered how he could afford it and John ended up promising to find a 1966 VW for Ella to match her eyes which he'd seen in Kericho Motors run by his friend the 'Flying Sikh' as he was known. John was really trying very hard to impress Ella but it didn't seem to be working.

'I'm sure Joginder would give you a good price for that green VW, Ella,' cajoled John. 'Shall I put in a word for you?'

'I won't have the money for a while, I'm afraid,' said Ella a little frostily. 'But at least I won't be trying to put oil and water in the boot now that I've learnt where the engine is.' Jan laughed as she told the story of how Ella had thought someone had nicked the engine of her yellow VW because it wasn't at the front. After they'd left, Ella confided in Jan that she felt there was something very disturbing about John.

'Nonsense, you've just got the hots for him,' Jan pointed out.

'No, it's not that,' Ella replied pensively. 'There's something he's hiding and something tells me he's not really a teacher.'

'I'm sure you're imagining it,' Jan put in.

'And, for the record,' retorted Ella, 'I don't even like him, far less fancy him.'

'Uhu,' was all Janet said. 'That's two conquests you've made in a week, Ella Mackay. What's your secret?'

'Charm and beauty,' joked Ella forgetting her reservations. 'Which one would you choose, then?'

'Oh, I'll have the other one's brother,' said Janet. 'What's his name? Drew, was it?'

'Hey, you know that Haidee's a friend of the Kilpatrick family.'

'How do you know that?' Janet asked.

'Mike told me when he asked if he could come and visit.'

'Mmm, you kept that quiet. Drew didn't ask if he could come and visit me.' The two girls carried on the banter for a while before getting off to sleep, happy and strangely full of anticipation.

Ella's happy feelings were disconcertingly tinged with confusion and anxiety. She'd met two gorgeous men who seemed to like her but there was something sad and mysterious about both of them and she wasn't at all sure if she wanted to become involved with either of them.

CHAPTER 8

The Windmills
of My Mind

The girls at Kipsigis Girls' School continued to be a delight. Walking into a classroom was like going on stage in front of a captive audience. If anyone even whispered out of turn it was, 'Shush, the teacher's talking.' And silence would reign once more.

Resources were another thing. Without any duplicating facilities and very few text books, things like English Comprehension were very difficult to deliver. Ella found herself skipping breakfast after dorm duty, writing furiously on the roller blackboard with any colour of chalk that was left. She was copying out the passage for comprehension and would have to read it along with her pupils before moving the board up. Then the multiple choice questions were copied on to the board, one at a time because there was no more space, and the girls given a minute to answer each one. It was a laborious but unavoidable procedure. David, who had to do the same thing, reckoned the exercise did wonders for the girls' speed reading and powers of concentration; if they didn't pay attention, and quickly, the blackboard was moved up and the words were gone. Luckily the teachers were working with the cream of Kenya's girls who were also desperate to learn. Most of them were destined for university and some of them would be awarded scholarships to study overseas, mostly in UK or America.

Ella sent an aerogramme to Caithness asking her Mum and Dad to organise a raffle at Altnabervie Kirk Sale to raise funds for a Gestetner and copy paper. The problem was it was a seven week turnaround for ordinary letters so it might take months for anything to happen.

It was nearly six weeks into term and the following Saturday was October 14th and Ella had booked the weekend off duty to travel to the Thorn Tree to see if any Eland House delegates would turn up in response to the message on the tree. She'd asked Jan to come along, mostly because she would enjoy her company and the lift in her VW would have been useful.

As luck would have it, Jan's car was having a few problems and Ella went with Janet to take it into Kericho Motors for repair.

Joginder Singh, the safari driver and John Francis's friend, was there, in his scruffy not famous capacity, and announced he would need a couple of days to get parts—and it was already Thursday. They wouldn't be driving to Nairobi. He offered to drive them out to the school.

'You must be Ella,' he surmised. 'John Francis said he'd met a pretty red head from Scotland. He said you might be interested in the green 1966 Beetle. It's a great little car, 1300 and tough enough for any road. What about if I let you have it with a deposit and you can pay the rest later?

'I might think about that.' Ella replied. 'I'll come and have a look when we collect Jan's car. Thanks. That's really good of you.'

The girls decided they would hitchhike to Nairobi from outside the school gate. They didn't tell Mrs King who might have had a holy fit if she'd realised what they were up to. They were right.

However, before they'd had a chance to set off a familiar Ford Anglia with fins rolled up.

'I hear you were planning a trip to Nairobi and your car's broken down, Jan. I thought you might like a lift.' This was John Francis looking sporty in a white shirt and looking very handsome in daylight outside a grocer's shop Ella was thinking. He was also paying her no attention.

'Well, we were going to hitch,' Jan said, 'but why not?'

'We? Oh, were you thinking of coming too, Ella?' John threw at her nonchalantly. He was probably remembering the frosty treatment after the bridge game.

'Well, actually it was my plan in the first place,' Ella said politely. 'I've got people to meet. Why? Would it make a difference to your offer?' she added unable to resist the jibe.

'That depends,' John said, equally politely.

'On what?' Ella asked.

'On whether you can stand my company for three hundred miles.'

That winded Ella temporarily so while she was thinking up her next reply John continued, 'Jean Pierre wants to come too. I've just rescued him from an RVP taxi journey. We have to pick him up outside the bank.'

'Fine,' Ella squawked but it was one of those Caithness 'fines' that didn't really mean fine at all.

After hoping nobody (especially John) had noticed her looking for the boot where the engine was, Ella piled her haversack into the Ford Anglia beside Jan's.

95

'It's only VWs that have the trunk at the front,' Jan whispered.

Ella managed a quiet chortle despite her embarrassment and shot into the back seat behind the driver's seat hoping to keep her distance from John. Too late. She could see his big brown eyes making contact with hers in the rear view mirror. They were smiling. Or were they mocking her? She decided to sink into 'in between' time and admire the view. She'd leave Jan to make conversation.

She wasn't handling her feelings well.

Jean Pierre provided some very welcome comic relief on the long journey. With his amusing English in a French accent and his unique Parisian view of the world, a potentially tense journey was fun.

'Why do zey not geev deez Kikuyu women a–how you say–veelbarrow for their bundles? Soon zey weel 'av no foch-head left,' was one of his many quips. 'Ees not kind.'

Of course everyone knew he was playing to the gallery for laughs. His English in the classroom was nigh on perfect.

John pulled up by the roadside as dusk was falling over the escarpment. He jumped out calling out,

'I need tea. Nice thick sweet African tea.'

'I'll get it,' Jean Pierre offered. 'Come and 'elp me Jan.' They could see a little dukha about fifty yards along the road.

'Come on, Ella,' John whispered gently. 'I want to show you something.' And before she could protest, he took her hand and walked her over to a viewing point over that very famous vista across the Great East African Rift Valley.

'Wait,' John said, 'and watch.'

The two shared some silent minutes as the sun turned into a big red ball and sank below the horizon at a phenomenal speed.

Ella shivered, or perhaps trembled–and John put his arm around her shoulder. She was paralysed. He was gentle. Eventually she said,

'That was just so spectacular.' And then she had the good grace to let her defences down far enough to say, 'Thank you, John.'

'My pleasure,' John replied. 'I thought you'd appreciate it.'

'And thank you for putting a word in for me with Joginder, I might consider that green VW–now that I know where the engine is.' Ella replied. She was beginning to realise, in retrospect, that she had, in fact, been neatly hijacked this weekend. She'd have to watch out.

'Good,' said John rather smugly. 'Where's that tea?'

They trundled into Nairobi by six thirty and John dropped the others at the CUSO haunt, the Fairview Hotel, announcing that he had to quickly see some family but could they meet later for food and a film as he had business the next day.

An hour later they were all outside the cinema.

'Well, it's "Yellow Submarine" or "The Thomas Crown Affair" or "The Lion in Winter"–oh no that's coming soon. What do you fancy, Ella?' Jan was asking.

'Cartoon with Beatles music or Steve McQueen? What a choice. Mind you, I thought this was the *bundu*. These films haven't hit Caithness yet.' Ella was answering. 'What about you guys?' she added picking up Jan's lingo and also dropping her previous frosty treatment of John, the sugar stealing, bad bridge player who was really quite nice underneath it all.

'I'll have Faye Dunaway,' John said predictably.

'Moi aussi,' oozed Jean Pierre kissing his fingertips. 'Mwah!'

After a quick Chinese curry at the Chowpatty restaurant the four just made the nine thirty performance.

Ella was at the inside end of a row next to a wall with John next to her. (How did that happen?). She was very aware of his proximity and conscious that she was hemmed in. Nobody had quite expected that steamy chess scene with Steve McQueen and Faye Dunaway or that longest kiss on record in the cinema world and some very delicious erotic feelings were washing over Ella in waves as John took hold of her hand and held it tight.

'If we were alone –.' John whispered.

'Well, we're not,' whispered Ella demurely. But the prim little side of her nature was receding into the background and she was definitely beginning to wish they were.

They all tumbled out of the cinema with Jan and Ella singing bits of 'The Windmills of Your Mind,' where they could remember the words and humming where they could only remember the melody.

'What a great song. I just love it.' Jan cried. 'I need to get the single. Who sang it again?

'Noel Harrison,' Ella said. 'But I doubt if we can buy it here.'

'I didn't know you could sing, Ella,' John said.

'Well, there's a lot you don't know about me,' Ella flirted.

'Can't wait to find out,' John teased.

However, all this 'sassiness' (Jan's word) would have to wait. John dropped them off at the hotel and went off to his 'some family'. There was still something that didn't add up Ella thought.

They had agreed to meet at the Thorn Tree at three o'clock on Sunday for the journey back.

Ella was excited to meet some of the Eland House group and find out how they were getting on and Jan was infected too. Jean Pierre had disappeared to spend the weekend with friends.

'The only problem is. This guy has said meet him on October 14th but he doesn't give a time.' Ella observed.

'I guess we could go there early morning and leave a note saying "MEET YOU HERE AT 1:00PM. ELLA FROM ELAND HOUSE NOW IN KERICHO", Jan suggested, '"WITH CANADIAN FRIEND JAN" of course. Then we could go shopping.'

That's exactly what they did. First stop was Nelson's Bookshop for chalk and a few books. Next stop was Bazaar Street where spicy smells, vibrant colours and noisy clamour didn't cost a cent. Open hemp sacks lined the street filled with brightly coloured powders, red chilli, yellow turmeric, brown cumin, coriander and garam masala and more bags with whole spices, green chillies, cloves, cinnamon sticks and countless other exotic ingredients the girls couldn't put names to. Other shops were crammed full of wooden, soapstone, ivory and green malachite animals in one corner, many coloured beads, sisal mats, skin shoes, bags and belts in another, elephant hair, haematite, ivory, copper and malachite jewellery here and the widest imaginable variety of *kitenges* and *kikapus* there. One shop was full of saris and shiny shoes and another of nothing but paintings of African scenes. The girls were entranced but broke. They made up their minds to come back with a car and after they'd saved a bit of money. Ella managed to afford a pretty kikapu to carry essentials.

As they arrived at The Thorn Tree at a quarter past one, Ella recognised a face from London.

'Are you Jim Sawyer–from Kakamega? I'm Ella and this is Janet.'

'Hi there, I remember you–but I'm not Jim. I just read his note and thought I'd come along. I'm Robin Smith from Kisumu. Good to see you. I had a horrible feeling nobody was coming.'

'Have you no faith in the message on the tree?' Jan piped up. 'Isn't it a neat idea? Who needs stamps or telephones?'

At this point a group of three girls and two guys rolled up and rescued Robin from his shyness.

'Dotty!' Ella fell on the friend who had made them all laugh so much over the two stuffed shirts in London. 'Jan, this is Potty Dotty Watty.'

'Excuse me, but that's Dorothy Watson in real life. My God,

you look great in a sun tan Ella.'

'You too, Dot. How's it going in ... um?

'Kisumu,' Dorothy said, helping her out. 'I see it's not too far from Kericho–and it's terrific. The kids are just so brilliant. I'm in a boys' school and they all work so hard at Science because they want to be doctors. I just wish there was enough in the lab to teach them a bit more.'

'It seems to be the same all over,' Ella added and then, 'Oh, look, here comes Toby Pickles–a bit like a beetroot.'

Poor Toby's fair skin had, indeed, suffered under the tropical sun but his grin was as wide as ever and he was happy to see everyone.

'Oh God, do you remember old Randy and Teddy?' cried Dotty. 'And that song of yours Toby–"Randy and Teddy were lovers"', she crooned at top volume. Then they all made Jan laugh with the stories of their induction course and the two pompous old men who were terrified that they'd set loose a bunch of loony rebels on an unsuspecting East Africa.

'Sounds like they weren't far wrong,' was Jan's observation.

Many more young mzungus had congregated including some who had not been at the induction course at Eland House but were still looking for new friends. There were Peace Corps volunteers from America, CUSO volunteers from Canada (which pleased Janet), British VSO volunteers and various others from Norway, Sweden, Australia, New Zealand, France and Germany. They weren't all teachers and included nurses, secretaries, engineer, medic and vet students and agriculturalists. They all had their stories to tell of their journeys and jobs and experiences and all seemed to have one thing in common–a fresh, young forward-looking outlook on the world which was full of hope for the rapid advancement of the new post-imperial, post-colonial Kenya. The Mau Mau war between the British colonials and the Kikuyu people with all of its killings and sacrifices was felt to have cleansed the country of the evils of the recent past and there was no other way but onwards and upwards.

If there were any cynics in the group, they were keeping it very quiet for the moment.

Next day at three o'clock, Jean Pierre and John arrived at The Thorn Tree to find Jan and Ella surrounded by purchases.

'I see you've been busy,' John said.

'Only things we need,' Jan said, 'and a thank you present for you.'

'I got something for you too,' John said. 'Here.' It was the single of 'The Windmills of your Mind'. Before she could stop herself, Ella had given John a big thank you hug which he seemed to enjoy because he wouldn't let go.

'I can't wait to work out the chords,' Jan said. 'We can do it together Ella. That was a great present John. Sorry we only bought you a shirt.'

'I zeenk I'm meesing out heah,' Jean Pierre joked. 'No presents?'

'You're not the driver. Sorry. But we do love you,' Jan ribbed.

The journey back was fairly uneventful. The two girls sang bits of 'The Windmills of My Mind' until they dozed off in the back seat while John and Jean Pierre chatted inanely.

At one point, Ella overheard Jean Pierre ask John, 'Who was the big African chap I saw you with in Kenyatta Avenue?' He was using his 'good English' voice and he sounded quite serious. 'He looked important.'

'Which chap?' John asked. 'It must have been a passing stranger.'

'Et je suis Jacque Réné Chirac,' Jean Pierre muttered. 'Phoof.' John's French wasn't good enough to pick up the implication, but Ella's was. Something close to fear gripped her and she asked herself why she was allowing herself to fall in love with this man.

Everyone was tired by the time John had dropped them at the school gate before heading back to Cheptonge.

Haidee had been waiting anxiously for Jan and Ella's return as, like the mother hen she was, not only was she in loco parentis for her pupils, her teachers were so young that she felt the same burden of responsibility for them.

'How did you get to Nairobi?' the anxious head asked. 'I hear your car's in the garage, Jan. You didn't say good-bye, either.'

'Oh sorry Haidee. John Francis from Cheptonge gave us a lift,' Jan answered. 'And we had Jean Pierre with us. You shouldn't worry you know.'

'Anyway, I'm glad you're back. Oh and, by the way, the Kilpatrick brothers from Kisimot dropped by to visit *me* they said–but they seemed a bit disappointed you were both in Nairobi.

'Oh really, that's nice,' Janet ventured. Ella could only blush.

CHAPTER 9

Behind
the Tall Dividing Trees

For a while, Ella clambered off the crest of that wave of enthusiasm and eroticism and retreated into that 'place in between' where she could make objective observations and take stock.

She needed some bonny views like over the bay on the Pentland Firth or across the valley from Hillside farm. Instead she found a view across the emerald carpet of the tea plantations from the top of the sports field–the only place in the school campus you could get a clear view of it apart from the headmistress's house.

The campus was surrounded by a fence and high trees and, what hadn't occurred to Ella, there was no easy way out. There were askaris at the front near the big gate and there was an askari at each of the three little gates at the back of the teachers' houses–probably to allow the servants access to their homes in the villages–a whole new world without tar roads, cars, running water, electricity, brick houses with windows or any of the amenities so apparent in the school and in the larger towns. Otherwise, near the classrooms and dorms the perimeter was impenetrable.

Ella decided to ask Arapbet if she could take a walk in the reserve as it was called and was surprised at how delighted he seemed to be. Still following his programme of total immersion in Swahili, he kept saying, *'Asante sana Memsaab Kidogo. Mzuri mzuri.'* Ella understood that he was inviting her to his home to meet his family so she packed her new sisal *kikapu* with a few things the children might like but not chocolate which would melt outside a fridge. She found some coloured pencils and a notebook she'd brought from Scotland in the big trunk which had just arrived a few weeks late, and a tin of soor plooms which her mum had sneaked in to surprise her. She thought the children might like the bright green boiled sweets from Scotland–and Arapbet's cooking was playing havoc with her waistline anyway.

The two set off from the house, down to the bottom of the now partly cleared garden. In six weeks, carrots, cabbages, lettuce and onions were doing well and there would soon be, maize, pineapples and tomatoes. This earth was good–naturally fertile and rained and sunned on for three hundred and sixty five days a year.

There was a large green patch of some plant Ella didn't recognise and the shamba boy seemed to be concentrating his attention on it. As they got closer, Ella recognised the smell of marijuana and decided to play the innocent and ignore it to save any embarrassment.

'You want *banghi* memsaab?' the *shamba* boy said. Marijuana was legal and accepted as part of the culture in Kenya–like cigarettes–so she needn't have worried.

'*Hapana penda,*' Ella said. 'I don't like the stuff.'

'*Shauri a Mzungu,*' he replied which Ella took to mean, 'That's your problem because you're a mzungu,' but she wasn't too sure.

The askari at the little gate was somewhat surprised to see Ella but allowed Memsaab Kidogo through the gate–but only because she was accompanied by Mzee Arapbet, a respected old man.

Now, this really was another world. The whole area must have been like this before it was carved out and pummelled and flattened into the shape ready for the endless acres of tea, the cash crop which was going to make some people very rich.

The valley was steep sided and criss-crossed with dozens of paths worn out in the red earth and beaten down until the ground shone like a polished red floor. At the bottom of the valley was a stream and a pool where goats and cattle could be seen drinking. It was afternoon when the sun had come out after the daily lunch time rains and this new world looked freshly washed.

Patches of maize and bananas were interspersed with pineapples and vegetables near the bottom of the hill and the steep valley sides provided pasture for the cows and goats.

Dotted along the sides of the pathways were round thatched mud huts in groups of three or four, while some huts were isolated and higher up the side of the valley away from the main paths. Some chickens were clucking and scratching around the front doors of some of the huts.

A few people were beginning to stir from the daily siesta necessitated by the midday rains. Ella thought she'd experiment with her Swahili so she tried,

'*Lala kwa mvua,*' which she hoped meant, 'People have been sleeping because of the rain'.

'*Ndio,* Memsaab,' Arapbet said but he was laughing so she reckoned that wasn't quite right.

Ella's experience that day was life changing. The welcome that awaited her from the old man's three wives and umpteen children was overwhelming. The little ones clambered on to her lap as she sat on a low stool outside wife number one's hut and they couldn't resist stroking her hair that was shining in the sun. Sweet milky tea was brought in a cup with no saucer and some cream biscuits which had been bought especially for her.

The children shared the notebook and coloured pencils impeccably, each one taking a turn while the others watched and waited for his or her turn; Ella thought how kids at home would have been squabbling. An older teenage daughter who was at school explained to Ella that sharing was a very important part of the Kipsigis culture. She told Ella,

'If a traveller is walking many miles away from home and he passes a field with food, he is allowed to take one piece for his hunger and it is not stealing. He does not need to ask. If he takes more than he needs it is stealing—and he can be beaten.'

There was an analogy which Ella couldn't banish from her mind. Did the travellers who took the land to grow the tea take more than they needed? And did that mean that they should be beaten?

She noticed that the tin of soor plooms hadn't been touched and when a little one brought it to her with a questioning look, Ella opened the tin and popped a sweet in her mouth and screwed up her face with the sourness and made a loud sucking noise. The children screamed with delight. Eventually, one of the bigger children found the courage to try one. He too screwed up his face, giggled and shouted, 'Lemoni! Lemoni!' Then they all descended on the tin and that was the end of any talking for a little while as nothing could be heard but loud sucking noises.

A few days later Arapbet was to come along and ask, 'Iko ngini soor plooms?' A little later a surprised Mary Mackay got a letter asking if there was any way of getting a few more soor plooms to Kericho.

Ella was overcome by just how happy the people were in the village. They had no electricity, water, or anything of material value beyond the basics needed for survival. Food and drink came from the crops, cows, chickens and goats on their subsistence farms on the whole and a few crops were sold for cash to buy a book or biscuits perhaps or batteries for the only radio in the village which happened to belong to Mzee Arapbet. Heating and lighting were provided by charcoal and there were one or two candles for emergencies. The aroma of charcoal filled the air and clung to hair and clothes and to the people it symbolised home and security.

Ella could feel tears streaming down her cheeks and when the little children looked upset she just said, *'Furahi furahi,'* which she hoped meant happy. Arapbet's wives smiled knowingly at each other. These were good people untouched by greed and corruption and the ways of the city; they were people who could still love where others could only hate. The old social order was surviving here, hidden away, behind the tall trees, from the trappings of the western way of life, and those who had the wisdom to understand its value wanted it to stay that way.

That day Arapbet wanted Ella to meet someone important but there would be a ten minute walk. Ella agreed to this but felt grateful that her bare feet had now got worn into the orange rubber flip flops everyone wore at all times. His daughter who spoke English asked,

'Shall I come too, Ella?' Eleezabet said for that was her name–Eleezabet Chebet, daughter of Arapbet.

'Yes, please, Eleezabet,' said Ella, grateful for the language support because here, in the village, the language was the Kipsigis dialect rather than Swahili, the lingua franca, which was a mixture of African dialects, Arabic and various other influences including English which meant you could more or less make yourself understood.

The only Kipsigis word Ella knew was *'Chamagai'* which meant hello and Eleezabet taught her how to respond with *'Yamonai'* which meant, 'Fine' and they left it at that deciding to let Ella communicate with smiles, nods and handshakes.

Everyone in the 'reserve' was curious to meet Ella so the ten minute walk turned into a half hour walk as Arapbet proudly presented his memsaab kidogo from the schooli. Ella shook hands with everyone they met and greeted or responded with *'Chamagai'* or *'Yamonai'* depending on who spoke first. She was hoping that she'd got the etiquette right and wasn't offending anyone.

'My father is telling everyone you are a good Madam and that you are giving good teaching to their girls and that you have no bad ways,' Eleezabet told Ella. 'But he says you are too young to be away from your mother.' When Ella looked surprised, she continued, 'Do not worry. This is a good thing. Some of our girls go to the city and do not come back. They get into bad ways and are no longer too young to leave their mothers–but they are many years younger than you, I think and it makes the old people sad.'

Ella noticed the young girl was wearing a dusty but fashionable kitenge dress, her hair was plaited and she was wearing red nail polish which was almost worn off.

'And are you sad?' Ella enquired.

'No,' replied Eleezabet Chebet, 'I am not sad. There is little in the village for young people and much in the city.'

This made Ella Mackay feel very sad.

As the three walked along, Ella had a new awareness that the villages were made up of mostly old people and mothers with children and only a few teenagers and young men. She wondered what would happen if all the young people left. Would this way of life disappear forever?

As they neared a small hut, high up a valley side, Arapbet

shouted 'Hodi'–'May I come in?' which brought the response from within the hut, 'Karibu'–'Welcome'.

A tall, strong man of about thirty with very short hair and prominent cheekbones greeted Arapbet with a long handshake and eventually turned to Ella and spoke in impeccable English,

'I hear you are a teacher at Kipsigis Girls' School. How do you find your pupils?'

'They're wonderful. The best pupils I'm ever likely to work with. They so much want to learn,' said Ella, wondering why this man's appearance seemed familiar to her. 'I know we haven't met but I feel I know you from somewhere.'

The man laughed and Arapbet said something in rapid Kipsigis out of which Ella managed to grasp 'medali' and 'meheeko' after which the man went into his house and brought out a package wrapped in kitenge material. He unfolded the kitenge with great care and brought out two leather boxes of slightly different colours. He paused for effect like an actor on stage and opened the newer-looking box. Inside was a shiny new silver Olympic Medal from the 1968 Mexico Olympic Games which had just taken place a matter of weeks before.

'You're Wilson Kiprugut, aren't you?' Ella gasped. 'I've seen you on television at home in Scotland. You won a medal in Tokyo, didn't you?'

'A bronze yes–and now I've brought home a silver medal from Mexico for the 800 metres.' He opened up the other box with equal care and revealed the Tokyo bronze medal with its crinkled ribbon in blue, yellow, black, green and red.

'These are for my people, here–to make my village proud of my achievement. I'm not sure that they all understand how important these medals are in the outside world but they're happy that they are important to me.' Wilson Kiprugut paused for another minute and continued, 'I hope I can inspire new athletes one day–if the money can be found to train them.'

'I am very proud to meet you Mr Kiprugut,' Ella told him. 'I'll never forget this day. You must be Kenya's most famous athlete.'

Kiprugut replied, 'No, I leave that honour to Kip Keino the policeman. He has also won a silver medal and a gold. He is a good man and like me he wants to help the young people of Kenya. Kip Keino and I we both decided there was too much to dislike in the outside world to stay away from our homeland. The evil has even reached our sport.'

'But doesn't sport bring people together? Ella asked.

'You didn't hear what happened in Mexico,' he said and Ella had to admit that she hadn't heard. 'Two young black Americans, John Carlos and Tommy Smith won medals. But they were angry at what happens in America. They talked of Martin Luther King.'

'Yes, I remember.' Ella said. 'He was shot earlier this year.'

'These two, Smith and Carlos won the gold and bronze for the 200 metres but when they had to stand up on the podium they raised their fists with the Black Power sign. It was very impressive but do you know what the officials did?'

'I'm sorry,' Ella replied, 'I've been in Kericho without a radio and I haven't seen any newspapers. What happened?'

'They threw them out of the American team and sent them from the village because they said they had shamed America,' Kiprugut went on. 'Kip Keino said that it was America that had shamed them and all the Africans and African Americans. He was very angry and so was I. We wanted to leave for home straightaway to find what was valuable in our own land and, from now on, that is what we will try to do.'

'I can understand that.' Ella added. 'I come from a place that is far from the city in the far north of Scotland. Many of the people are still living a simple life there. They might know what goes on in big cities and other countries but they choose not to be part of it.'

The athlete nodded in empathy and changed the subject.

'Mzee tells me you read our African books all the time and ask him questions. It's good that you are trying to understand.' The world famous athlete was humble enough to refer to the old houseboy as Mzee, the sign of respect for the elderly and wise.

'I find it very interesting,' Ella told him, 'and I'm getting ready to read Ngugi's books with the girls next term. I'm sure they will teach me a few things–in return for what I teach them.'

Wilson Kiprugut said, 'Teach them well, Memsaab kidogo,' and he raised his hand in farewell.'

'Come and show the girls your medals one day,' Ella shouted back. He shrugged his shoulders. He never did visit the girls' school but he did go along to the boys' school at Cheptonge.

It was still hot on the journey back and Ella's feet were aching. The sounds of singing and pounding echoed across the valley as the women pounded maize into meal in giant mortars with long poles. Three women pounded into the mortar in time to the music one after the other and not once did they knock another pole. Another woman was grinding nuts and leaves using a small stone on top of another large, flat stone.

Along the road another family were roasting whole maize cobs on some netting over an open fire and, yet another family were cooking chicken pieces. It was time for the evening meal and Ella needed to get home for study duty that evening. She said farewell to Arapbet's family, a lengthy process with many handshakes, and Eleezabet 'escorted' her back to the gate into the school campus.

'It is very important to escort our guests,' said Eleezabet.

'Thank you,' said Ella, charmed. 'It's very nice to be escorted. Thank you for all your kindness. I will never forget today.' And she never did.

When she got home Jan greeted her with,

'Whoof, where have you been? Burning charcoal?'

'Ask me when you have a couple of spare hours,' Ella replied.

'Tell me now,' Janet cajoled.

'Later,' Ella said and retreated into her room. She needed a whole lot of that 'in between place' to consolidate her thoughts. Before that however, feeling a little guilty she added, 'Too tired, sorry Jan.'

After a little while Ella emerged, had a bath, washed her hair picked up her guitar and began to put music to the words she couldn't stop herself from writing:

> *The Shadow of a Dream*
>
> *I can hear the children singing*
> *Beyond the tall, dividing trees*
> *This side is a white world*
> *And the other side is black*
> *I can hear the cowbells tinkle*
> *As to the stream they wind their way*
> *And in the sky I thought I saw a place*
> *Where every face was middle grey*
> ***Chorus**: But it must have been the darkness*
> *Of the shadow of a dream*
> *Oh it must have been*
> *The shadow of a dream*

The Shadow of a dream

CHAPTER 10

Handel's Messiah

NOVEMBER 1968

As well as a down-market area with bicycle shops, a garage, market stalls and a night club cum bar and an 'upmarket' area with a row of dukahs, a large general store, butcher, greengrocer, tailor, restaurant, bookshop, Bata shoe shop, cinema, post office, bank and the Town Hall known as The Boma the little town of Kericho had a modern Roman Catholic church, a Mosque, a Sikh Gurudwara and a beautiful, very English-looking, ornate Anglican church called The Holy Trinity church. It looked so much like a Norman church that it was hard to believe it had been built only sixteen years before in 1952. Not only did the building look at odds with its surroundings–one doesn't expect to see banana trees and tall maize plants in an English pastoral scene–but it also had an incongruous, multi cultural congregation though it appeared that harmony reigned.

113

Music teacher Mary Lou from Springfield, Illinois had persuaded a fair number of the staff at Kipsigis Girls' School to join the choir of The Holy Trinity Church; in fact anyone who could hold a note in their head had been roped in to perform in a pre Christmas production of Handel's Messiah which was to take place at The Holy Trinity Church. Mary Lou and her husband Brad were clean living mid west Americans who had found the most suitable place of worship in the area before their first Sunday in Kenya.

Mary Lou was thrilled when she found a kindred spirit in the organist, a youngish English woman called Ruth. Both were rather large women who usually wore chunky shoes, box pleat skirts and unflatteringly tucked in short-sleeved shirts. The two soul mates drooled over sheet music they had discovered in a chest at the back of the church and played endless duets on the organ.

Ruth had been keen to arrange a performance of Messiah for some time but the dearth of choir members had always made it seem impossible. In fact the 'choir' had consisted of Ruth herself, alto, singing while she played, a nurse from the local hospital who sang soprano and the African manager of one of the tea estates who had the most amazing, bass voice which Ruth reckoned rivalled Paul Robson's. That was it. Mary Lou had pulled out the stops, 'pardon the pun', as she said, and transformed the choir in number if not in quality. She had advertised in all the schools, hospitals and shops for miles around and made the auditions sound fit for Broadway. In fact auditions included a performance of the scale from middle C up and down and a rendition of 'Doh a deer a female deer'. Ruth and Mary Lou had usually made their decision by 'Fah a long long way to run' as to whether or not the candidate could be trusted not to ruin the performance.

That was how Ella, Jan, Jenny, David, Jean Pierre, Bob and quite a few others became lambs to the slaughter. Conspicuous by his absence was John, not because he couldn't sing but because he flatly refused to be auditioned, despite all kinds of cajoling from various directions. He would enjoy being part of the audience. That was that. At any rate, he only went to the Catholic church.

Rehearsals were punishing but to everyone's surprise, and her credit, Ruth had a sense of humour.

'Choir, please,' she yelled one day, 'you have to get your lips around the men or you lose the impact!'

This raised a snigger, not unexpectedly, so a blushing, gauche Ruth stifled her guffaws with, 'No, No! I meant you have to get your diction on the Amen clear!"

This raised, 'Stop digging Ruth! You're in a hole!'

'Oh really,' a mock impatient Ruth hissed. 'Just make sure we can hear your 'm' in Amen.' This strange, old fashioned banter went on throughout rehearsals with a combination of laughing with and a bit of laughing at the obviously talented, but somewhat nerdy Ruth. It made rehearsals for the non-musical, not very Christian conscripts to the 'choir', if not exactly exciting, at least bearable.

For the genuine volunteers and especially the four soloists, bass, tenor, contralto and soprano, who had extra rehearsals, Ruth was a true inspiration. Under Ruth's guidance, and despite the inadequacies of the chorus, the soloists raised the performance to the standards of an oratorio worthy of the Royal Albert Hall in London–minus the orchestra of course–which had to be replaced by the organ, played by Mary Lou, and the violin, expertly played by young Manuel Menezes, the son of Dr and Mrs Menezes who had risen above their Catholic loyalties to allow their son to darken the doors of an Anglican church.

There were to be two performances, on Friday evening and at eleven thirty am on the following Sunday.

Ruth and Mary Lou had been fired by an ecumenical spirit

so, for the Sunday performance, had bribed and browbeaten various members of the different faith communities in the area with the promise of a rousing concert and a spot of lunch. The Sikh community and the Moslem community had come back straightaway with offers of donations of food–probably to make sure that there would be something more palatable than sandwiches, biscuits and bananas for the occasion.

The Friday evening performance came and went pleasing Ruth, Mary Lou and the small congregation which was made up mainly of Ruth's closest acquaintances in case everything all went horribly wrong. It didn't. It was competent, Ruth told them, but she wanted more passion and verve for the Sunday performance. There were important guests to impress. Ruth was the star. She conducted the proceedings with a gusto and enthusiasm worthy of Handel himself and even wept surreptitious tears of joy at the beauty and majesty of the words and melodies resounding around The Holy Trinity Church, Kericho, in the heart of the highland tea estates of Kenya. Ella was struggling with the incongruity of the situation.

The day arrived for the much publicised performance of Handel's Messiah and it had attracted a culturally diverse audience from miles around to swell the numbers of the normal Christian congregation of the protestant variety.

Ella, with little responsibility except to chip in and follow the others when it came to the alto bits, was people watching from her 'place in between'. She was reflecting on the unadorned bareness of Altnabervie Kirk, back home in Scotland, with its polished wooden floors and pews and its grey, leaded gothic windows without a hint of stained glass anywhere. Had it been only four months ago that the Mackays had knelt on the hard, unpadded kneelers to pray for the safety of the youngest member of the family who was off to face the dangers of Africa? She remembered the Caithness congregation dressed in grey and black and recollected fair-skinned faces with hair ranging from blonde, through sandy, red and dark brown. She could see red noses and ears and freckles and smiled as she pictured Copland, the oraman (general worker) on Hillside farm, flat cap in hand, sporting a shiny, very white, bald head above a line which cut him straight across the forehead, below which was the ruddy, sun tanned windswept complexion of a man used to working in the open air. She almost laughed out loud as she recalled the story of how his mates had bought him a packet of Kirby grips so that he could grow his hair long on one side and pull it over the top and fix it to the other side with a grip to form some sort of home grown toupee. He had finally given up on the idea but not until everyone had enjoyed the fun for quite a long time.

Mary Lou's sudden blast on the organ jolted Ella out of her daydream and the stark contrast between her memory of a bleak Scottish Kirk and the kaleidoscope of bright colours which were trickling into this gaudily decorated church as the audience congregated made her think of full Technicolor being infused into a black and white movie.

The choir were seated a little higher than the 'body of the Kirk' from which they could get a good view of all present. Ella was delighted to see Arapbet, his first wife and their daughter Eleezabet, whom Ella had met; they had come to see their two Memsaabs Kidogo singing. He was very proud of them. He had reconciled having three wives with being a Christian. Haidee King was there too on one of the rare occasions when she left the school at the same time as her rock, Elizabeth Kiprogot who was seated beside her. Elizabeth had a beautiful voice and was a member of the congregation but had declined the offer of a chance to perform Messiah. Her duties at Kipsigis Girls' School were too pressing, especially as most of the teachers were involved in endless rehearsals.

Ella was feeling spiritually uplifted, not just by this incense-filled, lavishly ornamented church or even by the prospect of magnificent music but by the cosmopolitan array of colours and cultures in the faces and attire of what she perceived as the most amazing Kirk congregation she had ever come across or would ever be likely to see again.

What was the intangible force that had brought all of these very different people together? Her thoughts switched to philosophy lectures and Teilhard de Chardin's 'hour of choice'. For these two hours would 'mankind abandon defiance of integration and find that faith in the unification of mankind'. Was Chardin's vision of Evolution going to come true where Mankind, to progress further, would sustain itself through finding a powerful collective faith?

Mary Lou's overture ended as suddenly as it had started and Ella was dragged out of her 'place in between' into the real world, not Caithness but Kenya. And Kenya, in all her cosmopolitan splendour, was displaying her exotic plumage in all its glory. Shiny black, brown and tanned white faces seemed to be glowing with health and there was an array of brightly coloured clothing that seemed to twinkle in the Sunday morning sun that streamed through the tall stained glass windows.

Darshan Singh, his pretty little wife and five pretty little daughters were twinkling in their gold-trimmed saris and forming a splash of colour in the front row. What would they make of Handel? Dotted randomly around the pews were beaded Kipsigis and Masai with enormous dangling ear lobes and crimson robes but no spears or red ochre hair mud so no flies. Multi coloured kitenges were everywhere. Here and there were conservatively dressed Mzungu colonials, the men sporting neatly pressed safari suits and the ladies decked out in subtle hues of patterned silk dresses and Kashmir stoles in pastel shades and the statutory straw hats, with matching floaty hatbands streaming over their shoulders. The Goan community had missed (or perhaps supplemented) mass and turned out in force to support young Manuel Menezes on the violin, which added a touch of floral dresses and black lace headscarves for the ladies and the inevitable black suits, white shirts and sober ties for the men. The children were impeccably dressed in black suits and white shirts for the boys and frilly dresses, shiny shoes and white socks for the girls. The young expatriates had turned up en masse with no attempt to be anything other than 1960s casual trendy whether they were educationists, medics, agriculturalists or engineers. Some didn't consider themselves religious but they were curious. Why were so many people so keen to attend a performance of classical eighteenth century music in 1968 rural Kenya? Jan wondered if they'd just come for the free lunch. A young, bare-breasted African mother in green Jinja cotton was comfortably feeding her baby next to Priscilla Cavendish who didn't seem to be batting an eyelid. (African tradition allowed nudity from neck to waist but it wouldn't do for even an ankle to be revealed.) Hugh Cavendish was there too but Ella reckoned young Emily had gone back to her Vet studies in Bristol. The local African community in sober, western dress and the white farmers and Brook Bond Tea employees made up the bulk of the congregation, as it was their local church, but the Sikh, Hindu and Moslem businessmen, the Irish and Italian priests from the nearby Catholic mission, Mary and Betty of Indiana from the World Gospel Mission and even Amos Goldstein from the Standard Bank and his wife Renana had all responded to Ruth and Mary Lou's vigorous advertising campaign.

On that day anyone might have been forgiven for thinking that representatives of a complete cross-section of the widely diverse communities in the area was present in that church for those two hours, on that one Sunday morning, in early December, 1968. That would have been forgetting the many African traditional religions, the Jehovah's Witnesses, the Quakers, The Seventh Day Adventists and a myriad of minor faiths that had found their way into the 'Dark Continent' in an attempt to bring enlightenment.

Handel would have wept for joy to witness his music, after more than two centuries, gripping this cosmopolitan audience, bringing them together and, for a short time at least, raising them above and beyond their differences.

Was this a fleeting glimpse of a global inter-faith meeting of minds?

Isabella Mackay, in her 'place in between' allowed herself the luxury of believing that it was. After all, Ewan Campbell, her old dominie from Balnahuig Primary School, had told her it would happen one day that the peoples of the world would unite–and she had trusted him implicitly.

Jan, also a mere alto, dug Ella in the ribs and whispered, 'Do you see who's sitting over there?' indicating the Kilpatrick brothers. 'That must be the father. I wonder where the mother and sister are,' she added, making it sound significant.

Jan was making eye contact with Drew and the two were wearing silly grins when Ella had to return the nudge to Jan as Ruth prepared to conduct them into, *'Every valley shall be exalted, and every mountain and hill made low; the crooked straight, and the rough places plain–'*

Ruth's rookie choristers enjoyed this part because she had described how the composer had made the melodies sound like a description of the words and they liked the bit where the word *'mountain'* dropped from very high to very low on the two syllables of the word.

What Ella wasn't conscious of was that, throughout her reveries, she had been sitting in a ray of sunlight which had been streaming through a tall window behind her, which was making her red hair shimmer above a face that seemed transfixed by some hidden joy.

Two young men had been watching her–two men from very different backgrounds, both intense, both troubled and both equally spellbound by this mysterious and beautiful girl. The concert was just about to reach a climax with 'Hallelujah' when Nature intervened. The entire congregation had just risen to their feet for the rousing chorus (as requested to by Ruth–according to tradition), when the sky darkened and a roll of thunder followed by a crack and flash of lightning added to rather than interrupted the performance. It was pure theatre. A startled Mary Lou recovered immediately and began to press the organ keys with even more gusto and a few seconds later an equally stunned Ruth, fixed them all with a steely eye and began conducting with a manic fervour. It took young Manuel a few minutes to recover before he was able to join in with a feeble violin. As the tropical rain hammered on the roof of the church as no other rain can, the entire congregation, of every creed and colour, joined the choir in the loudest, most rousing if not most tuneful version of the Hallelujah chorus ever not recorded.

As suddenly as it had begun, the daily storm had ended, but not before a number of people had developed the feeling that they had witnessed some kind of supernatural event or divine intervention.

As it was a pre-Christmas show, Ruth had adapted the performance so that the last chorus would be, *'Behold, a virgin shall conceive, and bear a Son, and shall call his name Emmanuel, God with us.'*

By this time, even the most unwavering non-believers were beginning to question their convictions. Ella's thoughts had returned to Pierre Teilhard and his intriguing theories regarding one universal faith which she felt fitted in perfectly with her strong belief in the fact that 'We're a' Jock Thamson's bairns' or Adam and Eve's or Mary Leakey's newly-discovered, Olduvai Gorge 'Nutcracker Man' or any other common ancestor a study of human evolution could come up with. For that moment Ella was overcome by the sensation that some inescapable force of evolution had finally brought together the peoples of the world and moved them up into a new form of human consciousness which raised them above and beyond their differences. The common origins and common destiny of mankind had come together, in her mind, like a full circle, and it all seemed completely logical. The problem was, if there was to be global unity, what would happen to the chaos of all the different faiths? Where were the threads that would join them together? The twenty two year old decided to keep her new- found discovery to herself for the time being as it was much too confusing to grasp. But the concept was to haunt her in varying degrees of intensity for the rest of her days.

By the time the concert was over and the audience were emerging from the church, the sun was shining once more and the storm puddles on the concrete pathway had already almost dried up. Trellis tables had been unfolded and sandwiches, mandazis, biscuits, bananas and sweet milky tea from a huge urn, were ready for consumption. A minute later, steaming metal trays of rice, curries and samosas were rushed off the back of a white van from Kericho Wagon Works and the feast was underway. Handel's Messiah had been stirring though perhaps alien to many present–but the food would make up for it.

Bob, who had toned down his loud, American tenor to blend in with the choir was enthusing, 'Gee, was that not awesome! Hey, Ruth, how did you get the guy in the sky to provide us with that drum roll?'

Squirming uncomfortably, but smiling contentedly, the maestro of the day replied, 'Just good management, Bob–as usual.'

The Vicar, Darshan Singh and Abdul Aziz, a local solicitor were deep in conversation and as Ella was making for some food she could hear phrases like 'from an inter-faith perspective' and '–overcome the pernicious influences of the outside world–'. She was just thinking to herself that there were plenty of those around in 1968 if you considered Vietnam or the Middle East or Rhodesia when a voice behind her said quietly, 'How's Ngugi coming along then, Elsa?' This was Mike Kilpatrick looking at her with eyes that could melt a girl. He was rather too conspicuously smitten.

'Um, Oh,' replied Elsa a little flustered, 'Fine, actually–in fact, fascinating.' She hesitated. 'Sorry, it's just a bit difficult to switch from the Messiah to 'A River Between'–but I'll be ready for the English lessons in January.'

'How much harder do you think switching from Handel must be for some of the people here, then?' was Mike's considered reply. He was making his Elsa think.

'You're right. But did you see the terrified look on some of the faces when the thunder struck? Even I was thinking it must be some sort of cosmic sign.'

Mike laughed and added, 'I don't think Armageddon's quite here yet–and the locals all expect a midday storm around here. I'm sure your Ruth timed this show carefully. Listen, when's the next free time you have to come and raid my library? The masses are going to cave in on us in a minute.'

'I'm free next weekend from two o'clock on Friday,'

'Pick you up at three.' And they lost each other to mingling.

Jan and Drew Kilpatrick had decided to abandon the effort to mingle and were having a quiet chat over their paper plate lunch.

Ella found herself behind Dr and Mrs Menezes in the queue for lunch. In front of them was John Francis looking strangely sheepish. Ella couldn't help overhearing Carmen Menezes say,

'And how is your Aunty Emma getting along in Canada? Such a horrible tragedy.'

'The last I heard she was well,' John was saying, 'and the two little ones are okay. It's Linda who's having the worst time. She's nine now and still having nightmares.'

'It was good you were over there to help them settle,' Dr Menezes added.

Ella could see an odd look of panic cross over 'John's' face as Carmen caught sight of Ella and said, 'Oh hello, you're Ella, aren't you? We met at the Tea Hotel.'

'Yes, how are you?' Ella answered politely. She was about to say how well her son had played the violin when Carmen went on,

'Ricardo, have you met Ella? She's at the girls' school – '.

'Yes, we've met, Aunty Carmen. In fact we've been bridge partners recently,' John said lamely.

Agnello butted in, 'I didn't know you'd added bridge to your talents, Rick. Is he any good then, Ella?'

'I haven't made up my mind yet,' was Ella's enigmatic reply delivered with a puzzled grin.

'Rick' alias 'Ricardo' alias 'John' was looking very uncomfortable so Ella was relieved when Ruth came on the horizon.

'Excuse me,' Ella said politely and turn to speak to her.

'Well done there, you did a wonderful job. Were you pleased?' Ella said to the deserving Ruth.

Ruth gushed with delight at how well everyone had sung and Ella responded, quite truthfully that the whole experience had been divine. Her added comment was, 'Wasn't it wonderful to see all those different people together?' Ruth beamed with pleasure.

The rest of the lunch went by in a whirl of socialisation where diverse groups fused and united and promised to perpetuate this glimpse of inter-faith reconciliation. Ella was very aware of this until jolted out of her reverie.

Jan and Bob were reminding Ella that it was John's turn to cook the dinner and host the bridge game, but where was he?

'He's over there, talking to his relatives,' Ella spat out.

'Hey John,' yelled Bob at the top of his tactless voice, 'When can we come for bridge?'

'How about Friday?' John replied adopting the same American accent. 'Sorry, Aunty Carmen, Uncle Agnello, I need to sort out my social life. It was nice to see you. Bye.'

'Bye dear,' Carmen said bleakly with a bewildered expression.

After John had ushered them away, Bob piped up, 'Don't introduce us to your relatives then. Are we that bad?'

'They're not my real aunt and uncle. We just have to call all adults aunty and uncle to be polite.'

'What about Friday then?' Jan asked.

'I can't do Friday,' Ella interjected. 'In fact, I can't do this week. I'm up to my eyes.' She was remembering her invitation to the Kilpatrick's library and she wanted to read as much Ngugi as she could so that she'd have something to say. Also, this 'John' was disturbing her. Her stomach churned at the thought of him and turned over at the sound of his voice–but she was scared. There was something she didn't trust about him. Besides, Mike was better looking.

'John' was looking miserable and just grunted, 'Okay, maybe next week then.'

When they were alone Ella confronted him,

'What's this Ricky, Ricardo bit then? Is there anything else we don't know about? Sorry. I suppose it's none of my business.'

'Oh, it's nothing -just a family nickname.'

'I thought you said they weren't family.'

'Close friends of the family. Look, you're right. It really isn't your business. Can we drop it? And please don't mention it to Jan and Bob.'

Ella would have felt much better if he hadn't asked her to keep his pet name secret but then asked herself why she should bother. There was going to be no future for this friendship.

'Ella,' John said surprisingly gently. 'Please don't worry.

One day I'll tell you. There's no great mystery.'

'If you say so,' Ella just smiled but secretly thought there must, indeed, be some great mystery.

'Will next Wednesday be okay for everyone?' John asked when the four were back together.

'That's ok by me,'

'Me too,'

'Fine,' said Ella but with some trepidation.

Back at school Ella had her hands full with nearly all of the subjects for Form One but she flew through the work so that she could get to bed early with her African Literature in English which was beginning to get under her skin and make her question so much about what had been happening in Africa over the past century.

Arapbet had been an interesting commentator on the so-called inter-faith triumph at the Anglican Church. He shook his head in surprise and wonder at the presence of so many different people–*Kalasingas, Waslimu, banyani na Wayahudi*–Sikhs, Hindus Muslims and Jews

'*Lakini kanisa kikristo*'–but it was the Christian Church. He said it was all very confusing and he didn't understand the music. He liked his own church because it had his own African music and he could still believe in Jesus and have three wives.

Jan and Ella couldn't find much wrong with that.

By this time, Arapbet had appeared with his beautifully written shopping list and announced, 'Would you mind bringing these things the next time you're in town, please?' He had conned them into learning very quickly by pretending he couldn't speak English. Total immersion.

Friday was looming and Ella was getting very excited about her visit to Kisimot farm, or her date as Jan described it.

'I'm going to borrow some books–that's all,' Ella protested. 'All in the cause of education,' she added with a twinkle.

'Lucky old you,' Jan responded feeling envious because her chosen brother, Drew, was off on one of his many safaris so they hadn't made any definite arrangements to get together. Ella tried to get an early night on Thursday to finish reading 'Weep Not Child' her second novel by James Ngugi. She had managed to finish 'The River Between' which had left her wanting to read more despite feeling more than a little disturbed by some of the themes and sentiments. She was slowly unravelling her feelings. Why instil Handel or Shakespeare into young African minds when traditional African literature could be a reflection of African life? Surely that would be a better starting point. Frustrated, she decided to tackle Elizabeth the only African teacher in school but Elizabeth felt no inclination to talk about such things. 'Least said, soonest mended, Ella,' she had said in her usual matter of fact way. 'Just get these girls through their exams. Their families have sacrificed a lot. Then God will see them through. But you're a good girl, Ella–better than most.' That would have to do. Elizabeth was a devout Christian and a devoted teacher and wanted a different life from the village life. It would sustain her.

So, apart from the schoolgirls, Ngugi and Achebe and perhaps even Mike Kilpatrick would have to be Ella's sounding boards for the moment.

Jan had said, 'He's definitely got the hots for you, EL SA. Don't kid yourself otherwise. Come on, you fancy the pants off him, don't you?'

'Well. I'm not just going to jump into bed with him–even if it is 1968. Anyway, I can't. I'm not on the pill–and I'm never going to be.'

'What? Unbelievable! Which plane did you fly in from?'

'One my big cousin never got a chance to go in.'

'Why not?' Jan asked breezily.

'She died. It was a stroke. They blamed endovin–and she was only twenty seven.'

'Geez Ella, I'm sorry. That's no joke,' murmured Jan.

'Perhaps having Rory at home was an excuse,' Ella confided.

'You won't always feel like this Ella,' Jan said and gave her a hug.

Ella had been footloose and fancy free in the swinging sixties but flower power, pot and the pill hadn't quite filtered through to Caithness in a big way–at least before Ella had whisked herself off to Africa.

Butterflies in her stomach, a bit scared and buzzing through lack of sleep, Ella flew through the day with her cheery Form One girls and managed to swap her lunch duty with Jan's so she could wash her hair and get ready for her date.

Mike Kilpatrick was no Rory Henderson. He was bigger, browner and better looking and much more exciting. She also knew he was carrying his heart on his sleeve so she wanted to look her best and be at her most interesting–and of course mysterious. One thing she'd learned about 'saving herself' for Rory was that the more she kept her distance, the keener the boys became. Today was going to be purely to look at his books she told herself.

CHAPTER 11

To Kisimot

At three o'clock a shiny haired shiny eyed Ella with lips coated with the latest shade of burnished copper and clad in her appropriate (but flattering) green kitenge answered the door to a rather dusty looking Mike whose jeep was parked nearby.

'I see you scrub up well but can I make a suggestion?'

'What's that?' Ella asked.

'Put that pretty dress in a bag and get into something scruffy. My brother's taken the closed truck on safari and I guess you haven't seen our road.'

'Oops. Hang on. I'll just get some jeans and a T shirt,' was Ella's too cheery reply when she really wanted to say, 'Huh. I took ages to get all dolled up.'

'And have you got something to cover your hair?' he shouted through from the living room.

Ella came back suitably dressed but without her dress in a bag.

'You'll need that dress later on–and perhaps a shower.' Mike said in that same polite but masterful tone that Ella had noticed the first time they met in the Tea Hotel.

'Really?' Ella shot back pretending to look shocked.

'Don't worry,' laughed Mike, 'My parents have invited a few Tea Barons home for dinner and I'd really appreciate your company.'

'Oh, won't they mind me coming?'

'Of course not–and you might like to put a toothbrush in case it gets too late to bring you back tonight.'

'Now, hang on a minute. I'm really not too sure … .' Ella was beginning to lose control of the situation and was feeling too much at the mercy of this smooth operator when he interrupted.

'Please don't worry. You'll probably be sharing a room with my sister and I'll take you home in the morning. The roads are really not safe at night.'

'Wait here,' Ella said briskly before rushing off to her room to collect herself. She could get out of this hairy situation now– just say no–but something told her she could trust this man. 'What's the matter with me? He's gorgeous–and I'm worried that his parents aren't going to be there at all,' she thought.

'Are you all right, Elsa?' Mike called after a while.

'Coming,' shouted 'Elsa' while packing dress, make up kit, toothbrush, nightie and, as an afterthought, dainty little leather sandals for the evening.

'I need you to meet someone. Wait here a minute,' Mike said and disappeared out of the door. Was there no end to the surprises?

He came back with a large golden dog on a lead which didn't look too friendly. Mike put his arm around Ella's shoulder and stroked her hair.

130

'Now, stroke his head,' said Mike.

'He's beautiful,' Ella said. She loved dogs. 'He's almost like a golden Labrador but not quite. I think he likes me. Look, he's wagging his tail.'

'He's a Rhodesian Ridgeback. Look. Feel the ridge. His name's Simba. Simba, meet Elsa. Her hair's the same colour as yours.'

'Doesn't that mean lion?'

'That's right. A dog needs to be brave around here and unless he knows you, he'll attack.'

'In that case,' Ella declared while stroking his head, 'I'm very glad we've been properly introduced, Simba.'

Mike and Ella laughed as Simba licked Ella's hand and rubbed himself against her legs.

Ella thought to herself, 'How can I not trust this man?'

'There's just one more thing we have to do before we set off,' added Mike.

'What now? Life's certainly not boring around you, is it?'

'I hope not. I have to go and see your boss with a message from my mother. Our phone keeps breaking down. I thought you might come with me so I can explain why you might not be home tonight. You know what a mother hen she is when it comes to her young teachers who've come fresh from the old country.'

'Yes I do,' said Ella. 'How is it that you know? How many other young teachers have you swept away for the night, I wonder?'

'Would you believe me if I said not one?'

'No.'

Haidee was having tea when Mike and Ella were shown into her living room and she didn't seem at all surprised to see them.

'Your mother's phone is working now. She told me to tell you,' she chortled. 'And I hear you're invited to dinner, Ella.'

'Well you probably knew before I did then,' Ella replied, relieved that everything seemed to be above board.

'You won't need this letter now,' Mike said, leaving it on the table anyway. 'How are you Mrs King?' the polite son asked his mother's friend.

'Busy but fine, thank you. And you Michael?'

'Can't complain.'

'So I see,' the older lady surmised.

'Mike's going to let me borrow some of his collection of African Writers. I've only got two and I'm taking over the literature from David in January, remember?' Ella announced, tailing off a little at the end.

'Of course my dear,' said Haidee, raising one eyebrow. 'Good idea.'

'I'll make sure she gets back safely, Mrs King. Don't worry. I've got Simba in the jeep.'

'Good,' Haidee said, thinking what a lovely couple they looked and that Simba wasn't going to be the best protection for young Miss Mackay.

'I've got something for you, Ella. You can bring it back sometime. No rush.' Haidee went off to fetch a very colonial looking lady's hat with a huge silk scarf loosely tied round it.

'Michael will show you how to wear that. Otherwise your bonny ginger hair will be the colour of the dust,' Haidee added in a very bad Scots accent.

'Thank you, Haidee,' smiled Ella and hugged her.

'You take care of her, Michael Kilpatrick. Do you hear me?'

'Yes madam,' he replied with a Boy Scout salute.

As they clambered into the jeep, Mike said, 'Watch out you don't step on the mastitis stuff I got from the vet,' Ella laughed and told Mike that it could have been her father saying the same thing in Caithness.

Out on the road, at long last, Ella's excitement was rising. She'd never been off the beaten track apart from walking to the villages in the reserve behind the school.

'I look like one of those 1920s film stars in the vintage cars,' moaned Ella after Mike had instructed her to shove all her hair under Haidee's hat and tie it on with the scarf over the top and secured under her chin while leaving enough free to cover her face if necessary.

'Don't complain, young lady. You'll thank me soon,' was the curt reply.

The emerald green carpet of tea seemed to go on for miles and then suddenly the well-maintained tar roads stopped and the vegetation changed to savanna–grass dotted with umbrella trees–and for a little while the road seemed to disappear.

'There is another road to the farm from the other side which we use to get the milk out to the dairy,' Mike explained. 'This one's a bit more scenic though.'

'I can't really see the road,' Ella yelled above the revving as the jeep dived down into another pothole, kicking up a cloud of dust. 'Now I know why all these women wear big hats and scarves. It's not fashion, it's survival,' she went on, covering her face except for her eyes. 'And I bet that's why the Arab women are covered up in the desert. It's nothing to do with modesty!'
Another lurch and Ella panicked for a second. Mike was driving along as if all was normal so she willed herself into going with the flow, bumpy though that was. Simba was sleeping peacefully so he'd probably seen it all before. All along both sides of the road were villages and little pockets of green where the little subsistence farms or shambas seemed to be using every little corner of land to produce a wide variety of food crops like vegetables, maize, pineapple and bananas and a few small patches of sisal, tea or coffee. A few villages had some big old trees were mango, passion fruit, pawpaw or avocado.

'The soil here is good if it's looked after,' Mike explained, enjoying seeing his homeland through the eyes of a newcomer, 'and these shambas are well tended. Look how the farmers have interplanted all the different crops in rows. Next year they'll change the rotation. They'll use the manure from the goats and cattle and the sun and rain does the rest.'

'Not a chemical anywhere. That's good,' was Ella's comment.

'If they had the money, they'd probably slap them on as much as the tea estates do,' Mike suggested.

'How much do the farmers sell?' Ella enquired.

'They usually sell just enough to buy a few things they can't produce on the farm–but some farmers are going over to cash crops at the expense of the family food. That's becoming a problem.'

'But they have to find school fees from somewhere,'

'Then,' said Mike, 'they usually sell a few cows.'

'One of the schoolgirls told me her father wants her to pass her exams because he'll get more cows for her when she gets married. Is that true?' asked Ella. She was keen to start pumping Mike for information.

'Yes, it's true. That's why the families are willing to make huge sacrifices to send their kids to school. Unfortunately the boys are getting the first chance at the moment.'

'I know,' Ella added, 'Elizabeth Kiprogot, the vice head at school gets het up about that. She tells the girls, 'Educate a man and you educate a person but educate a woman and you educate a family.' That really fires them up–not that they need it. I wish the kids at home could see how hard they work. Our kids in Scotland don't even want to be in school half the time and these kids here are desperate for an education.'

'My worry is this,' Mike continued. 'Will there be the jobs and the infrastructure for them when they get that education? Most of them just want to escape from the village and the streets of Nairobi ain't exactly paved in gold.'

Ella cut in beginning to feel depressed about the situation, 'Where are the giraffes and the elephants? I haven't seen a single one yet. I've only seen the flamingos on Lake Nakuru from the main road.'

'Sorry Elsa,' laughed Mike. 'You won't find any around here. It's too cultivated. I'll take you down to the Masai Mara sometime. That's teeming with wildlife–you'll love it–except the roads aren't too great.'

'You mean this is a good road?' yelped Ella as the jeep revved its way out of another gully.

'At least it's a road. Down there it's usually a "no road" that you have to go on–straight for the lions,' boasted Mike.

'There's Kisimot,' cried Mike pointing at a row of trees a little way up a hill. 'We'll be there in five minutes.' She could see he was proud of his home and excited to be taking her there. Someone had done a lot of work on this part of the road which was now made up of crushed stones–to allow the rains to drain away as Mike explained so the last part of the journey was blissfully smooth. Simba had woken up and was wagging his tail and barking happily.

'He only sleeps on the bumpy bits,' Mike told Ella. 'Daft dog.'

'Maybe he just knows he's nearly home when he hits the smooth bit,' Ella pointed out.

'Clever clogs. You're probably right. Here we are. Home.'

Ella was too entranced to feel nervous about meeting Mike's family or worry about the dust in every pore of her body. This place was magnificent. They had approached the side of the sprawling old single storey house through an avenue of high conifers some of which had crossed over forming an archway over the road–and when they emerged from the avenue Ella gasped. The large house, backed by more trees, was perched high on a hillside overlooking a wide panorama of Kenyan plains in the far distance in the middle of which was a huge splash of emerald–like a lake–which was the vast acreage of tea around Kericho. Isolated mountains like mole hills jutted out of the flatness beyond the rolling hills in the near distance. Even more amazing, and in contrast to the surrounding scrubby savanna, an oasis of manicured lawns, shrubs, trees and splashes of brightly coloured exotic tropical flowers revealed itself to an astonished Ella. She recognised the purple bougainvillea draped along the walls of the house and around the fences providing what seemed like endless curtains of vivid colour which served to show off the rest of this immaculate and fascinating, mature garden.

'This garden would be open to the public in Scotland. You could charge a fortune,' Ella told Mike, transfixed, hardly able to take in the combination of the sumptuous garden and the breathtaking view beyond it. 'How on earth did they manage to do this right out here in the sticks?'

'You can ask the lady herself. Meet my mother. Mum, this is Ella.'

'How do you do, Mrs Kilpatrick,' said Ella at her most respectful.

'Shona. Hello Ella. I take it you like gardens,' Mike's comfortably plump and healthily bronzed Mum said with a smile, shaking Ella's outstretched hand.

'Well, I like this one. How did you do it? It's exquisite.'

'I'm glad somebody appreciates it,' said Shona with feeling. 'My two sons and my husband keep telling me it's too much work and a waste of time. And the Africans just shake their heads and say you can't eat flowers.'

'Och, dinna listen to them. It's the bonniest garden I've ever seen.' Ella piped up slipping into the Scots dialect as she detected Shona's familiar accent.

'What about the view?' Mike chipped in. 'Isn't it the bonniest view you've ever seen?'

'Nearly,' said Ella, feeling a little defensive of Shona, 'though you can't beat some of the bonny sights in Scotland.'

'My granddad called it the MBA–Miles of Bloody Africa,'

went on Mike. 'He tells the story of how he found this spot back in the 1920s and decided there and then, he was going to build a house here.'

'And he did,' was Ella's pointless reply.

'And I call this garden my little bit of Scotland,' Shona added. 'When I came here in 1937 to marry Mike's dad, it was just a bit of scrub–but it did have the stream and good volcanic soil and when Angus got the animals going, there was plenty manure so I wrote to my brother in Perthshire with a long list of plants. He had a terrible hassle keeping them alive but they got here. Look, heather–even white heather. These conifers arrived as babies too and now look at them! Thirty feet high, would you say? Some of these other plants have come from all over the world. The eucalyptus is from Australia–'

Ella was then subjected to a long lecture on what was in the garden, how and from where it had got there–and bombarded with names from hibiscus to magnolia–canna lily (related to the banana plant) to bird of paradise (strelitzia)–this flame tree was from Australia but that Nandi flame is native to Kenya and so on until Mike came to the rescue.

'Steady on Mum,' her son piped up.

'It's OK. It's interesting,' Ella countered. 'My mum loves flowers. My Dad says my brother and sister and I had a PhD in Botany before we were five–but I dinna ken a lot of these plants.' She was feeling very comfortable with Shona.

'I'll leave you to it for a bit then,' Mike said, gratified to note that the two seemed to have hit it off so well.

A tall, craggy faced man of around fifty in grubby, green shorts and shirt and huge, battered farmer's hands strode across the lawn from a gate at the bottom of the garden and sat himself down in a saggy chair near a low wooden table on the verandah where a tea tray had suddenly and mysteriously appeared.

'Did ye get the stuff from the vet?' he said brusquely, 'Old

Maridadi's struggling.' One of the milkers had a bad dose of mastitis and the dairy farmer needed to treat her straight-away. 'Where's that lassie you were threatening to invite to dinner?' he added with a vestige of a Scots accent picked up from Shona and visits to the family in Blairgowrie.

'Look over there. She's another flower freak,' Mike mum-bled, pointing over to the far end of the garden where the two were deep in conversation near a massive, rambling passiflora which was covered in blooms.

'I wish we could grow this in Scotland,' Ella was saying.

'You probably could but you'd only get the flowers for a day and no fruit. Did you know this is where the passion fruit grows?'

'Wow,' the young girl gasped, genuinely amazed.

The farmer decided to dig the two women out and strode across the lawn.

'This must be the bonny lass from Scotland. Hello there.'

Shona made the introductions, 'This is Ella. She's from Caithness and her dad's in dairying and her uncle lives in Perth—and she's been telling me about the Castle of May gardens.'

Angus was pleased to note the affinity that had developed so quickly between the two women. His wife so needed a kin-dred spirit.

'Delighted to meet you,' boomed Dad. 'I'm Angus Kilpatrick. We enjoyed the Messiah last Sunday. I was telling Shona she'd missed out on a rare bit of culture out here in the bush.'

'Yes. Ruth did well, didn't she—especially as most of us were a bunch of amateurs,' Ella admitted.

'How's the cow?' she asked, changing the subject. 'Mike was telling me about the mastitis. It makes me feel I'm back at home.'

'Not too good. In fact I'd better get down to her now. Listen, sorry, I'll see you later,' and Angus Kilpatrick disappeared through a gate in the high fence.

'Tea, you two?' shouted a neglected Mike from the verandah.

For a moment or two, Isabella Mackay had been transported back to Hillside Farm and her own parents. Her own mother was as dedicated to her flower garden as Shona Kilpatrick was and her own father would be fretting in a very similar way over his cows as Angus was now. She felt strangely comforted.

'Did you say you had a sister, Mike?' Ella asked tentatively as there had been no mention of her. Before his reply, she detected a furtive exchange of eye-contact between mother and son.

'Oh, she'll be back before dark. She drove over to one of the schools this morning. She likes to help out when she can.'

'Is she a teacher, then?' Ella asked.

'No. my dear, I'm afraid not,' Shona answered gravely. 'She couldn't cope on her bad days. She's not exactly, um–well, you see–but she's looking forward to meeting you. Michael hasn't stopped talking about your visit for days,' she added. This was all moving along far too quickly for Ella's comfort.

'Mum, we're going to dig out some books,' Mike said, 'I promised Ella she could borrow some of the African Writers.'

CHAPTER 12

Secrets Too Dark
to Handle

The library at Kisimot was from a bygone age. Rugs over a
polished wooden floor, chintz curtains, two huge, soft, sag-
ging sofas with piles of cushions, an enormous green leather
chair with extra wide arms and a smaller chintz armchair with
matching footstool. The room was dominated by a huge open
fireplace with large, neat piles of wood on either side. One
wall, also wooden, was covered in animal skins and paintings
but the rest of the wall space was packed from floor to ceiling with books which, on closer inspection, seemed carefully
catalogued. Ella noticed that there was a space for Scotland
and a verse from Robbie Burns stitched on to a sampler in a
glass fronted frame. She would ask Shona about it later.

'This is my favourite room–especially in the evening with

the smell of burning cedar.' Mike told her. 'I love the peace to read–with only the sound of the crackling fire. I think it's because I never got the opportunity to study before things went horribly wrong.'

'Something tells me you want to tell me about it,' Ella suggested.

'At some point, yes, but not quite yet,' Mike replied. 'I wouldn't want to burst that happy bubble, my little Elsa.'

'I'm not your little Elsa–firstly–and secondly, if the things that "went horribly wrong" were anything to do with the Africans hitting back at a bunch of decadent and racist snobbish toffs who were treating them like dirt, then I'm not in any bubble and I don't need to be protected. If I'm going to be any good as a teacher of literature out here, I need to try to understand more than the world press have allowed us to find out–and I need to find out which questions to ask–or not ask. I thought you were going to help me there, Mike.'

'Right,' retaliated Mike, reeling back from the unexpected vehemence of this hitherto bubbly, carefree girl. 'It's not a pretty story though. I've been trying to make sense of it since I was a kid. And for the past few years, I've been digging around in the writings of the Africans in search of reasons for it all.'

Mike called Ella over to the big window which overlooked the back of the house onto what looked like a large village of traditional round huts and tin roofed brick houses and some larger, stronger looking buildings.

'This place is beautiful isn't it? My grandfather chose it well for its view out at the front. It's also a large project designed to help the Africans with housing, ten acre shambas for each family, schools, a shop and a clinic. That's what you're looking at. But, what you need to know is, my part of the family hasn't always lived here–but we've made it what it is today. The land you see here once belonged to my uncle and his family who decided they were going to hightail it back to Scotland in 1954 before, as he put it, "they were all butchered and skinned alive"–which was an overreaction as nothing had happened to them–and the local Kipsigis and Kisii were not directly involved in Mau Mau although they did want their stolen land back from the Mzungus. The feelings didn't run so high around here as in the White Highlands north of Nairobi. Much of the Kip and Masai land wasn't what the whites wanted–it was only good for grazing and wild game–and the tea and sugar estates around Kericho and the passion fruit factory near Kisii were good employers.

My parents, Drew, myself, Nan, my sister and little Donald moved from here to live on a farm near the foothills of Mount Kenya. I remember we could see that mountain through a window like this one and the Kikuyu children used to say that God lived in it. When we were young, Drew, Nan and I went to the Mission school with the Kikuyu children and we also went to the villages and learned about their language and culture. Mum and Dad were pleased because it was a Church of Scotland Mission; they weren't "decadent and racist toffs" as you put it. They were good mzungus who genuinely wanted to help–sounds pathetic doesn't it–considering what happened.

Anyway, you've read about Mau Mau which means different things -like Out Out or Mzungu Aende Ulaya Mwafrica Apate Uhuru–Whites go home so the Africans can have freedom–or whatever. The Kyuks called it Muingi–The Movement. Well, the loyal Kikuyus–loyal to the Mzungu farmers that is–would probably not have terrorised their bosses if they were being treated well but there were enough white bullies who treated their workers so abominably that all of the whites were tarred with the same brush in some people's eyes including the likes of my parents who were doing their best. Perhaps they didn't have the full blown missionary zeal like the American fundamentalists who were always falling over backwards to drag the Africans up by the bootstraps but they tried to do what the Africans thought was best. I remember my mother used to really get annoyed if she heard us using wog or nigger. She said only stupid ignorant people showed such lack of respect–which left us without much respect for a good few of the whites around at the time.

'Do you reckon there are a few of them left still?' Ella asked, beginning to see where this tale was leading to.

'For sure,' said Mike, 'but they tend to keep their mouths shut in the wrong places. Things can get nasty.' Mike then continued, 'Enter the black politicians–who played on the fear and superstitions of their own people and their anger at being exploited–and boom–full scale insurrection with some bloody, murderous, oath-taking which was meant to cleanse the land and protect people from the evil spirits–or cure a man of being a white man's nigger. I've never really understood it and I don't think I ever will.' Mike was shaking now. Ella put her hand in his but said nothing.

'Little Donald must have been about three when it happened. One night he disappeared and we never saw him again. It might have been better if we'd never discovered what happened to him but, unfortunately, we did. The son of one of the workmen came to tell us and screamed his apologies and wailed his heartbreak. Then he ran away into the dark and they found him hanging from a tree in the morning.'

Mike was silent.

After some time Ella asked gently, 'Can you tell me?' Mike looked at this young girl who was giving him strength and after some time managed,

'I don't think I've repeated this to another living soul since I heard it. I was hiding behind a door and nobody knew I'd heard. These men had wanted a big oathing ceremony–the biggest–and they wanted to make a sacrifice of someone who was both white and Kikuyu–and my mother had agreed to allow Donald to take part in some initiation ceremony into the Kikuyu tribe so he was both white and Kikuyu. She said she wanted to show the people that Jesus could accept different cultures and could forgive their sins–you know–you can still be a Christian and have four wives and thirty two children type of thing.'

'Then what happened?' said Ella, feeling that this emotionally damaged boy needed to get this whole poison out of his system.

'Well, this Kyuk who topped himself had been made to swear that he would kill any Mzungus who tried to prevent Uhuru coming and if he told anyone what had happened there that night, he would be killed–and they were right–he told my parents and he died–except he killed himself. They chopped my little brother into bits–and–and–though I've never been able to believe this–they made people eat bits–and swear allegiance to Uhuru.'

Ella felt herself reeling as if she wanted to throw up. 'Oh, Mike–I'm so sorry. How could you ever forgive that? How could anyone ever forgive that?' An icy shudder ran through her body and she could feel herself beginning to lose consciousness. She had read about rumours of cannibalism and sacrifices but had felt detached–but this was something different; hearing about it first hand from someone who seemed to be falling in love with her was spine-chilling. She had a feeling there was something more that had to be told. Mike didn't need her to go to pieces right now. She clung on to his hand until he stopped shaking and finally he spoke.

'You have to think that these were just a tiny minority of deluded people. And there was so much anger against the whites. Drew says in a way it's not very different from a lion kill but he's wrong. He's so wrong. My mother and father will never be the same. They couldn't bear to be at Kisimot without

Drew or me. That's why I've never gone away to study.

'Mike, tell me about Nan. I'll be meeting her later and I'd like to be prepared.'

'Nan was such a beautiful little girl with long curly hair and the bluest of eyes. She still has that but– –. They wanted to leave a permanent reminder as a warning. I sometimes feel it would have been better if she hadn't survived.'

'No Mike, you should never say that–'

'You don't know what it feels like to be reminded every day of what happened–to have to constantly think that it's not the Kips or the Luo or even most of the Kikuyus that were to blame–only a few deluded puppets of evil, manipulative and probably educated politicians who did that–to fight for forgiveness in your heart. Sometimes I want to burst. I want to wake up from the nightmare–but we can't! My mother potters around on the edges of reality and buries her broken heart in the frangipani and works her socks off for the schools and the shop and the clinic which is financed by our family–not these bent politicians in Nairobi. She's purging the guilt of the idiots in Happy Valley which you've no doubt heard about. My father and I slog keeping the smallholdings going with the help of some good African managers–with a wary eye on our backs to see if one of the black saviours in the city is going to destroy our efforts–in case people think we are doing their job. As for Drew, wonderful charming Drew, he prefers animals to people you see–they don't answer back and they only kill for food. He drops back into the farm for air and a good bath every now and again and then escapes to spend the rest of his time in the Mara taking money from Americans who want to look at the animals. Perhaps he's right. He's always telling us to chuck in the farming and leave the land to the *watu* and join him in opening an upmarket Safari Lodge. He reckons it'll do the country more good than competing with them for the one thing they want–the land that they consider has always belonged to them. But that's crazy logic. Uhuru's one thing but you don't suddenly know how to produce wheat or coffee or milk or mend a tractor unless you are taught–and, my dear Elsa, we don't have to travel very far from here to find near as dammit Stone Age life going on.'

Ella wasn't sure she liked the patronising 'my dear Elsa' bit but hoped the outburst had succeeded in expunging some of the heartbreak that must have been tearing Mike apart. Mike practically spat out the last sentence and collapsed drained of emotion on one of the floppy sofas.

Ella's comment surprised even herself, 'Then your parents are right. There's still a lot to do. The white farmers, the medics, the engineers and the teachers–we all have a part to play as long as the people want us to help and as far as I can tell they are desperate for this help. Our job will be done when they kick us out when their own workforce is ready to take over. Do you know there is only one black teacher in Kipsigis Girls' School–and she's the most competent–because she's the only one who truly understands what the kids want and need?'

'I knew you were going to turn out to be a very special girl, Ella Mackay and I can tell that my mum and dad like you already,' Mike said brightly, relieved of a secret burden.

'Mike,' Ella felt prompted to say, 'I'm glad you've been able to tell me all this but we're still only friends, aren't we? We're a long way from being special to each other yet. Give it time.'

Mike leapt out of his floppy seat and visibly pulled himself together. 'Okay. Let's look at these books. Have you read Ngugi's play, "A Black Hermit" yet? Oh and this is his latest "A Grain of Wheat"–I was lucky to get that one so soon. How did you get on with "Weep not Child"?'

'I love the way he writes,' Ella said. 'And I'm learning a lot– but it made me cry. After hearing your story, though, I'm wondering if Ngugi's been sparing his readers the gory details.'

'I have a feeling he'll be writing a lot more before his career is over but I suspect he'll keep his wrath for the politicians or any that's left over from the missionaries,' Mike replied.

The two were interrupted by Shona calling out, 'Mike, it's time you showed Ella to her room. There's plenty of hot water for a shower. You both look in need of one. The guests will be here at seven.'

Mike ran his fingers along his very neat bookshelves and said quickly, 'Take this one–and Achebe's 'Things Fall Apart' and Soyinka's 'Kongi's Harvest' for the moment. Then you can come have more another time.'

'When do you think I'm going to find time to read all these and prepare my lessons too?' Ella joked.

'You will. You're hungry–and I want you to come back for more–books I mean,' though he didn't mean books at all by the look in his eyes.

As Ella was languishing in a hot shower, she realised that Mike hadn't actually got around to telling her about what had happened to Nan–only that she would have been better off dead. She was thinking it must be something pretty awful and she was scared. She didn't want to react with shock and Mike had said she would be sharing her room–although you couldn't tell. There were two beds but absolutely nothing was out of place in the spotless room. She was thanking her lucky stars that her hair usually looked at its best curling into shape while damp and was finishing off the last touch of bronze metallic lipstick when there was a gentle tap at the door.

'Come in,' Ella called brightly. Nothing happened and then there was another very gentle knock. Ella's stomach churned. She didn't want to hurt this girl. She got up and opened the door. 'Hello. You must be Nan.'

The first thing that struck Ella were the huge blue eyes staring at her a little anxiously so she smiled as she looked straight into them. The girl nodded her head vigorously and said something in sign language that obviously meant yes.

Ella decided to bite the bullet and try to make herself and this girl feel at ease.

'Can you hear, Nan?' This was followed by another nod but she placed her fingers on her bottom lip.

'You can't speak, can you?' A shake of Nan's head confirmed that this was true. 'I'm Ella, a friend of Mike's, and I'm very happy to meet you.'

Nan cupped one of Ella's hands in both of hers and smiled a sideways twisted smile which shone out of her eyes. One side of Nan's face was badly disfigured which Ella hadn't noticed at first as the girl had carefully draped her long fair hair over it. As the hair slipped back, Ella was thankfully just able to stop herself from gasping as she realised that Nan had only one ear.

'I hear you have spent the day at one of the schools. Was it ok?'

Nan kept on smiling and nodding.

'Good,' said Ella, 'I'm starving. What about you? Shall we go and eat?' Nan's face clouded over as she shook her head and signed something that Ella couldn't understand.

'Okay,' Ella almost whispered. 'I'll see you later. I have to go.'

As Ella returned the gesture of clasping one of Nan's hands between both of hers, Mike's young sister smiled gently and nodded that she understood and that it was fine.

Unlike the desegregated microcosm of 1968 Kenyan society who had made up the party at the Tea Hotel where Ella had first met Mike, the dinner guests that evening were all white and well turned out for dinner according to colonial custom. Gin and tonic was the tipple with the quinine's reputed anti malarial properties—as a purple faced, paunchy gentleman informed everyone. Ella was conscious of everyone's curious eyes on her as the only newcomer.

Ella recognised Hugh and Priscilla Cavendish but none of the others. Priscilla was looking particularly *maridadi*—a

Swahili word meaning 'all tarted up' that Ella loved. She smiled to herself as she remembered that Angus's cow with mastitis was called Maridadi. She'd be keeping that comparison to herself tonight as she wasn't sure Priscilla's sense of humour would stretch that far.

'Ah, Ella, how nice to see you again; I was telling Shona about your "doing a Queen Mum" thing–marvellous idea. I was saying that at last there was a suitable girl around here to catch young Michael's eye. He's such a stay at home slogging on the farm or nose in a book. It's not good for a young man like that.'

Ella couldn't get a word in edgeways and was thinking of holes in floors or any other escape route. Mercifully Mike still hadn't appeared, probably because he knew what the level of small talk was likely to be, so they were both spared further embarrassment.

'Hm,' thought Ella. 'That explains all the attention.' She felt distinctly ear marked and what was worse was that Mike seemed more than happy to go along with it.

The son and host presented himself immaculately dressed in a cream jacket and cravat and Ella had to admit he was very good looking.

'A girl could do worse,' she told herself, 'and wouldn't he please the folks at home.'

Mike's etiquette was impeccable as he made the introductions though Ella was feeling a mixture of warmth and discomfort at the way he was holding her elbow in a little too proprietorial a manner. Something told her she needed to go along with the pretence so that Mike could save face–and she liked him enough to do that.

'You look lovely, Elsa. I'm so proud of you,' Mike whispered when he had the chance. 'Why so quiet?'

'I'm sussing out the situation. Not sure if I've got much to say,' Isabella Mackay whispered.

Shona had organised a table for twelve that wouldn't have shamed a top class hotel–with full silver service, an array of crystal glasses and pristine white, heavily starched serviettes folded into a fan shape. The table was extra wide and had not one but two resplendent flower centres using blooms from Shona's own garden.

'Did you arrange those, Shona?' Ella enquired glad of the chance to say something. 'They're beautiful.'

Before Shona could reply, Priscilla butted in loudly, 'Oh yes, Shona always does her flowers. She's so talented you know.'

Ella thought she detected a glimmer of a wink from Shona who was wearing a fixed smile.

'I'm sure your mother likes flower arranging too from what you've told me, Ella.'

'She does. She's tried teaching me but so far I haven't found the patience. Perhaps some day I'll get around to it.' Ella told herself to keep it simple. Small talk only.

'Purple and Paunchy' was busy lowering the tone as quickly as the host and hostesses were trying to raise it.

'Kip,' he shouted at the houseboy who was clad in white kanzu and red fez, *'Lette gin ngini–upesi. Mimi hapana penda wine*–Bring me another gin quickly. I don't like wine. Sorry, Angus what did you say your boy was called?'

'Take it easy Ron,' his little wife was saying looking as if she was taking a big risk in opening her mouth.

Angus simply said, 'Solomon, our guest would like a little more gin, please,' and nodded at his servant who had previously been warned to go heavy on the tonic.

'Well now Ellen,' the by now squiffy Ron went on, 'What do you think of life in the Tropics eh?' And before she could answer, he launched into what was probably a well worn party piece,

'They say there are only three ways to survive in a place like this. You can go all to Hell with religion, all to Hell with women or all to Hell with drink. That's why I drink gin. That way I please my wife.' He laughed loudly and alone and then stayed more or less silent for the rest of the evening. Everyone seemed to know each other well so, inevitably, Ella, as the newcomer, was targeted after Ron's little outburst. After endless questions on her background and how she had landed up teaching all Africans in Kipsigis Girls' School and did she need to have a teacher's qualification to do that, all of which Ella just managed to answer politely, the query that broke the camel's back came from a tea baron's wife called Trish,

'And can you manage to get any decent work out of your wog, sorry, boy?' she asked in a tone that suggested that she herself was not successful in that task.

At this point, Isabella Mackay came out of her shell. 'I ...just–don't believe you asked me that question,' she almost spluttered in annoyance. 'What in the world gives anyone the right to bully someone into doing their dirty work for them, pay them practically nothing and then complain that they're not willing to do it–most likely because they've been criticised for it?'

All eyes were on Ella and they'd heard every word so the various conversations had been abandoned.

'And for your information, we don't refer to Arapbet as "boy". In fact we address him as Mzee–as we should, because he deserves the respect–because without him we wouldn't be able to do our job. Let me tell you what he does–willingly might I add–because we show him appreciation. He arrives at five am, lights the wood stove for hot water, makes us a cup of tea, gets us up and fed and sent off to school by six on dormitory duty days, launders our clothes, cooks, cleans and nags us to mark our books and teach the children well–and he's the best language teacher I've come across. And do you know what? I'm bloody ashamed that we don't pay him more than the pittance we do. Oh–and he welcomed me to his home in the village and introduced me to Wilson Kiprugut who won an Olympic medal in Mexico and isn't that proud of it–and he walked all the way with his wife and daughter to the Holy Trinity Church to see us in the Messiah. And the only person who thought of offering him a lift home was Haidee King.'

There was a horribly noticeable pause before a now calmer Ella managed to say, 'Does that answer your question?'

'Clearly,' said Trish petulantly while fingering her expensive-looking ear rings. 'I hope you're not suggesting that I might be bullying my servants.'

Ella had to dig deeply into her diplomatic skills and was glad she hadn't made a direct accusation–which was lucky.

'No, I didn't say that. I was simply saying that the lovely old man who looks after Jan and me has been like a father to us. He calls us his memsaabs kdogo and tells us he's the bwana in the house so we call him boss and we all laugh about it. I think it's because a bit of mutual respect goes a long way. He sees us getting stuck into our job so he gets stuck into his.'

At this point 'Purple faced and Paunchy' piped up again, 'Stage One.'

'Not again dear,' his wife said. 'We could do without your potted philosophy this evening.'

For the moment Ella was not to discover what Stage One was but suspected that everyone else knew.

'We could do with some more wine, Solomon,' Angus said quickly.

Solomon made a point of starting with Ella. Looking immaculate in his white kanzu and red fez and with a bottle in each hand he said, 'Red or white, Memsaab?'

'Red please, Solomon,' and she smiled into his eyes. He smiled back, nodded and went on to serve Trish with equal decorum. She had the good grace to smile and say thank you.

Shona, perfect hostess, stepped in to save the ambience, 'Priscilla, tell us about "doing a Queen Mum" again. How does it work?'

'Clever lady,' thought Ella. 'She knew I couldn't handle that right now.' Ella was sorry that Mike wasn't on her right or left. She could have done with his support–though she wasn't going to apologise for anything.

After Priscilla had organised the one to one conversations with ladies to the left and men to the right–which involved a little chair switching and hanging on to serviettes and wine glasses–Ella found herself talking to Roger from Brook Bond Tea with the chance of talking to Mike later on as, thankfully, he had engineered his way to her other side.

'Nice one, Elsa,' Mike grunted before launching into a conversation with Roger's wife and Trish's friend Hermione– about Peter O'Toole in 'A Lion in Winter' which was showing at the Kericho cinema. Ella was left wondering whether there had been any sarcasm in his voice.

'I enjoyed your little performance,' Roger put in quietly. 'It's about time someone put that spoilt cow in her place. She's always complaining about this boring place where there's nothing to do.'

'I bet she complains about no milk and newspapers on the doorstep,' replied Ella sensing an ally.

'I've heard her on about lazy postmen. Resents going down to the post boxes,' Roger went on. 'I doubt whether she reads any newspapers. She keeps saying Hermione's her only friend–and poor Hem's lumbered.'

'I don't suppose I'll be invited back here though,' Ella surmised glumly.

'You might be surprised,' Roger answered.

'I don't think Mike was impressed though,' Ella added. 'I should've kept my mouth shut.'

'Anyway,' Roger went on changing the subject. 'Have you taken the schoolgirls on one of our educational trips round the tea estate?'

Everyone survived the dessert, coffee and liqueur with

its stilted conversation–and eventually the last of the guests dribbled away before Angus Kilpatrick laughed loudly and hugged little Ella round the shoulders.

'I thought you'd throw me out,' Ella cried, relieved that this big, cuddly, father figure of a man had forgiven her for offending one of his guests.

'You were magnificent.' Angus said. 'Did you see the look on that woman's face? Come on. Let's get the hot chocolate. Nan, where are you?'

Shona, Mike, Angus and Ella went through to the kitchen where Nan already had a pan of milk on the wood stove and was lolling on a chair with Simba at her feet.

'Best bit of the day,' Shona told Ella. 'Whatever happens, we all get together for a nightcap–the whole family.' She arranged six mugs on a tray and picked up a big tin and a spoon.

'Hot chocolate all round?'

'Wonderful,' said Ella.

'Let's have it in the library,' Mike suggested. 'The fire's still going strong.' Nan signed that she'd been there all evening. 'Lucky you, Nanny,' he continued. 'Some of these guests we have can be pretty boring.'

Nan signed in Ella's direction and everyone laughed.

'She says she likes you though, Ella,' Angus translated.

'Good. I like you too Nan,' said Ella–and meant it.

'What have you been doing tonight?' Mike asked his sister and, in reply, she took Ella by the hand and led her through to the library. She opened up a wide drawer and pulled out an artist's pad and handed it to Ella.

'That's brilliant,' Ella said as she found a smiling portrait of herself staring back at her. 'But you only saw me for five minutes. How could you remember?

Nan shrugged her shoulders, spread her palms upwards and outwards with a tilt of her head and a smug smile which said, as clearly as any words could, 'I'm a genius.'

'Yes, you are a genius,' said Ella and Nan's vigorous nod and wide grin showed how delighted she was that Ella had understood.

Mike was thrilled to see the two of them getting on so well and when Nan insisted on giving Ella her picture he said, 'Can you do another one for me?'

'Tomorrow,' Nan signed. She signed some more for Mike to translate. 'She's sorry she didn't come to the dinner party. Some people make her feel uncomfortable.'

'That's ok,' said Ella. 'I feel the same sometimes.' Everyone laughed. Shona and Mike got involved in a sign language chat with Nan so Ella decided she'd ask Angus about something that had been bugging her.

'What did that guy mean by Stage One?'

'Oh it's just a little observation he's made about all these new expatriates who've been coming out to Kenya since Uhuru–like yourself I suppose. He's been here all his life so he reckons he knows it all. Stage One is when people have just arrived and the African can't do anything wrong. Then there's Stage Two, when disappointment sets in and the African can't do anything right. Stage Three is when you realise that there's good and bad in the Kenyan like there is in any race. In our case, it's just been a bit bloody hard to forgive and forget–but,' said Angus, 'we've taught ourselves and our kids to see everyone as an individual–and we've had to learn how to trust. I like to think we're in Stage Three.'

'That Ron's not so silly after all, is he? I thought it was just the gin talking,' Ella added.

'He's struggling a bit–trying to get out of Stage Two, I think,' Angus said. 'As for that airhead Trish–I don't think she realises Uhuru is here or what it means–like a lot of people unfortunately. I doubt if she's ever got to Stage One.'

'I'm glad I said what I did then,' said Ella.

'Yeah–maybe you made her think.' Angus said. 'But a word

of warning. You're very lucky with your Mzee; not all servants are as wonderful; there's a lot of ill feeling around too.'

'I gathered that from tonight's little discussion. I hope I've skipped Stage Two and become a wise Stage Three with your help,' said Ella.

'I hope so too–but keep your wits about you,' Angus advised her.

'My Dad's treating you to the benefits of his wisdom is he?' Mike teased. 'Come on Ella, Nan's excited about you sharing her room. She wants to show you some more drawings.'

'Only a few because I'm very sleepy,' yawned Ella, needing no sign language to convey her meaning.

'Good Night Elsa,' Mike whispered. 'I'm jealous of my sister tonight.'

'Good Night everybody, thank you for a lovely evening,' Ella yawned again, allowing herself to be given Mike's good night hug. The Kilpatrick family had done their best to make Ella feel at home but before she could sleep she wept–tortured by the family's pain. Nan had proudly displayed her drawings of people and animals–many with anguished or tortured expressions. She was relieved to note that her own portrait was smiling. Ella showed her appreciation as enthusiastically as she could despite her sleepy yawns. As the young Scottish girl struggled to find sleep she couldn't get the picture of a framed sampler that Shona Kilpatrick had 'stitched by herself' in the long lonely African days. Ella had instantly recognised the verse:

Then gently scan your brother Man,
Still gentler sister Woman;
Tho' they may gang a kenning wrang,
To step aside is human:
One point must still be greatly dark,
*The moving **why** they do it;*
And just as lamely can ye mark,
How far perhaps they rue it.

When Ella had admired the picture which was purple and green and decorated with white heather Shona had sighed deeply. Her comment had been. 'You know it has to be an awful big *why* because it was much more than just a 'kennin wrang'. Ella wasn't sure if Shona knew that her son Mike knew the whole truth about the family tragedy and was quite certain that she had no idea that she, Ella, had been told about it. Ella had been too choked to speak. Now horrific images were disturbing her sleep. Where did Nan find her courage? What could she remember about the brutality? How could this family still be here in this country where such unspeakably grisly atrocities had been foisted on their baby boy? Could it be true that Mike had never spoken a word about it before? If so, how much responsibility did that leave Ella with? Yet, they seemed strong–living their lives. But why was Mike behaving as if his relationship with Ella was much further along than it was. She saw Mike's face–trusting her–believing she loved him as much as he seemed to love her. She saw 'her' Rory in her dream and how she had kept all the other boys at a distance. She had perfected the pose–not stand-offish enough to be unfriendly but not close enough to be accessible. But the biggest, most vivid image of all was her father. Charlie Mackay who had wanted her–expected her–to marry into the farm next door and pretended not to be disappointed when it didn't happen. The image faded. Another darker face appeared. A scream followed a distant shot. A brown arm loomed out in front of her about to steal–but the sound of a familiar song–a beautiful song–interrupted the dream–like a circle in a spiral like a wheel within a wheel–and the world is like an apple whirling silently in space–the autumn leaves were turning to the colour of her hair. That's his favourite line. He says my car is the colour of my eyes; he fixed up for me to have that car–he said trust me–please trust me. She woke up with a start, tears streaming down her face. Nan was holding her hand and stroking her forehead. Nan opened her mouth wide in a silent scream. Then she smiled, shook her head and pushed her palms together and laid one cheek on them.

'Was I screaming? – Sorry.'

Nan stroked her new friend's forehead for a little while longer until she calmed down. Ella remembered something. 'I used to know another Nan Kilpatrick. I went to school with her in Scotland. Isn't that strange?' Nan raised her eyebrows and then closed her eyes and did that palms together on cheek thing again and went back to bed blowing out the candle she had lit when Ella had screamed. Lying in the dark, willing herself to stay awake to keep the nightmares away, Ella's thoughts turned to John the enigma. Who was he? Why did she sense danger? Why was she so attracted to him? She thought of her family's struggle with Morag marrying an Englishman. The gossips in Caithness loved to think that the Mackays needed to be pitied. What on earth would they think if John appeared within their midst? No, it just couldn't happen. But – another image of her old Dominie came to mind. Ewan Cameron was telling the bairns that we're all different but all equal. Aunty Lizzie's voice was saying, 'Don't be silly Jeannie. Give it a century and we'll all be coffee- coloured.'

Why was she here at Kisimot? It wasn't right. She'd leave in the morning and later write a polite thank you letter and that would be that. She didn't want to hurt this family. If she stayed around any longer she would. It was time to be aloof.

CHAPTER 13

An Offer Ella
Could Refuse

After a healthy Kenyan breakfast of pawpaw slice topped with fresh pineapple chunks and passion fruit, Ella was given a guided tour, by Mike and Nan, of one of the ten-acre small-holdings, the school, shop and clinic which were all located close to the farmhouse and main dairy and bulk tank for the milk which had to be kept chilled by its own generator. Mike was full of enthusiasm for the project and anxious to show Ella how industrious and successful the African farmers were. Wilson Kirior, project manager, was in a small office with a tin roof, surrounded by paper work. When he saw Ella, he remembered her from the Tea Hotel and stood up to shake hands. She was conscious of his piercing eyes regarding her with a hint of cynicism.

'I see you have come to see what happens outside the school-room Miss Mackay,' he said with an outwardly friendly smile.

'Yes, I was kindly invited,' Ella replied a little wary of saying the wrong thing. 'How is your project coming along? Mike's been telling me a little about it.'

'It seems to be coming along well. The farmers are tending their crops lovingly now that their land is their own–again,' Wilson went on, with an emphasis on 'again', 'but I'm not sure if the hand milking of their two or three cows for sending up to the bulk tank is going to work.'

'Mike, can you come and have a look at this cow. We might need the vet,' Ben Chepkwony was saying. Mike and Nan both went off leaving Ella with Wilson.

'How was dinner?' Wilson asked and when Ella couldn't control a sigh he added, 'You don't have to tell me. Some of these characters are in their own world. Uhuru might as well not have come'

Ella wanted to tell him about her outburst but decided to say nothing so he carried on. 'Your Mike is better than most. He tries to understand what's going on in the minds of the *watu*. There's no Bwana this and Memsahib that if he can help it and he's trying to be fair. But he's an idiot if he thinks he can carry the can for the colonial bullies before him.' His fiery eyes were glittering and Ella suddenly wanted to spring to Mike's defence.

'But surely you believe in the project. He seems to trust you. You're on his side aren't you?' Ella asked.

'Perhaps–but before long there will be people, black not white, who will be doing his father's and his work. That, I believe, is how it should be.'

'Why are you telling me this?' Ella asked. 'Have you said this to Mike?'

'Yes but he doesn't believe it will happen. But you, teacher can tell the girls at the school. They must believe it,' Wilson

160

said with a scary intensity.

'No, sir,' Ella said defensively. 'It wouldn't sound right coming from me. But what I *will* be doing is reading Ngugi and Achebe with them and I will ask the girls what they think. I won't try to indoctrinate them.'

'Then how will you teach them?' asked Wilson.

'I'll let Ngugi's 'The River Between' teach them–and then let the girls make up their own minds–maybe through debates.'

'I think, maybe you are no fool, teacher. I wish you well.'

Mike and Nan returned with the news that Angus was going to dose the cow with more medicine.

'Don't listen to this one Elsa,' Mike said of Wilson, 'he's a raging rebel,' and the two men laughed together. Ella felt uneasy.

The school was closed because it was Saturday; it was equipped with benches and a blackboard, the walls were covered in the children's writing, number and artwork and a table was covered with clay models and home-made toys. Inside a single, rickety cupboard was one exercise book per child and a stock of slates and chalk.

'When the chalk runs out, it's sticks in the sand,' Mike told Ella.

'Can you see Nan's influence here?' he added, pointing to the pictures and the models. 'She enjoys working with the children.'

Nan started to sign frantically and took Ella by the hand.

'She wants you to say hello to Precious,' he said and turning to his sister added firmly, 'only five minutes, Nan, because I have to take Ella back to her school.' And, because it was obvious Nan didn't want her big brother around, he added, 'I'll see you back at the house.'

Nan nodded her agreement and the eighteen year old wordless girl and her twenty two year old companion set off through a break in the garden fence. Within minutes the two were surrounded by little children and Ella could see that they were all fond of Nan and curious about herself. They found Precious roasting maize on a charcoal stove outside the door of her traditional, round, thatched hut. After Nan had communicated in sign language for a while, she said,

'Hello E l l a–I am Precious, the teacher at our school. Nan says you are a teacher. Where do you teach?'

'I'm at Kipsigis Girls' School,' Ella replied.

'I know that school,' Precious said. 'I wanted to go there but the tests were too hard. Only two girls in one hundred can go there–but I passed my KPE and I can teach here but we need more teachers. Do you think you could like it here with Nan and me?'

'I'm sure I could,' Ella replied, 'but I have to teach at Kipsigis Girls School for at least twenty four months.

'Oh, that is a very long time to wait,' said Precious. 'Perhaps you could tell them you want to change your school.'

'I don't think that could happen. I've signed a contract. Perhaps you can find another teacher,' Ella suggested.

Then Precious said something which made Ella want to beat a hasty retreat back to Jan and back to normality.

'Nan says it has to be you because when you marry Bwana Mike you can live in the big house and just walk here soon.'

This was why Nan hadn't wanted Mike to come with them. She wanted to see Ella's reaction. Did she want to find out if Ella was a suitable wife for her brother? Had Mike told his sister he was planning to marry her and if he did where had he got the idea she might say yes? All these questions were buzzing round in Ella's head; she found herself blurting out,

'Has Bwana Mike talked about this to you, Precious?'

'No,' was the reply, 'only Nan has.'

'Then please, Nan and Precious, promise you won't say anything to him. It's not the right time.'

'I promise,' said Precious.

'And you, Nan.'

There were tears in Nan's eyes but she nodded sadly and circled her closed fist around the middle of her chest.

Precious translated, 'She is saying she is sorry.'

Ella could feel her own heart breaking for this lonely, damaged girl who was looking to her for friendship and hope–so she hugged her.

'Maybe one day I can come. We'll see, but I don't know yet. I hardly know your brother.' Then Ella added, 'but I very much like you and all your family and I want to be your friend. And Precious, it was good to meet you too–and good luck with the school.'

Nan and Precious both managed to smile.

Back at the farmhouse the whole family, including Simba, had congregated to say good-bye to Ella before Mike (and Simba) set off to take her back to Kericho. Ella thanked them warmly and added,

'You've made me so welcome and I'll never forget this visit.'

(She almost added, 'I feel as if I've got a whole new family,' but stopped herself, thinking that it might be misinterpreted.)

Some of the emotional pressure was released as the jeep rattled and lurched its way through the MBA back to town, but Ella was still conscious that this intense, young Mike was going to have to be handled.

'What do you have to do today, then–apart from swot up Achebe and Ngugi?' Mike asked cheerfully.

'Not a lot,' Ella foolishly replied, 'as long as I get the tests ready for Monday. It's the last day before the girls go home for Christmas.'

'Right,' said Mike decisively, 'Tea Hotel. Lunch. There's something important I want to talk to you about.'

Something about his tone suggested she'd better not protest.

'Lovely,' she said trying to keep the apprehension out of her voice, 'but I'm really not hungry after that dinner–and breakfast.'

'Just a quick snack and a drink–it's the ambience I'm after,' he announced, 'and I'd like you to meet someone.'

Ella had to admit she was enchanted by the Tea Hotel in daylight. Tea and a small platter of sandwiches had been served on the terrace where a green ocean of tea plants stretched as far as the horizon beyond the manicured gardens where peacocks and crested crane were picking their dainty way across the lawn. This was the epitome of British colonial Africa. Ella felt as if she was in a bubble that was about to burst as she reflected on the extraordinary visit to the Kilpatrick farm which was in the process of being sold off over a period of time to a group of Kenyan farmers who had never felt that the land had belonged to the Kilpatricks in the first place. Mike Kilpatrick knew this. He wasn't so sure that his father had ever admitted this. At the moment the family were rich. Angus was keen for that to continue so the land had to be made profitable and it had to be sold–bit by bit. However, his understanding of the concept of *harambee* was not so keenly developed as that of his son. Harambee–self-help–let's pull together to make progress was the buzz word of Jomo Kenyatta's era so Ella knew exactly what was meant when Ole Kiplangat greeted Mike Kilpatrick with a warm handshake and a hearty, '*Harambee, rafiki iangu.*' The two men were obviously close.

'Elsa, meet this Masai cum Kip who's been my friend since we were children. I'd trust him with my life.' Mike said.

'I remember you Elsa. You're at the girls' school, yes?'

Ella had a vague memory of seeing this incredibly handsome young man now dressed in jeans and snowy white shirt.

'Last time you saw me I was behind the bar but I'm off duty today. In fact, I've got a new job–with Brook Bond.'

'Oh yes, I'm sorry,' Ella said, warming to him, 'You look so different. Congratulations.'

'That's brilliant news, Ole,' his old friend Mike said. 'You deserve it after all the hard slog. Well done.'

'How's the project coming along, then?' asked Ole

'Good, I think but I'm struggling a bit with Wilson. He's a bit negative. I'm not sure he trusts my motives,' sighed Mike. Ella found herself saying, 'Perhaps it's his motives you need to be worrying about,' and then wishing she hadn't said it. Ole's nod seemed to show that he knew exactly what Ella meant but Mike turned to face her saying,

'When did you pick up on that?'

'Oh, just something he said this morning,' she replied.

'Ah well,' Mike said sadly, 'I just have to hope that he's with me until we manage to sell off all the shambas.'

'I think Elsa might be right. These students at the Agri College get all fired up with land grabbing ideas. "It never belonged to the Mzungus so we'll have it now." They're worse than the whites were before. They want Blacks, not Whites in control and very especially not Reds. I heard all the talk but I don't agree with half of it.'

'That's because deep down you're just a commy Masai,' said Mike.

'What does that mean?' Ella asked.

'Have you got a couple of hours? Our Ole's about to get on his soap box,' laughed Mike with a mixture of teasing and pride. Ella could see there was a warm friendship between the two men.

'Don't listen to him! I'm not a Communist. I have my beliefs in the spiritual world of Africa—but some say there are similarities.'

'I don't understand,' said Ella

Well, in our tradition, on my mother's side more because she is Masai, but also on the Kipsigis side, the land belongs to nobody and everybody, the living, the dead and those still waiting to be born. We only borrow it to meet our needs for a short time.'

'That's a beautiful concept but can it work?' Ella asked.

'It's the only way we nomadic pastoralists can survive. If the world would leave us alone it could work,' Ole pointed out.

'You say "we" Ole, but you're going to work on a tea estate owned by a huge multinational company. How does that fit in? Surely you have abandoned your traditional way of life.' Ella guessed.

'True–but not completely; this tea should bring much needed money for the part of the population which now needs it. Their roots have been pulled up and they will need money to survive. The profit should go to building up the infrastructure of the country.'

'What about you. Ole?' asked Ella. 'Have your roots been pulled up?'

'I hope not. I try to go home to the Mara whenever I can and live in the manyatta and follow the traditional customs. I have killed my lion and become a warrior even though my father was part Kipsigis. My mother made sure I was brought into the tribe.'

'It must be very hard to live two lives,' said Ella.

'No, not hard,' said Ole. 'This life I have now in the hotel and the estate house is not really real. When I go home and wear my blanket and relax there is nothing hard about the decision. I'm home and the roots go deep.'

'I think you should write a book,' Ella said. 'I'm reading "The River Between" at the moment and the Kikuyu way of thinking is so different.'

'Perhaps one day I will write a book and perhaps one day the Masai and Kikuyu will see eye to eye–but that day has not come yet.' Then Ole added, 'For now, Mzungu Mike and I see more eye to eye. Where did you find this Elsa, my friend? She thinks a lot–perhaps too much.'

'Oh, I just picked her up in a bar. In fact, right here at the Tea Hotel,' Mike joked and they all laughed.

'Anyway, I must go and see a man about a tea-estate,' the suave Ole declared as he stood up. 'Enjoy your lunch. *Mwethia*

Mzungu Mike. Go and save your corner of the world.'

'I like him,' Ella told Mike, 'What's Mwethia?

'It's just Masai for harambee. We've always talked about this since we were kids. He grew up on Kisimot together but, suddenly, out of the blue, the whole family moved to the plains and back to the old traditions.'

Ella went on cautiously, 'I meant it when I said I'm not too sure about Wilson.' When a cloud passed over Mike's face, Ella asked, 'What was it you wanted to talk to me about?'

'That's all the most important people now–so I can tell you now,' Mike announced mysteriously.

'What?' Ella pleaded impatiently.

'Look around you. Isn't this the most beautiful place you've ever seen?'

'Probably,' the girl ventured.

'And you feel comfortable with my family?'

'Yes, but we've only just met.'

'And you like Ole, my best friend?'

'Yes.'

'And you can stand up to the neo-colonial idiots you met last night?'

'Not sure about that one.'

'And you want to breathe new life and hope into Kenya through the young people.'

'I'd definitely like to but I'm not exactly certain if and how I can.'

Then, this intense young man launched into a lengthy speech on his hopes and dreams for the future of Kisimot where a new harmonious community would develop into a modern village with modern amenities and a school for the people which Ella could run. It would be a symbol of hope which would atone for the sins of the past.

Ella was astounded. 'Are you sure anyone's looking for a great white saviour? And anyway I can't break my contract to go and teach in a Harambee school.'

Mike came to the point and Ella was taken aback. 'I think I should marry you, one day.' Just like that. No warning. Not even a romantic kiss.

'Were you thinking of asking me first?' asked Ella too flustered to feel flattered. She was beginning to wonder where this guy had been when they handed out the social skills.

'I'm asking you now. I would have asked you before but I needed to know if you were the right one–the one I've been waiting for. I needed to see how my family reacted to you–especially Nan–and it was important that you liked Ole. Elsa, you have passed all the tests. Please say you will think about it. I can give you a wonderful life.'

'No, Mike I'm sorry I'm not ready to think about marriage yet; I've only been in Kenya for three months and this is only the third time I've met you. Perhaps I'm not the Elsa of your dreams. You've taken too much for granted. Can't we just be friends for a while and see what happens?'

'Is that a definite no to will you marry me?' a crestfallen Mike said very quietly.

'I'm not saying that because I think you're lovely–but it's just too soon–much too soon.'

'So you'll think about it–and you'll come and spend Christmas at Kisimot with us?'

'I'll give it some thought–but I just can't come for Christmas. Things to do and places to see in Kenya–and people to catch up with,' Ella went on briskly impatient to shake off the shackles.

'What people?'

'I've promised to get in touch with all the people in the group who came out to Kenya at the same time as I did. We plan to meet at the Thorn Tree.'

'Oh, I see. I envy you all these contacts. Life in the bush has been lonely. I never did get the chance to meet other young people after High School. I had to come home. Things were bad.'

There was no way Ella was going to let herself be dragged into another long saga so she just breezily said, 'Mike, I've had a wonderful time but now I've got to get back. Next week's going to be hectic as we want to get all the exams marked and reports done before the break.'

'When will I see you, then?' asked Mike.

'Let's leave it until after the New Year. We might see things more clearly then,' she said as firmly as she could muster. She didn't want to hurt him. The more she was getting to know him, the lonelier and more vulnerable he was turning out to be. She was fairly certain she didn't want to be trapped inside his bubble.

Back at school, and after a toe tickling, gut-wrenching, kiss and hug, Mike deposited a dusty Ella and her bag on the doorstep. Simba jumped out of the jeep and snuffled around her looking for some attention.

'See, even Simba thinks you're perfect,' Mike said still not losing hope. 'You will think about me won't you?' he added.

'You can be sure of that,' Ella replied. She just didn't say what she would think about him.

As the jeep sped off a much relieved Ella shouted out,

'Jan! Jan! Oh Jan, you won't believe the weekend I've had. It was like a whole lifetime.'

'Wow, Sounds intriguing. What happened?'

'Mike made me an offer he thought I couldn't refuse.'

'And did you?'

'What?'

'Refuse.'

'You bet I did.'

And for the next two hours she recounted her experiences in as much detail as possible for a fascinated Jan. When she had finished Jan just said,

'Heavy.'

There was no need for any translation across the pond.

After a dream-filled night's sleep, Ella woke up early and took her rubber-tipped pencil and her journal out to her thinking spot overlooking the green ocean of tea. In the heat of the sun she continued working on the almost finished outpouring, frantically rubbing out the bits where she had changed her views as a result of the trauma and conflict of the eventful weekend at Kisimot with the cast of characters which would stick in her memory forever.

Conflict

'We must stay,' quoth Mr Smith,
'For I'm sure you would not wish
Another Congo on your conscience.'
'Whose conscience?' spoke naivety.
'I am not responsible for History gone wrong.'
'They must go,' quoth Kariuki
'As their infuriating presence
Witholds us from the progress
Which is every man's desire'.
'Progress,' roared Mr Smith,
'Cannot proceed unguided
Since there's one and only one way
That the task can be approached.'
Naivety stands back and views the situation
With an inkling of perception that reveals the heart of man
I think that Mr Smith is proud of his ability.
He knows the way the world is going.
He's sure that he is right
As he views things in the 'only' way
With a cool, indifferent, economic eye.
He feels the fellows want to rise
To become just like himself
And, in secret, though he'd never say,
He fears they want to better him.

'And hang it all, if not for us they'd still be in the bush!'
Mr Smith, oh Mr Smith
You do not know how much I wish
That your pedestal would crumble
And you'd fall where you can see.
Naivety, though young, has eyes which can perceive
A pride which has been hurt beyond repair.
Mr Smith, you were a bastard
And self-righteous along with that
And, what's worse, what you've created
Are a million like yourself.
Kariuki is a bastard now, near worse than Mr Smith
Triumphant in his freedom to kick our Smith around
Human nature is a harsh and true reality.
Man is proud and man must be
Respected as important in the eyes of the world.
Oh Kariuki, Kariuki, do not be deceived
Into thinking that by crying out
The world will hear your voice.
'Go to Hell you lousy bums.
Let us find the path to follow.
We do not want to constantly
Be watched and criticised.'
I can hear you Kariuki
And I understand you well.
Do not be surprised because I do
While I am white and you are black.
I understand so well because I too
Had to fight for independence
Not so very long ago in the tender years of youth.
Youth can go two ways in life
According to its strength
Parents are the ogres who threaten
That development of character

Which comes from you alone.
But do they really threaten?
Or is it in the mind
Of he who wants to prove
That he can do it by himself?
Parents are well meaning
But often do not know
What burns in youthful hearts
That desire to be a person
An individual, wholly on his own
So pay heed to Kariuki for he constitutes
A people who are growing towards an existence
Which is not of their creation
Africa has two sets of parents
Which one will she follow?
As the wheels of 'progress' grind throughout her
Will one set have to die?
Mr Smith says it's inevitable
That progress is her fate.
'After all, the world cannot continue
With such an economic gap
Amidst the people of her soil'
Inevitability, inevitability, the father of fate
Tell us the answer before it's too late.
Youth can go two ways in life.
It can conform or can rebel.
Youth in a person is like youth in a people.
But Africa has no choice.
Conform to the new or conform to the old.
One side rebellion, the other rebellion
Banish a heritage or banish the world
Wallow in proud isolation or join in the fight
Africa, oh Africa, you can create, like Youth can create
New values, new ideas, new life

Discard what is bad, adopt what is good.
Be individual but, above all, be honest.
You are young, blissfully young,
But pride is the cause of many mistakes.
Banishing a heritage without a thought
About what you might lose
Is like disowning your parents who gave you your life.
Once you do that, the story ends
For nothing is deep but the need to succeed
Ambition comes, corrupts and forgets
About life and humanity and all that's affectionate
'I am fighting the fight,' cries the young politician.
'I know what to do. The rest of them don't.'
And the old lady at home weeps for her son.
He is lost, forgetting but not forgotten.
He cares not, for the Mission taught him,
'All that is new is everything good
All that is old will get you nowhere.'
But much that is new is a skin on a skin
And much that is old is deep in the heart.
New silver, old gold, gold sold:
The bargain seems poor sad–
Like the death of an old friend.
Fight, Africa, fight!
I will never deny you the right
To compete freely and openly
I do not fear so I do not oppress.
History, they cry, will never learn.
Each man has to be top dog.
God knows why!
Don't fight for what the other man has.
It's not what you want.
It will be your downfall
Fight for what's good and human and fair

Don't forfeit self respect for what the world terms
Affluence and power
Look to your people, the gold in the soil.
Don't feather your nest, empty but for you.
Compete but compete fairly, not by example.
Power is no excuse for exploitation.
An eye for an eye, a tooth for a tooth
Good God, man, who stole the eye?
Not your people, not your own.
And the tooth of the one you blame
So readily for bringing you down
Is still unobtainable
The man with the tooth gave you the chance
To fight for your rights in the world
You know and you know you can't bring him down
So don't pick on the poor and weak of your own.
By the way, who brought you down?
The white men who came and made us feel small
He is the one to answer for all
Now, answer this question
Why did you not visit his land
Like him, not to conquer but to see?
'Not to conquer!' you roar. 'What a lie
A typical, hypocritical, white man's lie'
Be careful what you say
Now you are free. What does this mean?
Does it mean there's no power, no weapon no bomb?
Has the white man surrendered?
Do not expect him tomorrow
To plunder, to rob and to seize
He could do it with ease.
But he won't–is my hope.
My hope is he respects you as part of the world.
He gives you take. You give, he takes.

174

Independence but interdependence–harambee, Mwethia
He respects so respect
But mistrust and he mistrusts
Fear and be feared
But give, and be given
Give what is yours that you need not
Take what is his that he needs not
Therein lies equality
Within equality, however, lies inequality
You are you. He is he.
You want this. He wants that.
What does it matter?
You have learned from him.
Some things good some things bad
It's not fair to him to forget the good and remember the bad
It's not fair to you to practise the bad and forget the good
But there's good in the old
Of the land of your birth
'But they never would learn from us
As our life and customs were lowly'
Not true
Now you can teach what you've learned from both sides
Good is good so find it where it lies
Show the world how you feel deep down
Below the thin skin of conformity
Must you die to save face in the eyes of the world?
Respect yourself and the world will respect you
Each man can teach and each man can learn
Fight Africa fight
In peace

DECEMBER 1968, KIPSIGIS GIRLS' SCHOOL

Exhausted and empty of all emotion, Ella prepared to hide the journal under its silk scarf in the drawer and turned her face towards more light hearted activities. Her 'in between time' thoughts were once more captured and put down on paper where they wouldn't get lost.

(Many years later a much older Ella was to look through her journal and come across 'Conflict' and cringe. As a literary piece it was unbelievably bad, she decided, but as a record of her feelings at the time, she would not change a single thing. It was there as a reminder of the tragic story of family who had recovered from a nightmare for which they blamed themselves and for which they wanted to make amends–a family at the end of its tether who needed a new symbol of hope and a new source of strength. It was there as a reminder of the early days of post–colonial independent Kenya and the many different peoples with as many different conflicting views who were involved in the building of the new nation. And it was there as a reminder of how truly naïve she was to believe that the global forces of interdependence could be trusted to respect the emerging nations and stop the plunder and the manipulation of power.)

Now she was thinking that after the hard work of the last week of term, the team of young expatriate teachers would be ready to explore the spectacular and infinitely varied beauties of Kenya.

Ella had made up her mind to keep her sights set on two fancy free years in Africa, after which she would go home to share her experiences with the family and community she loved. All thoughts of entanglements with John Francis or Michael Kilpatrick, however appealing, she would put to the back of her mind. John, she couldn't trust because it was obvious he was hiding something. Mike was too much of a responsibility; he had taken it for granted that she was someone that fate had sent to be some kind of saviour. It was all too complicated. She was happy to be free.

CHAPTER 14

A Mystery and a Party

While contemplating her determination to stay solo in Africa and take her chances with the men in Scotland, Ella was neatly folding a silk scarf to cover her secret journal in the drawer.

She could hear Jan frantically calling her name. It was nearly four o'clock in the afternoon on Sunday and Ella realised she must have been outside writing since early morning. The rains had not come that day, as often happened towards the end of December, so she had lost all sense of time. She hadn't told the sleeping Jan she was going out.

'Oh, thank God you're OK,' Jan gasped. 'We've been looking for you everywhere.'

Bob came crashing through the door yelling, 'Have you seen him?'

'Who?' asked a confused Ella.

'We thought you might be with him,' Jan added unhelpfully.

'I don't understand,' a calm Ella said quietly. 'Slow down.'

'John Francis seems to have disappeared.' Bob shouted much too loudly.

'Don't be so melodramatic.' Ella scolded. You thought I'd disappeared a minute a go. He's probably gone visiting or something.'

'That's what everyone thought until they went round to his house.' Bob pointed out. 'The car's sitting outside the house doors wide open and car keys and house keys the lot–on the table next to a cup of coffee–not drunk–and a half-eaten sandwich! What does that tell you?'

'Then I got scared this morning when I couldn't find you Ella.' Jan complained. 'Bob came to see if John was here and there was no sign of you either.'

'And your car was outside!' Bob went on. (Ella was very proud of her new green car which had been delivered by Joginder Singh after they'd got back from the Nairobi trip; he hadn't asked for payment up front and her heart sank as she remembered that it was John, this man she was trying hard to distance herself from, who had put a word in for her. She couldn't forget that.)

'It's like the bloody Marie Celeste!' Bob spluttered. 'Nobody's seen him since Friday afternoon. It seems like he's gone AWOL before. He didn't come back for ten days last time.'

'Then he'll come back like before,' said Ella. 'I've often thought there's something strange about John. I don't think he's who says he is.' Ella went on to tell Bob and Jan about the doctor and his wife calling him Fernando or something she couldn't remember and how cagey John had been about the whole thing. She told them, 'He just said not to worry and we'd soon know about it. Very odd.'

'The other 'odd' thing is he's left a whole pile of Chemistry papers that need marking before Wednesday–and I'm going to have to bloody mark them!' Bob went on unsympathetically. 'At least he got his exam papers ready for tomorrow's lot, I suppose. Oh no–they'll have to be marked too.'

'And who teaches Chemistry with a Political Science degree?' Ella asked. 'And he seems just too clever for his own good,' she went on using her mother's meaningless phrase. She felt angry with John but couldn't help adding, 'I hope he's all right.'

As all their exam papers were ready, the three decided to cook a meal, flatten a bottle of wine and stop worrying. Instead they decided to speculate on how much fun John Francis–or whoever he was–was having or what kind of danger he was in. Bob reported that a strange, black car had been seen around the compound after dark on Friday but nobody could recognise the occupants. Dolph Daley the Principal knew something, Bob was sure. They reckoned a political scientist could get mixed up in all kinds of skulduggery in 1968 Africa. Nairobi politics stank to say the least but they reckoned their friend was a good guy, working to uncover the scandals. Maybe he was a CIA agent, a Communist, indebted to the Mafia or an assassin. They thought they knew him well enough to know he couldn't be an anti-communist or a neo-colonial. How did they know this? They weren't sure but it was all hypothetical anyway. But why did he never, but never, talk about his time in Toronto? Perhaps he'd never been there or had been involved in some scandal so had to travel incognito. What did Dolph Daley know? Why was he covering for him?

The most likely scenario, they decided, was that he was an undercover agent for the Canadian government protecting business interests from Nairobi Mafia. Jan dismissed this on the grounds that there didn't seem to be much Canadian business going on in Kenya. Ella remembered another snippet of that conversation outside the church. She thought it had to be connected to some tragedy in his family. She was sure Canada was mentioned–and a little girl having nightmares. Bob went along with the anti corruption theory and was almost sure that 'our John' was a communist sympathiser or at least an anti-capitalist–or a socialist of the pink variety–but not too red and dangerous. That would have been too much for the mid west American, soon to be born again Christian. Bob thought he knew John so well; he seemed to be a pretty good Catholic.

None of this speculation altered the fact that life and work had to go on. The girls decided they were worrying for no reason and went to bed early to prepare for their busy week.

Later that night as Bob was blowing out the candles to go off to bed, he heard a car engine and the crunch of wheels on stones on the other side of the hedge. There were no headlights switched on. He quickly and silently unbolted the front door and crept across the grass in the moonlight to the gap that he and John often used to pass sugar or cooking oil through to save them walking around. A torch light went on.

'I think I must have left my keys at home,' John was whispering. 'Your security lot didn't give me a chance to get organised. Let me see if the door's open. Damn. Never mind there's a window at the back. Anyone could open it with a butter knife. I've got in that way before. You'd better go. No, don't get out of the car. I'm fine. You need to get to Kisumu before dawn. Go now–and take care. Do you hear me? Watch your back.'

'Aagh, you worry too much–the lot of you. I've survived so far. I can't see anything happening now.'

'I hope you're bloody right,' John said. 'Now go!'

As the car drove off without lights, Bob was rooted to the spot. 'My God. Was that who I think was? Impossible.'

He didn't move, or even breathe until he was sure John was inside and then he tiptoed home and crawled into bed without daring to light a candle again. What the Hell was John doing with one of the countries top politicians, Tom Mboya, and why was it so secret and what danger was he in? He decided not to breathe a word to a soul–especially not Jan and Ella. He also decided he'd go out of his way to make sure that John thought he hadn't seen a thing. He was scared. Like Ella he didn't trust John. He was not the friend he thought he knew.

Next day John waltzed into school as if nothing had happened so Bob decided to adopt the breezy approach.

'You left your door open and your car keys on the table so I locked up for you,' he said handing John back his keys. 'I guess she must have been pretty,' He was hoping John would come clean.

'If only,' said 'John'. 'Family problems, I'm afraid–sorted now. Thanks for that. Sorry if you were anxious.'

'No worries. Just thought you were big enough and ugly enough to look after yourself. When did you get back, by the way?'

'A friend gave me a lift last night.'

'Oh, I must have been fast asleep,' said Bob nonchalantly. He thought he could detect a look of relief on John's face–or whoever's face it was. Bob wasn't going to say anything unless John confided in him.

Now Bob knew a thing or two about world politics but where did this guy John fit in? He was obviously trying to protect this guy Tom Mboya but why? His imagination was running riot and he had figured out that someone might want to jail Tom Mboya or even bump him off because he wasn't a Kikuyu and after the Presidency or he could uncover some corruption in high places or he could upset the balance of power in the Cold War. Any of these explanations seemed feasible. Invigilation of exams gave Bob plenty of time to mull over all these possibilities but he came up with no real answers. He did manage to get a phone call through from Cheptonge

181

to Kipsigis to let the girls know that John was back, safe and sound, having sorted out some family problems.

'You do realise the girls were worried sick about you?' Bob told John as they waited for the call to go through.

'I'm really sorry Bob. Shit happens. I really don't want to discuss any details. Why did you have to tell the girls anyway?'

'I thought you might have gone off somewhere with Ella, now that she's got her car. Otherwise I wouldn't have worried them.'

John, by way of an apology, said he would throw a BYOB (Bring Your Own Bottle) party on the Friday to celebrate the release from the hard slog.

'Geez, the guy's got a hard neck,' Bob told himself. 'Maybe I'll spike his punch and loosen his tongue.'

By Thursday, all the teachers were completely exhausted as the system was geared to exams at the last moment, students going straight home and reports being ready by Friday. In theory they could wait until mid January as there was no way results could be posted to the remote villages–but you were a bad colleague if your results were not ready to put into the reports before the break–so Haidee had wisely made a Wednesday deadline for marking and Friday midday for reports which she then had to sign and put comments on. Result–complete but euphoric exhaustion, which, coupled with John Francis's famous punch and plenty of loud music, made for a good party for those with the stamina. The others just conked out in the nearest corner.

John's BYOB parties were a bit of a con really, like himself. He had a mate who ran an off-licence in Kericho where he bought a few beers and wine bottles on a sale or return basis. Then he had another mate who brewed the local pombe at ten cents a bucket. Add some lemonade and loads of fruit juice to a pombe punch and you have a pretty palatable drink with a kick like a mule. Then, if you're like John, you hide away the polite people's posh plonk–under his bed in his case–until everybody's so smashed they can't have any more and you say, 'Oh dear, we didn't manage to finish all this,' and when the guests are too polite to take it back, you take it back to your mate at the off-licence (where they probably bought it anyway as it's the only off licence in town) and you get your money back (which is really theirs)–and you make a tidy profit.

Ella watched the first half of the con, with amusement, from a fairly sober point of view as she never was able to drink too much. She was nursing some passion fruit juice pretending it was punch when she witnessed the host stashing yet another bottle (of vodka this time) under his bed. 'Huh, caught you,' she hissed. He didn't even have the good grace to look sheepish.

'Just doing a bit of rationing–everyone's getting too sozzled too quickly. I might bring it out later.'

'I might spread a rumour that the punch has been poisoned,' Ella teased. 'That looked like a rather nice bottle of white wine I saw disappearing under there a little while ago.' Always the gentleman, John was quick to offer some and started to dive under the bed to get it.

'No thanks. Not drinking tonight,' Ella said and flounced off. Predictably he rushed after her stammering a little after a few drinks.

'I wouldn't mention anything. Bit embarrassing,' and after Ella gave him a long stare and said nothing, he added, 'Please.'

'Only if you'll come clean about who you are and what you're up to,' Ella found herself saying after her one (strong) glass of punch. 'You don't fool me for a minute.'

'Oh God,' was John's reaction. 'Ella, don't ask me here–and don't ask me why.' He was suddenly sober again and sad and scared. 'Come with me.' He took her gently by the hand and led her out on to the verandah at the back of the house.

'I asked you to trust me.'

'How can I? I'm not even sure what your real name is and –'
David and Jenny from Kipsigis had followed them out and
next second Ella found herself wrapped in a pair of masterful
arms being kissed like she'd never been kissed before.

'Oops. So sorry,' said little Jenny wren, with a giggle, before
scuttling off back inside followed by a grinning David.

'Oops. So sorry,' aped John after they'd left, 'except I'm not.'

'I suppose that's one way to shut a girl up. I'm not going to
read anything into that–and I still want some answers.'

'I know you do but I just can't give you them at the moment.
It might not be safe,' murmured a John she didn't recognise. He
was trembling but through fear or emotion, she wasn't sure.

'Are you telling me you've signed the Official Secrets Act?'
said Ella taking a stab in the dark at what might be the truth.

'You don't want to know that,' was the cryptic reply.
'There's only one thing I'm going to tell you. I have to be a
bodyguard for someone very important–and who it is has to
remain a secret. He doesn't even think he needs protection–or
even from whom, because I can't even tell him that.'

'Okay, stop John, I believe you,' Ella said quickly, covering
his mouth with her hand because he was beginning to talk too
loudly. 'Ssh–you've had a few drinks so don't tell me any more.
You're right, I don't need to know this.' In reply, John buried his
face in her hair and muttered, 'Damn and blast and bugger!'

'Come on, there's Ob-La-Di Ob-La-Da,' Ella cajoled. 'Let's
go and dance. Let everyone think what they like. They will
anyway.'

They gave themselves up to the dancing and looked like
any other couple getting to know each other except Ella was
thinking, 'I can pick 'em. Two fruit cakes in a week.' This time
she wouldn't be confiding in Jan. Like Bob, she was scared.
But she didn't know what Bob knew. And Bob didn't know
what she knew.

The partygoers were dropping like flies as the music graduated from Marmalade to Marvin Gaye's 'Grapevine', then from 'Hey Jude' to Simon and Garfunkel–and the punch took its toll. Mary Lou had long since been driven home by a concerned Brad in her polka dot dirndl skirt and her fit of the hiccups, Jean Pierre had passed out on the sofa and looked like he was there until morning and most of the Cheptonge lot had managed to slope off to their own beds. This left Bob in the kitchen boiling a pan of water on the wood stove for coffee. Dolph was threatening to switch off the generator.

'No generator, Dolph, no music, no party–so pleee–ase have another drink,' Jenny wren was pleading. Jenny wren and David weren't going to miss any details of a budding romance between Ella and John while a very squiffy Jan was trying to negotiate a bed for the night.

'Can I ask you some questions, John?' she managed to utter.

'Only if they don't take more than one brain cell to answer–I've had enough questions for one night,' he said watching Ella squirm.

'Okay, have you got flour, eggs, sugar and milk in your larder?'

'Of course,' John replied, relieved.

'Then, can I crash in your spare room if I promise to make some Canadian pancakes for breakfast? I can't take Beetle home tonight.'

'Jan,' a gallant John said, 'you can crash in my spare room even if you don't make the pancakes. Go ahead.'

Something like panic struck Ella when she remembered she'd got a lift in Jan's car so she said, 'Keep a space for me too.'

'Shuit yrshelf,' Jan slurred and with a nod in John's direction she added, 'Shilly girl.'

'Coffee,' yelled Bob in a much too loud for comfort voice.

'No–going to sleep,' Jan managed–so it was coffee for seven before Dolph went off to plunge everyone in darkness but not before John had found some candles to stick in empty wine bottles and a torch for Bob to guide Jenny and David home to crash in his spare room in the house next door. Fifteen miles along a deserted and bumpy road was too far to drive after a skinful of punch. And then there were two, washing up enough mugs for the morning since John had invited Bob, Jenny and David for breakfast on the strength of Jan's promise to make Canadian pancakes. The silence apart from the clinking of china was deafening. Ella started collecting glasses and putting stuff in the bin outside. She couldn't handle this. This man had almost revealed dangerous secrets to her and all evening they'd been pretending to get together and she didn't know what to say—so she just got busier—'I'll empty this ash tray. It stinks.'

John grabbed her arm. 'Stop it,' he said. 'You're doing Joseph's job. He'll want to reuse the bottles—and not everything goes in the incinerator bin.'

'Just a bit more—I hate a big mess in the morning,' Ella fussed but she wasn't fooling him.

'Listen. There's only one single bed in the spare room but there are two beds in my room.' John said tentatively. 'Please—have the second bed. Don't worry. I promise to be good. I'm too knackered to try anything, anyway.'

'I didn't think for a minute you'd want to.'

'You don't know me very well then, do you?' John said searching Ella's face for a response.

'That's the problem,' a weary Ella sighed. 'Where's that bed?'

A loud snore reminded them that Jean Pierre was still crashed out on the sofa and, when Ella and John both laughed, a little bit of the tension was released.

True to her word, Jan produced an enormous pile of delicious pancakes for breakfast which went down as quickly as it grew despite Jean Pierre's silly comments.

'Your crepes, zey are too theek. In Paris vee can roll them so nicely round ze most deleecious fillings. These Canadian ones are blobs,' he said in his strongest possible French English accent which he knew everyone laughed at.

'Zat's because zey are pancakes–not crepes–dummy,' Jan shot back, imitating his accent very badly.

'Phoof, I zink I go to ze Congo vere zey understand me better,' countered Jean Pierre laughing, ' but perhaps zey keek me out.'

Ella was glad of the light hearted banter with Jenny wren's eyes following her everywhere, obviously dying to find out if there was a new romance in the offing. David was having a fragile moment while John and Bob looked like bears with sore heads.

'Great party JF,' Bob grunted without much enthusiasm.

'Glad you enjoyed it,' muttered 'JF' in reply.

'Hey guys, we're on vacation, now. What are we all doin'?' Bob asked with as much vim as he could muster. He'd given up on the idea of pumping John for the truth.

'I'm for Christmas Day at home–Kipsigis Girls' School. Any takers?' Ella volunteered.

'Mark will be here from Canada,' Jan reminded everyone.

'It's back to the family for me,' John said. 'My mum always insists.' (Ella wasn't sure if she felt relieved or disappointed.)

'I'll be there,' cried Bob.

'Me too,' David added. 'My flight home isn't until the 29th.'

'We'll make it your farewell party, shall we?' Jan declared.

'Do you think I could invite a couple of friends from Brooke Bond?' said Jenny. 'They're only here for a few weeks.'

'Tomorrow, I hope to be swimming in zee Indian Ocean,' piped up Jean Pierre. 'Mitul has invited me to visit his friend in Mombasa. How could I refuse?'

'That makes a table for eight so far,' Ella said doing a quick mental count up to keep her mind off John Francis.

'I'm looking for some company after Christmas,' Bob said. 'My plans fell through so I was just going to find someone in the Peace Corps office–but pot luck's kinda risky.'

'Sorry Bob,' Jan said. 'Mark and I have booked our Safari.'

'Well, it's gonna have to be some pot luck Americans, then.'

'Speaking about Americans, I don't envy the risks these guys in Apollo 8 are taking.' John pitched in. 'They've just launched today and should be going round the moon on Christmas Day.'

'Shoot, how do you know that?' a flabbergasted Bob asked. Normally such news took days to get to the sticks or weeks if it was an overseas newspaper. Hardly anyone had radio coverage beyond Kenya and even that was crackly–and local news coverage was so censored it often became meaningless. John's access to news, he believed, was significant. Why?

Who was financing all this? Not his teacher's pay.

'I heard that too,' Ella whinged with a yawn, 'very early in the morning. He's got this posh radio–and it only crackles a bit.'

Ella ignored Jenny's grin. Nosey cow.

'It's a Beolit 1000 transistor. There aren't many around. I can get world news from most places on it,' John said. '–I like to keep in touch.'

'Is that why you've got so many batteries?' Ella enquired.

'These nine volt Ever Ready jobs are hard to get so I stock up.'

'Bloody expensive system if you ask me,' Bob said so vehemently that everyone jumped. It was so out of character. 'Why do you need it so badly?' he asked. John just inclined his head to one side.

Meantime, it was time to go home and Jenny wangled a lift from Jan and Ella and sent Jean Pierre off with David. She wanted the gossip.

'That was a lovely hug good-bye you got from John, Ella.'

'There's nothing to report,' Ella declared.

'You mean it was *non consumatto*?' Jenny asked. 'I don't believe you.'

'That's horrible Latin,' retorted Ella, 'and you'd better believe it.'

'But he's gorgeous,' Jenny said.

'Maybe he is but I'm not sure.' Ella told the eager gossips. 'I've said I'll meet him in Nairobi in January but only if I'm not somewhere else more exotic. He's going to look for a message at the Thorn Tree.'

Jan just had to add, 'She's got two gorgeous men keen on her. Did you know, Jenny –'?

'How are you getting along with Matthew? I hear he took you to the cinema, Jenny?' Ella butted in. And so the subject was avoided.

CHAPTER 15

A Tropical Christmas

After an early night and a long lie, Ella woke up with her head spinning from not just the party two nights before but the weekend at the bush farm, the performance of Messiah and the huge learning curve of trying to understand the Kenyan culture.

She suddenly felt homesick never having been away from home on Christmas Day. Christmas cards had been posted home inside a parcel of goodies sent in October but there was no guarantee they'd get there. Morag and Jamie, her sister and brother, were both married now but she hoped they'd keep her Mum and Dad company on Christmas Day. Would they miss her? She had a little self-indulgent cry and then remembered what her Mum had taught her. If you're feeling down, think of someone worse off than yourself and do something for them.

She jumped out of bed and hit the kitchen. There was no

Arapbet because it was Sunday so she lit the fire and went to get dressed while the wood stove heated up. She would bake some rock cakes with pineapple instead of raisins for Arapbet's children.

Then she had a guilt attack and decided to write an overdue thank you letter to the Kilpatrick family (not just Mike) to show what a 'weel brocht up Caithness quine' she was. It began with Dear All, thanked them for their excellent hospitality and told them what a pleasure it had been to meet them all and see their lovely home. She also said she hoped they would have a pleasant Christmas. She signed it Isabella Mackay and posted it to The Kilpatrick Family, PO Box 22, Kericho. She hoped this note was polite enough to be distant but warm enough to be kind. That episode in her life, she told herself, was well and truly over–apart from having to return a few books.

The rock cakes turned out fine, almost like her Mum's, so Ella wrapped them in foil and hid them from Jan's hungry eyes and her own.

She put John Francis out of her mind again, told herself she didn't intend to let him under her skin and turned her mind to preparing for a very strange and different Christmas.

With the arrival of Potty Dotty Watty and the addition of a few motley hangers on, the table had grown to fourteen so it was decided that they would take a risk with the weather and put tables from different houses out on the grass at lunchtime and spend the evening indoors with the leftovers. It was to be a typical 1960s BAD and BYOB (Bring a Dish and Bring Your Own Booze) occasion except for an oversized turkey that had been dumped on Africa, via chilled air freight. A Norfolk reject probably. It took Bob and David half an hour to cut the creature in two with an axe and a hammer to fit it in the ovens of two wood stoves. The warmest, driest time in Kericho is around Christmas so, with the need for half a forest of wood to keep the stoves going for long enough to cook the monster turkey, the woodchoppers were sweating with effort and any cooks around the kitchens were red-faced and glowing. Everyone had agreed that the servants should have Christmas off which was just as well because this was the time of year of initiation ceremonies for adolescents in the Kipsigis tribe. They wouldn't have come anyway.

After having been in the oven since early Christmas Eve, the beast was finally pronounced edible so there was a big rush to put more wood on to cook the vegetables before allowing the fire to blissfully go out and allow Jan and Ella's house and David's house to resemble hell's kitchens a little less.

The spread was over three tables and thankfully there was no rain. One end had all kinds of exotic Sikh dishes that Mrs Singh had prepared and the other end had the traditional turkey and all the trimmings minus the Brussels sprouts and cranberry sauce but plus maize and pineapple stuffing. The starter had been pawpaw with passion fruit so there was nothing new there but, lo and behold, Mary Lou had produced a huge Christmas pudding, custard and a tray of mince pies made from ingredients brought all the way from the USA. Finally, when nobody could eat another thing, Mrs Singh, now happy for everyone to call her Narinder, appeared with little glass bowls of an ultra sweet dessert which looked and tasted like miniature spaghetti and condensed milk. It was called *sevyan* and everyone liked it so much that later she used to send it along to their houses at regular intervals. Everyone called it Narinder's vermicelli pudding.

'We'd be going for a long walk after this in England,' said Jenny the vicar's daughter. 'I reckon we need some exercise.'

'Clear up first,' yelled bossy Bob and after the suggestion of putting the hosepipe on the dishes in a wheelbarrow turned out to be pretty inefficient, a proper job was done in the various houses on the school campus before everyone met on the school field for a game of rounders with a tennis ball and racquet which was all that could be found.

Jenny's two friends turned out to be Californian pilots sent out to seed the clouds to prevent giant hailstones falling on the tea plantations. Some kind of strange cloud formation over the hills caused super cooling which caused three inch hailstones. 'Happy Chepkirui landed up in hospital after one of those storms,' said Jenny. 'It was awful.'

'You should see what one of those storms does to the tea plants,' Jeremy was drawling. 'They're completely pulverised. Our job is to get under those clouds and shoot off canisters of silver iodide. That raises the temperature and causes the hail to fall as rain. Simple but brilliant.'

'Anyone fancy a quick flight? We got plenty of sick sacks,' Hank the other pilot enthused.

Dotty was up for it there and then, 'When can we go?'

'How about tomorrow?'

Ella just knew it was coming. Dotty was going to try to persuade her. 'Who's coming with me?' Come on. What an adventure!'

Nobody responded so she turned to her friend, 'What's got into you, Ella? I thought you were up for anything.'

So Ella was finally persuaded to spend Boxing Day flying—on condition that they were home in time for her to prepare for a trip to Nairobi and then on to Mt Kenya with Bob and some of his American Peace Corps friends. That meant on Christmas night it had to be good bye to Jan and Mark who were off to view lions in trees in the Ngorngoro Crater and a final farewell to David who was returning to a grammar school in Surrey at the end of his contract.

Next morning, as promised, the two American pilots arrived to pick up an excited Dotty and exhausted Ella who didn't go to sleep until the house was cleared up. After a half hour drive to the Brooke Bond airstrip all four were soon strapped into the tiny plane, Hank and Jeremy in the front, Dotty and Ella in the back. Next minute they were being whisked up into the clouds with stomach churning speed. For a little while, Hank flew the plane smoothly enough for the girls to enjoy the view which was truly amazing. From high above, the edges of the green carpet of tea could be seen with the brown savannah beyond–showing just how much cultivation had gone into the estates. Then he buzzed Kipsigis Girls' School with a bit of scary low flying so they could clearly pick out the dormitories, the classrooms, the dining hall and all the houses on the compound surrounded by a thick green hedge and separated from the red murram and patches of green of the villages in the African 'reserve'. Hank then flew them over the hills of the Mau Forest which seemed dense and impenetrable apart from a few patches in the middle which appeared to have been cleared for some reason. There was one area which looked fenced in containing some buildings and a high metal tower. Ella thought she could recognise Cheptonge nearby.

Ella thought she heard Jeremy muttering, 'That must be it,' and Hank replying, 'I think it is.'

'What are you looking at?' Ella asked.

'...Oh–nothing...', was the reply which Ella felt was evasive. She decided she would ask Bob later about the tower on the hill.

'How about some real action, girls?' Jeremy asked with a sadistic grin. 'Hit the bottom of that cloud at 275 degrees, Hank. You've got ten seconds before it falls as hail. Sorry girls, we need the training.' The strong restraining harnesses kept the passengers still but they went from upright to horizontal to upside down, back to horizontal on the other side and then upright again in a matter of minutes. Dotty was laughing with delight and the pilots were unaffected but poor Ella was filling her sick sack and almost passing out.

'I'm fine,' she growled with her eyes shut and, with sheer determination, she was–until the pilots had done another couple of loops and come to a gentler than usual landing on the smooth tarmac estate runway. Ella was relieved and decided she wouldn't be rushing to make friends with the pilots. They would have to find some other girls to show off in front of. They dropped Dotty and Ella off at the Girls' school and after a quick cup of coffee, disappeared from whence they had come with an address from Dotty who thought they would be fun friends to have. There was something Ella didn't trust about Hank and Jeremy.

Next morning, Bob, (who couldn't afford a decent car) Dotty(who still hadn't bought a car) and Ella set off for Nairobi in Ella's green VW Beetle (which hadn't been paid for yet). Dotty was meeting a friend who was travelling with her to the Tsavo Game Park. Bob had received a letter from another Peace Corps volunteer with a meeting place and a plan to climb Mount Kenya. Along the way Bob suggested they visit Lake Nakuru.

Thankfully VW Beetles can tackle most roads and although the road to the lake was bumpy, it wasn't too far off the main road. From miles away, swirls of pink could be seen swooping across the sky and settling around the fringes of the pale blue lake which was backed by rolling hills, like a picture postcard. Ella had managed to master the Kodak camera her Dad had given her and was busy snapping away for her collection of 35mm slides for the eager audiences in Caithness. The area was deserted apart from the three young teachers and as they walked along the salty shores, the birds ignored their presence. The girls picked up a bundle of pink, red, white and black feathers from the carpet by the lake side. The exotically beautiful birds were striking different poses. Some stood on one leg with their heads tucked under their wings, some proudly held their heads making intricate curvy shapes with their long necks and others were feeding from the shallow waters. Occasionally a couple would fly above the others revealing dramatic black feathers under their wings. A

photographer's or artist's paradise. The three were overcome
by a silence which needed no interruption as they drank in
this spectacularly beautiful scene. Here was an undisturbed
corner of the world in all its glory. They wondered how long
it would stay that way. All of a sudden, for no apparent reason, the entire flock rose into the air circled over the hill and
landed at another section of the lake shore, forming another
fringe of a different shape. The sound and movement were
like a wind whistling through pink blossom. Unwillingly, a
strangely humbled trio dragged themselves off so that they
could reach the city before darkness fell.

They finally chugged into Nairobi, quickly dropped Dotty
off at her friend's house and reached the Peace Corps Hostel
in time for a fairly unappetising supper of hot dogs, coffee
and slices of pineapple. Ella found herself the hanger on for a
while as the old mates caught up with their news of the different volunteers and made their comments on the imminent
American Presidential election. The big excitement was a
newspaper article in the New York Times with the headline:

3 MEN FLY AROUND THE MOON ONLY 70 MILES
FROM SURFACE, FIRE ROCKET, HEAD FOR EARTH

A guy called Rich, who seemed to be dripping in zoom
lenses was expounding on nobody ever being able to land on
the moon while another skinny guy was arguing strongly that,
if conditions had been right, Apollo 8 would have been there
for Christmas. Even Ella was getting excited as the three as-
tronauts were due to touch down that very day in the Pacific.

'We won't hear though unless someone has access to cable lines,' Rich was saying sounding very pompous and
knowledgeable.

(Ella's thoughts turned to John and his expensive radio.)

Next day Bob, Ella, Rich and Dave (the skinny guy) were ex-
amined by a Peace Corps doctor and pronounced fit for a climb
above the level of altitude sickness. After a bit of shopping, it was

Ella's car that everyone piled into to head North in search of the big mountain. After all, British MOD teachers were supposed to be better off than Peace Corps volunteers. That didn't stop Ella from asking them to share the cost of the petrol, however.

Some time later, Ella produced the following record of the trip which arrived at the offices of 'The Caithness Courier' well in time for the Christmas Number of the following year, 1969. Her family were bursting with pride and Ella received a nice cheque which she hoped would come in useful when she got home to Scotland:

NEW YEAR ON TOP OF THE WORLD

(Isabella Mackay, a former pupil of Balnahuig Primary School, Sinclair's Institute, Altnabervie and a graduate of Kings College Aberdeen and the Aberdeen Teachers' College is teaching at a boarding school for African girls near Kericho in the heart of the tea estates of Kenya, East Africa. Recently she had an adventurous climb to the top of Mount Kenya. This is her account of the experience.)

There it was, like some great, prehistoric monster looming out of the ocean. The ocean was the flat plains of Africa and the monster was the 17,058 feet of Mount Kenya. I could see the snow-capped volcanic peak jutting out above the swirling clouds, dominating the horizon for miles around. I could understand why the Kikuyu people had named it 'Kirinyaga' White Mountain, and believed it to be the home of their God, Mwene-Nyaga, Possessor of Mystery or Whiteness.

We still had a twenty mile drive before we would have to start climbing. Feelings of excitement and awe were rapidly turning into sheer panic. How on earth had I, a simple Caithness farmer's daughter, born and brought up at altitude zero, got into this? The only climbing I'd ever done was to the top of Cairngorm from the ski-lift.

It had all started on Christmas Day when a group of young teachers, all going through the strange experience of their first tropical Christmas away from home, inevitably began reminiscing. This of course led to snow and the only place in Kenya above the 14,500 foot snow line is Mount Kenya. Before we realised quite what was happening, we were rushing around getting the essential medical check ups, poring over maps, and packing up an old VW with food, boots, warm clothing, haversacks, cameras and vast quantities of aluminium foil.

Our leader, Bob, was an all American Peace Corps volunteer who had once run an outward bound school and luckily, we thought, had been up a few respectable hills. Then there was Richard, the fanatical photographer, also American, who was usually to be found stalking giraffes or lions with zoom lenses but was evidently not averse to zooming in on high mountains. The third intrepid mountaineer, Dave, was rather an unlikely looking candidate; he was thin and pale and always seemed to be purging his third world guilt. He turned out to be the geographer who was to keep our spirits up with tales of glaciers, eroded volcanic plugs and giant mountain lobelia.

I later discovered that I'd been brought along to make the porridge.

SIGNED IN

The plains from which Mount Kenya rises have an elevation of 6000 feet but we were to drive through the rolling foothills to 8000 feet before beginning our climb. Here we signed in at the gate of the Mount Kenya National Park; it was comforting to know that a search party would be sent out if we hadn't signed out within thirty six hours, especially since we weren't relying on pack mules or porter guides.

We set off with our packs on our backs in a pleasantly warm temperature. As we watched the peak in the distance we could see it constantly changing shape as clouds formed and then dispersed into the rarefied air. We were now going through open rain forest which we knew to be inhabited by animals such as elephant, buffalo, black rhinoceros, bush buck and many others. We were hoping to catch a glimpse of the rare bongo but apprehensive about meeting elephant or buffalo.

As it turned out, apart from monkeys, which areas common as rabbits in a Caithness garden, we saw a tiny duiker and a bush pig close by and a herd of elephants at a comfortable distance. Underfoot in the hardened mud, however, one could see the footprints of the different animals using the trails, which helped us over our disappointment. 'Old man's beard' or Spanish moss was draped over the cedar trees and the giant podocarpus, a conifer, dwarfed us completely. I was surprised to see butterflies at 9000 feet.

The vegetation gradually changed to bamboo forest, some of which must have been 40 feet high. Bob suggested we each cut a bamboo to use as a walking stick for the steeper slopes ahead. While we were taking a short rest, we could hear buffalo crashing noisily through the forest not very far away and suddenly we heard a low wailing sound and an eerie creaking right next to the path. Just as we were beginning to let our imagination run away with us, another climbing party, using zebroids as pack animals, caught up with us. A zebroid is a cross between a zebra and a horse and is ideal for mountain climbing as it has the stamina of a zebra and the tameness of a horse. We rather envied the group's lack of weight on their backs but were relieved when they told us that the moaning sound was merely the wind blowing over the hollow stems of dead bamboo.

At around 11,000 feet the bamboo forest opened out into moorland and the ground became distinctly soggy beneath our feet. Richard, who had already snapped every animal and butterfly within a mile as well as 62ft giant bamboos, was busy clicking away at the brightly coloured mosses and the gigantic heaths. It occurred to me that, though the heaths were up to thirty feet in height, they couldn't match the bonny purple of the heather on Dava Moor. Dave told us the story of 'Icy Mike' an elephant who had been found frozen, high up in the mountain. This has been the fate of many animals whose frozen bodies have remained intact for years above the snow line.

MOONLIKE

As dusk was beginning to creep in, we found ourselves in a strange, moonlike barren land above the moorland. The twin peaks of Batain and Nelion seemed much bigger now, rocky and sheer and partly covered in snow. We could see Lenana to the right, the third highest point which could be reached over gentler slopes. This was our destination. We had decided to leave the sheer precipices to the experts equipped with rope and ice-axe.

All around us were the dark rocks of the steep valley sides and long fingers of moraine; we were in Teleki valley, a fine example of the work of an ancient glacier. Our main concern was to get to Teleki hut for the night as darkness tends to arrive very suddenly near the equator. Bob was spurring us on. Dave was enthusing about glaciation, Richard was reluctantly putting the cover on his camera and I was leaning very heavily on my bamboo walking stick by this time.

We had paid a few shillings to book into the hut for the night, before our final assault on the peak next day. The fact that Lenana is known as a tourist's peak didn't dampen our spirits in the least. Bob had collected a large bundle of dead heath which is excellent for burning; we soon discovered how cold it can be at an altitude of 12,000 feet on the equator and, yet again, how sensible Bob had been. Thick porridge made from outward bound style fortified oatmeal and water from a nearby stream was on the menu and I made sure it had its fair share of lumps. Bob informed us that porridge sandwiches are considered a delicacy in outward bound circles, and a nutritious substitute for the fresh food that can't survive long expeditions. We had them for breakfast the following morning but I haven't been able to face them since, I'm afraid.

We had to be in bed by eight in order to manage a four o'clock start up the scree before the sun melted the ice which was the only thing stopping the the boulders from slithering and sliding and slowing us down. 'Bed' was a wooden bunk, well above ground level, with a thin mattress. Fully clothed, apart from anoraks, boots, gloves and socks, we began the tricky process of wrapping ourselves in aluminium foil and sleeping bags as protection against the elements. I felt like the Christmas turkey I hadn't eaten that year. We kept our feet moving to try to stop our ankles swelling because of the altitude. With that, and other mysterious scrapings and scratchings we were later to discover the reason for, we rustled our way to the sleep of the exhausted.

ALARM CLOCK

We woke to the sound of an alarm clock inside an old tin pot we had found lying around and the by now familiar twang of Bob's 'Let's go!' Somehow our limbs got forced into a vertical position and we proceeded to find socks and boots. It must have been bitterly cold; our socks were as hard as bricks, frozen stiff. There was nothing for it but to knock them against the wall of the wooden hut and prise them on. Spare socks were a luxury we hadn't thought of. By now our ankles were twice their usual size.

Breakfast proved to be another problem as some marauding thief had chewed the bag of oatmeal and devoured half the contents. This was no tiny mouse; the noises we had heard through the night had been hungry hyraxes which I can only describe as enormous rats with long thick fur and big canines. We cut the left over cold porridge into thick slabs and slapped it between bits of bread from our emergency sliced loaf and washed it down with warm coffee. The boiling point of water is lowered by altitude.

At this point, as we gave a backward glance at the hyraxes laughing at us from a rocky twenty yards away, I almost gave up. Whether it was porridge sandwiches, or the altitude sickness common at about 13,000 feet, I can't say, but Dave and I were both violently ill. However, with the help of a few sympathetic noises and a bit of pushing and pulling, our little party set off once more. We made short work of the scree with the help of our trusty bamboos and were soon enjoying a gentler climb through rugged terrain which was, for the entire world, like the Cairngorms. All traces of altitude sickness had gone. After a few hours we started walking through snow with the sun beating down mercilessly. You can get nasty sunburn in such conditions, and, despite precautions, we lost all the skin on our noses and cheeks, the only exposed parts.

Around ten o'clock, we came to a perfectly circular frozen lake called the Curling Pond, another reminder of Scotland. We didn't come across any curling stones but, to our amazement, we discovered an old pair of skis perched up against the wall of the nearby Top Hut. A few tents were pitched on a rocky path away from the snow and we could see two tiny figures in orange perched half way up Batain which was rising steeply just to our left by now. Tracks of pack mules crossed the ice and we found a hole where someone had chopped through the ice in search of water.

EXCITEMENT

Lenana was now looking much more accessible and our excitement was rising. We had to give ourselves enough time to make the downward trip before nightfall so we set off up what appeared to be a pleasant climb along a snow clad ridge. However, the snow was soft and deep, making our bamboos more of a hindrance than a help and, as we trudged on clumsily, we kept losing sight of the summit. We only kept going by telling ourselves that the next slope would be the last one and finally it was.

We literally ran to the cairn built by previous climbers, leant against it and drank in the view. Twenty photographs later and after the excitement of just being able to see the distinctive outline of Mount Kilimanjaro, two hundred miles away, someone cried: "Oh! Happy New Year!" We'd forgotten! Bob unearthed a miniature bottle of medicinal brandy and we drank to the New Year and our achievement before setting off contentedly for lower altitudes.

(If any Caithness Mountaineers are interested, details can be obtained from the 'Mountain Club of Kenya', PO Box 571, Nairobi, Kenya.)

Ella was rather proud of her article especially as everyone at home would be reading it and talking proudly about someone from their own village doing such an adventurous thing as climbing a mountain on the equator. She could hear them now,

'Of course, ye ken that's the Hillside Mackay. My Davy was at school with her –'

Her Dad's comment had been, 'Excuse me, but I'm not a simple farmer.'

Meantime, the exhausted quartet got back to the hostel in Nairobi where it took them three days to recover from the exhaustion and the nasty sunburn. Bob and Dave both felt they needed to get back to their respective schools but Ella was armed with some books for somewhere quiet but exotic so Rich suggested a trip to Mombasa where he knew a Canadian nurse with a house on the beach. Apart from being rather boring, Rich seemed an uncomplicated guy so Ella agreed and after a long, hot journey they rolled up at this girl's house along with half the volunteers in East Africa, by the looks of things. The poor girl had a notice pinned outside her door:

'Friends free: Others 5 shillings: You know who you are: Please shop for pancake ingredients.'

Ella left Rich in the company of some people he knew and escaped. She could do without being in a queue for pancakes.

For the first time since she'd arrived in Kenya, Ella was completely alone. She realised that she needed that time to consolidate and to get things into perspective. So much had happened and her emotions had been battered and bruised and she felt confused. It was time to be uncomplicated. She had some money so she decided to book into a little hotel called Whitesands where she could have a decent shower, a comfortable bed and peace to read. The tiny single room had a verandah leading on to the beach and palm trees with fronds that dropped on the roof and frightened her until she knew what they were.

'I just need to rest,' she told the English hotel owner, 'so please can you spoil me.'

'You look as though you need it so that's just what I'm going to do,' the lovely lady said. Ella sighed happily.

Next morning with dust and sweat scrubbed off, a night's sleep and lashings of cream on her by now peeling mountain sunburn, Ella almost felt like a new woman–apart from the exhaustion which was still making her arms and legs ache. She found a tea tray with toast and marmalade on the verandah and a bowl of fruit. She demolished the tea and toast and a banana and collapsed on the bed again with the verandah door wide open to allow the cool sea breezes to circulate through. She felt safe in the knowledge that a motherly lady was keeping an eye on her–so she settled down to read 'Things Fall Apart'.

It was beginning to get dark when she heard a voice,

'Miss Mackay. I think you should wake up now. The day's almost over. I hope you don't mind but I took the liberty of having your clothes laundered. They're ready to wear. Dinner will be ready at seven–or earlier if you like seeing as you've missed lunch.'

Ella didn't realise she had fallen asleep again. 'You're so kind and I don't even know your name.' she said.

'It's Joyce.'

'I'm Ella.'

'I know. You signed in. Ella's better than Miss Mackay. You're too young for that. My daughter's older than you I think.' So Joyce spoiled Ella for five whole days, feeding her fish and fruit and all things healthy and she left her alone to read. Sometimes Ella walked along the beach, swam a little and collected shells from the rocky pools but otherwise she went nowhere. After a few days rest Ella remembered her guitar which was stuck in her room in Kericho and felt inspired to write a little song which she could try out when she got back. It fitted her mood perfectly:

Let's Pretend

Let's pretend there's no tomorrow
Let's pretend there was no past
And the moment that we're in now
Might turn out to be our last

Chorus: *Let's pretend, let's pretend*
That right now will never end

Let's pretend the bombs are banished
Let's pretend the world is free
And the boundaries have vanished
Except the mountains and the sea

Let's Pretend

After the fourth day, with the glow back in her skin and the shine in her hair, Ella set off in search of The Fontanella, the open air café her London induction group had been advised to use as a rendezvous in Mombasa. She had put it to the back of her mind but now she felt confident enough to wander in there casually and see if there was anyone who might want a lift to Nairobi as she didn't fancy making the long trip by herself. She had given herself another night at the Whitesands just in case there was nobody there that she knew. She needn't have bothered.

'Ella, how ARE you?' and 'Gosh, you're brown,' and 'You look great,' and a few other expletives greeted her and it was lovely to see the fun-loving, uncomplicated 'educationists' who were going to be working hard and playing hard for the duration of their two year contracts. They talked about their schools and their sight-seeing trips and new friends and Ella's story about Mount Kenya was fun enough to share. Her more lugubrious experiences and her fives days of being on retreat, she kept to herself.

The outcome was successful. Two girls, Suzy and Clare had been planning to get a train to Nairobi which was going to be very slow so Ella offered them a lift. They decided to leave after two days and stop off to see the monkeys at Mzima Springs and the elephants in Tsavo along the way. Ella worked out that she'd arrive in Nairobi in time to leave a message for John on the Wednesday and she found herself looking forward to seeing him.

The trip was fun with the monkeys and the elephants but, after having to fork out on a safari lodge, Ella and the others were left with only enough money for the scruffy VSO hostel in Nairobi. Ella couldn't complain because Whitesands, though quite cheap had been a wonderful touch of luxury.

Ella said good bye to Suzy and Clare telling them she had to meet someone. She hoped John would respond to her message at the Thorn Tree but it wasn't certain that he would. Her heart skipped a beat when she heard his deep voice behind her; she was pleased she was chatting to a couple of acquaintances when he arrived so that she could appear to be casual. He looked strained and tired so Ella dropped the pretence.

'How was your holiday?' she asked as they slipped away from the carefree bunch of youngsters to wander along the street.

'Well, it's been a bit hectic.' John said a little sadly. 'I've been up country in Kisumu with some of my relatives and down in Nairobi with some others. I didn't manage to get away at all but I suppose I rested a bit. What about you?'

'Oh I climbed Mount Kenya and walked by the Indian Ocean, flew in a small plane and saw flamingos and monkeys and elephants. That's all,' she rattled off. 'Seriously, though, it was amazing. I think I've got ten rolls of film to develop!'

'Good. I'm glad you had a good time,' John said smiling. 'I hoped you would. Was Christmas in Kericho good?' That prompted an exchange of descriptions of their Christmas experiences but Ella could see that John was tense so she cut down on the enthusiasm. Eventually he spat it out. 'I think I need to explain why I'm so miserable sometimes. I'm – not just a teacher. I have another part time job as a secret body-guard. I can't tell you who I'm guarding though.'

'Why are you telling me this now, John? Ella asked feeling the benefits of her battery-charging holiday draining away.

'Because, if we're going to see more of each other,' John said, 'I need to explain why I'm sometimes not around–and I do want to see more of you, if you're happy with that,'

'I did miss you,' was all that Ella could say. Her resolution to stay aloof was crumbling. 'Isn't this job a bit dangerous?'

'It could be if I wasn't careful but there's a big organisation backing us. I'd understand if you decided to back off.' John declared.'

Ella said. 'Maybe it just wouldn't work. I'd be scared and you'd be hindered. I probably don't want to know more, do I?'

'One day I'll explain–everything.' John said in reply. Their evening ended early before lock out time at the VSO hostel– with an arrangement to meet for lunch the next day. John's words before he kissed her good night were, 'I hope you'll decide to take a chance on me.'

As he enveloped her in his protective arms, Ella felt safe and not at all aloof. She would have to once again wrestle for control of her feelings.

Next morning, Ella had once more persuaded herself she was completely ready to tell John that they were just good friends until he arrived looking visibly shaken and with a very earnest request.

'Ella, I really need you to do me a huge favour – '

'It depends what it is.' Ella said with her heart in her mouth.

'I need you to deliver some flowers to an address and make sure that someone gets a message. I'm sorry Ella. It's life and

death. Not for you but for someone very important.'
'I'll do it,' Ella said feeling the urgency. 'But only if you tell
me who–and why me–and I need some more answers.'
'I'll fill you in on the way to the flower shop. Jump in. We'll
use my car now–but it'll have to be yours later.' John seemed
to be thinking quickly on his feet.
'OK Ella, here it is. You know Tom Mboya is so popular
with the people and they hope he'll be President soon. Well he
has a least two sets of enemies–maybe more. The Americans
don't want him in power and neither do some of Kenyatta's
cronies.' Ella was looking bamboozled so John added, 'I'll
explain it later. I belong to an agency that wants to protect
him–make sure he becomes President. Now there are corrupt
officials, African and American who would rub us out along
with Mboya as soon as look at us if they knew who we were;
there are nearly a hundred of us dotted all over Kenya–and
another lot in USA. I know they, whoever they are, have details of some of the agents. One of them has already been shot.
I can't be seen anywhere near Tom's house–and there's no way
I can contact him. His driver, a Luo, is one of us–but it's too
dangerous for him to use radio contact–they're hacking in all
the time these days.
'Who are "they"'?
'Your guess is as good as mine–the enemy.'
'So this is where I come in?' Ella said–not scared any more.
She was coming out of that place in between–and fighting for
justice again. 'What do you need me to do?' she said excitedly.
'Good girl,' John said, squeezing her hand. 'If I wasn't driv-
ing I'd kiss you. This is the plan. Listen carefully. We have
to be quick. The message we received says the assassination
attempt is due to take place within twenty four hours–and if
that fails–another should take place before the election.'
'Which election?'
'The US Presidential election.'

'Why on earth…Oh, my God–'

'The other problem is–Tom won't accept that he's in any danger. You have to be convincing. Do you think you can do that? He needs to organise tight security and get out of Nairobi, now. OK?

'You bet I can,' said Ella finding some Isabella Mackay spirit.

'Right I have a coded message Tom will trust and understand. You must give it to him and tell the driver Tom is in danger. Say the message is from me, John Francis. But to get to the house you need cover–so–everybody knows Pamela Mboya loves her flowers and she often has them delivered. Today, you're the delivery girl. Make sure someone lets you in–say you need to arrange the flowers–anything–just get in there–and pass on the message to Tom and nobody else–without saying a word. Ella I don't want any bug finding out you're involved. That's important. Understood?

'Understood,' said Ella but she was feeling distinctly sick by now–as the realisation of the danger she was in washed over her.

The flowers, in Pamela's favourite pink and purple were bought, and John drove Ella back to her car.

'Follow me–and I'll take you to the end of the road. When I signal right and go straight on–you take the right turn.'

'OK,' said Ella concentrating very hard.

'The Mboya residence is fourth on the left. It's the only one with shields on either side of the gate. Tell the askari you have flowers for Mrs Mboya. They'll be expecting them.'

'How?'

'We got someone to phone saying there was a gift of a bouquet and a professional florist to arrange them. That's you.'

'Who?'

'The professional florist.'

'Oh–I can do that–arrange flowers I mean.'

210

'You won't have to–probably. When you leave get back to the VSO hostel. I'll see you there.'

All went to plan. Ella announced herself, was let in through the gate, passed on John's message to the driver, told him she would inform Mboya, got herself into the house and handed over the note to Tom without saying anything–and waited while he read it.

'More rubbish. Thank you young lady but I've got an important meeting here tonight and these clowns aren't going to stop that.'

'Please, Mr Mboya.' This was Ella being persuasive. 'I've been told to tell you to take this one very seriously.'

'I'm sure you mean well–but tell John I'm fine. Sorry I have to go. Leave the flowers.' With that Tom Mboya rushed out of the room leaving Ella to see herself out.

'He doesn't believe me. He says he's hosting a meeting tonight at home,' she whispered to the driver who swore loudly and swept his eyes round all corners of the grounds.

'Right. Get yourself out of here and keep driving. Don't stop.'

Ella got out through the gate and headed towards the VSO hostel. Machine gun fire reverberated in the distance.

CHAPTER 16

John's Story

EARLY 1969

Back at Cheptonge, safely behind locked doors in front of the fire, John finally spoke of his secret double life.

'Ella, I have to tell you everything now. I've put you in danger and I'm sorry–but if I don't make you understand what's going on you might be even more at risk. But, please–none of this can go beyond these four walls. Lives could be at stake and a lot more besides.'

'John, you're scaring me,' Ella whispered, trembling a little. 'I promise I won't say a word.'

'OK, I believe you. Where do I start? Well, first of all my real name isn't John Francis–as you've guessed. If some people knew my real name and who my family are they could link me to an enormous Socialist Pan African movement, which isn't popular with quite a few mega powerful people in Kenya and worldwide, especially in America as you can imagine.'

'You're a red under the bed basically,' Ella said, trying to clarify the whole concept in her naïve brain as yet uneducated in the intricacies of world politics.

'It's no joke, I'm afraid–and it isn't as simple as that. You have to take it seriously,' John went on.

'Sorry,' Ella replied, 'it's just that I don't understand.'

'Right. You know I was a Political Science student in Toronto. Well, I wrote this essay on the situation of impoverished black peasants all over Africa and how I felt they were better off in countries like Tanzania with a leader like Julius Nyerere, whose economic policies were based on the African traditions which are essentially a unique type of socialism which fits in with their culture. I believe that, by the way. Anyway, fortunately or maybe unfortunately, I'd grown up in a family with extreme anti capitalist, anti colonial views and I had an uncle who carried those views so far that he died for it, very horribly and publicly leaving a wife and three young children. They came to Canada soon after the assassination and I met them. He was my mother's brother so word had got to me that they were coming and could I help them. It turned out that the Kenyan government had given them a lot of help.

People blamed the money grabbing Kikuyus–now called the Kiambu Mafia–for shooting him but Auntie Emma wasn't so sure. She said she believed Jomo Kenyatta when he denied it. He and my uncle talked about reconciliation, detribalisation and multi racial harmony she said. She also said he kept asking how that dreadful thing could have happened and the country owed so much to Uncle Pio etc. etc. Some people said she was just too trusting and that Kenyatta was covering up for his hoodlums who were corrupt up to their eyeballs.

The point is Uncle Pio was one of a long line of people in Africa who have died under violent, but mysterious circumstances–like Patrice Lumumba to name one. They say

Eisenhower gave the direct order to bump Lumumba off so America could get its hands on the uranium in the Congo— you only have to look at the cable lists to Africa at the time. Anyway, I wrote all this in my essay and a few other things I'd gleaned from family chats and handed it in. When you're twenty, you'll splurge anything on a bit of paper for a few marks. That would have been–um–1966 about eight months after the murder and I was feeling pretty cut up. My little cousin was with him when he was shot and she was horribly traumatised–still is.

Anyway, the next day, I get called into the faculty professor's office and asked if this was a piece of fiction I'd produced. Something told me to keep my mouth shut or pretend that it was. So I just asked him if he thought it was and said no more. He sat and stared at me for a long time and then asked me how I was related to Pio Gama Pinto so I told him he had been my mother's brother. I remember his exact words.

"So you're not bull-shitting, kid–and I have a job for you." Then he took my essay and ripped it into shreds and burned it in a metal waste bin and said, "You didn't write this. But you've got an A. But, listen up–never write or talk about this again unless you're absolutely sure of who you're talking to." Then he went on to tell me that Auntie Emma had been right when she thought it wasn't the Kenyan Mafia who had bumped Uncle Pio off and that it was part of a much wider scenario. He wouldn't give me the details–for my own safety he said–only that he needed me to be part of a large team of undercover agents who would be watching over the movements of the next target–Mboya.

Anyway Mboya's story goes back to 1958–or maybe 1950 when the guy was sacked for agitating the Kenya Labour Workers Union when he was twenty. In 1958 there was this All Africa People's Conference in Ghana where Tom met Kwame Nkhruma who, in case you don't know, was the first president of an Independent nation, Ghana, and they call him the 'Father of Africa.'

(Ella felt patronised here but didn't 'say' anything.)

Tom was so impressive they made him Conference Chairman–at only twenty eight–and ever since then, he's had only one purpose in life–to turn the whole of Africa into a federation of Socialist states each relevant to their own tribal societies. Now I don't need to tell you where that idea sits in the state of play in the Cold War at the moment. Tom Mboya's no fool and neither is Jomo Kenyatta and they know exactly what kind of government the USA favours for Kenya. Kenyatta is telling the west he wants a capitalist state and would welcome business investment in his country but that it has to be ethical capitalism where the poor in Kenya won't be exploited. America says fine–but at the same time *Mzee* is well in with Tom along the same lines of Pan African Socialism and as Tom's a Luo, the second biggest tribe in Kenya, he wants to show he is his right hand man and likely successor, but he's got a bunch of crooks swanning around him who reckon capitalism means grab what you can while the going's good and give it to your own tribe and nobody else. He has to play a double game. Now, the other double game Mboya has to play is with the Americans. That's where I come in. They've made me a CIA agent on a project known as Camelot which looks after the safety of people deemed to be at risk of assassination by anti- communist forces.

'What I don't understand,' Ella had to butt in. 'Why does America need to hang on to Kenya? She doesn't have any uranium or gold or diamonds–or anything.'

She was finding it hard to keep up with the whole jumble of unfamiliar concepts that were tumbling out so quickly–while John was finally unburdening himself.

John continued, 'True–but America desperately wants a pro-western state to counter the communist threat they are so

215

paranoid about. They feel there's a real danger that if Kenya goes the way of Tanzania, Somalia, Mozambique and any other pro Russia states, they could lose control of the whole of Africa. Look what they've done to Nelson Mandela because he dared to say he was a Marxist. They believe they have to keep the socialists out.

Now, Kenyatta and Mboya know how America feels so they're both playing a double game with them too. They think they are fooling the Kiambu Mafia on one side and America on the other–but they never lose sight of the Pan African dream. Activating the trade unions in every little corner of Kenya is essential–and the tricky bit is that it has to be done in secret. The corrupt politicians in high places shouldn't know how extensive the socialist movement in Kenya is or how potentially successful it would be in overthrowing the present government. As I said before, that's the role of people like me. My patch is the sugar estate along the road. Quite a few of the workers there are Asian and they're being exploited as badly as the blacks so, when I disappear from time to time, I'm training and activating Union officials.

Another crucial part of the job is the protection of Tom Mboya who comes along to speak from time to time. He's really charismatic and very popular so when they get the word to do something they'll follow him. There are hundreds of undercover agents like me around–in every business, factory or big farm in the country–apart from parts of Central Province where the Kikuyus don't want anything to happen–for their own selfish reasons. Most of these undercover guys were recruited when they were studying in Canada or The States and they were all black or Asian Kenya Nationals with an axe to grind against the colonials or their capitalist bosses–or a reason to be grateful to Tom Mboya.

You know one or two of them, Ella, except you don't realise it.'

'Ole at the Tea Hotel,' Ella gasped.

'Spot on.' John said, amazed at her perception. 'He wanted to recruit your friend Mike Kilpatrick as a token white who understood the cause. That would probably have been a disaster because his father hasn't kicked the colonial views.'

'What about the two Project managers on that farm?' Ella asked, ignoring her dismay that her 'friendship' with Mike Kilpatrick had obviously been under scrutiny, 'Are they –?'

'Both of them are. One of them, Ben, is fine but the other one is pretty fiery. He absolutely hates Kyuks and tends to overreact.'

'That would be Wilson. I suspect he's not too keen on Mzungus either,' Ella said and surprised John who thought he was telling the story.

'So you've met him?' he said, to which Ella replied, 'Briefly.'

'Where was I? Oh Yes. Tom has had a steady stream of students to recruit from–about five thousand of them between 1958 and 1962. Fewer since Kennedy died which upsets him but still enough.

Tom became a personal friend of the Hagbergs who helped organise the airlift of students to USA and Canada. Maybe you've heard of Granny of the Airlifts, Gloria Hagberg, who prepared these students for flying and for their life and studies in USA. Well, at one point, around 1960, scholarship funds had been raised for the students but there was no grant for airlifting them. At that time the USA President had stepped down in March (LB Johnson I think) so the State Department was in charge and had just decided not to finance the project. Tom went out there to sort it out but they still refused to budge so he badgered JF Kennedy who finally agreed to give the airlift project $100,000 dollars from the Kennedy Foundation if the State Department still refused to give the money. They did refuse and after Kennedy made the offer the State Department came up with the same offer saying Kennedy was trying to outbid the State Department–and accused him of electioneering. In the end, Tom took up the Kennedy offer and rejected the Government offer. Remember LBJ had resigned in March so the Presidential elections were in full flow–Kennedy finally beat Nixon by a narrow margin and Tom thinks Nixon blamed the airlift funding fiasco.

More important, Tom says Kennedy told him that Nixon signed a document signing over thousands of dollars grant every year for 'further funding of education projects in Africa'– and nobody has seen any of that money since. Tom can't stand Nixon but he plays his tune in public because Kenya needs America's help. He doesn't see him as a threat but CIA intelligence tells us that Camelot recognises "an unidentified threat to the person and projects related to Mr T Mboya". We don't know what that threat is or where it's coming from and Mboya has just dismissed the whole thing as nonsense. I sometimes wonder if Nixon could be sitting on that grant. It seems unlikely but who knows?'

'A tidy sum for an election campaign, in fact,' Ella surmised as she grappled for understanding. This was a huge and complex scenario.

'Who knows?' John repeated. 'I'm speculating here but I reckon Nixon could be Tom's enemy number one. Just think. Tom could embarrass Nixon if he could prove the 1960 stitch up of Kennedy–and put him in real trouble if he started asking questions about the missing money.'

'Has Mboya threatened to do that?' Ella asked.

'No, I suspect he wouldn't dare to at the moment. He wants to keep him sweet for now. He reckons Nixon doesn't even realise he has the information because he didn't know how close he was to JF Kennedy. He thinks it wasn't Americans who issued that threat to murder him.'

"Who does he think it was?' Ella asked. 'I can't imagine a message coming across from America about a threat from the

Kiambu Mafia.'

'Tom says why not? They've got enough money to hire the most sophisticated professional assassins,' John countered. 'I suppose he could be right.'

'The timing seems odd to me. Why a week before the Presidential Elections?' mused Ella.

'Coincidence maybe?' suggested John. 'It'll be interesting to see what happens over there … It's pretty close, they say.'

'One thing has been confusing me. How come you always seem to know what's going on?' Ella asked. 'The phones around here hardly ever work–not even from here to Nairobi or even from school to school. And the papers are about a week late'

'Sophisticated and expensive communications–only available to a few,' John explained. 'They've spent a bit of money there, I can tell you. They've set up around six INTELSAT II series telephone circuits around East Africa so they can communicate straightaway. There's one about two miles as the crow flies into the forest from here and about five miles up the hill behind the World Gospel Mission. I have to check in there every Sunday morning or if ever there's a problem. Great cover eh? I can pretend I'm a born again Christian if anyone finds me. I don't drive–I just cut through the trees.'

Ella remembered the two Californians who were buzzing the clearing on top of the hill.

'Is there a metal tower and a fence all round the place?' she asked John and when he said yes she described how Hank and Jeremy were taking an interest in it.

'Might be significant; they're not our agents. I didn't know they were around.'

'That explains why they found you this job for you at Cheptonge then,' said Ella

'That's right. They made me the co-ordinator for the area within a hundred miles of here. Dolph Daley thinks I'm on a research project.'

'I didn't even know that place existed,' Ella said. 'Come to think of it, I once saw a helicopter disappearing into the forest on top of the hill.'

'There's a bit of a clearing on top of the hill big enough for helicopter landings–but only for emergencies. Otherwise very few people know the centre's there ... There's no road and when you get there, you need a pass to get through the gate. Most of the people at the Mission don't even know what the place is all about–apart from it having something to do with National Security. There's one American guy there, Paul, who's undercover and he fobs them off and sorts out all the agents within the same hundred mile radius. Bob knows him as an accountant at the Mission, which he is in real life.'

'And what are you in real life, John Francis or whoever you are?' Ella asked, suddenly feeling overwhelmed and a bit panic stricken.

'Just call me John Francis for while. Right now I can handle the Science and PE teaching if I work hard. I got good grades at school and the Sports are great. For the moment I'm a teacher but that's not my life plan. I just have to get Odhiambo Tom Mboya through to a position of power so he can clean up the corruption in this country and set up better working conditions for all the people–maybe within eighteen months or so. Then I'll see what I can do about having a new life with no secrets. I have to admit it's getting me down now; I'm glad I've found you to share it with.' John added.

'Oh, I don't know, John. The whole thing sounds very dodgy to me,' Ella protested. 'How can you be sure you can trust the CIA? They might be using you guys as intelligence for all kinds of reasons–like weeding out all the commies or avoiding a coup or setting up an assassination and blaming it on internal politics. You said they needed Kenya to be pro-west.'

'I've thought about all that but it doesn't make sense. Mboya's doing everything right as far as Operation Camelot is concerned–ethical capitalism and no dealings with Russia. He's just what America wants. My only worry would be if Nixon gets in and decides Mboya is a threat to his credibility.'

'Don't you think his Pan African Socialism might be seen as a communist menace?' Ella asked.

'Don't you see?' an exasperated John was saying. 'We're seeing the two sides of America. Camelot Intelligence wants a peaceful, harmonious move towards fair working conditions under someone like Tom Mboya. They're the clandestine socialists who have seen how Tanzania works well and they think it's the best answer for Kenya. The other side of America–which we'll find out about on Sunday–say Nixon's government if he wins–wants Kenya to appear pro-west and definitely anti-communist. And Mboya is very good at that. He believes African Socialism can exist within the context of the west. It has to. Kenya needs investment and business enterprise to provide employment but if the corrupt side of capitalism goes on it will just mean the rich will get richer and the poor will get poorer. Tom Mboya could put a stop to that if he got in. And I'm here as part of the plan to make sure he does. Mzee Jomo Kenyatta knows the country needs Tom Mboya too. He's a tired old man now–and they say the booze is addling his brain. He won't be able to control his Mafia–and he'll be just a puppet.'

Ella was feeling exhausted by all this intense political discussion and had come to the conclusion that John had been brainwashed and that perhaps he was trying to make his dead Uncle Pio's dream come true.

'But John, it's so dangerous. There's already been one attempt on his life. Whoever it is will probably try again.'

'I need to get up to the phone and find out what happened.' John said. 'I can use my emergency key.'

'Can we not find out from the radio?' Ella pleaded. 'I don't fancy being alone right now–especially in your house. Anything could happen.'

'I don't think we're going to hear anything on the radio. Nairobi will hush it up, I'm sure. Don't worry, I won't be long.'

'Please take me with you.'

'I can't do that. Just blow out the candles and climb into bed. I'll lock you in and I'll be back as soon as I can.'

He clasped her face between his two hands, kissed her on the forehead, locked the door and disappeared into the dark night.

The night sounds echoed in Ella's head now that she was alone and the fire had stopped crackling. She couldn't bring herself to go to bed but sat bolt upright on a dining chair listening to the distant bark of a dog and some loud Friday night beer voices in the village beyond the Cheptonge school compound boundary which had a similar high hedge to the one at Kipsigis Girls' School.

Ella wished she had taken John's advice and gone straight back to the Girls' School but, with Jan still away, she had been too scared to be alone. She peeped through the curtains and saw that there was bright moonlight. At least John would be able to find his way–but then she was gripped with fear when she thought about some unknown enemy who could find him easily. Too many things were not adding up. Since when were the American government likely to support a socialist movement and how did John think that one man, however powerful, could stop the rich getting richer and the poor getting poorer. Perhaps Tom Mboya was already dead.

Ella had left her car at the house of a friend of John's because she was too shaken to drive home alone. As she and John were leaving Nairobi in his car they could hear the police sirens in the Starehe district.

'I hope they don't recognise this car,' John had said. 'It was at the scene of another attempt on Mboya's life. His last driver got gunned down then. He died after three days. '

'Now you tell me!' Ella had gasped and broken out in a cold sweat.

Back at Cheptonge she was scaring herself even more so she decided to carry a candle into John's bedroom and find the radio. She switched it on and carried it back to the living room where the dying embers were still warm. Eventually after interminable irrelevant items –

'This is the BBC World News––unconfirmed reports of an attempt–leading Kenyan politician–outside his Nairobi house within the grounds–policeman–trusted long term–arrested–unharmed but visibly shaken–no explanation–as yet.'

'Where are these bloody batteries?' she said to herself out loud as she walked around looking in drawers. She found one and managed to change it with a struggle. She'd lost the World News wavelength and as she was fiddling around an American drawl came over.

'Voting is close between Hubert Humphrey, the Democratic Candidate and the Republican Richard Nixon in their race for the White House. Humphrey is known for his support of liberal causes while Nixon's campaign has been based on law and order issues. Senator Wallace who is courting the segregationist white vote is lagging well behind. Humphrey is believed to have captured almost the entire Black and Hispanic vote whereas Nixon believes he has appealed to the "silent majority" who wish to see an end to the Vietnam War and have "peace with honour" – campaign marred – assassinations – Martin Luther King – Senator Robert Kennedy during 1968 – Results are due – new president will be appointed on Sunday January 20th 1969 – '

Ella's brain was buzzing with all this political information she would normally absorb passively and forget about. Now it was taking on immense significance and she found herself being dragged into the shadows of John's clandestine world. She kept the radio on to see if USA would report anything on the Nairobi incident but by the time John got back there was nothing.

It had taken him ten minutes to race along one of the several routes he used to the communications centre. He'd been trained not to use the same path because it would become well trodden and easy to follow. As he was getting his key out, a voice startled him and he heard the gate creaking open. It was Paul.

'I thought you might come. I heard what went on. What the Hell were you and that girl doing near Mboya's house?'

John explained how he'd been in the Nairobi Communications Office and there had been a message over the main phone from Washington to get Mboya the–out of his house as there had been a threat planned for after dark on the Thursday evening.

'I knew I had to contact his askari who's one of us as you know,' he told Paul but I couldn't risk being seen around Tom's house so Ella, that's her name, and I thought up a plan–

Ella turns up in her car, delivering flowers as a cover, drives through and gives Wesley the warning. She gets to see Tom alone and he rubbishes the message and goes off to get ready for a meeting. Ella has to leave because he won't listen–so she does–and tells Wesley what has happened. He tells her to get out of there fast. The next thing I hear is loud machine gun fire. I know I should have scarpered but I couldn't help it; I ran up to the house and found Wesley just standing there like a wally. He'd thrown the gun on the ground and had his hands on his head. He just yelled, "The stupid ass wouldn't listen to me. He thinks he's immortal. Now the place will be crawling with police and they'll *have* to protect him." He'd emptied his gun into the back of Mboya's car as it was the only way he could draw attention to the danger he was in.' John explained.

Paul went on, 'He'll cop it for attempted murder for sure because he won't be able to tell them about the warning–or at least where it came from. Bloody brave though. He's saved his life.'

'Bloody stupid,' John replied. 'But I'm sure Tom can get him off if he knows why he did it.'

'Word is Wesley's been arrested and there's an armed guard around the house–which, I suppose, was the right result,' Paul declared. 'And there were reports of a green VW beetle, an Asian man and a European woman with red hair. The Nairobi centre told me it was you. What happened straight after the shooting?' Paul asked.

'Wesley just yelled get the Hell out so I did. Ella had already gone back to her hostel. We picked up her stuff and went round to my friend's house–and they offered to hide her car in the garage and we decided to take mine back here to Kericho before we were missed. Ella was too shaken up to drive anyway–and someone must have spotted the VW at the scene. I'm pretty sure nobody noticed my car though–it was around a corner.'

'There's been no more word about the threat to Mboya's life,' said Paul, 'And Camelot hadn't a clue where it came from. They denied they had anything to do with it. In fact they're trying to find out who hijacked their communications line.'

'Is there anything on the wireless?' John asked.

'Only stuff about the election–it's a close run affair, they say.'

John left quickly feeling anxious for Ella who was probably terrified alone in the house. At least he felt Mboya was being protected now and that maybe he'd start taking threats to his life more seriously. He found Ella with his radio on her lap listening to a crackly American News bulletin. His arrival startled her and she gasped and screamed for a second.

'Sorry,' John whispered. 'It's all right. I don't think anyone can connect us to the incident,' he lied. There was no point in adding to her panic. 'Paul explained what happened. Wesley just emptied his gun into the back seat of his car to scare him and get the attention of security. It was as simple as that. Nobody was going to attack him tonight with all the kerfuffle–so he probably saved his life.

'BBC World News has an unconfirmed report with no details and there's nothing from USA,' Ella said pleased to be trying to help.

John thought, 'Shit! The Americans will know that someone knew enough to prevent it.' Instead of revealing his thoughts to Ella, he said,

'Don't worry. We're safe now and we'd better get some sleep so we can appear to be normal tomorrow. It's school on Monday.'

'What can I do about my car?' Ella suddenly remembered.

'I'll take you home tomorrow and then I'll get a message to Nairobi so they can send a driver up with it. We'll just say it had broken down and needed repair–and you didn't want to be late for school,' an authoritative John said without hesitation.

'I love it when you're so masterful,' Ella whispered feeling safe at last. John's response was to sweep her up in his strong arms and bundle her through to the bedroom. Much later, however, he came back for the radio which was still trying to broadcast the latest news across the world. Isabella Mackay's resolve to be aloof and inaccessible had crumbled.

CHAPTER 17

Like the Images You Find

NOVEMBER 2006

Ella clambered up from her 1969 storyland gasping for breath.

A kaleidoscope of images and quotes was swirling around in her head in an uncontrolled and surreal spin. She had finally closed up her lap top at two in the morning and was being woken up by the digital clock radio thirty eight years later.

'Flamingos and waves on a sandy beach – I'm running away – the sound of gunshots – Is Prime Minister Tony Blair really expressing deep sorrow for what happened during the slave trade two hundred years ago? – Another voice is saying forgiving the debt could be compensation – I'm trying to sleep in the back seat of a car – speeding, speeding, down and down, round and round – I'm alone – Will it be Nixon or Humphrey for

President? – A big, round African face with a huge smile – saying thank you for saving my life – Granny of the airlifts is full of hope – the cover of Time magazine – another face and a caption : "Why Barack Obama could be the next president" – mother white American – father Kenyan – I must read his book "The Audacity of Hope" – spin spin – the cradle of mankind will inherit the earth – evolution of faith – fusion – Balnahuig Primary school – Ewan Cameron was right – 'We're a Jock Thampson's bairns! – the world just doesn't know it yet – spin spin – Lawino, a beautiful Ugandan girl is asking – but who made the clay that God used to make us? – Obi Okonkwo dies and Things Fall Apart – Weep Not Child – more death – no forgiveness – spin spin around – celebrities snap fingers – another child dies – a bell rings in a school assembly–another refugee is created – Make Poverty History – a white rubber bracelet can't feed a hungry child – one hundred and fifty children can have lunch for a year because of a 'No Presents but Please Donate' birthday party – cynics don't give money – fear of corruption – corruption exposed–but not eradicated – nothing changes – Ngũgĩ wa Thiong'o no longer James – too much hate for the Scottish missionaries who pulled up the roots and killed a tribe – Did it have to happen? – Petals of Blood – spin spin – no – no – no – no – Senegal is a paradise everyone wants to flee – What shining example of progress? – boatloads to the Canaries – drowning bodies – quote: 'In Senegal, like everywhere else in Africa, the poor go on getting poorer and the politicians live like kings – '

Spin spin spin – violence on the London Streets – the tragedy of human trafficking revealed – a young suicide bomber believes he's going to Paradise – a cruel deception – spin spin spin a dramatic Kenyan sunset a giraffe and an umbrella tree – a trip to the World Travel Market at ExCel London Docklands 2006–Freedom Passes – drawn to the Kenya stand – two journalists – one Kikuyu one Luo–saying a murderer wouldn't take his victim to hospital. Was he defending Thomas Cholmondeley for shooting an African warden?–He must be the new baby Haidee talked of on the very first day I set foot in Kenya–1904–100 year lease on Masai ancestral lands–Did the Masai understand the colonials?–I think not–ran out August 15th 2004–century old scramble for land–quote: There is a strong feeling even among white farmers that Masai land claims are justified–40.000 Masai around Laikipia–violence–no no–need reconciliation–Ngũgi won't return–self imposed exile–such a tragedy–Petals of Blood is a good book–you must read it–Lumumba, Pinto, Mboya–dead communists–all dead–no good for Kenya–ambiguous–

2003 St Petersburg 2004 Dubai–wonder of wonders Kericho 2005 Globalisation for the Common Good–an interfaith perspective–held in a massive Sikh Temple–little town of Kericho immortalised by Africa's largest Gurudwara–Honolulu 2006 Istanbul 2007––the children of Adam are limbs of each other–hope for the future–World Gospel Mission huge influence in Kenya–hospitals colleges universities–Mano Singham, philosopher–"All your ancestors are mine, whoever you are, and all mine are yours–Ewan Cameron *was* right–

Only false religion destroys–paedophilic priests–sexual frustration endemic among young Muslim men obliged to live with parents unable to marry–sexual taboo–bombs–spin spin–greed–How Africa developed the West–USA–why do I equate the two?

–spin spin back back towards 1969–why are there no mobile phones, no internet, no television?–we desperately needed them in our little corner–fear–danger–hope for the future–change, equality–wipe out exploitation and corruption–repair a broken pride–too late?–I have to go back–conquer the panic–I must tell the story–perhaps nobody will want to read it but I have to tell the story–I'll shut my eyes to block out the present–pretend that all hasn't been for nothing–History matters–then why aren't things any better in this world – ?

Power must stay with the philanthropic – no money for war – money for the poor, the starving, the weak and exploited.

Mboya still alive – Mandela still lives – hope – Let Abraham Lincoln and Martin Luther King not have died for nothing – Barack Hussein Obama – Who can fund his cause? Where's Cora Weiss, the Red Queen of Peace? Where's the justice – the recompense for sufferings instilled by the west? Is Mwalimu Gloria watching him? – as the images unwind, like the circles that you find in the windmills of your mind.

Gasping for breath, reluctant and in a slight panic, Ella returns to the story she feels she must tell.

CHAPTER 18

Just Good Friends

'Wake up Ella. Joseph's asking if Memsaab Kidogo is still alive.' John whispered sitting down on the edge of the bed. 'I thought you might like some tea.'

'Is it morning–and are we still alive?'

'We're still alive and there's only five minutes left of morning.'

'What have we done John?' asked Ella.

'Quite a lot really. I think we might have fallen in love for starters but we'll have to put that on hold for a while. I'd better get you back to school seeing as it's Friday and term starts on Monday.'

'You're right. I'd better get going.'

'You haven't got a car remember,' John pointed out–and the whole scenario came flooding back leaving Ella in a trembling state of panic.

231

John took both her little hands in his big hands and said very calmly, 'Listen Ella. Listen very carefully. I'm sure you're perfectly safe. What you must do is carry on exactly as normal. OK?' She nodded dumbly. 'Remember, your car broke down and I had to give you a lift back from Nairobi–and my cousin a mechanic is driving it back for you. Are you remembering that? Nothing else happened.' Ella nodded again.

'But why did I come and stay here last night?' Ella asked foolishly.

John looked at her sideways with a grin and said, 'Nobody would be surprised if you left that to their imagination, now would they?'

They both had to laugh.

Back at Kipsigis Girls' School, Ella had to struggle to clamber out of the trauma of getting dragged down into the shadowy world of espionage. She desperately wished she could confide in Jan but as this was out of the question she covered up her anxiety with ultra cheerfulness. The two girls swapped travellers' tales and enthused about getting back to the pupils. It was, to Ella, as if nothing had happened.

She was now mentally ready to tackle the challenge of preparing her girls for their Literature in English exams–which Elizabeth Kiprogot, pillar of the staff at Kipsigis Girls' School, had said was all that was expected of her. It was good to get back to the task in hand and to be part of a team that was prepared to pour in everything they had to do the best job possible in the short time they had to 'do their little bit' to recompense for the sins of their forefathers. Ella always felt uncomfortable when this sentiment was expressed and preferred to think that kids were kids were kids wherever they were. These girls were no different–except in one sense. They were all highly intelligent.

Keeping very busy was just what Ella needed to keep her mind off her complicated love life. Both Mike and John had come to visit but she had managed to avoid going on a date with either of them.

She returned Mike's books with thanks as she had been given a little funding to spend in Nelson's bookshop in Nairobi to add to the school's tiny but expanding library. She'd used some of her own money to buy some simple readers to send to Nan and Precious for their small Harambee primary school at the farm and had sent a flamingo feathered ornament which looked like a flower arrangement for Mike's mother. Otherwise she was really *much too busy* to visit–which was in fact true.

She and John saw each other as they chaperoned Saturday evening school dances involving the girls travelling to Cheptonge on a covered bus, which was expensive but protected their elaborate hairdos and pretty dresses and the boys travelling on a lorry to Kipsigis Girls School–which was cheaper because they didn't have to stay so pretty. Nothing was said about their adventures in Nairobi–although they did talk about how Nixon had got in by a whisker and was proceeding to play the good guy by trying to put an end to the Vietnam War. Again Ella was *much too busy* to go on a date but one Friday she invited John for dinner with Bob and Jan–reckoning there would safety in numbers. 'Can't wait to see how your bridge is coming along,' Ella said breezily as she tried to keep things light.

'Oh we'll whip them this time,' John replied. He too was hesitant about the relationship and had seemed strained and tired. He wouldn't say why but Ella was sure Tom Mboya was still in danger–and that meant John could be too. How she wished he wasn't involved in this whole mess. Jan then inadvertently added to the complications by inviting Mike and his brother Drew when she bumped into them in town that same day. Drew had returned from one of his many trips to the Mara where he was hoping to set up safari trips for tourists and Jan thought they could add to the conversation over a meal for four.

'Oh Jan–I know it's not your fault but what am I going to do? I don't think I can face this.'

'Geez I'm sorry, Elsa. What have I *done*?'

'For goodness sake don't call me Elsa.'

'Oops, sorry that's Mike's pet name, hey?'

To even up the numbers the girls decided they would invite Jenny wren and her new housemate, a shy girl from Liverpool who had come to teach Science. On the menu was a giant shepherd's pie using vegetables from the garden to make it stretch. The evening wasn't up to the Kisimot standards of befezzed and bekanzued servants and silver service but the nosh and plonk were passable and the girls managed to sparkle with interesting descriptions of holiday trips and funny stories about school. Bob too was loud and entertaining in his truly American manner and Drew turned out to be an enthusiastic and entertaining raconteur. He was on to his third long story, which happened to be about zebras taking the initiative in crossing crocodile-infested rivers in front of the wildebeest migration, before Ella realised that neither John nor Mike had said more than a few words all evening.

She decided she would have to use all her diplomatic skills to pull them out of themselves so she told everyone else to stop hogging the conversation and let them have a word in edgeways. Later, Jan accused her of trying to work out which one was the sheep and which the goat–but that wasn't at all how Ella saw it.

Mike was the more confident and immediately countered with, 'Well, we can't all go on exotic holidays to entertain our guests with. Some of us have to keep the home fires burning.'

Predictably Bob came up with, 'Well, how are they burning, Mike?' and everyone was subjected to a progress report on the dairy, the shambas, the shop, the clinic and the school. John carried on staring into his glass. As Jan and Ella were clearing away the main course and getting dessert ready, Jan whispered,

'Round One to Mike.'

'Jan, you're awful. Help me out here will you please?' Ella pleaded. So Jan persuaded John to tell a few sporty stories culminating in one about a visit to Cheptonge by Wilson Kiprugut and his Mexico Olympic medals. The evening was rescued, on the surface. Ella was hoping that the message had been put across that she was happy to be friends with both Mike and John as long as she could stay fancy free. What was closer to the truth was that she could have been tempted by either of them but couldn't decide which one. Mike was the rich one that her parents would approve one but John was the more intriguing, Mike was better looking and taller but John was more athletic and had a nicer voice and eyes. She also knew that Caithness was not ready for anyone like John Francis. Oh no–and before long it would be time to go home and pick up the threads of life in Scotland. Also, both of these men were carrying too much baggage. She had made a decision to move on. The evening ended with little hugs for 'just good friends'. After all the guests had gone, Jan found Ella sitting on the floor in front of the still blazing fire hugging her knees.

'Why is it Jan that there are either no men or two men?'

'Maybe you should go to Tibet. There's polyandry there.'

'No thanks. One man's enough. I think I'd better wait until I go home to Scotland. Though –'

'Which one do you prefer?'

'Sometimes I think I know. I keep thinking what my folks would think and then I think I shouldn't consider that–but anyway, I think I've lost them both after tonight.

'No way–they're both mad about you. I reckon it's going to be pistols at dawn if you don't hurry up and pick one.'

'I can't. Oh Jan I'm so stupid.' She burst into tears. She wished she could tell her friend all about Tom Mboya and the danger she'd been in. 'Oh, crumb Ella, they're only men.'

'Yep,' said Ella. There was nothing more she could say.

CHAPTER 19

Nairobi Tragedy

It was decided that the Girls' school needed a hockey team as a donation of thirty hockey sticks, ten balls and some funding for a place on a 'hockey course' at Kenyatta Teachers' College in Nairobi had arrived from some overseas benefactor. Nobody really wanted to go on the course so Ella was nominated after she foolishly admitted that she'd once captained a school team. She set off on a Tuesday for Nairobi in her VW which had been returned by John's friend Shashi, whose family lived in Kericho. John always seemed to have his finger in all sorts of useful pies. Ella had given Shashi a lift into town and he had told her a long story about what was happening to his family who were preparing to emigrate from Kenya to Britain though it was the last place they wanted to go.

'Why you want to go where you're not wanted?' Shashi had said to Ella. 'But if you haven't got a Kenyan passport, you've got no choice these days. You can't even go India.'

Ella was horrified to hear about what was happening and sympathised with Shashi and his family. The business they'd built up over the years had been confiscated–or Africanised to use the euphemism–and, on top of that, the restrictions on the export of currency were crippling. His story was repeated all over Kenya. Uganda was even more vicious under Idi Amin. Shashi was bitter because, as he said, the Asians had helped the Kenyans to gain independence from the British Colonials and then they'd got a kick in the teeth. Shashi went on to say,

'They are jealous of our money so they are taking over our businesses and breaking them–destroying all of it.'

Ella agreed that this was hard but the conversation had to come to an end as she needed to get back to school. On the way home, Ella found herself reflecting on yet another facet of Kenya's cosmopolitan society. Less than a year before, the only non-whites Ella had met had been her sister's friend from Guyana and one fellow student at Aberdeen University from Barbados (whom she'd fancied). 'How many other things have gone wrong because of the arrogance of the British Empire builders?' she asked herself. She decided she would now call herself a cosmopolite. In the meantime she'd got her car back and was now bombing her way down to Nairobi for the three day course. She booked into the hostel and presented herself for the induction meeting–and was staggered to find that the session was being led by none other than John Francis. When he saw Ella, John registered surprise for a split second and continued to lead with aplomb. He knew what he was talking about having regularly played for a club hockey team and been in the under sixteen national team.

'I didn't know you were coming on this Ella.'

'I wasn't expecting to see you either. Bob told me you'd been AWOL again for a couple of weeks but I thought it was ... you know.'

'Part of it was–you know. Listen, I'm tied up tonight but shall we get together tomorrow. It's been ages. Good to see you, green eyes.'

'Good to see you too, brown eyes,' Ella replied before she could stop herself. That wasn't very aloof.

After hostel supper with some other hockey students and fending off questions about how she knew this gorgeous man, Ella managed an early night. The next day's training was fine but John wasn't going to let her out of his clutches at the end of the afternoon session.

'Ella, there are a few people I'd like you to meet,' he said with a ring of authority in his voice. 'Can you smarten up and I'll pick you up at seven.' She almost said she couldn't make it but had absolutely no excuse and couldn't invent one quickly enough. Later she was glad she'd made a bit of an effort because John presented himself very smartly suited and booted and they sped off across Nairobi. The date was July 2nd 1969 which was to become imprinted on Ella's mind forever.

John and Ella drove up to one of those large ex colonial houses with grand carriage drives and swept to a halt. They were greeted by a pleasant European lady in her fifties who shook Ella warmly by the hand and greeted her as if she'd heard all about her. Ella was puzzled.

'There's someone very special who would like to speak to you. Please come through,' she said ushering Ella into a large room where a round faced man and a tall, very pretty African woman were standing as if waiting to meet her.

'I don't understand,' Ella said recognising the man.

'Let me introduce myself. I'm Gloria Hagberg.'

'Oh,' Ella said astounded. 'Aren't you Mwalimu Gloria of the airlifts? It's an honour to meet you.'

'I'm glad you've been taking an interest in the successful young students from Kenya. I believe you are a teacher too.'

'Yes, I am and I love it. The girls are a pleasure to teach,'

Ella said with complete sincerity.

'You're absolutely right. I'd like you to meet one of my students who went to USA to study a few years ago when she was only twenty. It's Ella isn't it?' (For once John Francis was struck dumb, overcome by the occasion.) This is Pamela Odede as she was and now she's Pamela Mboya.' Ella gasped and shook hands with Pamela and waited to be presented to her husband who was none other than the illustrious and controversial Minister for Economic Planning and Development in Jomo Kenyatta's government, Tom Mboya.

'We've met, I believe, briefly. I'm sorry if I was rude to you Miss Mackay and thank you for possibly saving my life,' Tom Mboya said in his resonant voice which filled the room. 'I'm sorry you were traumatised by the whole experience. John says you haven't been quite the same since.'

'Oh,' said Ella without contradicting this interpretation. 'Do you think I really did save your life or could it have been a hoax?'

'I have been persuaded by many people, including John here, that I can't afford to take the risk of it being anything other than a genuine threat—so I'm trying to be careful.'

'I wish that was true,' Pamela scolded. 'He seems to go all over the place without a guard.' Her husband laughed his loud laugh and said,

'Nobody's going to take a pop at me in broad daylight—and we're always guarded at night.'

'I hope you're right,' the beautiful young woman said. 'You have a wife and five children to think of.'

Gloria had ordered snacks and a glass of wine to be served and after everyone had chatted about Kipsigis Girls' School for a short time she excused herself saying that she had another engagement so John and a completely gobsmacked Ella left. Tom Mboya and Pamela also took their leave as he said he was flying to Addis Ababa very early in the morning.

Ella was never to forget that brief encounter.

On Saturday July 5th 1969 Tom Mboya was gunned down as he left Chhani's pharmacy in Government Road. This time no warning message from USA over the CIA communications line was sent. They never did find out who had sent the previous warning.

John was completely and utterly devastated and blamed himself which was totally irrational. Mboya himself had sent his driver cum bodyguard home and driven himself to the chemist's shop which was owned by his friends who were also acquaintances of John and his family. Mrs Mohini Sehmi described how she had heard two gunshots outside the shop after Tom left and when she went outside he fell into her arms. There was blood on his red shirt. She described how they laid him on the floor of the shop before calling an ambulance and the police. Mr Chhanni remembered how the ambulance men had tried to resuscitate Tom using a contraption called **Res Q Air** which he knew to have been dumped on Africa because tests in the USA had proved it to be completely useless. Tom Mboya died. It had been such a professional assassination that he would probably have died anyway.

John and Ella were about to go to the cinema in Nairobi when the news reached them so they abandoned the idea in a state of complete shock and John took Ella back to the widowed mother and a sister whom she'd heard of but never met. It turned out they were not his real family but a cover for John when he was in Nairobi on agency business. The cover was no longer needed and his surrogate 'mother' said that she was sorry the man was dead but very glad that all this undercover secret nonsense was over. Ella now heard that John's real family lived in Kisumu near the shores of Lake Victoria. He had a mother, a father three brothers and a sister. His mother was Olga–Pio Gama Pinto's sister.

That night John announced that he would never again get

involved in Politics, especially not in Kenya. He had missed his family and no longer felt he could put them in danger. He would study for one more year and qualify as a teacher he added. Ella felt numb and though her heart went out to him, she couldn't comfort him in front of these strangers who were not his real family. She just said,

'I think you would make a wonderful teacher.'

Next day the two drove back to Kericho in convoy this time saddened by an experience they could never tell the whole truth about. Ella was allowed to tell people she had met Mwalimu Gloria Hagberg, Granny of the Airlifts–and coincidentally Tom Mboya but was not allowed to reveal the fact that she had probably once helped to save his life.

Camelot was abandoned and Kenya's corrupt capitalists were not brought into line. It was the beginning, however, of an investigation by all of the agents scattered around Kenya who had given their loyalty to Tom Mboya and his socialist ideals for a better Kenya. John Francis, though not at the centre of the investigation, was very much involved. The investigation started with an agent based in the Treasury Office getting a copy of a very long letter to William Scheinmann, American philanthropist and sponsor of the scholarship student airlifts around the time that JF Kennedy agreed to the funding of the airlifts from the Kennedy Foundation. Further digging turned up a cable with the order to go ahead with the removal of OTM and it was signed by the initials JEH. When it was pointed out that Tom Mboya's mother had named him Odhiama it was felt that the target of the message had been identified. The other set of initials no one dared to identify but, as John said, it stank of the FBI which in turn, stank of anti communism. Others pointed to the FBI as the servant of the then President of the USA, Richard Nixon, about whom Tom Mboya probably knew an embarrassing secret which could not be revealed.

Meanwhile a scapegoat assassin was charged and the world was persuaded that internal factions, notably the Kiambu Mafia, were highly likely to be to blame. When questioned, the assassin said, 'Why don't you ask the big man?' Which big man did he mean?

One strange fact that bothered some people was the sudden departure of the two Californian pilots in the middle of the Kericho cloud seeding project. They had said no goodbyes. Their project was abandoned, unfinished. Ella was struggling with a memory of a Boxing Day jaunt where these two Americans were buzzing what could well have been a communication centre on top of a hill in a clearing in the Mau Forest which couldn't be accessed by road. When she told John, he nodded as if he agreed with Ella that the fact was very strange–but significant.

John Francis would never forget the death of his uncle Pio Gama Pinto and his predecessor Patrice Lumumba or the fact that Tom Mboya's greatest wish was to develop the Kenya branch of the Lumumba Institute.

After Mboya's death, John cut all ties with the hero's idolatrous followers and sank into depression for a while.

'No doubt others will carry on–but not me. With a British passport, I'm not even welcome here.'

'Perhaps we can both be cosmopolites,' Ella suggested before she told him why she had decided that that was what she was going to be.

Not aloof at all.

'Mandela still lives. Perhaps one day he'll succeed,' was the cry. The intelligentsia of Kenya, the recently returned scholarship students from overseas studies, understood exactly what that meant.

CHAPTER 20

Back to School

Back at Cheptonge Boys' Secondary School John Francis remained John Francis for the time being and headmaster Dolph Daley was delighted with the sudden upturn in his young teacher's efficiency and enthusiasm. John had informed Dolph that he had given up the 'part time research project' that had taken him away from school from time to time but that he had enrolled in a post graduate course from January so would be leaving the job. He didn't say where the course was and omitted the fact that it was leading to a teaching qualification. Only Ella knew the details and she knew how to be discreet.

Ella immersed herself in her job and grew to love the girls more and more. She strove to keep up with their ambition and perseverance by producing more and more material for them to absorb and she pushed their thinking skills to the limit. She shared their dreams and their traumas and cried at the tragedy of Elizabeth 145 who never returned from an initiation ceremony. She had died from an infection brought on by a botched circumcision. Ella, being Ella, voiced no opinion on clitorectomy but encouraged her students to debate the pros and cons as part of the character study of Muthoni in Ngũgĩ's 'The River Between'.

The months flew by. The hockey team flourished and Kipsigis Girls' School shone at the Nairobi Music Festival in Choral Singing, Drama, International Dance, Traditional Dance, Solo verse and Choral Verse. Mary Lou's superb choir and the Kipsigis traditional dance team trained by Elizabeth, both gained firsts. A traditional play written directed and acted by the students got a second and Evelina Mboga (mboga, rather unfortunately means vegetable) was third for her recitation of Rudyard Kipling's Boots which was the prescribed piece. Ella had a hand in training Evelina and was convinced the poem was chosen with the sole purpose of challenging the sound confusions between traditional African languages and the English language. The first challenges were the b/v confusion and the fact that all words end in a vowel sound of which there are only five pure ones in most Kenyan languages–so the first line began as 'Vootsee vootsee vootsee vootsee mahcheen ap an dan agenee' and, after a long time finally ended up as a crisp 'Boots boots boots boots marching up and down again' of which Ella was very proud . Another contribution of Ella's was a team of Scottish Country Dancers performing 'Hamilton House' who were second out of three teams. How bizarre was that?

The most satisfying achievement for all concerned, however, was a first and a special commendation for a choral recitation of Hilaire Belloc's Tarantella. The adjudicator had praised the diction, the rhythm, the shading of expression and the enthusiasm of the choir but was almost sure that he detected a distinct Scottish accent; he didn't say whether or not that was a good thing. Ella was delighted because it had taken a very long time indeed to iron out the aforementioned language problems to which were added the l/r and the d/th confusions. This led to horrors like, 'And the heepee hoppee hapee of the crapee of da handsee' which didn't sound at all like the 'hip hop hap of the clap of the hands' and was totally out of sink with the flamenco beat it was supposed to represent. However, Ella was tempted to think that the 'Voom' of the far waterfall sounded better than the 'Boom' of the far waterfall but still worked as hard on changing it as she had on changing 'the tething and the sprething of the stlaw for a bething' into a beautiful 'the tedding and the spreading of the straw for a bedding' and 'the frees that tease in da High Pylenees' into 'the fleas that tease in the High Pyrenees'

It would seem that there was enough to keep Ella's mind off the recent traumas but she still felt desolate at the thought of John leaving in a few months time and couldn't help feeling close to him after all they had been through. They didn't see each other for weeks because they were both throwing themselves into their work but when Bob organised a bridge foursome at his house, they found themselves clinging to each other in tears as soon as they had a private moment supposedly making coffee in the kitchen. The trauma had been shattering and they both felt they needed to distance themselves from it but it didn't stop them pulling themselves together to thrash Jan and Bob by three rubbers.

That night John finally snapped. He decided, since it was all behind him, he was going to trust Bob and Jan with most of the truth about being part of Tom Mboya's security net. Ella allowed John to reveal the selected facts in his own way and took his cue about what still had to remain secret. Jan was flabbergasted and Bob finally admitted what had been eating him up for a year–that he had seen Mboya outside John's house late at night under spooky circumstances. The air was cleared and there was relief all round–and a huge amount of sadness at the loss of a good man who had already done so much for his people in Kenya and who may have continued had he lived.

Bob and Jan, as far as John and Ella knew, kept their secret while they were still in Kenya but when their time was over and they went home they never did keep in touch beyond Christmas letters for a few years. Such was the transient quality of many of the expatriate friendships formed in the tropics. However, Ella was quite certain that they had never forgotten those days.

CHAPTER 21

Holiday of a Lifetime

As promised, Ella had booked a twenty four day holiday for her Mum and Dad over the Christmas and New Year period which wouldn't interfere with the farm commitments in Caithness and would give them the chance of a holiday of a lifetime in the sun, away from the cold Scottish winter.

Charlie and Mary Mackay had never been on a plane before and Ella had never been on holiday with them except to her uncle's farm all the way down near Edinburgh. They would fly from Inverness to Heathrow and pick up a direct flight to Nairobi where Ella would meet them with the details of the itinerary which had been arranged by the travel agent in Nairobi. This was a major trip so it had to be especially well planned. Now the Scots know better than many what happens to 'the best laid schemes of mice and men' and the inevitable happened. There was to be a week in Kericho over Christmas,

248

New Years Eve at the Naivasha Hotel, a week in Nairobi at the Westlands Country Park Hotel and then a week in Mombasa at Hotel Coraldene.

Despite efforts to call it a day, John and Ella were still being drawn together so they made arrangements for the two sets of parents to accidentally on purpose bump into each other at Hotel Coraldene, Mombasa. His family would be staying with relatives in Mombasa for the whole month of the school break. Ella had never met John's parents so this was going to be a crucial moment in the development of their relationship. The tenth of January was arranged—two days after Charlie, Mary and Ella were expected to have booked in. Ella had no idea where John and his family were staying in Mombasa and had absolutely no way of getting in touch with them. On December 22nd the travel agent in Nairobi had apologised profusely but had unavoidably had to change the Mombasa week for the Nairobi week because of several double bookings and they hoped it wouldn't make any difference to the enjoyment of their holiday.

'That's it,' Ella thought with her heart sinking, 'John and I were never meant to get together.' She felt that fate had taken over. She did, however, plan to leave a message at Hotel Coraldene for John to pick up after she and her parents were due to have left for Nairobi.

After one night of luxury at the New Stanley so that they could recover from their flight, Ella bundled her awestruck parents into the Beetle to drive them to Kericho amid exclamations like,

'Look, Dad—purple trees!' from Mary looking at curtains of bougainvillea and,

'Are there nae fences aroond here?' from farmer Charlie as Ella manoeuvred her way through yet another herd of goats on the road.

The three laughed and joked and drank in the new experiences with childlike wonderment—Ella seeing things anew through the eyes of her parents on their first visit to the Kenya she felt she knew so well now. Mary and Charlie were entranced and Ella was delighted that she'd been able to bring them. Arapbet had waited to meet Memsaab kidogo's Baba na Mama and had baked a cake to serve with tea. He greeted them in English and with great respect. They were mzee like he was and there was no need for them to learn Swahili. He told them that their daughter was a very good teacher and the children loved her and thanked them very much for letting their daughter come to Kenya. Charlie and Mary were charmed but rather diffident.

'I don't think I could be doing with somebody cleaning my house and cooking for me,' Mary said after Arapbet had gone home.

'I said exactly the same as you,' Ella told her Mum, 'until Haidee King came and put me right.' Charlie and Mary enjoyed the story.

Later in the evening the lady herself, Haidee King dropped in with an invitation to Christmas lunch to join her seventy five year old mother who was on holiday from Birmingham. As if on cue, Mary pootled off to the bedroom and returned with home made Christmas pudding and mince pies which she had hidden among her knickers, she said, because they might come in handy. Haidee giggled with delight and Christmas day was organised. Christmas lunch was perfect for the older generation though Ella was feeling the loss of Jan's company as she had flown off to Canada leaving a silent void in her domestic life. She had had a good cry and got it out of her system but she was going to miss her desperately.

After lunch Haidee had her usual visit from her old friends, Angus and Shona Kilpatrick. This rather threw Ella and she was glad of the offer of another glass of port. Mary and Charlie were rather taken aback by the warmth of the greetings that Shona and Angus were offering Ella and wondered why they were calling her Elsa. Shona told Mary when she thought Ella wasn't listening, 'Our Michael seems to be keen on your Elsa but I don't think it's come to anything yet.' Ella could feel her ears burning and a blush spreading. She thought to herself, 'What does she mean by yet?' The upshot was that the Mackay family were invited to visit Kisimot one morning and stay for lunch so that the two men could talk farming and the two ladies could wander round the garden. This would leave Ella at the mercy of Mike unless Nan and Drew were around. Another visit had been added to the visits to a tea estate, sugar plantation and passion fruit juice factory Ella had planned for her Dad.

For her parents the visit to Kisimot turned out to be the highlight of their trip. The two sets of parents hit it off straightaway as they had a lot in common, including a Scottish heritage, and enough different experiences to interest each other. As Ella had suspected, Drew and Nan were 'busy' which left Mike and Ella to entertain each other. They decided to take Simba for a walk and the conversation naturally turned to how remarkably well their parents were getting along. Small talk about school and the farm and Ngũgĩ's novels went on until Mike could stand it no longer.

'How's John Francis? Are you still seeing him?' he blurted out quickly.

'I'll probably never see him again,' Ella replied, realising that this was upsetting her. 'He's leaving Cheptonge to do some post graduate course.' She remembered to be discreet about the details.

'Ole told me all about Camelot, by the way, so you don't have to be cagey,' Mike said, which astonished Ella. She wasn't quite sure if she trusted Mike and certainly didn't want to be drawn into any tricky conversation so she simply said, 'What's Camelot? I don't know what you mean.' This must have been the kind of situation Patrick Smith-Jones' father was referring to when he was advising her to be discreet.

The conversation stopped dead after Mike mumbled, 'Oh, don't worry about it. It's not important.'

After some time Mike finally said, 'Elsa, I still think about you a lot. Do you think we might have a chance?' Ella was quiet for some time before she said, 'I'm not sure Mike. I'm not ready for anything permanent and I need to go home to Scotland for a while to get everything back into perspective. '

'You're not due to go back for a whole year yet. If I promise to be easy-going, can I take you out from time to time?'

'Just as friends?' Ella asked.

'It'll be hard but it's a deal,' Mike sighed and put his arm around her shoulder which was how they were when the two mums spotted them and gave each other a knowing look.

'You're a sneaky woman, Shona Kilpatrick—a bit like myself,' Mary Mackay laughed. 'But I'm not at all sure I want my youngest to be living so far away from home—even if it is such a bonny place.'

'Ah, but it would be a fine excuse to visit, eh?' Shona replied. 'Anyway, the chances are that we'll leave this place in the not too distant future.'

It had been a wonderful day and after Ella and her parents had said their good-byes, it occurred to her that neither Nan nor Drew had appeared on the scene. Ella decided not to mention them.

'Let them keep the beautiful memory,' she thought feeling protective of her parents. She also didn't want them to worry about her until she got home in a year's time.

The rest of the holiday was a dream despite a few hiccups of the 'it could only happen in Africa' type. Number one was when the right back wheel of the Beetle sheered off and bounced along the road in front of the car. Miraculously Ella managed to stick the car in a muddy bank at the side of the road and nobody was hurt. Kericho motors fixed it in a jiffy and they were off again. Number two was strange more than anything. The Naivasha Hotel had put on a wonderful meal and music for New Year's Eve to make a perfect ending to a day of flamingo–viewing. In the old fashioned way a page boy was walking around with a sandwich board and a bell announcing a phone call for Charlie Mackay from Ian Mackay.

'What's the silly blighter ringing me here for?' Charlie said thinking it was his brother Ian from Perthshire putting through an international call. Mary panicked a bit thinking something might be wrong. Ella said she would go and take the call. She was sure it must be a mistake knowing how difficult it was for international calls to get through. Sure enough a very drunk Ian Mackay, complete with Scots accent, wanted to talk to his brother Charlie at the Naivasha Hotel, Ella fetched her Dad and the two men talked for half an hour before they realised that a completely different Ian Mackay from some farm in Kenya had been wanting to talk to a completely different Charlie Mackay who was his brother but not Ella's Dad. Mary and Charlie dined out on that story for a long time. Number three (because things always come in threes and Mary was waiting for it) was when the trio arrived at the Coraldene there was no booking and the receptionist said she couldn't let Ella leave a message for John, especially if she wasn't exactly sure of his name.

'Please,' said Ella, 'if a John Francis asks for Ella Mackay, just give him this letter. It's important. Thank you.'

The document from the travel agent meant nothing. The hotel was full. It was suggested they could try Diani Beach which was thirty miles south of Mombasa. Everything was fully booked there too but Ella's wee mum put on such a pathetic face that they cleared a boat out of a boat house and set up three camp beds with pristine cotton sheets, a mirror, a table and a chair. Add to this the silver service tea tray and you have the best room in the hotel with sea breeze air conditioning and direct access to the beach and the Indian Ocean.

Ella's Mum thought it was the best bit of the holiday. At six in the morning, there she was, alone in the Indian Ocean, in her navy blue and turquoise paisley pattern swim suit with its stiff pre-formed bra cups and sturdy concealed corset which was only one size too big for her slim little body. It was the only thing she could buy (as usual) at Altnabervie Drapers. Charlie had brought a swimsuit which he called his *dookers* which looked like bottle green boxer shorts without a fly. He never did get around to wearing them and only turned up his *breeks* and took his socks off for a paddle after Mary had nagged him until he gave in.

'No chance of a midnight skinny dip then Dad,' Ella joked.

From a trip to the coral reef in a glass-bottomed boat to a visit to a giant 300 year old tortoise and all the attractions of historical and beautiful Mombasa including the famous Mombasa Tusks, Ella's Mum and Dad missed nothing–not even the luxuries in the Diani Beach hotel from swimming pool to five star restaurants–except for the room. They felt the boat house as the best room of all. They also made little use of the restaurant by the time they had sampled all the roadside delights like *mandazis, matoke,* roasted maize, *choma nyama,* samosas and stuffed chapattis–which had been rolled thin and thrown high in the air until they were the size of an umbrella before being stuffed with spicy fillings and folded. Those were Ella's favourites. Crayfish masquerading as lobster in the posh restaurant was delicious but not that much better than the street food.

Ella tried to contact Joyce at the Whitesands Hotel but she had gone to England for Christmas and the hotel was fully booked but she was allowed to take her Mum and Dad for a walk along the silvery white beach to the rocky pools where she had found so many exotic shells. They stopped for some tea and Charlie's gaffe was to put sand in his teacup and stub out his cigarette in the sugar. The two substances looked almost identical so he was forgiven.

Ella went back to Hotel Coraldene the day they had to leave Mombasa but there was no message from John. As he wasn't coming back to Cheptonge, she'd have to rely on him getting in touch with her. Why would he want to do that now that she'd let him down? He'd think it was deliberate–or that her Mum and Dad hadn't wanted to meet him.

Back in Nairobi after an exciting visit to a Tsavo game park where they were chased by a rhino and Ella's normally calm Dad had been prompted to yell at the top of his voice, 'Step on it Ella!' the three scruffs presented themselves at Westlands Country Park Hotel and came across some of the worst kind of snobs who could be politely described as neo-colonials. Ella was delighted at the short shrift her parents gave them and told them she was proud of them.

'Don't they think they're somebody?' Mary had said in her strong Caithness accent as she witnessed some rudeness towards one of the African staff. 'You'd think somebody could tell them good manners don't cost a penny.' Much to Ella's satisfaction, this was said just loudly enough for everyone around to overhear.

Another whirlwind tour followed–this time of Nairobi and its surroundings. Red, yellow, brown, green, chilli, haldi, garam, coriander, jos sticks, cinnamon and countless other exotic ingredients–an array of colours and a concoction of aromas–Bazaar street, Nairobi. Business seemed to be less brisk than when Ella last visited and the faces longer. Talk was of Africanisation and queues for vouchers and moving away to that cold, dark, unfriendly country with no servants and no businesses to run–UK. Suddenly, choosing a British passport over a Kenya passport was turning out to be a cause of insecurity. Charlie had got into a long conversation with a shopkeeper who had sold him a short sleeved shirt. Charlie was saying to Gulam who'd been giving him his life story and sharing his fears,

'I don't blame you. I can't say I'd like to live in that London either–too many folk for me.' Ella hid a smile and dragged them off before Mary could add to her collection of a wooden giraffe, an elephant's hair bracelet (which looked plastic) and a kitenge which would make a good tablecloth. The rest of the shopping trip was in and around Government Road and the pristine and modern shops around the rest of Nairobi City Centre.

Ella spared her parents the story of the assassination outside Chhani's Pharmacy. As they walked past it her heart felt heavy and she hoped they wouldn't need to buy anything there. She did, however, take them around all her other haunts like the Snocreme Ice Cream Parlour, Chowpatti the Indo-Chinese restaurant and The Thorn Tree.

'Oh look there's a message for me from Potty Dotty Watty,' Ella told her amused Mum and Dad. 'She's a Science teacher. Oh I've just missed her. She's gone back to her school.'

'Now that's what I call thrifty,' Charlie said with a chuckle. 'Nae stamps and nae phone bills. Marvellous.'

As a treat Ella took them for lunch at the brand, spanking new Hilton which had been opened in December 1969 Next day they lost Charlie for a whole day. He was interested in having a look at the dairy industry and Angus Kilpatrick had given him a contact at the Kenya Cooperative Creameries, KCC Headquarters. This fellow turned out to be from Orkney so it was nearly bed time before a normally tee total Charlie was delivered to the hotel in a slightly inebriated state.

'Sorry Mrs Mackay,' Sandy McBain was saying. 'I can't understand it. He's only had a couple of Tuskers.'

Well, that's two more than usual,' Mary said with a grin. She wasn't quite as sanctimonious as her 'elder of the Kirk' husband. She wasn't going to let him forget this.

There was just time for a trip to Treetops to see the leopards at night, view the game from the wrap around balcony and see

Mount Kenya from a distance, before it would be time for Ella's Mum and Dad to go home. The journey north from Nairobi was full of interest for the tourist parents. Every piece of land was cultivated–even right up to the road and Charlie was fascinated by the intercropping and Angus had told him about the crop rotation. Ella explained that this was the Kikuyu area. Unlike the Masai who were nomadic pastoralists, they were cultivators who valued their land highly. Bananas, maize, millet, yams, carrots, cabbage, lettuce, tomatoes, beetroot, potatoes, watermelon, cucumber, pineapples, avocado, mango, passion fruit–and a few more besides–everything was growing in the volcanic soil. Cattle and goats wandered everywhere and Charlie reckoned nobody could go hungry in Kenya. They stopped by the roadside and shared the biggest pineapple they'd ever seen and Ella bargained for a colourful *kikapu* that her Mum wanted. Ella showed her how to carry it around her forehead like a traditional Kikuyu woman–so Mary spent the next few days looking for grooves in foreheads.

Much too soon, the holiday was over.

'It's all about making memories, isn't it,' Mary told her daughter as she said good-bye. 'Thank you for the best holiday ever.'

'And weren't they great memories, eh Mum?' Ella replied. She had been careful to make sure that their experiences would be nothing else but happy–and fortunately she had succeeded.

'It was good to see your neck of the woods for the rest of the year lass,' Ella's Dad said. 'Now, you look after yersel and come back in one piece. We'll see you for Christmas.' Charlie Mackay looked happy.

Charlie, Mary and fifteen 35mm films flew off into the night sky. Ella hadn't expected to feel so desolate.

CHAPTER 22

Lonely–and a Trip to Masai Mara

Ella analysed her depressed mood as she drove home alone to Kericho. Jan, her soul mate had gone home to Montreal. John was at Kenyatta College and would probably never get in touch again after she hadn't turned up in Mombasa (Why hadn't she left a message at the Thorn Tree?). Bob had announced that he had become a born again Christian so Ella reckoned there'd be little contact there any more. Even Jenny, Mary Lou and Brad, Jean Pierre and Mitul had left. Kenyan citizens African and Asian would be replacing them. Ella felt there was nobody left she was close to. She thought she'd pop in on Haidee as soon as she got back before going back to the house she would now be living in alone.

She found a distraught Haidee surrounded by packed tea

chests in a house that was almost stripped bare.

'They've chucked me out,' she said flatly.

'Who have? They can't do that. The school would collapse without you,' Ella said, realising just how much she meant that.

'Oh yes they can. They can do whatever they want. They're calling it a transfer. I'm to be vice principal at a bigger school–vice principal to an African principal. That means I'll get all of the work and none of the kudos.' Ella didn't point out that she thought she was probably right. Haidee had been given a week to pack and get to her new school and very little explanation as to why. Haidee thought it might have been because she'd let Mary 98 sit her exams just after her baby was born.

'I bet your replacement is African,' Ella said, 'Africanisation is all they're talking about around Bazaar Street.'

'She's called Poppy Ogola, twenty four and about to give birth,' said Haidee with a wry smile. 'I wouldn't mind if it was Elizabeth or someone else half competent but this one's got a granny who's a university professor and a lot of string-pulling attached to her.' Ella didn't say that she'd bought some children's books written by a Poppy Ogola for Nan Kilpatrick and Precious's school. Haidee was obviously distressed and didn't need to hear that.

Competent Haidee left and young and fragile Poppy arrived. She was very decisive except her decisions were perhaps not the wisest. The funds for setting up the new Advanced level courses were squandered on eight clocks and eight framed pictures of Jomo Kenyatta, one for each classroom which left everyone gobsmacked. It took six months before the teachers finally got the textbooks they needed. The decision that most upset Ella personally was when she was ousted from her house and allocated a room in someone else's house in town. The other tenant in the house was a Kenyan nurse at the hospital and very nice but she was no soul mate.

She was also hardly ever there. The move meant a lot of driving—even at night after study duty which wasn't a lot of fun. Ella worried about Arapbet but then assumed he'd have a new job with the new tenants. She gave him a bonus and a banana skin wall hanging and wished him good bye and good luck holding back the tears. Within two weeks, you could have knocked Ella down with a feather when she opened her door on a Saturday morning to find Arapbet wanting to help her. He'd got hold of a bicycle and must have cycled for miles. It was agreed he would come on a Wednesday and a Saturday to do her laundry and a bit of housework. The new tenants were not to his liking. Ella didn't discover why and didn't ask.

Ella waited and waited for a letter from John and when none arrived, it confirmed her fears that he'd assumed that her parents had refused to meet him. After all he was used to that happening in his own community. He'd often talked of parents' disapproval of their children's choice of girlfriend or boyfriend.

Mike on the other hand did come to visit but found Ella gone and when he found Poppy ensconced in Haidee's shoes, he asked where Ella was and was told the information was confidential. Poor Mike panicked and came to school on Monday morning, saw the Beetle and pulled Ella out of class. When he found out where she was living, he was none too impressed and said he would visit in the evening. Before sunset he was there with a friend—a puppy in his arms the same colour as Ella's hair and just like Simba. She christened the kitchen floor with a puddle so Ella christened her Tana after the river in Kenya.

'She's yours,' Mike said.

'But I've got nobody to look after her,' said Ella.

'Yes you have,' Mike answered, 'I want you to take her in the car wherever you go. Will you promise me that?'

Next day Ella took a day off sick feeling she deserved it after the treatment she'd had. She spent the day getting to know her new little friend and training her not to make any more puddles in the wrong places. Arapbet came on Wednesday and promised to look after the puppy for the day. As soon as Tana was house trained, she and Ella became inseparable. She sat under the blackboard during lessons and the schoolgirls spoiled her during breaks. She loved the car and barked if she was left alone. She probably would never have tackled a thief or an attacker but nobody knew that so Ella felt safe.

The teaching went on but the team spirit at school was broken. Elizabeth Kiprogot did her best but was hardly ever allowed to make any decisions except when Poppy went away to have her baby. Within three weeks Poppy was back with her mother and an *ayah* to look after the baby boy–ready to take over and become a hindrance once more.

Mike was there for Ella and for that she was grateful and she visited the school at Kisimot a couple of times which pleased Nan and Precious and delighted the children because she taught them a few language teaching songs. For a few brief moments she wondered if a life in Kenya, more precisely at Kisimot, would suit her–but by now, she was thinking of going home and it couldn't come quickly enough.

Ella kept hoping that one day John would get in touch but by the August break there was still no word. An aerogramme from Jan brought the news that she'd married her Mark and gone to live on a Greek island–and please could Ella stop off on her way to Scotland. Ella's reply to Jan was factual but she tried not to make it sound as bad as it was.

During the August holiday, Mike invited Ella to go on safari to visit his brother Drew in the Masai Mara. She went along and they found the plains teeming with game. It was a magical experience following the wildebeest migration and witnessing a lion fight and a cheetah kill. Sleeping in a tent with the night noises much too close for comfort was exciting–more so because Drew could identify the animals and tell them how close they were. His tales of close encounters told around the fire added to the atmosphere and Ella had no doubt he could make a go of his safari tours when his lodge was finally built. The two brothers were very different and there was a good deal of sibling rivalry. Mike felt Drew should be back on the family farm instead of wandering across the plains after animals whereas Drew felt that developing safari holidays was the only way he could survive in independent Kenya. They always ended up agreeing to disagree. A highlight of the trip was an invitation to a Masai wedding for the three of them plus Simba and Tana who had become firm doggy friends. Drew's Masai was fluent and he was obviously well liked by the group. Probably the most unpleasant thing Ella had ever had to do was to drink some horrendous concoction of milk, blood and charcoal which had been left to ferment in a large gourd. It was considered a delicacy and was called *mursik*–so Ella called it 'more sick' as she toasted the happy couple with a smile which hid the urge to retch.

'I wouldn't want to have to drink this stuff all the time,' Ella said to Drew, 'but otherwise you seem to be enjoying life alongside the Masai.'

'I don't interfere with what they want to do and they let me get on with my stuff,' was Drew's down to earth explanation.

Ella was, indeed, struck by the harmony. There did seem to be a peaceful co-existence between the Masai people and the wildlife around them and between Drew and his team and the Masai. During the day animals and people seemed to be wandering freely across the plain. It was hard to believe a young Masai had to kill a lion before he was considered to be a man. But the thick thorn tree fences around the *manyatta* to protect the cattle and goats from predators told another story.

At one point when Drew and Ella were alone he confronted her bluntly, 'You know my brother's pining for you Elsa. What do you think? Are you going to marry him?'

'I honestly don't know, Drew,' was the only answer Ella could give. 'I am very fond of him but maybe that's not enough. Let's see.

CHAPTER 23

Two Letters

Two letters arrived for Ella about a month before she was due to fly home. One was from her mother telling her that there was a job going at Sinclair's Institution in Altnabervie. Could she please write immediately if she wanted the job because, although John Gunn, the Principal, would dearly love her to have it, he would have to find someone soon if she didn't want the post. Ella wrote back and accepted the position straight-away because it made it easier to leave if she had something definite to look forward to. It wasn't until later that she realised that she didn't even know what subject was on offer.

The other letter was from John. The one she had been wait-ing for and given up all hope of. He said he would be going to Zambia in January but could he drop in to see her on his way to see his family in Kisumu–for old time's sake? It was a tentative letter and Ella didn't know how to interpret it. She decided he just wanted to say goodbye to her as someone who had shared some traumatic times with him. Nothing more. She wrote back to John saying please come but he'd have to come to school during lessons first so that she could show him where she lived. Then she told him all about Haidee leaving and all the changes. At the end she said she trusted he'd got the message she'd left at Hotel Coraldene explaining the mix up with the booking. It was around this time that Ella wrote a second verse for the song she had written after her first visit to Arapbet's home.

> *My heart is full of longing*
> *For the one whose love is mine*
> *As I look into my mirror*
> *I can see our skins entwine*
> *The sun shines down upon the earth*
> *With rays of one mid hue*
> *I call it happy colour*
> *Which brings to all a life anew*
> *Chorus: But it must have been the darkness*
> *Of the shadow of a dream*
> *Oh it must have been*
> *The shadow of a dream.*

She made up a pretty melody for the song and worked out the chords. When she played it the music club, the girls thought it was beautiful. Mary Chepkirui saw the tears in Ella's eyes and said,

'I think you must love him very much, Madam.'

'Perhaps I do but I might never get the chance to,' replied Madam.

A few days later, first thing in the morning, there was a phone call to the head teacher's office with an urgent message for Ella. She panicked thinking it might be bad news from Scotland. It was John. It was a very short call. He just said, 'I didn't get your message. Why didn't you try again? I'll be with you at the school before three o'clock. Wait for me.' Before she could say more than, 'OK, I'll do that', the line went dead.

'Thank you Mrs Ogola,' Ella said. Poppy insisted on Mrs although everyone knew she wasn't married. 'I really needed that message.'

'Don't let it happen again during class time.' Poppy just had to say something. Ella didn't reply. It had been the one and only call she'd ever received at Kipsigis Girls' School. Phone calls were that rare.

Ella managed to drive home at lunch time to make sure the house was presentable and quickly wash her hair and put some of John's favourite burnished copper lipstick on. (She slipped it in her bag as an afterthought.) She sped back to school on a cloud. Who was she kidding? He was going to Zambia and she was going home to Scotland. There was no future there–but she still had to look her best. It had been nearly a year since they'd seen each other. Would he have changed? She knew she had. Overwork and no dinner parties or Arapbet to spoil her every day meant that she'd lost weight and were these dark circles under her eyes?

At long last he arrived–in a blue VW beetle just like her green one. When he stepped out of the car he had that little boy lost look that Ella remembered when they first met. He was anxious too then.

'What happened to that lovely Ford Anglia with the fins?' said Ella trying to sound business like in front of the curious schoolgirls who were hanging around. She thought she heard her melody being hummed and a voice singing,

'It must have been the darkness of the shadow of a dream
It must have been the shadow of a dream–'

'Just wait until I see you lot tomorrow,' Ella thought as she was desperately trying to cover up a blush.

'I had to sell it to find the fees for Teachers' College,' John was saying. 'Joginder gave me this VW and some cash for it which was handy.'

'You mean you came to Kericho and didn't try to find me?' Ella complained and immediately wished she hadn't.

'I didn't think you'd want to see me. And there was a rumour that your parents had visited the Kilpatrick farm.'

'Whose dog is this then?' John asked as Tana did her usual tail wag and bark job before going in the car which she loved.

'This is Tana. She goes everywhere with me. I feel safe with her. Come on,' Ella said briskly. 'Let's get out of here. Follow me.'

The two little Beetles, one green followed by one blue left the school compound amid waves and cheers from (mostly) Ella's music club.

Pancakes and scrambled egg (again) and a bottle of plonk were on the menu and John and Ella explained and explained and explained again how they *had* tried to contact one another but when that failed why they had thought that the other wouldn't want to be contacted. Yes, Ella had left a message at Hotel Coraldene and no, the woman hadn't passed it on. Yes, Ella's parents had gone to Kisimot but only because Mr and Mrs Kilpatrick had met them at Haidee's and invited them and yes, she had seen Mike and he'd given her Tana as a puppy but no she certainly wasn't in love with him.

'And do you love me?' John finally said–very bluntly.

There was a very long silence before Ella at last ventured,

'I don't know. I haven't seen you for nearly a year.'

By the time John Francis had left Ella Mackay's house for his family home in Kisumu (very early in the morning) the two were very much along the way to falling in love. With that came the endless questions. What were they going to do about it? This wasn't going to be simple so they had to be very sure.

'Let me wind things up at school,' Ella said, 'and then we

can spend some time together.'

'I'd like you to meet my family,' John said but when he saw Ella's panic-stricken face he added, 'Don't worry, I've taken loads of white friends, male and female home before. They'll think you're just another friend.' And so it was arranged that Ella would spend a few days in Kisumu after the school term ended. John decided that was too long to wait so he invited himself to Kericho for the following weekend. 'Can I bring my little sister, Rosie? You'll like her and I know she'll like you—and she goes to sleep early.'

'I hope she does,' Ella replied enigmatically,'—like me I mean.' She might have got her man—and he did seem to be in it for the long haul but it didn't mean she couldn't drive him mad by playing hard to get. After all, she'd had years of practice. After he'd gone, a strange mixture of love, excitement, apprehension and fear came over Ella. This was going to be the longest of hauls and who knew where it would lead them?

Now she had to concentrate on finishing off her work at school and packing up and shipping off the vast amount of 'stuff' she had collected to take back to Caithness. What she had felt would be a smooth operation was now tinged with uncertainty and her stomach was in knots. Why hadn't she stuck to her guns and stayed fancy free?

CHAPTER 24

Farewell or Au Revoir

The schoolgirls had worked hard and were ready for their exams; Ella was going to miss them and they made it very clear that they would miss her too. In the past few months in the absence of her old friends she had dedicated most of her time to their needs which they had appreciated. They showered her with home made cards and small gifts and she was going to find it very hard to leave them.

John and Rosie appeared two Saturdays before end of term and ten new visitors had joined them before the weekend was over. Tana had timed it well. At two o'clock in the morning she produced ten little pups of all different colours and Rosie was thrilled. Romance was knocked on the head for John and Ella because nobody went to sleep early. Ella called the vet (who lived two doors along) for two of the pups which were ailing and he decided that Tana was too young to cope with more than four pups and took six of them away. Ella and Rosie were devastated but John (by now Ricardo) was detached and sensible.

'She'll be much better with just four especially since she's going to be missing you after you go. Where's she going anyway?'

'She'll go back to Kisimot. She loves it there and adores Simba their dog. I will miss her though.'

A cloud passed over John (now Ricardo's) face as Kisimot was mentioned and he needed reassurance that Ella didn't feel she had made a mistake and that her parents wouldn't prefer her to marry a rich mzungu. Of course Ella assured him that was all nonsense and the cloud passed over. Rosie and Ricardo (formerly John–would Ella ever get used to it?) left with lots of exciting stories to tell the family. Rosie told Ella the family were already looking forward to her visit. Before they left, it was arranged that Ricardo (still John to Ella) would collect Ella from Kericho, take her to Kisumu for a few days and take her to the airport later–if she wanted to get rid of the car. Ella decided she'd hang on to the car just for a bit longer but she would accept the lift to his home.

After term ended and the girls had gone home and the staff farewell parties were over there were two weeks for Ella to get ready to leave. She'd sold the car back to Kericho Motors who would take it off her hands the day she was leaving.

Mike was devastated that John was back in Ella's life and he was finding it very hard to hide his feelings which upset Ella. She had never told him she loved him but Mike had assumed that one day she would. He had done all the right things, even Ella felt that, but it would never work she told him. When she thought of Mike's parents and Nan and Precious and Simba and Tana and even the remote Drew, she was heartbroken because in a way she had loved them all as, in a way, she had loved Mike–but not enough to marry him.

'I'm so sorry Mike. I'm not the one for you but I'm certain

there's just the right girl out there if you just get out there and look–like I told you to before.'

'But I'll never forget my Elsa.'

'And I'll never forget you and everyone at Kisimot.' And she never did. She couldn't bear to visit Kisimot to say good bye. That was how Mike arrived in the jeep, three hours later than expected, with Simba and a big box with blankets for Tana and her four pups. He had arrived to be confronted by two VW Beetles outside Ella's house–one green and one blue. The two men shook hands stiffly while Simba created a welcome distraction by going absolutely mental with excitement over Tana and her pups. Ella wasn't looking forward to saying good bye to the little family but was delighted to see Simba's reaction.

'Now, Simba, you make sure you look after them for me, won't you–and look after your master too.' At that, Ella dissolved into uncontrollable sobs; she was thankful of the smokescreen of Tana and her four dear little pups.

'Come on Ella, she's only a dog,' John, not Ricardo yet, was saying. But it wasn't only a dog. It was a damaged but brave family, a handsome young man with hopeless social skills and his heart on his sleeve, a beautiful girl now horribly disfigured, three year old Donald murdered in brutal circumstances, a brother who preferred animals to people, a mother who hid her heartbreak in a beautiful garden and dinner parties for appalling colonial bigots and a strong and wise father who was doing his best to keep them all together. And they'd been hoping, perhaps even expecting, that Ella could make it better with her optimism and energy. Now it was never going to happen. The young woman felt their pain and was consumed with a guilt that she didn't deserve.

Mike, as usual, the expert at smoothing surface things over (although totally useless when it came to deeper feelings) came to the rescue; they'd put Tana and the pups in the jeep and go to a 'nice place' for tea. How many times might the Kilpatricks have had to do that throughout the years of Mau Mau? Go to a 'nice place' and everything will be all right. They went to the Tea Hotel; that was where Mike had announced that he was probably going to marry Ella but it was here that he would say good bye to her forever. The irony hadn't escaped Ella.

Yes, tea on the terrace overlooking the green carpet of the estates was pleasant and uplifting but Mike wasn't going to mince his words. After the 'niceties' were over and they were drinking tea from fine china he announced rather pompously,

'You two won't be able to get married of course.'

Ella gasped but John was ready with a question the answer to which he predicted he could shoot down easily.

'And why not, Mike?'

'Because it will break her father's heart. He confessed to my father that the only thing that he prayed would never happen was that Ella would marry a black.'

It was John's turn to flinch. It hadn't been the answer he'd expected. Ella however, recovering quickly from the shock of finding out something about her father that she truly didn't know, was now angry enough to fight. And angry enough with Mike to know that she could never, but never, have married him.

'And what if it would break *my* heart *not* to marry John?' Ella protested in a loud and confident voice.

'There's no answer to that, is there?' … After a stony silence that seemed to go on forever Mike announced, 'I think it's probably time to go,'

As they all stood up to leave Mike shook hands with John and said, 'Make sure that the better man has won. Look after her.' John, now Ricardo, fixed Mike with a hard gaze and said, 'You can be quite certain that I will.'

After a few fond farewells to Tana, the puppies and Simba and a more polite farewell to Mike, Ricardo (she had to get used to it) and Ella set off to meet the family in Kisumu. The long–the very long–journey had begun.

When Ella and Ricardo (there, she'd remembered–and the days of John the spy were gone forever) arrived at the sprawling bungalow in the Indian neighbourhood which was the family home, it was dark. Ricardo's father was sitting on the verandah keeping well away from activities in the kitchen. Ella was aware of a massive morning glory winding its way over a trellis before she was ushered in to be welcomed into the bosom of the family–literally. Dad, paunchy but tall, Mum tidying her hair back into its Spanish style bun as she pulled off her apron then Agnelo, Jos, Carlos and little Rosie in height and age order lined up to give Ricky's friend Ella a massive Goaencar hug. Any friend of Ricky's deserved the warmest welcome they could extend. Ella was overwhelmed but delighted. She wondered if it would have been very different if they had known there were distant wedding bells in the air.

'Ricky says you'll be going back to Scotland soon. Have you enjoyed your contract?' This was big brother Agnelo taking charge.

Ella answered truthfully, 'It's been the most amazing experience of my life. I'm just wondering what it's going to be like when I get back to the snow and the long dark nights. But I've got a job fixed up so I won't have time to brood.' She could see Ricardo's Mum and Dad relaxing–they must have decided she posed no threat to their son. After that, with her easy manner, Ella got along well with everyone, especially little Rosie who loved all her funny stories about school and her travels as a 'tourist' expatriate in Kenya. The few days flew by with tennis games for the four sporty brothers, a fishing trip where Mummy wielded the frying pan by the riverside, card games with Rosie who taught Ella a new game 'fulus' which was not too different from flush. Food, with all its exotic names, was delicious but remained a mystery. As a guest, Ella was never allowed near the kitchen.

The only criticism was that Ella in her home stitched kitenge dress and rubber flip flops (now called chapals) was too scruffy to take to church. She did have some jeans and a T shirt and the leather chapals which she wore when she was 'dressed' but this was not suitable for Our Lady and St Joseph Catholic Church.

'Sorry, I'm afraid I've packed most things and shipped them already,' she lied convincingly. High fashion had never been Ella's strong point. Decency (for going into town) meant a kitenge round the waist to cover the mini skirt with your money tied in a knot in the corner. This was not the moment to mention that, however. The solution was found. Oscar de Souza, Dad's best friend and tennis partner of old was visiting and as a master tailor was carrying a tape measure in his pocket. Two seconds later a confused Ella had her arms in the air and hardly noticed she'd been measured up.

'What's your favourite colour, Ella?'

'Green I suppose,'

Rosie, Ella and Ricardo had gone down to the bazaar and bought some black shoes with a little heel and no open toes. Ella hated them and was to nurse the blisters they gave her for a long time despite them being half a size too big. Flip flops in hot weather were what suited her Scottish feet. But the black shoes were decent enough for church. Next day Oscar arrived with a neat little sleeveless dress with darts in all the right places and a hemline demurely on the knee–unlike her other 1960s minis. It fitted her perfectly like no bought dress had ever done and was in a shiny material with an emerald green pattern on a white background. Ella tried to insist on paying for it but Oscar wouldn't hear of it. Later on, Ricardo told her a bottle of whisky instead would do the trick–so Ella felt better about it. The most memorable and amusing part of the weekend, however, had been the trip to Our Lady and

St Joseph church. Roads, in Kisumu, were not the best in the world in 1969 and very often there were drainage ditches up to six feet deep or more located quite close to the edge of a road and there was no particular pattern as to where these might be. Parking was equally haphazard. You simply drew up and stopped at a reasonable distance away from where you wanted to walk. You just had to make sure you were well away from the middle of the road. Ricardo had wanted to take his visitor as close to the Church as possible since she was decked out in her new dress and borrowed white shawl with which she could cover her head and or shoulders as she wished. He had drawn up swiftly and jumped out expecting Ella to do the same thing. She had–except she had opened the front passenger door and stepped confidently into fresh air and landed neatly at the bottom of a six foot culvert. She couldn't move or speak, not because she was hurt but because she was paralysed with laughter.

'Has anyone seen Ella?' Ricardo had asked flummoxed.

'I'm down here,' a slightly winded and giggling Ella finally managed to say. 'I can't get out. You'll have to help me.'

Fortunately the weather was dry so most of the red dust brushed off but it was a rather ruffled Ella, rather than the perfect one that all the effort had gone into, who joined the family pew at Our Lady and St Joseph Church for all the Kisumu Goaencars to stare at curiously. Without a doubt, Ella had left a lasting impression on Ricardo John's family. When it was time for her to leave for Kericho and then on to Nairobi to catch her flight home in time for Christmas, they were as sad to see her go as she was to leave them.

Ricardo was with her all the way, helping her to deliver her car to Joginder Singh and transporting her luggage, including the now battered old guitar, down the bumpy road to Nairobi for the last time. They sang all the way, the songs people sang after generators and record players went silent and candles in wine bottles were lit: protest songs like 'Blowin in the Wind', Beatles songs like 'Hey Jude', songs they shared like 'The Windmills of my Mind', Scottish lilts like 'The Dark Island' and inevitably, 'Leaving on a Jet Plane' which made Ella cry and then laugh when John Ricardo pointed out,

'Planes do fly to Zambia – should you ever think about that.'

'I'll have to find out if my soul's in the soil of the land of my birth, first', Ella said with a touch of melodrama and a twinkle.

'Do you believe what that Kilpatrick said about your father?' Ricardo John asked suddenly serious. Ella considered her answer for a long time.

'I'll be very disappointed if it is true. Maybe it was just Mike's way of hurting us – oh, I don't know.'

The songs stopped and the silence in the car was ominous. The apprehensive lovers, sorry to leave each other, unsure if they would ever meet again and what trials they would have to face if they did make a future together, treated themselves to a dinner dance bed and breakfast at a sophisticated hotel. It was the perfect formula for romance and passion. Ricardo and Ella's new song which they danced to over and again was 'Malaika'. In Swahili that means 'My Angel'.

Neither knew what the future would hold so they clung to each other as if their lives depended on it.

CHAPTER 25

In Retrospect

AUGUST 2006

I can't believe it has been thirty eight years since all that happened. It seems like only yesterday. At the moment I'm working
on how best to tell the tale of what took place over the few years
that followed which could easily fill another couple of books.

To cut a long story short for now, life in Caithness after the
euphoria of being back among loved ones and being treated
like a mini celebrity, didn't quite inspire me to stay there.
My dad tried hard to find me a nice Wellington-booted rich
farmer and Ricky John Francis Fonseca my husband always
says he rescued me from that fate.

Perhaps if I'd never left Caithness I wouldn't have changed;
at first I thought everyone else had changed but they hadn't–
and I didn't want to turn into a 'when I was in Africa' type of
person.

Ricky found me a job in a mission school where the nuns might turn me into a good Catholic (difficult) and I took that 'jet plane' to Zambia so here we are thirty eight years later in a leafy North London suburb having got here via the metaphorical North Pole and a few other exciting places. We've had our adventures and our struggles–many of them interesting or amusing or just bizarre–but those tales will have to wait for another occasion.

For the record, Shona Kilpatrick and Mary Mackay (my Mum) exchanged letters for a few years and I was allowed some snippets of news: Michael married a Swedish girl called Inga, Drew married a vet called Emily who was helping him to run an animal orphanage and ' Nan (whom you (Mary) didn't meet) has had a book of drawings published.' When a copy was sent as a present, I was shocked to recognise my own face smiling back at me. To use Jan and Bob's lingo from across the pond, 'It all figured.' I should probably feel grateful that some of the other confidences they unburdened on each other weren't shared with me.

Now that retirement has come there's time to reflect. Did we make any difference to young Kenya with all our enthusiasm and hopes and dreams? We follow progress out there sometimes with despair but at times with hope. In 1977, for example, Wangari Maathai and some rural women, risking death, armed with spades began planting trees as a symbolic protest against illegal logging and corrupt exploitation of Kenya's resources. By 2004 Wangari had won a Nobel Peace Prize and Wanjira, her daughter, had spread the news worldwide of the Mazingira (Environment) Green Party better known as the Green Belt Movement with its 'a million trees a million dreams' slogan.

As for the rest of our planet–are there any real solutions to the problems or is the world still blowing in the wind? Will humanity find the common threads that tie us all together?

Can we envisage globalisation for the common good? Can we find that intangible ingredient which is essential for the further evolution of humanity? Could we destroy our world before we make it a better place? War, pollution, environmental degradation, global warming, climate change, poverty, discrimination and exploitation–it's all happening. Negative sweeping statements and accusations abound but in little corners in far flung places there are countless individual success stories which add up. For every destructive force there is a creative force, for every divisive action there is one that draws people together.

I like to think that in our own little corner, in our own little way, our little family might just have helped the melting pot of cultural fusion along its way. It's been a happy home with a welcome for all the different creeds and colours this cosmopolitan earth has to offer. It just happened that way and it felt like the most natural thing in the world.

Also, just before retiring from teaching in the local 'just out of special measures' comprehensive–probably London's most multicultural school, I had to write one more 'Life in the Day of'–to add to the ones written at Balnahuig Primary School and Kipsigis Girls' School in my first year of teaching.

A Life in the Day of Ella Fonseca

June 2006

*My body wakes up before my brain does because my bladder dictates it and I shuffle off to the bathroom. At least there's no queue nowadays since our only daughter Molly has gambolled off to new pastures without a backward bleat. We call her the **laat lamekin**–an Afrikaans endearment meaning 'late lamb'–the child of ageing parents. We picked up this expression in South Africa two years ago on our last holiday together as 'Paw, Maw and the (not so) Wee un'–that reference for you Sunday Post reading Scots.*

It's only 5:00am, still dark and chilly, so I totter off back to the

279

bedroom relishing the prospect of another blissful couple of hours of anxiety-free sleep delightfully infused with pipe dreams. Mind over matter equals dream fulfilment–but only until you wake up. But Ricky, my husband of 35 years, is on my side of the bed and he's got the entire duvet so I have to pull it back to his side and nudge him over from my bit of the bed without waking him or bang goes that extra sleep.

'I was playing golf with Tiger Woods until you woke me up,' he grumps.

'Were you winning?' I mutter. I've heard it before.

'No. He was laughing.'

'Was he laughing at you?' I reply. I play along with the little fantasy. It seems we're both on pipe dreams these days.

'Yeah. The same as I was laughing at Jack playing scrabble yesterday.'

I don't comment as that might lead to some more gleeful gloating. Ricky never tires of trouncing his fellow competitors in the North London Scrabble Championship.

'Go back to sleep,' I mumble. 'It's still midnight!'

We're wasting valuable sleep perchance to dream time here. We both snuggle down, back to back, duvet up to the chin.

But the brain has kicked in by now with all its worries and deadlines. The pipe dreams evaporate and that overflowing filing cabinet creeps into view.

'It's not the work you **have** done that makes you tired. It's the work you **haven't** done,' I hear my mother's voice emanating from beyond the grave and I wonder how many times I've harangued my less than willing pupils in the local comprehensive with this cry.

If it's Saturday, mind over matter can banish the thought. Otherwise action-planning mode kicks in and that's the end of the dreamy bliss. I switch on Radio 4 even before the alarm is due to come on–to try and take my mind off the almost definite hassle of the day ahead by listening to what is happening in that world out there that I'm not responsible for and can opt out of if I so choose.

It works for a while and then, there's nothing for it; it's time to get up and get on.

A hot bath later and the old joints and muscles are moving more smoothly now. It's really time to retire but we'll soldier on until July. We'll manage that, my bones and I, and even my brain should probably cope despite the odd senior moment.

'Miss, we haven't got registers!'

'What did I say? Oh, get out your **diaries** I meant. Hey, look after me here please. I'm an old lady!'

There's one little 'Okay Miss' but otherwise there's an ominous silence. Nobody's coming up with, 'You're not old Miss,' so I'm hoping they'll give me a break and start looking after me. No such luck. Silent reading is interrupted by Damien De Monteford, pint-sized bombshell, tumbling into class like a ton of bricks falling off a lorry. The De Monteford bit has connotations of academia which are definitely delusional but the demonic bit is fairly accurate. Why is it that all the boys called Damien tend to have behaviour problems? And why is it that they're closely followed by the Lees and the Waynes? Could someone please explain this to me?

'Late detention this afternoon, Damien,' I say in what I hope is a distant, inscrutable tone—the one that's supposed to be intimidating. I usually don't fool anyone.

'I can't Miss. My dad's waiting to take me to the doctor's today.'

'I'll ring him and check then, shall I?'

'Never mind, I'll do the detention miss.' This is followed by a wide, engaging grin.

I've just noticed another engaging grin and it's Dwayne, hoping I haven't seen the non-uniform trainers and the lack of school blazer.

'Uniform detention, Dwayne.'

'**Gorranote** Miss.' And he has, of course. 'Mrs Bloke is looking for a second hand blazer for me, Miss.'

What can I say? Mrs Bloke is the pupil services officer and she's the one who really runs the school, despite the protestations of the posers and the preachers in the Senior Management Team.

In our school there's an ailment that most of the teachers seem to be suffering from at the moment. I call it 'tenitis'. Every school has *one. That's the year group, all 200 hundred of them, who strike dread in the minds and fear in the hearts of anyone involved with them. Such a year comes around every few years, like a tidal wave, and it takes five years, from Years 7 to 11, for them to go through school like a dose of salts. If the school's really unlucky, the remnants continue to wreak havoc in the sixth form. The fashionable terminology would describe them as 'emotionally unintelligent'. Hmm.*

Right now, our school has just such a group and they're currently in Year 10. Hence the 'tenitis'. There's a further complication which I have named 'tendiitis' which is an acute form of tenitis. I'm right there. For my sins I have been co-tutor, form tutor, co -tutor, form tutor and now co-tutor of Form 10D since they were in 7D. Hence the 10Ditis. The disease has put paid to five tutors but I have survived, the only survivor, and I'm full of hope for my colleague, Helga, who is lucky enough to be co-tutoring them—for the moment. As I said before, it's really time to retire but we'll carry on, my waning sense of humour and I. Helga is younger, tougher and still optimistic enough to take them through year 11 and their GCSEs—but, by that time I'll be long gone, pottering into the sunset—though maybe with a gleeful backward glance from time to time -perhaps. There goes the bell. That's the worst bit of the day over.

*I rush to the sanctuary of the small group of EAL learners whose friendly smiles and enthusiasm more than make up for the rest of the rogues. EAL stands for 'English as an Additional Language' which speaks for itself. These kids arrive during the year from all corners of the world and are the most highly motivated and beautifully mannered in the school because they have to pull themselves up by the bootstraps to survive. They actually **want** to learn. They need to be accepted by teachers and are desperate to fit in with their peers- and their peers know this—which explains what happens first.*

Within a week, Abdul, Leonora, Chi Wai and all the other little 'New to English' darlings have acquired every F, C and B word the London-born Damiens and Courtneys can think of . Within a month, their spoken grammar is appalling and 'ain't done nuffink' and 'innit' are tripping off their lips in a very fluent fashion. This is what we call Language Acquisition. Language Development is when we have to work hard to undo the damage.

What happens in the end is often amazing and always very rewarding. The EAL pupils cotton on, work hard and outstrip their friends- but not before a bit of trauma has been gone through.

It's lunchtime and time for EAL pupils to come for help with homework, play language games on the computer or just escape from the rough and tumble of the playground. It's my duty day.

'Mees Fonseca, beeg boy takeeng peece out of me! I not like it.'

I know exactly what she's trying to say and I also have a good idea which big boy might be taking the piss out of her.

'Is it the tall boy with the blonde hair?' I ask, arm above my head to demonstrate tall and pointing to her own blonde hair to show what blonde means.

'Yes, Mees, he say I stoopid I not speekee Eenglish.'

'So what did you say? '

'Notheeng. After ten times I keek him on leg. I say **he** stoopid.'

There has obviously been a break down in communication here so it's time to activate plan A. Secretly, I admire her spirit and I'm wondering how she lasted as long as ten times, but I don't 'say' that.

Instead I say, ' Irina,' (She's a pretty little Russian girl.) 'You should never kick anyone. Why didn't you come and see me the first time he said that?'

'Sorry Mees, I not know what to do.'

'I didn't know what to do', I instruct, wondering what happened to the lesson on the past simple negative.

'I didn't know what to do,' she repeats obediently but haltingly.

Plan A includes teaching EAL pupils what to say in sticky situations and then finding the bullies and confronting them with what they have done.

After arming Irina with a few key phrases like, 'Actually, I'm learning English very quickly,' and, 'I bet you can't speak Russian', we arrange for the culprit to be delivered to the EAL department–familiar *ground for us but unfamiliar for him.*

He turns out to be not such a bad lad masquerading as a rather unpleasant piece of adolescent arrogance who knows what his rights are but not what his responsibilities might be. He has already gone straight to the top in the shape of the Acting Head Teacher, to complain about this wild Russian girl who has assaulted him.

I ask him to listen to what Irina has to say about how he has upset her and I ask him how he might feel if he had to go to a school in Russia where nobody spoke English. This usually works and he appears to be suitably remorseful. I leave them with a script each so that he can teach Irina some English by acting out a situation about making arrangements to go to somewhere like the cinema, a restaurant or the bowling alley etc. This usually works too and judging by the giggles a little while later, they seem to be getting along just fine. Sorted.

Meanwhile, down in the bowels of the school where the Senior Management Team are ensconced, the Acting Head Teacher has made a big mistake; he has passed the buck to one of his Deputies. This one has neither imagination nor a sense of humour and the flexibility of a toughened steel ramrod. She's fallen hook, line and sinker for the tale of the violent, disturbed Russian girl and is determined to DO SOMETHING ABOUT IT. She rumbles along to find Irina to start the sanctions procedure, convinced it is going to end in exclusion from school at the very least.

First she attacks the EAL department who, in her eyes, are 'responsible' for this fiasco Then she comments on how disgraceful it is that decent boys like Sean O'Leary should have to put up with vicious little Russian girls.

I know better by now than to counteract this tirade so I invite her to come along to the classroom where Sean and Irina are still engrossed, one in teaching and the other in learning and they're obviously quite good friends by now.

'Decent boys don't subject little Russian girls to verbal abuse because they can't speak English,' I say. 'Sean knows that now—and Irina knows she shouldn't kick people in the shins—because she doesn't

have the language to defend herself. She won't do it again and Sean won't be bullying her any more. Look at them.'

'Hi Miss. Y'allright?' pipes up Sean with a grin.

He gets a glare in reply.

'I don't believe you but let it be on your head!' is her last word before she stomps off. Two out of three people have learned a lesson today. I suspect the third person might be uneducable.

It's Year 11 English in the afternoon and I'm so relieved I'm providing in-class support for Harvey Sugar's GCSE class. Firstly I'm exhausted, frustrated, annoyed but perhaps feeling slightly triumphant after the lunchtime altercation and wouldn't have the energy to cope with a class on my own. Secondly, Mr Sugar's lessons are a haven of peace amid the chaos which rules in some other parts of the school. He also has a sense of humour.

'Obi!' Obi is wearing the latest fashion accessory on his head. It looks like one of those stockings that robbers used to wear to disguise themselves–except it only covers his hair.

'Yessir'. (Hats are not allowed in class.)

'Take that thing off your head. It looks like a condom.'

'Sorry Sir', he replies accompanied by stifled chortles. Nobody dared laugh out loud in Mr. Sugar's lessons.

'You don't want us to think you're a dick head, do you?'

Immediate result! The headgear shoots off his head and hasn't been seen since! But Obi has a sense of humour too. I can hear something between a splutter and a guffaw coming from the direction of his seat.

The others are stunned into silence and the lesson on Arthur Miller's 'A View from the Bridge' continues without further interruption.

The day ends in a wave of tension again today despite my efforts to provide a tiny bit of respite from the military operation which is the day to day reality of a school coming out of Special Measures.

The last confrontation is maintaining silence for the register while diaries and private readers are on the desk and a further expectation is that the thirty or so form tutees will read silently until it is time to go home. I feel this doesn't come naturally to most lively fifteen year olds so, after they are registered I tell them they can pack away and have a few minutes chat before the bell goes.

Just as the bell is about to go a flourish of aforementioned Deputy Head needing to DO SOMETHING ABOUT SOMETHING sweeps through the door, diagnoses the lack of silence as total chaos and bellows at the pupils.

'Stand up Year Ten!' (She doesn't know which form it is.) 'Where are your diaries and readers and why aren't you reading silently?'

'Excuse me,' I say politely hoping that she might infer that I'm implying that she might have considered saying that to me before wading in with both feet. 'I have just allowed them to pack away as the bell is about to go.'

'Well, it hasn't gone yet!' Half way through the process of the pupils taking their books out again, it rings. 'And you can stay here for five more minutes.' She stomps off without a glance.

'Do we have to Miss?' a little voice says politely.

'If you're quiet you can go now—and have a nice evening.' I reply. I reckon one piece of undermining deserves another. I think my form agree by the sound of the cheery good-byes and comments that I could not possibly admit to having overheard.

It isn't my day to do late detention or homework club so I shoot off home in my little green street Ka hoping to be in time for Countdown. I can sometimes manage to get there by the first teatime teaser just when Ricky has put the kettle on. I couldn't survive without him. He is supposed to be semi-retired and working from the loft when he feels like it but he seems to be putting in almost as many hours as when he went to the office. He does take a break for Countdown, however, and luckily for me has developed a passion for cooking.

We both settle down with a big mug of tea and a chocolate digestive and cocoon ourselves in the comfort of a spot of courtesy and culture which for me is a perfect antidote to the cacophonous chaos of the comprehensive. I tell Ricky this and ask if he thinks my bit of alliteration is quite effective and he thinks it is too. Once the Countdown conundrum, crucial or otherwise, has been worked out, usually by

Ricky first, I collapse in a heap on the sofa and wake up half an hour later. This is really a very middle aged thing to do but I tell myself it's a reaction to the stresses and strains of life at school.

If Ricky has cooked, I potter a little preparing a few things for tomorrow's lessons and then we have dinner. If he hasn't cooked, I throw together the quickest stir fry ever, then prepare for tomorrow. At busy times, the pottering can go on all evening which means I really need that half hour's sleep

When there's free time, TV viewing depends on who has charge of the remote control and as this is usually Ricky, I cuddle up on the sofa book in hand and Pepper the pussy under my chin. The alternative is watching replays of the replays of golf, cricket or golf so I let it all act as flickering wallpaper. Today, as can sometimes happen, I fall asleep on the sofa so I get woken up by a paw on my face belonging to a cat that needs feeding before we potter off to bed in search of those pipe dreams again.

You might be wondering where housework features. Well it sort of happens as we go along. I keep a favourite birthday card from my good friend which shows an elegant lady (not like me) on the front announcing, 'Housework? I sweep the room with a glance!' It also has a picture of a handbag labelled 'BETTER THINGS TO DO'. Then a lovely Vietnamese lady called Hai who actually likes housework and doesn't object to some extra money comes on Monday afternoons so when I get home from work, I say, 'Hi Hai' and later 'Bye Hai'—and the house is clean. But most important, for now until I retire (finally) my 'housebound' Ricky hoovers and cooks and talks about his househusbandly duties with pride. I have daughter Molly to thank for persuading her Dad that it's cool to cook. Her gorgeous boyfriend Michael from Manchester does. However Ricky is looking forward to relinquishing fifty percent of his duties as soon as I give up going out to work.

I'd better try to find a new occupation soon. They say housework expands into the time you have to spend on it. This is not going to happen.

As I said, it's time to sleep perchance to dream. Good Night.

DECEMBER 1ST 2006

Now, since retiring in July, I'm missing all the cultural fusion in that comprehensive school where on Valentine's Day we could say I love you in a hundred languages. Sometimes, however, tolerance went too far as when Clare, a white English girl, felt she couldn't prepare an item for International Evening because she was *'only'* English. Happily, on that occasion, she was persuaded to come up with a couple of songs including 'An English Country Garden' and she declared that she was proud to welcome so many people from so many other countries to *her* country. She got the biggest cheer of the evening and Ella Fonseca cried like a baby, behind the scenes where nobody could see.

As I said before, I like to think we've got our own brand of fusion at home. Ricky, a Goan, probably some kind of mixture of Portuguese and Hindu or Moslem Indian and Ella, that's me, likely to be some kind of mixture of Viking, Celt and Norman, got married and produced a beautiful daughter, Molly, who has only a tiny trace of her mother's flaming red hair. Molly is in love with a blonde, blue-eyed English boy, Michael, who is likely to be a mixture of Angle, Saxon and Viking. In theory they could have a red-headed baby. Another interesting bit of fusion in the family is that Rick's nephew, Sean Fonseca married Sarah, a granddaughter of Mzee Jomo Kenyatta himself.

That brings me back to 1953 when wee Ella asked the question, 'Why are we all different?' and Mr Cameron told her it was all to do with people crossing the sea and that it was good to be different: he told the little ones that we're all different but we're all equal. It was fusion then and, now that fifteen percent of the children in that London comprehensive of 2006 are of mixed race, it is fusion today. The point is most people welcome this or think it just doesn't matter.

Was migration right or wrong? Who knows? However, I will always remain convinced that it is wrong for one society to trample on the beliefs of another and then pull them up by the roots and leave the people to flounder in an alien society. By the time the world began to realise what had happened in Africa and what was still happening, was it too late to pick up the pieces? Unfortunately, the lost babes in the white man's wood are still being exploited by the unseen faces behind the huge multinational companies that control the world economy because money talks. Africa has truly developed the West. The richest continent in the world in natural resources is still being systematically drained of those resources by ruthless businessmen who would make the corruptions of the African politicians, who are being blamed for the self destruction of their own countries seem like drops in the ocean of world-wide, financial skulduggery. The Tom Mboyas of this world knew this and some of them, like Tom Mboya, died. If he had lived would Kenya have been a better place? Perhaps– or perhaps it would have disintegrated into civil war. Who knows? From where I stood then in 1968 I saw the remnants of a beautiful and harmonious rural society based on sharing and mutual respect which was named African Socialism. It had been going on for centuries peacefully bar the odd skir-mish over land or cattle. History records what happened next. East Africa long before 1969 had developed into three differ-ent countries carved out by the colonists. Queen Victoria had even had the audacity to present the Kaiser with the gift of Mount Kilimanjaro which explains the funny kink in the bor-der. (Perhaps that myth simply illustrates how arbitrary the borders were.) Tribal lands were ruthlessly cut in half and no-madic pastoralists ignored the borders.

Tanzania became the socialist country under Nyerere which developed relatively harmoniously, Kenya became the capitalist country where JM Kariuki, Mboya's friend, said he didn't want to live because it had ten millionaires and ten mil-lion starving, Uganda's nightmare regime was led by the gold smuggler Milton Obote closely followed by the murderous despot, Idi Amin.

History keeps on repeating itself. Men greedy for territory, gold or power have gone to war and when some succeed in getting more than their fair share, those deprived rise up in arms–or those who would protect them do so on their behalf.

Ewan Cameron had survived the war to end all wars and had a spectacular war wound to show for it. He taught his pupils to hope and to fight for truth and justice and to believe in universal kinship.

From where I'm standing now, in 2006, I see rich countries giving many (but not all) of their children too much too soon while in poor countries many (but not all) children are de-prived or dying because they are getting too little too late. I see powerful nations sending other people's sons and daugh-ters to fight wars that are not of their making and which can never be won. I see war leading to more war and sometimes in the name of religion–a never ending cycle.

Something from my dim and distant past drew me back to Kenya described by some as the cradle of mankind. I studied Ngũgĩ all over again and he is still a magical author. It is tragic that he lives in exile.

Research threw up a few surprises. The little town of Kericho which I came to know so well was host to the FOURTH INTERNATIONAL CONFERENCE ON AN INTERFAITH PERSPECTIVE ON GLOBALISATION in 2005. The confer-ence was held in Africa's largest Gurudwara or Sikh place of worship and it was chaired by an Iran born intellectual, Dr Kamran Mofid. The theme was 'Globalisation for the Common Good'. So some people are doing some good things around the world. But are there enough? For the moment I feel hope-ful that this is yet another piece of evidence to suggest that the world might be finally pointing in the direction of fusion.

While flicking through 'The Week' which claims to tell you 'all you need to know about everything that matters', I came across the face of a man who could be said to owe his success to among others, Tom Mboya and Mwalimu Gloria, Granny of the airlifts. His name is Barack Obama. His latest book is called 'The Audacity of Hope'. He is black as his father was Kenyan but he is also white because his mother is from Kansas. His father, also Barack Obama, was one of the students airlifted with the help of the funding from the Kennedy Foundation that Tom Mboya helped to arrange. Mwalimu Gloria prepared him for the flight and for his studies in America. The article in 'The Week' is headed, 'Is this the face of America's next president?'

Gloria Hagberg, aged 94, still lives in Nairobi. Wouldn't it be wonderful if she lived to see the day that the son of one of her Kenyan students became President of the USA?

That would be more than fusion. That would be justice.

CHAPTER 26

Fusion

Ella Fonseca had typed the last sentence of the last chapter of her first novel or so she thought. It was a short sentence but she felt that it spoke volumes. Just as she had been compelled to start writing she now felt the story had to end there with a hope for future justice and the harmonious mingling of migrants of many creeds and colours.

Then she realised that this was not an ending; it was a beginning. The story had hardly scraped the surface of the concept of cultural fusion. The story of Isabella Mackay was only one story of a girl uprooted from isolation. There were millions of migrants with amazing stories to tell. There were melting pots in metropolitan cities all over the world and Ella had often been reminded of her old auntie's words,

'Give it a century and we'll all be coffee coloured.'

The novel wasn't finished. There wasn't enough fusion in

'Fusion' without one more chapter. She felt it wasn't clear what she meant by 'That would be justice'.

She had to tell the world about what was going on in her daily life that would never have been going on if she hadn't got on a plane in 1968 and jetted off to Kenya leaving her sheltered Caithness existence behind. She wanted to tell the world how proud she was of Molly, who had inherited a tiny touch of auburn in her dark locks and a hint of greenish hazel in her dark eyes. Molly, who in her mother's biased eyes, was the prettiest of the Fonseca and Fernandes cousins who'd been seated with their parents in a very long row in a Catholic church in rural Northamptonshire at Midnight Mass. Molly's fair skin and bright smile shone across at her mother at the other end of the row. Ella too was conspicuous by her light skin amid the dark skin of the Goans–but now, in 2006, she was regarded with kindly acceptance by the local very English community.

She wanted to shout from the rooftops about how proud she was when Molly had eagerly answered a question which a young Irish priest had designed to inveigle his seven year old first holy communicants into saying how proud they would be to belong to the Catholic Church.

'I belong to the world,' Molly had said, her little hand waving frantically in the air. The young priest had been floored and had asked if Ella felt this was a childish answer or a well considered one. Ella, of course, had told him that it had to be the latter because Molly had been well taught about the equality of the races and the need for respect for all cultures. ('Thank you Mr Cameron,' Isabella Mackay Fonseca had whispered inwardly thinking of the big world map at Balnahuig School in 1953.)

'We had to explain,' Ella had told the priest, 'why it was all right for Daddy to be brown and Mummy to be white.'

She wanted to tell the world how angry she had been thirty five years ago at the prophets of doom whose ignorance had come up with phrases like 'abhorrent miscegenation' or 'half caste' or 'half breed' when Ella and Ricardo had announced their engagement to be married. She wanted to say how hurt she felt when her father had said, in all sincerity, 'You do re-alise that the two of you will be on the edges of two societies but you won't be accepted by either.' And to show just how good a father he was he had added, 'Even though you've bro-ken my heart, my door will be open to you when you need to come home.' She needed to point out how wrong and hurt-ful her brother Jamie had been when he had said, 'If you get married, it might be fine for you and Ricky but it wouldn't be fair of you to have children.' At that point, Ella was in her safe place 'between'–away from the world–protecting her-self. If it hadn't been Jamie, the brother she loved, she might have lashed out in anger and pointed out that he would be the first to admit that cross-breeding cattle was a good thing so why shouldn't it be the same for people? Had he not been there during Ewan Cameron's lessons on why the Balnahuig bairns all looked different? Had he not been the one who had asked, 'How does it work for dogs, Mr Cameron?' But she had kept quiet preferring to let things unfold in a way that she knew it would–and she felt sure that she would eventually have the satisfaction of listening to Jamie eating his words. He may even have forgotten that he had ever said such a horrible thing. In 2007, she wondered what he had to say about labra-doodles, the new designer dogs.

This novel had to announce Ella and Ricardo's glee when yet another celebrity or super athlete of mixed race hit the headlines: Dame Kelly Holmes, Jamaican mother and English mother, double gold medallist to add to the list headed by Daley Thompson MBE CBE, Nigerian father and Scottish mother and the first athlete to hold Olympic, World, European and Commonwealth titles simultaneously. Tiger Woods is in-teresting; his heritage includes an exotic one quarter Chinese, one quarter Thai, one quarter African American, one eighth Native American and one eighth Dutch. Peter Ustinov. Tina Turner, Yul Brynner, Ben Kingsley, Elizabeth Barrett Browning, Shirley Bassey, Halle Berry, Naomi Campbell, Cameron Diaz, Robert Mitchum, Elvis Presley, Iain Duncan-Smith, Colin Powell, Malcolm X, Rahul Gandhi, Kiri Te Kanawa, Enrique Iglesias, Jamie Cullum, Monica Ali, Keanu Reeves, Alexandre Dumas, Craig David and Molly Fonseca can be added to the list of successful people of mixed-race.

Thirty five years ago Ella and Ricardo had not predicted the twenty first century 'public fascination' with inter-ethnic relationships referred to by Professor Berthoud of the Institute of Social and Economic reform at Essex University. They had set off rather fearfully on their journey through what they expected to be a hostile society with few open doors.

But the 'intermix boom' has arrived in UK in the early years of this third millennium. Britain has one of the fastest growing mixed race populations in the world and the trend is likely to continue given the countless examples of mixed race relationships in TV dramas which reach into every living room in the country.

Teilhard de Chardin, Tagore, Gerald Heard, Mano Singham, Dr Kamran Mofid and countless other visionaries, philosophers and theologians have predicted some kind of coming together of all the peoples of the world for which they have given different titles like Humanism, Human Socialisation, Human Totalisation or Unanimisation, Religious Globalisation or Spiritual Evolution–to name a few. Somewhere up there on that higher plane, during her philosophy studies, Ella had been only vaguely aware of their abstract ramblings and mystical ideas which had a beautiful message which she never really believed could come true. Yet, one thought was coming through in her moments of reflection. Had the Darwinists and the evolutionary psychologists said that human nature had evolved from the 'survival of the fittest' instinct to an ethic based on mutually beneficial co-operation? Could this be happening? In 1997 in UK half the African or Caribbean men and one third of the black women had white partners and a fifth of Asian men and a tenth of Asian women had white partners. Why? Is it a basic, uncontrollable human instinct to diversify and widen the gene pool? Is it a rational decision made by evolved human beings to help them move towards utilitarianism–to provide the greatest good for the greatest number? Or, is there a conspiracy to manipulate the masses through the media into adopting a global, race blind, unified human species? (Ella, even in her most fanciful frame of mind, couldn't quite contemplate the latter.) Another argument she couldn't come to terms with was that 'God wants us to diversify so that human beings can evolve'. There were too many assumptions attached to that one.

But what's happening with religion? Are all the religions and philosophies embracing each other too? The Queen referred to 'our richly multicultural and multi faith society' with pride–but clearly not everyone believes that different faiths and cultures existing in a segregated fashion are the best way forward–so what's next? Will it be an all embracing global philosophy tied together by the common threads of moral codes from all the established mythical religions? Or will it be a totally new 'moral consciousness' which has little to do with traditional faith and much to do with a rational set of rules for the survival of cosmopolitan humanity beyond nationality? Or will mankind evolve into what Gerald Heard called 'leptoid' man who will leap into a wider consciousness freed from guilt or repression or the need to believe in life after death or mythical gods?

Ella clambered off her cloud number nine and decided there was perhaps enough fusion in 'Fusion' to justify its title.

Now it was time enjoy the first Christmas season of her retirement. Over the thirty five years of their marriage Ricardo and Ella had climbed the walls of convention and gathered a motley (in the nicest possible sense) crew of interesting and mostly like-minded friends.

By the end of the following few weeks, with her senses sharpened by her plunge into her long abandoned 'place in between' with its more mature and heightened philosophical awareness, Ella was going to look back and wonder if by most people's standards, it had been by no means a 'normal' few weeks.

First the Christmas parcels were posted off to the wee bairns on the Mackay side of the family. Thinking of the little Mackays brought Ella back to the isolation of her own childhood–before she had ever seen a person with a different skin colour. An image then sprang to mind of a bus journey she had taken in Kenya, thirty eight years before, when lots of little African children had been queuing up to stroke her soft red hair. These children had never seen such hair or skin. Two years later, in Zambia, Ella recalled being wakened up in the middle of the night aware that someone was in her bedroom and a little shadow was fumbling around at her back. As quickly and quietly as it had appeared, it had disappeared. By the morning she had dismissed it as a dream but when she told the story, one or two people were quite certain about what had happened. They were sure the culprit had been a small African child trying to confirm the rumour that, hidden under their clothes, white people had long tails like colobus monkeys. As she was contemplating that thought, Ella realised how much the world had changed since then. Were there any corners of the world where people had never seen different races?

'No more "book",' Ella told herself. 'Let's get back to reality!'

But that reality was 'fusion' all over the place. The social calendar read:

Sunday Dec. 9th: Mayor's Festival of Many Cultures
Monday: Zoey's birthday dinner (take a pud)
Wednesday: Chicken Shed Panto (inclusive theatre)
Friday: Dinner at Nisha and Ashok's with Shoba
              and Ajit
Saturday: Amrita and Altaaf's wedding–Moslem bit
Sunday: Meet Molly's outlaws in Manchester
Friday 22nd: Neighbours at home
Christmas Eve: Northampton so Molly can cook +
              Midnight Mass
Christmas Day: Kids do Christmas at Rosie's. Yes!
Sat 30th: Molly's Michael + more mates come
New Year's Eve: Golf Club Dinner Dance
Sat Jan 27th: Brentfield Rotary Club Burns Supper

'No more laptop, green eyes,' Ricardo said to his normally extrovert wife whose book he'd been dipping into. 'Let's just have fun with the fusion. There's plenty of it.' That was how the two cosmopolites, Ricky and Ella, joined together to play 'Spot the Fusion'. There was fusion on TV, fusion at the supermarket, in the newspapers, among the neighbours, on the streets; the stuff was everywhere. It had been there for some time but they hadn't really paid much attention to it. The social calendar was stuffed with fusion. There wasn't a single evening without it; even the neighbours were a cosmopolitan lot. Twenty five years ago, Ricky had been the first non-white in the street and he and Ella had joked over the American phrase, 'There goes the neighbourhood.'

On Sunday evening there were nine Mayors in the front row at the Metropolitan Peel Centre of whom four were ladies, one Mayor was Jewish, one Nigerian, one British Indian, one British Caribbean and the others white. The occasion was a multicultural festival of song and dance. All cultures and colours were represented. As the lady Mayor, Esther Goldstein began by saying, 'Today was all about getting together in unity.' One surprise for Ricky and Ella were the Bollywood UK champions. The girls dancing to 'Sayna Sayna' and 'Gujerali' were six milky skinned blondes.

'That's a different view on fusion,' Ricky said before Ella could.

Friday night at Nisha and Ashok's new house promised to be interesting. Nisha, the Nepalese princess married to the Hindu Bengali professor (of Evolutionary Psychology) had invited the Sikh couple Shoba and Ajit along with the Scottish Ella and Goan Ricky to dinner with no doubt some highbrow chat. True to form the small talk didn't last long and the group were soon involved in a lively discussion on whether secularism was the best ethos for a multi faith school and how the youth could be turned into good global citizens. Solutions included moderating all the traditional religions so that they would not stray too far from the evolving global culture which would consist of a transcendentalist world view. This was highfalutin stuff and Ella was sure she hadn't been the instigator.

'You'll never get the Muslims to moderate their views,' a more than usually dogmatic Ricky declared. 'The Koran tells them they must fight against all other religions until Islam dominates.' (He was entering into the spirit of the argument.)

'Absolutely true,' Ajit joined in. 'They're brainwashed and they can never understand democracy.'

Shoba came back with, 'Come on, most Moslems we know are perfectly reasonable, law abiding citizens who hate what the terrorists are doing.'

'I'm sorry but I think Ricky and Ajit are right,' Professor Ashok Naipur continued in a low voice of authority. 'There can be no appeasement. Unless the rest of the world realises that it isn't money or territory or oil or anything else but Allah that's driving the suicide bomber to commit these atrocities we are nowhere near finding a solution. The Koran was suited to the Middle Ages but today you can't have a closed dogma with no freedom to question and this religion still cultivates medieval and dangerous aggression as it has done throughout the centuries.'

'Okay, suppose the world does realise this. What *is* the solution?' Ella asked.

'Highly intensive cognitive behavioural restructuring therapies and psychological warfare to break the closed Islamic paradigm,' tripped off the tongue of the professor.

'Isn't that brainwashing?' Ella asked holding her fingers to her temples. Did anyone else feel like screaming?

'Sounds like hypnotism to me,' Nisha piped up. 'You can't do that.'

'It's either that or be forced into a world where Jihadi terrorism rules unless Islam dominates.' Ashok added expecting it to be the last word on the matter.

'Why can't we just take the best bits of all the established faiths and get on with it,' Nisha suggested.

'That's what the little kids do.' Shoba added. 'There's enough of a consensus about moral codes for it to work.'

'Huh,' Ricky the Catholic threw in. 'The Muslims are just waiting for the other faiths to weaken and leave the West in limbo before they pounce and take over. And if we question our own religion we weaken it.'

'Nonsense,' interjected Ella. 'Nobody ever got anywhere without questioning beliefs. If you ask me there's a lot wrong with both Islam and Catholicism because it goes against nature to keep young Muslim men and Catholic priests away from sex. All that pent up sexual frustration is bound to take its toll. Suicide bombers or paedophile priests—I don't know which are worse.'

'Now, who's talking nonsense?'

Despite it being a matter of great ethical concern, the group allowed themselves to laugh.

'I'm not so sure it is nonsense,' Ashok added looking thoughtful.

'How's the book coming along, Ella? Shoba asked to change the subject.

'Well, I thought it was finished but I've just realised it needs another chapter.'

'What's it about?'

'I can't tell you just yet.' Ella had just been overcome by a feeling of foreboding. 'Before there is fusion there needs to be heat,' she mused. Slightly tipsy on red wine Ella foresaw the world in flames and the phoenix rising from the relics of the old mystical religions freed from guilt and repression. A cold shiver spread through her and she wasn't ready to share her thoughts.

'We're going to a wedding tomorrow,' Ricky swiftly announced respecting Ella's reticence and getting her out of a jam. 'The daughter of my Hindu best man is marrying her Moslem professor.

'And his father was a Sunni and his mother's a Shia–and she lives in Swindon,' Ella added, coming back to earth with a bump.

Ricky, like all good Fonsecas, enjoyed a few drinks at celebrations and he had only one complaint about the Moslem Wedding. 'The one day I'm offered a lift from door to door, both ways, and it has to be a dry day! How about that?' he yelled in mock pain. 'But wasn't it a great day? Lovely people aren't they?' he added meaning every word.

'One more step in the right direction,' Ella reflected inwardly. 'There might be fusion without too much heat after all.'

Out loud she said, 'And now we've got another big day tomorrow. We have to be in Manchester by half past twelve to meet Mike's parents.'

Lunch went well and when the bill came Ricky tried to pay it but Mike's dad jumped in, 'I'll have that one. You can have the next one; it might be a wedding.' They agreed to split the bill and both sets of parents expressed their approval of their offspring's choice of partner.

Molly and Mike were spending Christmas with their respective families but Mike would come to London for a few days over New Year.

That night safely cuddled up on the London sofa Molly revealed to her mum that Mike's parents didn't go to church but he didn't think they'd mind if she and Mike got married in the Catholic Church.

'More fusion,' Ella let slip.

'What do you mean, Mum?' Molly asked thinking it was something alarming that her mother didn't approve of.

'Well, this book I'm writing,' she answered, ' is about all the people of the world who are embracing each other's beliefs and eventually that might lead to what I'm calling 'fusion' which is the best bits all melted together to make one set of rules that everybody agrees we should all stick to.'

'Heavy,' was the twenty two year old's reply. 'But, you know,' she added in her usual analytical way, 'Come to think of it–it's been happening to me and my friends all our lives– since play school even.'

'Do you know Molly,' Ella said, 'You're absolutely right. I didn't think of it that way.' And she gave her lovely daughter a great big hug.

'You owe me if it gets published, Ma,' Molly said pushing her luck.

'I don't suppose you want to come into your old school tomorrow morning, do you? You can see what the new Head has done to the old place.' Ella said–also pushing her luck.

"Sorry Mum, no can do. I've got far too much sleep to catch up on. Thought I might see you all in the evening,' Molly the party animal replied.

Next day Ella crept into the school she had retired from to deliver some Christmas cards to pigeon holes while she was sure the pupils were safely in class and wouldn't see her. She did bump into the new Head (a fellow Scot) however and his enthusiasm almost persuaded her to consider going back into the rough and tumble–but not quite.

On her way out she came across a wall display of Year seven work entitled CHRISTMAS IN BRITAIN. There were several different illustrated descriptions but the one that caught her attention read:

> *'Christmas in Britain*
> *is when people of all religions*
> *exchange cards and presents*
> *to remind themselves*
> *that it is a time of giving and loving*
> *no matter what religion your family believe in.*
> *It also shows*
> *that we are all the same really.'*

> By Priti Patel 7S

'Out of the mouths of babes,' Ella said to a passing ex colleague–smiling at the profound simplicity of this childlike statement.

'A year ago that one wouldn't have been considered PC enough for a wall display,' the vaguely familiar ex colleague replied. 'It's Ella isn't it? I thought you'd left.'

'I have,' Ella answered.

'Happy Christmas Ella.'

'You too. Enjoy your break.'

As she left the school behind Ella was thinking that Priti's description of Christmas in Britain perhaps doesn't tell the whole story and people might object to the Christian connotations but the process of fusion is constantly bubbling away as it has done since time began. Fair, dark and red-haired fused together into one 'race'. Is it now time for black, brown and white to blend spontaneously for no other reason other than that they want to? Is the human race about to embark on a whole new era in its evolution at the beginning of this third millennium? Ella could envisage the smudging of the lines between the races in the growing number of beautiful children born of more and more mixed parentage and felt a warm glow of satisfaction. She was certain that this commingling which used to be feared would one day, very soon, be celebrated as a triumph of evolutionary progress.

She rushed off home to finish getting ready for Christmas. This year was going to be special because Molly and her Fonseca and Fernandes cousins (and a couple of non-Goan boyfriends and girlfriends of a variety of ethnic backgrounds) had banned the oldies from Rosie's house and had taken over the task of cooking the Christmas lunch. The 'oldies' were quite sure the youngsters would do an excellent job and were more than happy to hand over the reins. It was time to concentrate on living in the melting pot. Fusion was in the air and fusion would breed more fusion–and that was that.

This time the lasting image was of the ever-expanding snowball reaching the top of the mountain and breaking into a thousand pieces of fusion which scattered around reaching into every corner of the world.

THE END

Epilogue

Is the world still blowing in the wind or are things improving? It would appear that over the years all kinds of do-gooders with every good intention have been drawn to the 'cradle of mankind'. To date this has culminated in the first World Social Forum on African soil which took place in Nairobi in January, 2007. They ask, 'Is another world, a better world, possible–a world without war, exploitation, environmental degradation, discrimination or marginalisation?' The whole gamut of human ills was on the agenda. The vision is there. The hard bit is implementing the practicalities. One telling observation was of shiny 4x4s brandishing the logos of well known NGOs from all corners of the rich world but the real grassroots delegates couldn't attend because they were too poor to pay the registration fee.

The speakers included Kenneth Kaunda, very elderly ex president of Zambia and Cora Weiss, extremely wealthy daughter of Samuel Rubin of Faberge fame whose vision was 'the pursuit of peace and justice and the search for an equitable reallocation of the world's resources'. 'K K' at eighty three might be forgiven for being a little out of touch and Cora Weiss, not 'Granny of the Airlifts' as has been suggested, but more 'The Red Queen of Peace' might be forgiven for viewing the plight of the impoverished of Africa as only one of her vast number of undeniably worthy causes throughout the world.

The other 'Granny of the Airlifts' of Kenya, Mwalimu Gloria, is watching in the wings. I'm sure she believes that a better world is possible–but perhaps the road to achieving it is going to be a long and bumpy one. One giant step towards that better world would be the success of the son of one of her protégées–the mixed race candidate for the Presidency of the USA. The significance of his connection with the 'cradle of mankind' might not slip by unnoticed.

Ella Mackay Fonseca is watching too as she *dares to hope* that the dark and brutal side of man's nature will recede and that peace will break out all over the world. In her Utopia the effects of migration and cultural fusion will result in such minute differences between races, creeds and cultures that there would be no longer be any need for war or that desire for power which drives men to manufacture arms for vast profits. The power would remain with the philanthropic and the vast wealth released from the abandonment of the arms trade and the exploitation of the weak by the strong would be diverted into health, education, the environment–and globalisation for the common good.

'Keep your face to the sunshine and you cannot see the shadow.'

HELEN KELLER

Glossary

Sukuma: v. push
59 askari: security guard
61 shamba: garden or small farm
65 Uhuru: independence
   pishi: n. cook
66 Bwana: Sir
   Skooli: school
72 Mzungu: n + adj. European
73 pombe: local African beer
   Mwalimu: s. teacher Walimu: pl.
75 Twende: Let's go
   Tutaonana: See you later
   Kahawa: coffee
   Sasa: now
   Tafadhali: please
97 bundu: bush, remote countryside
99 kitenge: brightly patterned cloth
   kikapu: round basket or bag made of sisal
104 banghi: marijuana
105 Hapana penda: (I) don't like
108 Chamagai: Hello in the Kipsigis dialect
   Yamonai: Reply to Hello
109 Hodi: Can I come in?
   Karibu: Come in / Welcome
126 lakini: but
138 maridadi: all tarted up (a great name for a 'cow')
145 watu: people – the masses usually
150 lette: bring
   ngini: another or again
   upesi: quickly
   mimi: me or I (whichever fits)
164 Harambee: the spirit of self-help and co-operation
   rafiki: friend
   iangu: my

Mwethia: the spirit of Harambee in the Masai
language
215 Mzee: elderly, worthy of respect. In this case Jomo
Kenyatta, President of Kenya
254 dookers: swimming trunks in N E Scotland
breeks: trousers
matoke: savoury banana
choma nyama: meat on skewers
261 ayah: nanny
262 mursik: a Masai drink made from milk, blood, urine
and charcoal
manyatta: Masai village with a circle of dwellings
protecting a central area to keep animals safe
NOTE The front cover picture is of Torrisdale Bay, near
Bettyhill, Sutherland in the far north of Scotland.
STOP PRESS: July 2007:
Ella Fonseca has just spotted more fusion. Could the
Global Elders of the Global Village (led by Nelson
Mandela and supported by Richard Branson) make
some wise decisions which would be listened to and
acted on?

ISBN 142512968-4